HONOUR

HONOUR

****

A Historical Golf Novel

RICHARD O'CONNOR

Library of Congress Control Number 2012930070

ISBN: 978-0-9836689-1-6

Published by:
Huntington Park Publications, Inc.
103 N Adams Street
Rockville, MD 20850-2256
www.huntingtonparkpublications.com

PRINTED IN THE UNITED STATES

O'Connor, Richard 1949-
Honour – 1st Edition
p.   cm.
First Edition
10 9 8 7 6 5 4 3 2 1

Cover photographs and composite: © 2011 *Jim Morris*

HUNTINGTON PARK PUBLICATIONS, INC. · MARYLAND

A NOTE TO THE READER

This book covers the period in American golf from 1909 to 1919. This is not an actual accounting of the historical events of the period. I have attempted to be accurate regarding the real people, places, and events which are mentioned in the book; however, the dialogue between the fictionalized characters and the real life historical characters is fiction. I have included a list of the major historical characters in the book as a reference guide for the reader.

The first rules of golf were written in 1744 by the Honorable Company of Edinburgh Golfers based in Murfield, England. There were 13 original rules and many of these early rules have been incorporated into the official rules we use today. The first rules were adopted by the Royal and Ancient Golf Club of St. Andrews in 1897. The current rules, which have been adopted by the United States Golf Association, consist of 37 rules and also include special rules for stroke play, three-ball, and four-ball matches. I have included the original rules of golf in the author's notes.

The period from 1885 until 1926 has been designated by golf historians as the Hickory Shaft Era. Modern day golfers may not be familiar with many of the rules and terms which were common during the Hickory Shaft Era. Wooden-shafted clubs were used in all sanctioned competitions through 1926, when metal shafts were legalized by the two ruling bodies in golf, the United States Golf Association and the Royal and Ancient Golf Club of Saint Andrews.

In 1895, fewer than 50,000 people played golf in the United States and there were fewer than 100 golf courses. By 1922, there were more than two million new players and one thousand new courses across America.

GLOSSARY

Birdie: One shot under par for a hole

Bogey: One shot over par for a hole

Calcutta: Open-auction pool wagering system in which bets go into a pot and shares are paid through bidding

Dogleg: A fairway with a sharp turn right or left

Dormie: In match play, leading an opponent by the number of holes remaining in the match

Four ball: Scoring in which only the best ball per hole counts for each team of two players.

Gutta-percha: Ball used before modern rubber-core balls; made from the sap of Malaysian Sapotaceae tree

Haskell ball: Ball made with rubber thread wound around its core; invented by Corburn Haskell in 1902

Hosel: The socket where the golf club shaft meets the head

Level: All even

Match play: Scoring in which the number of holes won by each player determines the winner

Medal play: Scoring in which a player's total score for 18 holes determines the winner

R&A: The Royal and Ancient Golf Club of Saint Andrews, the ruling body of golf in Great Britain and Ireland

Stymie: A stymie occurs when an opponent's ball lies directly in the putting line of another player and the two balls are more than six inches apart. The opponent's ball is not marked; instead, the player has the option of curving his putt around the blocking ball or playing over it. The stymie rule was eliminated in 1952.

Take the turn: Term derived from Scottish courses; a player goes out holes 1-9, at which point the player would take the "turn" and come back using the same fairways in reverse order for holes 10-18

Tee Box : A box with sand for making tees

Teeing Ground: The place where play begins on each hole

The National: The United States Open

The Open: The British Open

Trash: A form of betting on a match

USGA: The United States Golf Association, the ruling body of golf in the United States

CLUB NUMBERING

Golf clubs were not numbered until the late 1920's, after metal-shaft clubs were approved by the USGA. The following is the modern-day equivalent to the nomenclature used during the Hickory Shaft Era.

WOODS

Driver 1

Brassie................. 2

Spoon 3

Cleek 4

IRONS

Driving Cleek 1

Mid Iron.............. 2

Mid Mashie 3

Mashie Iron......... 4

Mashie 5

Spade Mashie 6

Mashie Niblick.... 7

Niblick................ 8-9

"A man's pride shall bring him low:
But honor shall uphold
the humble in spirit."

PROVERBS 29:23

CHAPTER 1

The morning mist floated gently across the practice range and obscured the tree line 300 yards away. Players who arrived early could hear the cry of the morning doves as they began their daily courting ritual. The Commonwealth Club's range was a place of peace and solitude.

The Commonwealth Club had been established in 1897 after a group from the Alston Golf Club left over a dispute about fees and the policy for admitting new members. Alston was a restricted club where only blue-blood Yankees could join. The dissident group bought the old Rich Farm and hired Macallister McKenzie to design a new nine-hole course. The membership grew to more than 100 members by 1900 and the two clubs became instant rivals.

In 1902, the Alston Golf Club won the Boston Area Inter-club Championships by defeating the Commonwealth Club team in the final round. The following year, the Commonwealth Club took the title by recruiting a little-known professional golfer, Harry Warden, to play on the club team. Warden was granted a "special membership" and won all of his matches. The Alston Club filed a protest with the local rules committee that Warden was a professional golfer, paid by the club, and shouldn't be allowed to play in inter-club matches. The Alston Club claimed simply that it was not proper to expect "true gentlemen to play against someone who had lowered himself to accept payment to play this hallowed game." The Commonwealth Club prevailed when the rules committee voted to deny the appeal only because there was insufficient proof that Warden was actually paid by the club. Just the same, Warden was known to boast to friends that the club had given him free food and free golf rounds for a year after the victory.

In 1907, the Commonwealth Club pulled off a coup by hiring Guy Rockham as their head pro. Rock was a name golfer, having played for over ten years in England and Europe with Harry Vardon, James Braid, and Sandy Herd. He had won tournaments in England, Ireland, and France, and had finished fourth in the 1902 British Open, a classic in which Herd beat Vardon and Braid in what is still one of the longest matches in Open history. Rock was a vibrant bear of a man, tall, handsome and muscular, with a long gait to his step. He weighed 290 pounds and wore a size sixteen shoe. He was a boisterous man and was as loud as he wanted to be. He had wavy brown hair streaked with white which he kept long and combed straight back. On cool days he always wore an ascot with a white silk shirt. He loved the feel of silk.

Rock had stumbled upon the job as head pro at the club. He had visited Connecticut in the spring of '07 to play in a series of exhibition matches with his old friend Donald Ross. Ross had been invited by James Walker Tufts to design a new course at his resort in Pinehurst, North Carolina, and Ross invited Rock to join him on the trip. What started out as a week of friendly golf and healthy carousing at Pinehurst turned into a series of exhibition matches along the East Coast. In three months they played 22 matches and cleared more than $4,000. Rock called it the "easiest money I ever made."

The exhibition tour ended with the only loss of the trip, a match at the Rockford Country Club, north of Boston. They lost to two local phenoms, 13-year-old Frances Ouimet and 17-year-old Clyde Rothschild. Ouimet shot one over par for the final eight holes and Rothschild birdied the final hole to win the match 2 and 1.

After the match, Rock was approached by Jacob Gustove, President of the Commonwealth Club. He invited Rock to visit the club and to meet the members. Two days later, Gustove asked if he would become the club's teaching pro. He offered Rock a generous salary, an opportunity to make additional money giving lessons, and time off to play in tournaments. But the particularly attractive aspect of the offer was the condition that he would also be a full member of the club. As head pro, Rock would be allowed to enter the main entrance of the club, eat dinner with other members in the dining room, and use the men's lounge as he pleased. No other teaching professional in the Boston area had this type of deal.

With little saved, and his 30th birthday close upon him, Rock accepted the offer and quickly became one of the guys at the club.

CHAPTER 2

George Riley sprinted down Homer Street, his golf bag tucked under his arm, toward the trolley stop at the end of the block. He was late to meet his friends for a golf match at the Blue Hills Golf Course. His after-school chores had taken longer than expected. As George approached the 1st teeing ground, he saw his best friend, Johnny Scranton, chasing a pig off the fairway. Johnny looked tired. Sweat cascaded down his face, and his shirt was soaked.

Blue Hills had been built in 1902 by the City of Newton on a portion of the Reeves farm. Sheep and pigs routinely wandered onto the course from what remained of the farm. The advantage to playing at Blue Hills for George and Johnny was that the city allowed high-school golf-team members to play for free - the city charged all other players 25 cents a round for the nine-hole course.

"That darn pig keeps making a burrow on the first hole," Johnny said, "I can't keep her away."

George glanced at the undulating fields. He was tall and thin and had wavy light brown hair. There was a small scar on his chin from a bike accident when he was six and he had warm azure blue eyes. At 6'1", he was the tallest member of his family.

"This is the shortest the grass has been all year," George said.

Johnny was one month and two days older than George and had started shaving long before his peers. He was 6'4" and his upper body was well formed from his daily, almost religious, weight-training program. He had been lifting weights with his dad for two years and it was beginning to show in his upper chest and arms. Johnny was the tallest boy in the 12th grade and also the most handsome. The girls fell head over heels for Johnny. He had big, baby blue eyes and a strong, square chin.

George noticed that Francis Ouimet had arrived with Paul O'Connell.

"Hi, guys. Where's Bobby?" George asked.

"He's at home. Got in trouble today at school and the principal sent him home early with a note for his mom to sign. He told me he was grounded for the weekend."

"Paul, how many times have you played?" George asked.

"This will be my second time. Francis has been giving me lessons in the backyard."

"If anyone can teach you to play, it's Francis."

"Okay, guys. Let's get going. I have to be home by 6:30. Today is my birthday!" Johnny exclaimed.

In unison they yelled, "We know. You've reminded us every day for the last week."

The boys checked in with the starter, Dave Cyrus. He had been the starter since the course opened in '02.

"Well, if it isn't Mr. Riley, Mr. Scranton, and Mr. Ouimet. You can tee off after the foursome." He looked over at Paul. "I've never met this lad."

"This is Paul O'Connell," George said. "He's taking Bobby Crimmon's place today. Bobby got in trouble at school today. He's grounded."

"Are you a member of the golf team?"

"No, sir," Paul said, embarrassed by the question. "This is only my second time playing golf."

"Okay, laddie. I'll waive the playing fee today. Don't be nervous. You'll do fine. These lads are some of the best young golfers in the Boston area. Watch and learn."

Dave slapped Paul on the back.

"Did I tell you I found a new Haskell Comet the other day?" George asked. "I found it along the edge of the 6th hole at the Commonwealth Club. It looks as if it's only been hit a few times." The boys moved their bags to the back of the 1st teeing ground.

The Haskell Comet was the latest model in the B. F. Goodrich line of golf balls. The Haskell was a revolutionary design invented by Corburn Haskell in 1902. He had developed a new process of winding thin rubber strips around a central core. The Comet flew farther and was more durable than the gutta-percha ball which had dominated the market since the late 1850's. The "gutty" was formed using the sap of the Sapodilla tree and frequently lost shape and often broke apart. At least they were affordable: the most popular gutty, the Bramble, cost only 15 cents.

In 1906, Goodrich introduced a variety of new balls, all based on the Haskell design. The Flyer, the Stag, and the Scotty burst onto the market. The new balls were expensive: a Flyer cost 75 cents. In January 1907 Goodrich introduced the Comet, which cost a full dollar per ball, the most expensive ball on the market.

"Let me see it," Johnny said. George took the Comet out of his bag. Johnny examined it closely.

"It's heavier than I thought. They have a special at Spaulding's," said Johnny.

"The grass is short today, so it will fly," Francis said.

The foursome teed off and headed down the first fairway.

"George, who enforces the rules in golf?" Paul asked as he examined the Comet.

"Each player does. Let me show you."

George reached into his bag and took out a copy of the 1908 Rules.

"The Honor Code is an integral part of the game. Rule 13

is a good example." He read from his rule book:

> *A player or caddie shall not press down nor remove any irreg-*
> *ularities of surface near a ball in play. Dung, worm-casts, or mole-*
> *hills may be removed (but not pressed down) without penalty. The*
> *penalty for a breach of this Rule shall be the loss of the hole.*

"So what does that mean to you?" George asked Paul.

"Well," Paul said slowly, "I guess it means that if a player or his caddie presses down on a ball or removes any items near a ball, the hole is lost."

"That's right. It's up to the player to call the violation on his own. If he doesn't, he's breached the Honor Code. I won't play with someone who violates one of the rules. Honor is the most important element of the game."

"What if I touch the sand with my club in a bunker before I hit the ball?"

"Ground your club in a hazard or trap, add a stroke," Johnny said. "If you whiff, add a stroke. If the ball moves after you address it, add a stroke. I had a situation in a match last week where the wind moved my ball after I had addressed it. I stepped back, told my opponent that the ball moved, and assessed a one-stroke penalty to my score. I lost the hole but went on to win the match."

"Did your opponent see the ball move?" Paul asked.

"No, I don't think so. But it didn't matter. The ball moved and I called the penalty."

"Gee, that must have been hard. You didn't move the ball, but you still had to take the penalty."

"That's part of the game," Johnny said as he anxiously waited to tee off. "The Honor Code is paramount in this game. Without it, we might as well be playing football. This is the only sport I know where the player enforces the rules. That's why integrity and honor are so important."

"Johnny, how do you make a sand tee?" Paul asked.

"Come on, kid, I'll show you. Besides, that group ahead of us is taking forever."

Johnny led Paul over to the tee box and scooped up some sand with his hand.

"Francis, you could've explained the honor code to Paul," George whispered.

"I thought it would be best explained by you and Johnny," Francis said. "The first time I played with Paul at the Fens, he whiffed three times. He didn't count the strokes and told everyone at school that he shot a par on the hole. He actually had a triple bogey."

"Okay. I'll keep an eye on him," George said. "Rules are rules."

Paul and Johnny re-joined the group. "George, how does the stymie rule work?" asked Paul.

With all these questions, it was going to be a long round, thought George.

He paused and took a deep breath.

CHAPTER 3

"Okay, enough of the rules lesson," Johnny said.

The foursome in front of the boys had finally moved onto the first green. Johnny stepped into the teeing ground, which was marked by two red metal rods placed six feet apart.

"Let's play a four ball. I'll take Paul as my partner. I'll flip for the honor."

Johnny took a nickel from his pocket and George yelled heads as the coin hit the ground.

"Tails it is. We'll hit first," Johnny said. "What are we going to play for?"

"How about 10 cents a hole?" Francis said.

"That's 90 cents," Paul said. "I don't have that much money."

"No, silly," Johnny said. "You can only lose 45 cents if your team loses all nine holes. That's not going to happen."

"My mom gave me 50 cents when I left home today. I have to buy corn meal and a quart of milk on my way home. That leaves 10 cents."

"I'll spot you if we lose," Johnny said. "But don't worry. We won't lose."

Two goats wandered onto the 3rd fairway.

"We'll need to move those goats on three if the group in front doesn't move them," George said.

Johnny grabbed a handful of sand from the tee box. The tee box had became popular in England in the early 1880's. A square box mounted on the top of a metal bar, the tee box held course sand and a sand cone. Before the city installed the tee boxes, staff would pile sand next to each tee area in order for members to form mounds of sand for their drives.

Johnny formed a sand mound, gently placed his Bramble gutta-percha ball on top of the mound, and selected a brassie from his bag. He couldn't afford one of the new Haskell Comets. He carried a blue canvas walking bag with eight clubs plus a putter. His clubs were made by Isaac Bell, a club maker in Newton. Johnny had worked for Bell during the winter and, in exchange for his work, Isaac had made him the eight clubs. He had a driver, a brassie, a spoon, a driving cleek, a mid mashie, a mashie, a mashie niblick, and a niblick in his bag.

Johnny's wooden-shaft brassie was shaped in the old Scottish style with a pointed toe and a shallow face. The brassie head had a deep face, and a brass sole plate on the bottom. Isaac had added molten lead in the rear of the head to heavy-up the club head.

Johnny became fascinated with the process of making clubs. It took Isaac over an hour to make each club. First, a new shaft was cut from a one-inch square stock of hickory or ash. The square stock was hand-shaved with a plane or a bow saw. Next, the tapered end of the shaft was inserted into a hole drilled on the side of the head and joined with glue. Finally, the glued joint was wrapped with fine fishermen's twine. This provided added strength to the shaft at impact.

Isaac used a hand-forged process to create his irons. He had more than 40 iron molds, each with a different loft and thickness. Molten pig iron was poured into the molds and shaped into a club face. Shafts were shuddered into an opening at the top of the iron and secured by a pin, which was inserted at the base of the club. The last step in the process was the installation of the grip. A coarse cloth was wrapped around the top third of the shaft. A roll of calfskin leather was wound over the cloth and secured with a tack. Isaac then placed a black medallion with a bold 'I' on the top of the shaft to complete the club.

Johnny took two practice swings before he hit his ball. He lunged into the shot and the ball initially headed right but suddenly turned to the left and landed in the middle of the fairway.

"Nice shot," George said. "Okay, Paul, you're up."

Paul was nervous as he addressed the ball. Paul was 5'5" tall, one of the smallest boys in the 12th grade, and he had a slight stutter. His sand tee partially collapsed as the club head descended. The shaft turned in Paul's hand and the ball hit the side of the club face. It dribbled into the long grass, no more than 40 yards from the tee box.

"S-s-sorry." Paul paused a minute. "Sorry, partner," Paul said again. His stutter became more pronounced when he was under pressure. He had learned to control the severe aspect of his stutter by speaking slowly and pausing when he felt pressured.

"It's okay. Stay focused," Johnny said.

George scooped sand out of the tee box with a new sand-cone he had bought at Spaulding's Sporting Goods in Newton Center. He pressed the cone down on the ground and gently lifted it up, creating an instant sand tee. George found it easier to use the sand-cone than form the sand tee with his hand. He placed the Comet on top of the tee.

He carried six clubs in his bag, all made by Wright and Ditson in Boston. His dad had given him three clubs the previous year for his birthday and he had purchased the additional clubs using money he had earned doing odd jobs in the neighborhood. His putter was a used Robish bulls-eye model which he had found in the trash at Blue Hills. George selected a driver from his bag. He took one practice swing and then smashed a shot straight down the middle of the fairway. The ball landed 20 yards beyond Johnny's ball.

"Wow! I've never seen you out-drive Johnny before!" Francis said.

"Boy, you've got something there," Johnny said. "I told you the Haskell was better than the gutta-percha. You can play over 30 rounds with that ball before it needs to be replaced."

Francis was next. He had an assortment of nine clubs from different club makers: a Wright and Ditson brassie, a Spaulding cleek, a Rohman niblick, and a Wilson spade mashie. He selected a brassie which glistened in the late afternoon sun.

"Did you polish the shaft, Francis?" asked Paul.

Francis smiled.

"I put three coats of shellac on last night to stiffen the shaft. Harry Vardon uses a pint of shellac a day. Some players at The Chase Club carry a can of quick dry shellac and apply the shellac during a match. The stiffness fades after six to eight holes. The hickory becomes whippy. There's a player at The Chase Club who used over 100 cans of shellac during the summer."

At fifteen, Francis was the youngest in the group. He was lanky and had jet black hair. He had a fluid swing and had impeccable skills around the green. Francis played with a Silver Tone gutty, the most expensive gutty on the market. He received six Silver Tones when he caddied back-to-back rounds during the member-guest tournament in April.

Francis placed a new Silver Tone on top of a sand tee and adjusted his grip before he addressed the ball. He hit his shot straight down the middle of the fairway and the ball landed 20 yards behind Johnny's ball. Francis was not a long hitter, but he was a steady, methodical player who hit most greens in regulation.

* * * * * * *

They finished the first hole with both teams shooting par. The second hole was a challenging 137-yard par three, with deep bunkers protecting the front of the green and a steep slope off the back. It was elevated from the teeing ground and the flag was cut in the right rear of the green.

"What should I hit, partner?" George asked Francis as he reached down and plucked some grass. He threw the grass into the air and watched it gently float behind him. He had seen older players use this technique to determine the speed and direction of the wind.

"I'd hit a spade mashie. It's playing about145 with the wind," Francis said as he gazed at the top of the tees. "It looks to be blowing harder near the green than down here."

"I don't have a spade mashie. Can I borrow your club?"

Francis handed him a Wilson spade mashie. It had been a gift from the President of The Chase Club and was in impeccable condition.

"Can he lend a club?" Paul asked.

"It's not against the rules," Johnny said.

The club head was heavier than his mashie and the weight was shifted toward the hosel. The shaft was extremely stiff, almost to the point of having no reflex. George took two practice swings. With a sweeping motion, he made contact with the ball dead center and the ball leapt off the club face in a high arc toward the left side of the green. The ball landed three feet from the cup.

"New local rule. No borrowing clubs!" Johnny said.

"As if that's going to happen," George said as he walked down the fairway toward his ball. "We all share clubs. Until we can afford to have our own complete set, then we will follow that rule."

* * * * * * *

The 3rd hole was the longest hole on the course. It was a 395-yard dogleg left with fairway bunkers 200 yards from the teeing ground. George hit a spoon and his ball landed between two goats munching on tufts of grass near the edge of the fairway. Johnny's drive cut the dogleg and landed in the middle of the fairway, 150 yards from the hole. Paul had his first good drive. It landed in the center of the fairway at the dogleg. Francis lifted his upper body as he hit his drive and hooked it into an open area of rough with rocks and exposed tree roots.

"Looks as if you might be in trouble, Francis," George said as they walked down the fairway. "Did I tell you? I went to the Americans game against the Washington Nationals on Sunday with my dad."

George immediately corrected himself: "I meant to say the Red Sox, now that they changed the team name again."

"I don't think that name will last," Francis said. "The team has had three names since they joined the American League in 1901. They've been the Americans, the Pilgrims, and now the Red Sox. They need to stick with one name."

"I agree," George said. "But I love to go with my dad to the Huntington Avenue Grounds to watch the team play, whatever they're called."

"How much is a ticket?" Francis asked as he reached his ball and examined the lie.

"My dad paid 25 cents for general admission. He told me the Braves are charging 50 cents for a ticket at the South End Grounds. Can you believe that? I can buy two gutties for that price."

Paul joined Francis as he examined the lie. His ball was located in the middle of rocks, and a large tree root was directly behind the ball.

"Francis, that's a terrible lie. Why don't you move it from those rocks?"

"Just a minute," Johnny said, standing in the middle of the fairway waiting to hit. "He has to play the ball where it lies or take a penalty drop."

"No. I don't want to move it," Francis said. "I can hit it."

Francis took his mashie and adjusted his stance so he could hit a sharp descending blow to avoid the nearest rock and tree root. As Francis' club descended, he hit a flat piece of ledge under the ball and the wooden shaft shattered in his hands. He advanced the ball 30 yards into the middle of the fairway. His hands stung as he picked up the broken club. He would have to re-shaft the head to be ready for the school-boy match on Friday. The mashie had been one of his favorite clubs.

As he walked up the fairway, he examined the broken end of the shaft. He would need to shave the shaft with a sharp knife, since the shaft had been forced further into the hosel by the force of his swing.

"Broke another one," Francis said. "Maybe my shafts are too stiff. It didn't give at all."

He used a mashie niblick for his third shot, which landed pin high, eight feet from the pin. Francis holed out to win the hole with a par four.

"Who pitched for Boston on Sunday?" Francis asked George as they walked to the 4th teeing ground.

"Cy Young. The Red Sox won 4 -1. Young pitched the entire game and only gave up two hits. Washington went with their new pitcher, Walter Johnson. You should see this guy. He's tall and has long arms that hang out from his shirt sleeves. He throws side arm and has an incredible fast ball. He struck out nine Boston batters. Cy Young is the best pitcher in baseball. He was awesome Sunday."

"You're crazy," Paul said. "Addie Joss with the Naps and George Mullens with the White Sox are better than Young. Young is getting old and doesn't have much left."

George turned to Paul. "I'll bet you Cy Young wins more games this year than George Mullens."

"You're on," Paul said. "The loser buys the winner a malt."

"Deal."

"Can we get back to golf?" Francis asked.

Francis had the honor. He took two practice swings and then hit a booming shot straight down the middle of the fairway. He had a wry smile as he stepped back to allow George to hit.

"Don't you give me that Cheshire cat smile, Mr. Ouimet," George said. "You've been saving that drive. Good shot. Let's see if I can beat it."

Francis continued to smile as George formed his sand tee and placed the Comet on top. George took two slow swings and then lunged into the drive. The ball exploded off the driver's club face and landed 250 yards from the teeing ground, 30 yards beyond Francis' drive.

Johnny was dumb-founded. "I've got to find a way to buy a Comet before the school-boy match on Friday!" he said.

"Nice drive, George," Francis said, still smiling.

* * * * * * *

For the next hour and half the boys slugged it out, each team winning two holes. George and Johnny finished the 9th hole with birdies, and the match ended in a tie.

"I'm really jazzed about our match on Friday," Johnny said as he and Francis waited at the trolley stop.

Francis played number one on the Brookline High School team and both George and Johnny played for Newton High

School. George and Johnny had traded the number one spot for two years depending on how each was playing.

"We have a solid team, but it's young," Francis said. "I might play number three on Friday. My drives have been off."

"What? We may not play on Friday? Are you ducking me in a school-boy match?" Johnny asked as George and Paul joined them.

"We'll see," Francis said. "Paul, you played well today."

"Thanks, Francis."

"After Paul's fine play today, I propose that we appoint him our official school scorer for the match on Friday," George said. "Newton couldn't have a better representative."

"Bravo," Johnny shouted. "I agree. We'll announce it at school tomorrow."

"Th-th-thanks guys." Paul paused. "Thanks. I won't let you down." Paul wondered what his new job entailed.

The first trolley to arrive was headed to Brookline and Francis jumped on the rider board before the trolley came to a full stop.

"Good luck Friday," he said as the trolley gained speed and sped toward Brookline.

"Good luck to you," George yelled.

Dust engulfed the boys.

CHAPTER 4

The sign outside of the Commonwealth Club's Pro Shop stated in bold letters:

LESSONS AND CLUB MAKING
GUY ROCKHAM
Golf Professional

As part of his deal with the club, Rock was given an area near the 1st teeing ground to build a practice facility. Rock attracted players from throughout New England to attend the new Rockham Golf Academy. He gave private lessons to members and non-members alike, and the Academy accepted all types of players: beginners, seasoned amateurs, professionals, Yankee blue bloods, and Irish street cleaners. If they could pay 50 cents a lesson, Rock's Academy was open to all. Rock signed a long term sponsorship deal with B.F. Goodrich and the Haskell became the official ball of the Rockham Golf Academy.

George's dad, Steve Riley, had met Rock at a Knights of Columbus meeting in early 1908. Rock had been a Fourth Order Knight back home in England and he loved the pomp and ceremony associated with the Knights. When he first arrived in Newton, he attended the nearest parish to the club, Saint Philip Neri in Waban. The Rileys were regular parishioners. When Steve learned that Rock planned to give lessons, he mentioned that his son and his son's friend played golf. Rock agreed to give the boys lessons, and in exchange, Steve agreed to install a new bathroom in Rock's home.

From the first day of practice, Rock took a special interest in

Johnny and George. He could tell that they had great potential, but they needed to work hard. He allowed the boys to hit balls after school, as long as they shagged the balls before he closed.

****

"What a great day," Johnny said as George joined him in front of school after their last class. It was a beautiful, clear May day and the apple blossoms were in full bloom.

"Let's go over to the club and see if Rock can figure out why my mashie keeps going right," Johnny said.

"Okay."

The boys caught the Commonwealth Avenue trolley, which stopped two blocks from the club. Rock was sitting on a bench near the pro shop, reading the Boston American as the boys entered the academy grounds.

"Hi, Rock," George said.

"Hi, lads. I didn't expect to see you today."

"I need your help with a problem I have with my mashie. It keeps going right every time I hit it," Johnny said.

"Okay, Johnny. Let's take a look at your problem."

Rock grabbed his walking stick and headed to the practice tee, lighting his pipe along the way.

The practice facility had a long expanse of bent grass, meticulously groomed. To the left of the practice tee, Rock had built two sand bunkers and a small green for pitch-and-run shots. The putting area was a large, two-tiered green set off to the right, so players could practice without disturbing other players on the tee. Stocked with hundreds of Goodrich Flyers, Comets, and Super Reds, it was the first complete golf training center in the Boston area.

"I'll get the clubs," George said. They stored their clubs in the members' storage room, which was in a separate shed near the 1st teeing ground. George ran back to the practice tee with both bags looped over his right shoulder. Rock noticed the top canvas bag had three holes in its side.

"George, have you been leaving your bag where the rats can gnaw at it? They love to eat the tarnish resin on the canvas." Before George could answer Rock said, "Can't have you wandering around the club with that ratty old thing."

"Okay, Rock."

Johnny grabbed his bag and selected a mashie.

"Okay, hit a few," Rock said as he moved directly behind Johnny. "George, can you shag?"

"Sure, Rock."

George grabbed the shag bag and positioned himself in the middle of the practice area. He turned and noticed Johnny was facing to the left.

George called out, "Hey. Turn. I'm over here!"

Johnny gave him a dirty look.

"All right. Hold on to your trousers. I'm moving," Johnny yelled.

Johnny was about to hit, but backed off the shot to gain his composure. George had rattled him.

"Remember. Keep your cool," Rock said. "He's only trying to help."

Rock was constantly trying to control Johnny's temper. This was Johnny's Achilles heel. Get him flustered and the ball could go anywhere.

"I want to shoot for the tree over to the left. That's my target."

"No, shoot for George. Better we get the ball back instead of hitting it into the trees."

Johnny addressed the ball and turned to face George. He

used the Vardon grip due to his slashing swing style. He dragged the club back in a flat plane and powered down on the ball. The ball jumped off the club face. About 50 yards from the practice tee, the ball veered and landed 25 yards to the right of George.

"Hit a few more shots," Rock said.

"See, I can't hit it straight," said Johnny, frustrated at the shot.

"Go ahead. Hit a few."

Johnny hit three more, exactly where he had hit the first one.

"I see what you're doing. You're dragging the club inside on your back swing and the blade is open on impact. Try to drag the club outside the line and square the blade."

The drag line was a favorite visual tool Rock used during practice sessions. He set out a string in a straight line behind each boy. He taught them to drag the club along the string until they could go no further, then lift the club up to the pivot point. Once at the pivot point, and with their shoulders parallel to the drag line, he would have them pivot and bring the club down along the line, forcing the club to accelerate through the ball. For each shot, they were to imagine the drag line in order to keep the club's arc consistent. Johnny's swing plane was flatter than George's, but the concept was the same for both boys. Johnny hit another shot and the ball landed near George.

"Good. Now hit forty more."

"Thanks, Rock."

Rock checked his pocket watch.

"I've got to go."

"Have a date tonight with Belle LaCree. We're going to the opera."

"Belle LaCree!" Johnny said in a sarcastic tone. "How did a mutt like you swing a date with a grand lady like Belle?"

"Watch it, bud. Who you calling a mutt?"

Belle LaCree was one of the richest ladies in Newton. She lived in Chestnut Hills in one of the grand mansions along Commonwealth Avenue. Her late husband, Robert LaCree, had made his fortune in the slaughterhouse business. Three years earlier, as he was crossing Cedar Street, a drunk driver from West Roxbury hit him. The police estimated the car was going 19 miles per hour. The driver was convicted of negligent homicide and sentenced to eighteen months in jail, the first auto-related conviction in Newton Superior Court.

"I thought Belle never went out," Johnny said.

"She wants to learn how to play golf. I've given her two lessons already. She invited me to the opera and I accepted."

"She asked you out? Way to go, stud. Get the rich ones to come calling!"

"Watch your mouth, son. She's a lady."

He winked and headed back to the clubhouse.

"See ya."

Rock had a swagger that Johnny had never seen before.

"Come on," George yelled. "I want time to work on my brassie."

Johnny hit 40 shots per Rock's directions. Thirty-six of the shots landed within two feet of George.

Rock stood on the veranda of the pro shop and watched as the boys traded shag duties. He never saw them goof off during a practice session. They were all business. He was amazed at how dedicated the boys were. On the wall of his office Rock had a sign which summed up his own philosophy: Practice makes perfect and perfect practice makes champions.

"These boys are going to be champions," Rock said to himself. "One day, they're going to make me a fortune."

****

The boys finished their workout with a short match. Each boy selected five balls and a mashie niblick. Each player shot to a selected target 130 yards out, and the player who got the closest to the target with the highest number of shots won the match. George was a master with the short irons. He put his fifth and final shot dead stick and won his third straight match.

"Damn. I can't believe it!" Johnny said. "Wait til I get you out on the course."

As the boys walked past the pro shop, they saw a new canvas bag hanging on the rack. It had a note attached: "Don't let me see you with that old tattered bag here again. We're a class act, not a bunch of muni players. Rock."

George smiled.

In 1907, the town of Brookline had built a new nine-hole municipal course at Long Pond. The Boston Traveler described the municipal players who played at Long Pond as a "bunch of hicks and low lives" due to their attire and the cheap wooden sticks they used. The "munis" loved to bring beer on the course and were rumored to be drunk by the sixth hole. Muni players had become a joke.

"Nice gift," Johnny said.

George ran his hand along the new canvas bag. The oil resin was smooth and clean. He slowly transferred his clubs.

"Yea. Rock is a swell guy."

CHAPTER 5

"What are you up to?" George asked.

"Oh, nothing," Johnny said. He quickly folded a paper he had in his left hand and stuffed it in his pocket. He was quiet as they walked home from school.

Suddenly he blurted out, "I've decided to play in the Blue Marsh Invitational. The application is due Tuesday."

"Don't you need a sponsor to get into the tournament?" asked George.

"They're opening the tournament to non-sponsored players because the best amateur players have refused to play in the tournament."

"Why won't they play?"

"They're scared. The Massachusetts Golf Association voted to prohibit any amateur player who enters the Blue Marsh from playing at any member clubs, even if they don't accept prize money."

"That's ridiculous!"

"The old guard considers professional golfers a plague and they're trying to stamp them out," Johnny said. "Look at what they did to Jake Longstreet when he played in the Secaucus Open last year. The best amateur player in New England. The association stripped him of his amateur status and forced him to return his trophies."

"Is Alec Campbell going to play?" George asked.

"I haven't talked to him. I'll find out."

Alec Campbell was the head pro at The Country Club. The Country Club set the standard in the Boston area for how to treat their golf pros, and the other established clubs followed their lead. When Campbell was hired in 1899, the Chairman had made it very clear that he would be treated as the hired help and he had to abide by certain rules. He was prohibited from entering the club through the front door, he was not allowed to socialize with club members, and he could not address members by their first names. He couldn't even enter the member's lounge.

Members were upset when he played in professional tournaments or even exhibition matches. He had played an exhibition match with the British Open winners, Barnes and Haught, when they toured the United States in 1905. He won $400 and some members demanded that he donate his winnings to charity. Alec respectfully declined.

"Did you hear Francis resigned as a caddie at The Country Club?" George asked. "The USGA recently voted to classify any caddy over sixteen as a professional. Francis loves to caddy, but he doesn't want to risk losing his amateur status."

"The old guard hates the idea of anyone making money from golf," Johnny said. "The pro game is coming and it will be bigger and better than the amateur game in a few years. There's nothing wrong with getting paid for doing something you love."

"So are you going to play?"

"You bet I am," Johnny said.

He pulled the application from his jacket and waved it in front of George.

"My dad lent me twelve bucks for the entry fee. He agreed I could take next week off from school to practice. Maybe I can play well enough to repay Dad and have some money left over."

"Twelve bucks! That's a lot of money. And if you accept any prize money, they'll strip you of your amateur status and you'll be black listed. I thought you wanted to get a job this summer at one of the clubs."

"I've changed my mind. I'm going to try my luck in a few pro tournaments. Screw the honorable gentlemen who claim that golf is for amateurs only. The pro game is coming and I want to be part of it."

Johnny raised his voice.

"I've won the Boston School Boy Tournament and the Chipper Tournament. I'm ready to try the next level."

There was no doubt that Johnny was ready to play at a more competitive level of golf, thought George. Johnny was the best school-boy golfer in Massachusetts. He held the lowest school-boy medal round in the state and he was undefeated in match play tournaments.

But to play at Blue Marsh and turn pro? George was reluctant to encourage his friend. He was only eighteen. What would he do if he failed?

The boys walked briskly but silently down Walnut Street toward Commonwealth Avenue.

****

Commonwealth Avenue was the main street which ran through the heart of Newton. In the previous ten years, the city had been transformed from a sleepy farming community eight miles west of Boston to a vibrant new commuter suburb. The expansion of the Boston and Albany Railroad line through Newton Center and four new electric trolley lines had changed the city dramatically. In 1904, the Boston and Albany expanded the station at Newton Center and added 15 daily commuter runs into Boston. The city had recently widened the road by two lanes in both directions and it was the first completely paved road in Newton.

The boys crossed at Walnut Street and stopped in the median

strip where the city had planted American elms and dogwoods. The dogwoods were in full bloom and the elm buds were starting to appear. George counted five varieties of dogwoods in the median strip: white, pink, rose, yellow, and a combination blue and white. There was a sweet amber smell in the air. A cobalt blue Stanley Steamer passed as they waited to cross the street.

"There are more and more cars on this street each day and fewer horse-drawn buggies," George said. "My dad won't come out here with his horse and buggy to compete with these new contraptions."

George wondered if there would be a day when all the horse-drawn buggies and wagons would be gone, replaced by automobiles and motor trucks.

"So. Are you going to join me?" asked Johnny. "Rock is going to play and has offered to give us a ride to Natick."

"I can't. I want to qualify for the Massachusetts Amateur and play in the Springdale Amateur in Rhode Island. Playing in the Blue Marsh Invitational would jeopardize my amateur status. But, do you need a caddy?"

"I was just about to ask you," Johnny said.

"Race you home."

"You're on."

George bolted across the street and took the early lead in the two-block race. As the boys approached Homer Street, they saw a Stanley Steamer parked at the corner. George glanced back and saw Johnny had stopped to talk with the owner.

George turned and asked, "Why did you stop? I've got to get home before we go over to the club."

"George, come see this." Johnny motioned for George to join him. The fire-engine-red Model R Roadster had oversized rubber tires with yellow spoke wheels. The color contrast was stunning.

"I'd love to own a Steamer one day. It's a real beauty!" George said. He noticed that the steam pot in the front of the car was venting steam out of the side instead of through the tail pipe. George had never seen a steamer with a side discharge vent. The driver was trying to get the boiler to work.

"There are no gears in the steamers," George said. "They hold the speed record for production cars at 65 miles per hour. I can't imagine going that fast."

"Steamers are on their way out," Johnny said to his friend. "Gasoline engines are going to put the steamers out of business. I'd like to own an EMF Light Four Roadster. Now that's a classy car."

"You're crazy. Steamers were the best selling car last year."

"I read in the Globe that they recently discovered more oil in Pennsylvania. Gasoline prices will drop and the new internal combustion engine will be the future of automobiles. With a steamer you have to wait for the boiler to heat up before you can drive. The new internal combustion vehicles have a manual crank that lets you start the engine immediately. You can jump into the car, have your passenger turn the crank, and the engine immediately starts. You watch. I'm right."

Johnny and George continued to debate the pros and cons of the steamer as a large puff of steam came out of the steam pot. Startled, the boys jumped back. The owner of the steamer jumped out of the driver's seat and poured a bottle of water into the steam pot.

"Don't be afraid," the driver said. "It won't hurt you."

"He has to cool the system to even out the steam flow," Johnny said.

Johnny was the smartest boy in their group, but he had not done well in school. He had a solid C-minus average. Too much time devoted to golf and girls.

Nancy Marchand came up behind the boys as they admired the steamer.

"Hi, Johnny," Nancy chirped. "Hi, George." She glanced quickly at George as she passed.

"Hi ya, Nancy," Johnny said. "Are you going to the dance at Norumbega Park Saturday night?"

"No one has asked me. Are you asking?"

"I haven't decided who to ask yet. I'll let you know. You're definitely on my list though."

Norumbega Park was the largest amusement park in the area. It had opened a new indoor dance pavilion, and the best bands played on Saturday nights. The park was on the banks of the Charles River, four miles from Newton Center. It had a huge penny arcade, an outdoor theater, and Nancy's favorite place, the zoo. The Commonwealth Avenue Street Railway trolley ran right to the front door of the park, which stayed open until midnight on Saturday.

"I'm on your list!" Nancy raised her eyebrows in mock surprise. "Johnny, you're such a tease. Some girls would be offended by that response. I'll wait. I know you'll ask me."

She smiled an especially sweet smile.

"You also know that we will have a really good time."

Nancy winked at Johnny.

"See ya." She stepped in front of the steamer and headed down Walnut Street toward her house.

George was amazed at how poorly Johnny treated Nancy. She was the best-looking girl in school and had an exuberance with her bubbly laugh. She was slim and had long brown hair and the most beautiful green eyes George had ever seen. Nancy and Johnny had been on-again, off-again, boy friend/girl friend for three years. Johnny didn't like to get tied down with one girl and Nancy was known as the school flirt. They were perfect for each other.

"Are you going to ask her to the dance?" George asked. "She really wants to go with you."

"Probably. I'm waiting to see if any other options open up." George shook his head in disbelief.

A buggy passed the boys and kicked up mud onto George's leggings.

"I can't believe they haven't paved our street," George cried out.

It had rained the previous night and there were large puddles in the middle of Homer street.

"My dad goes to City Council meetings every month to lobby for our road to be paved, but they continue to ignore us."

****

The houses on Homer Street were an eclectic mix of architectural styles – American Four Squares, Victorian bungalows, and Neo-Classical homes – all built during the late 1890's. The neighborhood consisted of Irish, Scottish, and German immigrant families, and the street regularly flooded during heavy rains. The Rileys moved to 10 Homer Street in 1897, one of the first houses built on the block. Johnny and his dad moved to 9 Homer Street in '05 after Johnny's mom died during the typhus epidemic the year before.

George and his sister, Maggie, who was four years younger, had their own rooms, and his father had built a large family room in the rear of the house. George thought it was the best home on the block.

"Okay, let's go play nine before it gets dark," Johnny said.

"I'll meet you at your house," George said. "I have a few chores to complete before I can go. I'll come over in about an hour."

Johnny walked across the street and said, "Okay. It will give me time to finish my last history paper. I'm writing about Roman battle tactics."

****

"Hi, Mom."

George entered the house through the front door, which had a blue and yellow stained-glass window. The panel glass had been a gift from George's uncle, who worked in Sandwich as a glass blower.

His mother was on the back porch washing clothes. She sat at a long table near the wash tub. Edith Riley was in her early 40's, and she had graying hair and deep age lines on her forehead. A petite woman, she was impeccably dressed, even in her work clothes.

"Hi," she yelled as she tried to crank the roller on the washer. "Can you help me for a minute? This darn roller keeps sticking. It'll only take a minute. The roller pin has come loose and I can't seem to adjust it."

George went to the cabinet where his dad kept a tool kit and he grabbed a pair of pliers and a crescent wrench. As he entered the wash room, he kissed his mother on the forehead. Then he methodically took the roller assembly apart.

"How was school today?" Edith asked.

"Okay. Nothing special today."

George removed the roller track, adjusted the roller pin, and in less than five minutes, he had the roller back on track.

He tested the roller by cranking through the last white sheet.

"As good as new."

"Thank you, dear."

Edith Riley was proud of her dutiful son. He never refused to help with items around the house and she felt truly blessed. If only Maggie, her youngest, would help out a little more.

"Will you be able to finish cleaning the attic today?" she asked.

"Yes. I have time before I leave with Johnny for the Comm."

George spent the next hour pulling out old furniture and boxes which had been in the attic since they moved in. It was a hot, sweaty job and he was surprised how tired it made him. Finally, the last piece was out and he changed quickly.

"I'll be back for dinner."

"Be careful when you're crossing Newton Street. Stay clear of the construction equipment for the new trolley line."

George bounded down the front stairs and grabbed his jacket just in case it got cool after the match.

"Bye, Mom."

Johnny was waiting anxiously for him on the front steps.

"What kept you so long?"

"I had to help my mom. The roller jammed on the wash tub."

"I read they're developing an electric wash tub roller," said Johnny. "A guy by the name of Maytag has filed a patent for his invention."

"How do you remember all this stuff but can't remember to bring your homework ?"

Johnny ignored the question and rolled his eyes.

The boys cut across the backyard of the adjoining neighbor and headed towards the old Wesimer Farm. The farm was on the highest point in Newton. They could see all of Newton Center: the new homes along Homer Street and the Newton Cemetery which bordered their neighborhood; the new City Hall under construction; Newton High School and the Rowe Street shopping district beyond the school; and the large homes along Commonwealth Avenue up to Chestnut Hill.

"Wouldn't this be a great place to build a house?" George said. "What a view! Some day I'll have enough money to buy the Wesimer Farm and build a grand estate."

"Sure, sure," Johnny laughed. "You'll need to rob a bank to get that type of money."

CHAPTER 6

Bob Johnson stood in front of a large green scoreboard in the Blue Marsh dining room frantically trying to organize the players' pairings for the first round of the tournament. He looked much older than his actual age of twenty-eight. He had a pudgy face and medium build and always wore a bow tie, his trademark. For the previous five years he had been an auctioneer in Braintree, but he had become bored with the auction business.

In 1907, he organized the first professional golf tournament in the Boston area. As the organizer, Bob received a percentage of the player entry fees, sold golf products during the match, and received a percentage of the gate. In the Salem Match Play Invitational in 1908 he cleared over $150.

"Okay, Charles McDonnell," Bob muttered. "Who shall I pair him with?

McDonnell was the marquee player in the Blue Marsh Tournament. He was the defending Leicestershire Open champion and recently had won four pro tournaments in England. The London Times declared him the next great English player. He had scheduled a series of exhibition matches in the United States for early May and June, so Bob invited him to play. But McDonnell had never responded. Bob checked the steamship records and discovered when McDonnell was to arrive. He decided to meet the elusive McDonnell at the steamship docks upon his arrival.

Bob immediately recognized McDonnell as he came down the gang plank. He wore an English tweed three-piece suit and sported a large handle-bar mustache.

"Mr. McDonnell. I'm Bob Johnson. I wrote you a letter

regarding the Blue Marsh Invitational."

McDonnell turned, a bit startled.

"Yes, Mr. Johnson."

He extended his hand to Bob.

"I'm so sorry I wasn't able to respond to your kind invitation before I left England. The post arrived with your letter just before I boarded the ship. I would be honored, sir, to play in your tournament."

Bob was impressed at how personable McDonnell was at their first meeting, a trait not common to most golf professionals Bob had dealt with at tournaments. McDonnell offered to pay the entry fee, but realized he had only pound notes.

"Can I pay you after I exchange these notes?"

"Of course," Bob said.

Bob recognized Tyler Summer from the Boston Examiner standing near the dock. He called to him as McDonnell found a porter for his bags.

"Tyler, I'd like you to meet Charles McDonnell from England. He's going to play in the Blue Marsh Invitational I have organized."

"Mr. McDonnell. An honor to meet you, sir," said Summer. "Can I ask you a few questions?"

"Sure, laddie."

Bob smiled as he helped the porter assemble McDonnell's bags.

The next day, the Examiner ran an exclusive front page story on the legendary Charles McDonnell and the Blue Marsh Invitational.

******

As Bob pondered the first day pairings, his assistant, Sarah

Knowles, came into the ball room. She was impeccably dressed in a taffeta dress, buttoned in front.

Sarah had worked for Bob as his chief assistant and secretary for two years. She was petite, with curly, long blonde hair and a firm body that turned heads when she entered a room. She had the refinement and poise that Bob lacked. Bob was amazed that she had not been snatched up by one of the many young men who followed the matches. But at twenty-three, she was not ready to settle down.

"There are 77 entries. Larger than Salem!" Sarah said.

She brushed back hair from her face.

"Who do you think I should pair Charles McDonnell with?" Bob asked. "I don't want him to be overshadowed by anyone."

"Why don't you put him with the kid from Newton," Sarah said. "Rock said the kid can play."

"That'll work." Bob made an adjustment to the pairing sheets. He was nervous as he worked on the pairings. This was his first major tournament and he wanted everything perfect.

"Are you going to play as the marker?" she asked.

"No. I'm going to send the last group off as a threesome."

Bob had decided to try a new format for starting players during the tournament. He would start players off the 1st and 10th teeing grounds simultaneously. Each pair of two players would tee off in intervals of seven minutes. By the time the first group from the 10th hole took the turn, the last group would have teed off from the 1st teeing ground. It was all a matter of timing and Bob hoped he could keep each group on schedule.

Bob tacked the last pairing on the scoreboard.

"There. That's the final pairing." He stepped back to examine his work.

"Great. I'll post the pairing sheets at the 1st and 10th teeing grounds tomorrow morning," said Sarah.

Bob looked at his pocket watch anxiously. He had only an hour left to get things organized.

"There's never enough time."

He still had to check on the setup of the reception room, and the caterer was waiting on a decision for the champagne.

CHAPTER 7

George and Johnny waited anxiously at the corner of Center and Commonwealth for the trip to Natick. George had decided not to tell his parents about the tournament. Friday was a slow day at school and he could afford to miss one day to caddy for Johnny in his first professional tournament.

"Gee, it was swell of Rock to offer to drive," Johnny said.

The boys heard the rumble of Rock's new Ford Model T as he crossed Commonwealth Avenue, two blocks away. The car had a cobalt blue finish, brass headlights, and a brass radiator cover. Rock had purchased two additional items, a windshield and a canvas retractable roof. These options added $150 to the $850 base price.

Rock's scarf was flapping in the wind as he pulled up in front of the boys.

"Come on. We're burning daylight," Rock said as he deftly threw the front of his silk scarf behind his head.

"Shotgun!" Johnny shouted, as he put his clubs in the back seat of the car.

"I want to get there by 8," Rock said. "Johnny, Bob called before I left the house. You're paired with Charles McDonnell. You go off at 8:40. I'm off at 8:30 on the back side."

"Charles McDonnell!"

Johnny's jaw dropped. His hands started to sweat and he felt light headed.

"Charles McDonnell," Johnny repeated.

Rock said, "You'll be okay. Just shake his hand, say hello, and focus on your own game."

"Charles McDonnell is one of the greatest players of all time," Johnny said. "He beat Harry Vardon last year 7 and 6 at Carnouste. He may be 34, but he still hits one of the longest balls and is a master on the putting green."

Rock rearranged his white scarf behind his neck again, released the brake on the running board, and engaged the clutch. The T lunged forward, throwing George and Johnny back in their seats.

"What route are you using to get to Natick, Rock?" George asked from the rear seat.

"I'm going through Newton Highlands and hook up with the Boston-Worcester Road west to Wellesley. Part of the road has been paved and it'll be quicker than taking the wagon trail through Lower Falls."

"I hear Blue Marsh has been criticized for hosting this tournament," George said.

He leaned forward so he could hear Rock over the hum of the four-stroke engine.

"No other course in New England would host the Invitational. Bob Johnson was turned down by all the local clubs: Woodland, Brae Burn, Salem, Nashua, Newport, and The Country Club."

Rock steered the T through a series of deep ruts in the unpaved road as they entered Newton Highlands and turned right on Lincoln Street.

"Why are you going this way?" yelled George. "The road sign pointed straight ahead for the Boston-Worcester Road."

"I want to show you guys something."

As they drove down Lincoln Street, Rock gave them a tour of the neighborhood.

"Fourteen houses are under construction on this street. The new train station at the corner of Center and Lincoln has sparked the recent building boom. They now have fifteen trains per day to South Station."

Rock stopped in front of a Queen-Anne-style home with a partially completed wrap-around porch and a large turret on the second floor.

"What do you think?"

"About what?" Johnny asked.

"What do you think of my new home?"

"New home!" said George.

"First home I've ever owned. I'd show you around, but we need to go."

"Wow, your own home!" Johnny said.

Rock engaged the T and eased back onto Lincoln Street.

"How much did it cost?" George asked.

"None of your business, young man. It's not polite to ask someone how much something cost. I'm paying for it out of my winnings at the Long Island Classic last month."

Rock had won the tournament in grand fashion, defeating his final opponent 5 and 4, and took home the first place prize of $500. He had also won a few long shot bets with the local bookies and pocketed an additional $1,000.

"Hold on," Rock yelled as they came to the narrow turn at Woodward and Lincoln. He shifted into low gear and gunned the engine, and the T glided smoothly through the deep ruts. George was impressed that the T was able to handle this difficult part of the road. The only other car with a low gear ratio was the Pierce Arrow, and that cost over $2,000.

The T strained as it climbed the steep grade from Woodward Street to the paved section of the Boston-Worcester Road. The maintenance of the Boston-Worcester Road had been recently transferred to the Massachusetts Road Commission, whose first job was to pave the section from Brookline to Newton Upper Falls. The next section from Newton Upper Falls to the Wellesley town line remained unpaved due to budget constraints. Rock double clutched and shifted into high gear. He periodically glanced at Johnny to make sure he hadn't fallen asleep.

"So let me tell you about Blue Marsh," Rock said. "Blue Marsh was built by Harry and Terry Namcoli. They're brothers, oriental rug dealers from Lower Falls. They bought 600 acres adjacent to Lake Tecumsah in '02. The course is not long, just a little over 6300 yards, but it's very challenging. They installed the new wide-open bunkers next to the greens and hundreds of the traditional pot-hole bunkers in the fairways.

"The club dues are steep, $1500 per year, but members include Irish, Jews, Armenians, and even Russians. Blue Marsh and the Comm are threats to the established clubs in the area. The others are controlled by established Yankee blue-blood families who are determined to keep this game pure and controlled by amateurs. Harry and Terry are trying to change the game and I'm in full support of their efforts. Today will be not only a great event, it will be a milestone for professional golf."

Johnny broke in! "That's all very interesting, but how do I play the course?"

"You're right. Let's talk about strategy. Make sure you keep the ball in play off the tee, away from the pot-hole bunkers. Water comes into play on six holes. The 12th hole is a 140-yard par three, but there's water in front and the small green is surrounded by bunkers. Use a mashie unless the wind is blowing in your face."

Rock approached the rutted section of the road near Newton Upper Falls. The engine noise increased as he hit the first deep rut and it was difficult for him to hold the wheel steady. He eased up on the accelerator and the lower speed helped to guide the car through the larger ruts. It took almost fifteen minutes to negotiate the two mile section of the road. As they passed the "Welcome To Wellesley" sign, the paved road returned. Wellesley had paved their section of the road in 1907, one of the first towns to do so along the 26-mile route from Boston to Worcester.

Rock continued: "I played Blue Marsh last month. Shot an 81 in a fierce rain storm. The course is tough, but fair."

"Will we be able to warm up before we play?" Johnny asked.

"Of course. They have a practice area next to the club house."

****

As they climbed the Devonshire Hill near Wellesley Hills Square, the Abby of the Holy Cross appeared on their left. The Sisters of Charity had built the Abby after the Civil War to treat soldiers who had experienced mental problems. In 1889, it became a convent run by the Sisters of the Holy Cross. George's Aunt Lucille was a non-cloistered member of the Sisters of the Holy Cross and had lived in the Abby for ten years. George and his mother had visited Lucille often. They would use the old buggy road through Newton Lower Falls and the trip took over an hour to get to the Abby. George noted that it took less than 20 minutes to reach the Abby in Rock's car.

They headed through Wellesley Hills and 15 minutes later arrived at Blue Marsh, which was located near the Wellesley-Natick town line. A large sign adjacent to the entrance announced "Blue Marsh Match Play Invitational Golf Tournament Today."

Rock drove twenty feet down the gravel entrance and was stopped by a man with tickets in his hand. He set the brake on the running board and eased off the clutch as the engine purred in neutral.

"Good morning, folks. Great day for a golf tournament."

"I'm Guy Rockham. This is Johnny Scranton. George Riley, Johnny's caddie, is in the back seat. Johnny and I are registered for the tournament."

"Yes, Mr. Rockham. I saw your name on the list earlier. Let me check on Johnny Scranton."

Rock poked Johnny in the ribs.

"Someday they'll know your name, kid."

"Scranton . . . yes. He plays Charles McDonnell. Mr. Johnson asked us to make sure you parked near the entrance. Head to the right and a porter will take your clubs. Good luck."

Rock engaged the clutch and slowly released the hand brake. As they drove down the driveway, the Blue Marsh clubhouse emerged through the trees. It was a beautiful setting. The club house was a low-slung, single-story structure with a shake roof and a large clock tower to the left of the entrance. The club was set back from the lake, and the Nemcoli Brothers had preserved most of the mature trees in front of the club house.

A porter approached and opened the passenger-side door of the car.

"Morning, sir. Can I take your clubs?"

Johnny was startled. This was the first time anyone had opened a door for him, especially a car door. He stepped out of the car and brushed off the dust from the ride.

Rock had to slide across the front seat and exit from the passenger side. This was one feature he didn't like about his car. Other car manufacturers had installed driver-side doors. Ford needed to relocate the hand brake from the driver's side and allow the driver to enter and exit the car from the driver's side.

"Come on, George," Rock said. "I'll show you where the caddy shack is located and we can check in."

Rock and the boys walked around the clubhouse to the pro shop near the 1st teeing ground. Sarah Knowles was standing behind a long registration table which had been set up in front of the pro shop. She was a stunning figure standing there with her golden strands of hair gently blowing in the morning breeze. She immediately spotted the dapper Rock dressed in his brown plus four with matching silk socks.

"Hi, Rock. I've got all your credentials ready. Who are your friends?"

"Hi, Sarah. This is Johnny Scranton and George Riley. George is caddying for Johnny today. Quite a fine player in his own right."

"So this is the Johnny Scranton you have told me so much about. George, it's nice to meet you. The caddy shack is over to the left."

"Hi, Sarah," Johnny said, extending his hand. The 5' 5" Sarah was dwarfed by the 6' 4" Johnny.

"Rock, you didn't say how handsome he was. I'll need to keep him away from the girls."

Sarah laughed and flipped her hair out of her eyes. She loved to tease the boys on the tour. Someday she would find Mr. Right, but for now she was content in playing the field. Mr. Right had to be rich, that was the primary criterion. She made a mental note to keep an eye on Johnny. He might be fun to date.

"Here are your credentials. Johnny, you're paired with Charles McDonnell in the opening round at 8:40. Rock, you go off at 8:30 with Billy Sullivan from Mattapan. Check in with the starter ten minutes before your tee time. We'll have a lunch for players and caddies after the first round ends around 1:30. The second round will begin promptly at 2:30. Top sixteen scores in stroke play qualify for the match play quarter finals tomorrow.

Good luck, gentlemen."

The mix of stroke-play and match-play in tournaments originated in the early 1890's in England. Prior to the 1890's, all tournaments were match play format only. As more players became eligible to play in tournaments, golf committees began to use the stroke-play format to select the field for the match-play tournaments.

"Sarah's quite a dish," Johnny said as they walked over to the caddy shack.

Rock laughed.

"Not in your league, son. You don't have enough money."

Rock was suddenly interrupted by a booming voice near the caddy shack.

"Rock, you son of a bitch."

Johnny and George turned to see a burly man with a long beard, bear-hug Rock.

"Cyrus Clyde, you old dog. What are you doing here today?"

Cyrus had been the caddy master at Balford Rapids, outside of St. Louis, in the first professional tournament Rock had won in the United States in 1905. Cyrus even carried a loop for Rock when Rock's caddy fell over a tree stump looking for another player's ball and broke his arm. They had been friends ever since. Cyrus had recently been appointed the caddy master at the Carlisle Country Club.

"Bob hired me to coordinate the caddies for the tournament. I've had a hell of a time recruiting experienced caddies. The USGA threat to declare them professionals has scared them off, but I've recruited some great lads from as far away as Springfield and Albany. I've got a nice kid assigned to you, Rock."

Rock turned toward George.

"Cyrus, this is George Riley. He's going to caddy for

Johnny Scranton."

"George Riley of Newton High School. You won the Boston School Boy tournament last summer. Won your last match, I believe, 5 and 4."

"Yes, sir," George said.

"Johnny finished third, as I recall. Lost on the final hole to Archie Moorefield."

"That's right," George said gleefully. "Boy, you know a lot about us."

"It's my business, son. I try to keep track of all the up-and-coming players. Come on, George, we'll set you up over here. You boys need to hurry and warm up. The locker room is just beyond the registration table. Good luck, lads."

Cyrus put his hand on George's shoulder and gently guided him toward the caddy shack.

CHAPTER 8

"Nice digs," Johnny said as an attendant led them to their assigned lockers.

The lockers were arranged in square bays with 28 lockers per bay. They were constructed of indigo mahogany with gold-plated name tags on each door. In each bay, there was a round card table with a green felt top, wall-to-wall embroidered carpets, a Tiffany electric lamp, and a fan which gently rotated from the ceiling. Johnny had never seen such an elegant locker room.

Inside Johnny's assigned locker was a gift basket from the organizing committee. It contained a sleeve of Goodrich Comets, assorted crackers, and a small bottle of Jameson Irish whiskey.

"Is every tournament like this?" Johnny asked Rock.

"No," Rock said. "They have gone all out. Since this is their first year, the tournament committee, and especially Bob Johnson, wants a reputation as one of the best tournaments in the country. Nice, huh? Come on, let's change. I need to hit some balls and practice putting before we tee off. The greens are really fast out here."

Johnny slipped on his shoes and remembered his dad's words: "We're with you. Do your best and keep a level temper throughout. Mom will be watching."

Rock shook Johnny out of his day dream.

"Ready?"

"Yes, sir. Let's go."

"Don't take unnecessary chances," Rock said. "The course will eat you alive if you try to cut too many corners."

****

They proceeded to the 1st teeing ground where a large score-board had been set up listing the daily pairings. Johnny had never seen his name in foot-high letters. At the sight of his name in bold letters he developed goose bumps and a slight chill.

"Largest field I've ever seen for an event. Seventy-seven players," said Rock.

"They all paid twelve bucks?" Johnny asked, amazed at the number of entries.

"Most did. Some players received a sponsor's exemption due to their finish at tournaments in Worcester and Springfield."

Johnny recognized a few names on the board: Philip Morris from Hyde Park, who had played in the Colonial School Boy matches the previous summer with Johnny; Shawn Hogarth from Needham, who had come in second at the Mass Amateur the previous year; and Billy Nugent, from Nehodine in Wellesley. He had played with Nugent in a charity event at Wollaston in April. Nugent shot a 78 and Johnny shot 81.

A man standing next to the players board approached Rock.

"Hi, Rock."

"Lucas. Ready for lots of action?"

Rock extended his hand to a tall, slender man in his early thirties with slicked-back hair and then gestured toward Johnny.

"Lucas, meet Johnny Scranton from Newton."

"Nice to meet you, Johnny."

"Glad to meet you."

Lucas Griffin was the starter at Salem Country Club and worked part time as a bookie for a syndicate from Haverhill. Johnny thought Lucas looked very smart in his three-piece, wool worsted coat. He figured it cost him over a hundred bucks.

"Lots of competition today. Largest group of bookies I've

seen at a pro tournament," Lucas said quietly to Rock.

In 1907 the USGA had prohibited bookies from being inside tournament grounds. The independent pro tournaments were different. The tournament promoters sold licenses to each bookie and they were allowed to set up a table in front of the clubhouse. Rock saw nothing wrong with this practice. There were bookies at baseball games, horse races, and boxing matches, why not golf? These "holier than thou" gentlemen of the game who controlled the USGA were too restrictive. Rock believed betting was good for the game and the pro game was going to get bigger and better than the amateur game because of it.

"Give me $100 on Charles McDonnell to qualify and $100 on my friend to win," Rock said.

Lucas looked dumb-founded.

"You want to place one hundred bucks on Johnny to win? I knew you were crazy. Okay, Rock, it's your money to lose. The boys in Haverhill are going to love this bet."

He took a small pad of paper from his vest pocket and made a notation.

"Odds are 3 to 1 on McDonnell, and the line on your friend is 40 to 1 to win. I've got you down. This is a really tough field."

Lucas leaned over and asked, "Are you sure you want to make this bet, Rock?"

Rock smiled.

"Let it ride. It's only money."

As he turned, he gestured to Johnny with his left hand over his ear.

"You didn't hear that."

"Hear what?" Johnny asked.

"Good boy," Rock said as they proceeded to the practice tee to warm up. "Remember the drill."

"What time do you have?" Johnny asked George.

"8:20. You have about 15 minutes to get ready."

Johnny started with his niblick and hit five to six shots per club. He finished with his brassie.

"I'm ready," Johnny said. "Let's go to the putting green."

George glanced at Johnny. His face had a stern and focused look. He had never seen Johnny like this before. He wondered what had changed him so quickly.

****

The putting green was immaculate. George had never seen such a smooth green. Johnny took out his Wright and Ditson blade putter. It was slightly beveled so he could lift the ball over a stymie. George noticed the stymie notch on the lower part of the hickory shaft. Johnny had added the notch after he won the Massachusetts School Boy Tournament at the Wollaston Country Club in September.

In that match, Johnny had defeated Brian Davis with a brilliant stymie shot on the final hole. He had used a spade mashie for his second shot on the 18th, and the ball landed eight feet from the flag. Davis got in trouble off the tee and hit a low punch and run shot for his third shot. His ball landed two feet in front of Johnny's ball. Johnny had the option of curving his ball around Davis's ball or trying to lift his shot over it. Johnny decided he had enough room to lift the ball. He cut down on it and hit the back rim of the cup, and the ball dropped in for a birdie. It was one of the most impressive stymie shots George had ever seen.

Six players were chatting on the green and they occasionally hit a few practice putts.

"Better to concentrate on your game," George cautioned

Johnny. "I've watched these guys. Poor practice habits."

George dropped three Haskells and Johnny started with a few short putts in order to get a feel for the speed of the green. He gently stroked each ball toward the practice cup. The balls rolled true and curved a bit due to the cut of the green. After a few minutes, a man interrupted the boys.

"Mr. Scranton. My name is Charles Howell. I'm the Rules Manager for today's tournament. We are checking each player's clubs to make sure everyone is playing with approved equipment. May I see your bag, sir?"

"Sure, it's over here," Johnny replied.

"Who made your irons, sir?"

"Isaac Bell, a clubmaker from Newton."

"I see these have been recently shellacked, Mr. Scranton. What did you use?"

"Linseed shellac. Last night I applied three coats."

"That's okay. Perfectly legal to apply shellac to your shafts, Mr. Scranton. What woods are you using?"

"I have a Bell driver, brassie, and spoon. I also have a Robish cleek which I purchased at a yard sale." Johnny smiled.

Howell examined the cleek closely.

"Interesting diamond-dot scored face on the cleek, Mr. Scranton. I haven't seen this type of pattern before on a cleek. Perfectly within the rules though."

He finished examining each club and put a tag on Johnny's bag which stated "Approved" in large, bold letters.

"This is the first time I've had my clubs inspected. Why the inspection?" Johnny asked.

"We're trying to prevent illegal clubs from being used in the tournament. One chap brought a spoon-like rake. It doesn't meet any standard set by the R&A or the USGA. Also, we're looking for clubs with metal rods inserted in the center of the wooden shaft. The rods are specifically prohibited by the rules."

"Do players really go to such lengths to win?"

"Yes. We see violations all the time. We want to keep this an honorable game. Due to recent changes in technology, we must vigorously enforce the rules, or the game will be ruined. Thank you, Mr. Scranton. Your clubs are approved for play today. We'll inspect the clubs each day. Time to report to the 1st teeing ground. You're up next. Good luck and have a pleasant round."

Howell headed back to the clubhouse.

"Can you believe that some players would put a rod in the middle of a hickory shaft?" Johnny asked, as he put the putter back in the bag.

"I can't believe it. How would they do it?"

George looked puzzled.

******

A large crowd waited at the 1st teeing ground for Charles McDonnell to appear. At precisely 8:30, McDonnell sauntered out and received a thunderous applause from the assembled crowd. Johnny immediately recognized him from his picture in the Examiner.

"Glad to meet you, Mr. McDonnell," Johnny said, extending his hand to the famous golfer.

"Call me Charles. I hate to be so formal."

Johnny was immediately put at ease by this big burly man, who was the same height as Johnny but weighed close to 300 pounds. He wore a long black evening coat, a pair of brown nickers, and a flat Irish wool hat. His signature handle-bar mustache turned up at the ends. Charles took out a pair of reading glasses as he reviewed the scorecard.

He noticed Johnny looking at his glasses.

"Blind as a bat. I need them to sign autographs. You'll get there some day, laddie."

Charles chuckled as he took a driver from his bag. The starter approached the two golfers.

"Gentlemen, it's time. I'll flip a coin to see who goes first. Mr. McDonnell, since you are a guest in the United States, will you call it in the air?"

The starter tossed a gold piece into the air and McDonnell yelled heads as the coin fell between the two players.

"Tails. Mr. Scranton, you have the honor."

Johnny took a few deep breaths as he tried to settle the butterflies in his stomach. He looked around the teeing ground for a level spot. The teeing ground at Blue Marsh was seeded with Kentucky blue grass and there was a sign on the tee box which encouraged players to use one of the sand cones in the box. They had two different sizes of sand cones. One cone was taller than the other. Johnny selected the shorter sand cone from the box, filled it with sand, and set his Comet on top of the sand tee near the left marker.

As Johnny addressed the ball, he was startled to hear the starter yell through his megaphone, "Ladies and Gentlemen. Now on the tee, from Newton, Massachusetts, John Scranton."

Johnny backed off the shot until the crowd noise subsided. Rock had advised Johnny that on the first hole he should swing gently.

"You'll be nervous and an easy swing will help steady the nerves. Also, the buildup of adrenaline at the start of a match will help propel the ball on your first shot."

The first hole at Blue Marsh was a 312-yard par 4. There were pot-hole bunkers on the left and right sides of the fairway and open bunkers surrounded the green on all sides. Johnny adjusted his stance, took another deep breath, and ripped into the ball. The ball started out to the right, then drifted left into the middle of the fairway about 220 yards off the tee.

"Next up from Lacstershire, England, the Royal Cup defending Champion and 1907 player of the year, Charles McDonnell." The enthusiastic crowd behind the teeing ground gave him a warm reception.

McDonnell ignored the sign on the tee box. He tapped the ground to create a slight indentation and placed the ball on the grass. The ball flew off the club face to the right and bounced into one of the pot hole fairway bunkers about 180 yards from the tee.

"Well, that was not a very good start, laddie! But a nice drive from you, young man."

"Looks as if we have a player with us," McDonnell announced to the crowd in a booming voice.

Johnny and Charles headed down the 1st fairway matching each other stride for stride. The nevous butterfly feeling in Johnny's stomach began to subside. He took a deep breath as he walked, drawing in the soothing lavender scent of the Azaleas bordering the fairway.

As McDonnell approached his ball, he noticed that the ball was lodged near the front lip of the bunker. He could only use a mashie niblick to get out of the deep bunker. He sprayed sand in all directions as he hit a massive shot out of the bunker to within 30 yards of the green.

Johnny approached his own ball and turned to George.

"What do you think?"

"Looks to be about 90 yards uphill."

"Yeah. The wind is a bit from the left. What do you think I should hit?"

"Hit the niblick. Keep right as the green slopes off to the left."

Johnny's ball was on a downslope. He adjusted his stance forward and took a full swing. The ball soared into the cloudless spring sky. The shot was so high that the ball seemed to hang endlessly in the air. It took one bounce in the middle of the green, spun back, and stopped three feet from the cup.

"Great shot," George said. "Let's get a birdie."

McDonnell hit a pitch and run for his third shot which landed seven feet from the cup. But he missed the difficult downhill putt and ended with a bogey.

Johnny examined his putt from three different angles. He had a straight putt up a gentle slope and he knew he had to be aggressive to get the ball to the cup. He steadied his putter behind the ball, dragged the putter head back, and boldly stroked the putt. The ball hit the right side of the cup, spun around, and dropped in. The crowd erupted as Johnny plucked the ball from the cup.

McDonnell patted Johnny on the back as they headed to the 2nd teeing ground.

"You made that birdie look easy. Great putt."

"Thanks, Charles."

Johnny wasn't sure if he should say anything about Charles' taking a five on the hole. He started to speak, then thought he should keep quiet. He remembered one of Rock's favorite adages: "Only praise good shots. Don't try to console people on bad shots."

Johnny reeled off eleven straight pars and then ran into trouble on the 13th hole. He ignored Rock's advice to avoid risks and he tried to cut the corner on the long, double-dogleg, par 5. His ball caught the top of the last tree and careened into the rough. He tried to hit a low second shot to get back into the fairway and caught a low-lying limb which knocked the ball down into the thick rough. His next shot careened over a bunker and lodged in the curl of the trap. He blasted out of the trap and finished with a double bogey seven.

George noticed that Johnny was flustered. The back of his neck was cranberry red.

"Take a few deep breaths. You need to stay calm. Remember, it's only one hole."

Johnny glared at George as he selected a brassie for his drive on fourteen. During the next five holes, Johnny made numerous simple mistakes and finished the round six over par, a 77.

McDonnell made a spectacular birdie on the 4th hole, chipping in from 40 yards out for a birdie, but got in trouble on the last five holes, and shot an 80.

"You had it going there for a while, laddie," Charles said as they headed to the scorer's tent.

"Yes. I got greedy. Good luck in the second round, Charles. You'll play better."

"I hope so."

Johnny carefully checked his scorecard before signing it. Johnny had failed to catch a mistake at a school-boy tournament two years before. His opponent listed a four instead of a five on a hole and Johnny had signed the card without checking each hole. He was disqualified for signing an incorrect score card. It was a painful lesson and he vowed it would never happen again. Johnny checked the card kept by Charles McDonnell with his own card and found no errors.

CHAPTER 9

Johnny was paired with Keith Lyons from Hempstead, Long Island, in the second round. Lyons was a short, wiry man, who weighed no more than 140 pounds. He loved to talk during a round and it was difficult for Johnny to get him to cease the banter. George and Johnny learned that he was in the paint business, had five children– three girls and two boys– and loved to eat candy while he played. They also learned about his favorite food, what music he liked, the new color of his house, how he hated dogs, and where he went to school. He never took a practice swing. He just stepped up and hit the ball.

Johnny had learned from his first round and decided not to take any risks during the second round. He was able to place the ball off the tee in better locations to set up for approach shots to each green. He quickly learned how to tune out Keith's banter, and he played well.

As they approached the last hole, the sun began to descend over the clubhouse, engulfing it with a golden glow. The players had a spectacular view as they walked down the fairway. There were thin, wispy clouds on the horizon, and the rays of the fading sun created a fiery portrait. "God," Johnny thought. "This is beautiful." Johnny seemed to drift off to George. He quickly snapped Johnny out of his day dream.

"Last shot, old man. Make it count."

The pin was tucked in the upper left-hand corner of the green and Johnny had over 180 yards to the front of the green. He selected a spoon for his second shot and used the strong interlocking grip Rock had taught him for these types of shots.

He dragged the spoon back slowly and descended sharply behind the ball. The ball leapt off the wooden club face, began a slight draw, and landed safely in the middle of the green. He two-putted for par and finished with a 75 for a two-round total of 152. Keith Lyons, the mouth, finished with an 84 for a two-round total of 167.

As George and Johnny approached the scoreboard, they glanced quickly at the scores. Only one score was lower than Johnny's two-round score of 152. Paul Corcoran from Rochester had shot 149.

Could it be that Johnny would place second in the medal round? thought George.

"There are only ten more scores to be posted, Johnny. Keep your fingers crossed," George said.

Johnny headed down the hill.

"Come on. Let's watch Rock finish on eighteen."

"I need to put the clubs away. I'll meet you at the hole."

"Okay."

As Johnny headed to the 18th green, Sarah approached him.

"Well, Mr. Scranton. A 77 and 75 today. Not bad for your first tournament. Maybe Rock is right. You do have game."

"Rock has talked about me?"

"Oh, yes. We've had long talks about your future."

Sarah smiled and then disappeared into the scorer's tent. Johnny wondered what exactly these long talks had entailed.

When Rock finished his round, he headed toward the scorer's tent, where he saw Johnny standing outside the entrance.

"I heard on the 17th teeing ground that you posted 152. Way to go, kid!"

"How did you do in the afternoon round?" Johnny asked.

"Shot 79. I made some dumb mistakes. Hope 159 will be

enough to play tomorrow."

"Looks as if you're in with that score."

"I need to sign my card first," Rock said.

Johnny decided to wait and watched the last group come into the 18th green.

George joined him with a piece of paper.

"I have the first fifteen. The sixteenth qualifier will be decided by this final group."

George showed Johnny the list of qualifiers:

Paul Corcoran --------- *Rochester Country Club* *149*

John Scranton --------- *The Commonwealth Club* *152*

David Stinson --------- *Teaneck Club* *156*

Guy Rockham --------- *The Commonwealth Club* *159*

Charles McDonnell---- *Leicester Club* *159*

Steve Riley -------------- *Elk Ridge Club* *159*

Forest Murphrie ------- *Springhaven Country Club* *161*

Larry McDermitt------ *Worcester Country Club* *161*

Keile Richmond ------- *Forest Hills Club* *161*

John Mitchel --------- *Upper Montclair Club* *161*

Tim Ross--------------- *The Hempstead Club* *162*

Jerry Rouise------------ *The Mattapan Club* *163*

Seith Iglasini ----------- *The Brooklyn Golf Club* *165*

Jeff Rice----------------- *Concord Country Club*.............. *165*

Joe Wentworth --------- *Gloucester Club* *166*

George added, "Terry Wilder has a chance for the sixteenth spot if he can make par."

Wilder hit a bad approach shot to 18 and landed twenty feet from the cup. Johnny noticed he used an open putting stance with both feet angled away from the ball and kept his right elbow tight to his side. He stroked the ball boldly and it rolled gently to the edge of the ridge, broke sharply, and gained speed as it came down the hill. The ball caught the left edge of the cup and dropped in for a four. The crowd following Wilder broke into applause as he gunned his fist high in the air.

"This guy could be a formidable opponent," Johnny said.

Johnny and George climbed up the slope to the scorer's tent, where three reporters from local papers suddenly surrounded them.

"Johnny! My name is Harrison with the Boston American. How does it feel being the youngest qualifier in the history of a professional golf tournament?"

"I didn't know I was the youngest qualifier. It feels great."

"Do you think you can win this tournament?"

"You bet. I'm ready to take on all comers."

For the next ten minutes, Johnny fielded questions about his round: How were the greens? Was he nervous? Did he have a girlfriend? George was impressed at how naturally and how calmly Johnny answered each question.

A photographer asked if he could take a picture.

"Only if my best friend is in the picture," Johnny said.

He grabbed a reluctant George and forced him to smile. Then a second photographer asked for a photo.

Rock stepped in and grabbed Johnny's arm.

"Sorry, boys. We have to go."

The sun was setting fast as Rock pulled out of the club's driveway and headed east toward Newton.

"What a day," Johnny said as he slumped down in the front seat, totally exhausted.

"A great day," George observed. "One of the best days of my life. Tomorrow will be even better."

CHAPTER 10

For Saturday's third and fourth rounds of the Blue Marsh Tournament the format changed to match play. Overall low score in the round didn't matter; the key to match play was the player's ability to win individual holes.

Johnny played brilliantly. The match play format suited Johnny's game. He defeated his opponent 5 and 4 in the third round and 2 and 1 in the fourth round.

On Sunday, Edith Riley went to the six o'clock Mass at St. Philip Neri to light a few candles. It was a cool crisp morning and Edith decided to walk home from church. The mile hike was invigorating. As she walked up the sidewalk to their home, a deep voice greeted her.

"Hi ya, Mrs. Riley."

"Oh!" Edith caught her breath, startled by Johnny's appearance on the porch. "Johnny, you startled me – my goodness gracious. Why are you here so early?"

"Couldn't sleep."

"Come in. I'll make you breakfast. George!"

Edith's loud voice reverberated throughout the house.

"Johnny is here."

"Okay," George said as he rushed down the stairs.

George directed Johnny into the parlor.

"How did you sleep?"

"I got a few hours of sleep. I kept turning over all night replaying the holes in my mind."

"Boy, that was a great match with Jeff Rice yesterday. I still can't believe you stymied him on the 17th hole. I was sure that you were going to lose that hole."

"Yeah, I got lucky with my fourth shot." Johnny smiled. "It landed outside the exclusion. I was surprised he didn't ask for a measurement."

"The stymie took the wind out of his sail. He looked dejected after the putt," George said. "He played 18 too conservatively."

Steve Riley came into the parlor.

"Hi, boys. I still have goose bumps from that match. I stopped at Cassidy's Pub last night and they were talking about your stymie shot on the 17th green, Johnny. You're starting to get a reputation, my boy. I didn't hear the other scores from yesterday. How did everyone do?"

"Rock defeated Paul Corcoran 3-2 to advance," George said. "Terry Wilder defeated Charles McDonnell 5-4. Tim Ross defeated Keile Richmond 4-3 and Johnny defeated Jeff Rice 2-1."

"What are the pairings for today?" Steve asked.

"Rock plays Terry Wilder and Johnny goes against Tim Ross. The winners advance to the final this afternoon."

"We're leaving early in the buggy to pick up Aunt Lucille on the way. Johnny's dad is coming with us."

"Aunt Lucille is coming!" exclaimed George. "She's a nun! Can they come to a golf tournament?"

"Non-cloistered nun, young man," said Steve. "She loves to attend sporting events."

"She'll be the only nun on the course."

"Don't bet on it. Half the convent is coming to watch Johnny."

George raised his eyebrows comically and smiled.

"Well, Johnny, you'll be the only one with a nun brigade in professional golf," he said.

"Yeah. Maybe they can muster some divine help."

They all broke into a long laugh.

Steve tried to keep them quiet. "Don't kid about Aunt Lucille. You know how sensitive your mother is about her."

There was a knock at the front door.

"Who could that be at this hour?" Steve asked.

He opened the door and found some thirty kids from the high school gathered in his yard. He immediately recognized Nancy Marchand.

"Hi, Mr. Riley. Johnny's dad said he was over here. Can he come out?"

Johnny appeared in the doorway and the group erupted in applause.

"Hi ya, Nancy. Hi, gang."

Johnny waved as if he were a seasoned politician. Nancy grabbed his hand and pulled him into the street.

"We have something to show you."

Parked in front of the Riley home was a 1908 Reo. The car was fire-engine red, and it had oversize tires with white spokes. Steve Riley thought it was the best-looking car in the neighborhood. Wayne Kankas had decorated his dad's car with banners which said "Scranton's Screeches," and on the back of the storage box was a sign that said "On to Victory at the Invitational."

"We're coming to see you play today."

"How can you afford tickets ?" Johnny asked.

He knew that Bob Johnson had increased the Sunday ticket to two dollars per person.

"Rock donated sixty bucks to the high school sports fund to buy a block of tickets. We had a lottery this morning to choose who would go."

Johnny began to feel flushed and his legs began to shake.

"Nancy, will you please excuse me for a minute. I really feel like I'm going to be sick."

Johnny quickly headed for the bathroom.

"George, what's the matter with Johnny?" Nancy asked.

"Nerves. He'll be okay once we get to the course."

Nancy nodded and then took charge.

"Okay, gang, let's go over to Charlie Wie's house. His dad is going to drive us out in his hay wagon. Don, Bridget, and Irene – go with Wayne in his car and we'll meet you near the scoreboard."

Nancy was acting like a drill Sargent barking out orders.

"Okay, Nancy. Bye, guys," George said. "Remember. Quiet on every shot and no running on the course."

"I've tried to teach them this etiquette thing," Nancy chimed in. "Bye, George."

"George, I didn't wake you this morning to attend church," his mom said as she came onto the porch. "I think the Lord will forgive you missing Mass today."

"Thanks, Mom. I was tired last night. I needed the extra sleep."

"I lit two candles for Johnny and Rock today. Not that the good Lord takes sides in a sporting match, but maybe he can help keep the wind down or keep the rain away."

"No rain forecast for today. The candles must have worked," George said sarcastically.

George knew that his mother believed in the power of prayer so he could kid her only so far on this point before she became defensive.

"Where's Johnny?" Edith asked. "I made breakfast."

"In the bathroom. Case of the jitters," George said.

"You should bring your shawl, Mother," Steve said as he grabbed his coat and hat. "It could get brisk in the afternoon. And check out the American story on page three. There's a picture of George and Johnny."

"Give me that," Edith said grabbing the paper from Steve.

"Look at this. My George in the paper. George! You should have brushed your hair."

"Yes, mother," George responded, with an exasperated tone.

"I'll read this on the way," Edith said.

Just then, Johnny emerged from the bathroom looking pale.

"Nice bathroom job, Mr. Riley. I checked out your tile work."

"Johnny!" Edith said as she put her hand on his forehead. "Are you all right? How about some castor oil? Always helps me when I have a stomach ache."

"No thanks, Mrs. Riley. This will pass."

"Well, we're off," Steve said. "We'll take the buggy road through Lower Falls, then cut over onto the Boston-Worcester Road at the Abbey."

"Give me a hug, Johnny," said Edith. "Good luck today. We'll be rooting for you."

Edith leaned over to kiss George on the forehead.

"Keep his temper under control," she whispered in George's ear.

"Maggie, are you coming?" George yelled. "Mom and Dad are ready to go."

"Yes, I'm coming," Maggie yelled back.

She came bounding down the stairs.

"See ya at the course, Johnny."

She giggled every time she spoke to Johnny.

"Bye, Muffin."

"I'm not a muffin!" she said.

Johnny patted her on the head.

"I'm a young lady."

With her curly brown hair, rosy cheeks, and wide open hazel eyes, she still looked as if she was the rag-a-muffin Johnny had played with as a child. As is often true with the baby of the family, wherever they went, Maggie had to be the center of attention. She had a crush on Johnny, but never dared tell anyone, especially Johnny.

"We're off to Natick," Steve said as they exited the house.

George waved goodbye from the doorway, then turned back toward Johnny.

"Let's get some food into you," he said. "A light breakfast will help your stomach."

George and Johnny were just finishing their meal when they heard Rock's horn.

"Come on, let's go," Johnny grunted. "I'm starting to feel better." George grabbed his tam-o-shanter and the boys headed out the door.

****

Rock was sitting in the T wearing a bowler hat and goggles.

"Well, this is the day. Are you ready, laddie?"

"Why the bowler, Rock?"

"I want everyone to know who is coming today. A bowler stands out, especially in this Tin Lizzy."

Rock dipped his head down a bit and stared at Johnny's pallid face.

"How you feeling, Johnny? You look flushed."

"I need a few minutes to let my stomach settle."

"Upset stomach?"

Rock glanced over at George.

"Did he throw up?"

"Yes, twice."

"He has the jitters," Rock said. "A slight nervousness is a good thing. Helps to sharpen your senses. I threw up once this morning myself."

"Johnny, why don't you ride in the back and lie down. I want to talk strategy with George."

CHAPTER 11

"Good morning, Mr. Rockham. Good morning, Mr. Scranton, Mr. Riley," the attendant said as he waved them through the barrier.

George was startled.

"He knew my name."

Rock smiled.

"Yes, sir. You're famous, son. Your picture is in every Boston newspaper."

The head porter met them at the entrance.

"Good morning, Mr. Rockham, Mr. Scranton, Mr. Riley. We'll park the car for you."

Rock and Johnny headed to the club's dining room. Bob Johnson and his tournament staff had set up their office in the ornate columned room. Bob was busy counting the receipts from yesterday's gate. He looked up as Rock and Johnny entered the room.

"Seven hundred and forty-two paid attendance," he said. "A record crowd for a pro tournament in Massachusetts. Today, we may break that mark. Did you see the newspaper stories in the Globe, American, and Herald? What a spread."

Bob shuffled through some registrations.

"Rock and Terry will go off on one and Johnny and Tim Ross will tee off on the 10th. Is that okay?"

"Okay with me," Johnny said. "Will you let everyone know in advance? My friends think I'm going off one."

"Sure. I'll have our starters announce the pairings and Sarah will post the pairings on the board."

Johnny picked up the Herald. Rock grabbed the paper from

him and pushed him toward the door.

"Come on, son. I don't want you to get a big head. You need to focus on the first match."

Johnny glanced at Sarah, who was hand-printing the pairing sheets. She was wearing a blue dress with a small yellow bow around the waist. The dress came down to mid-calf length and she was wearing dark stockings. He had never seen a girl wear such a short dress. He had heard about this new style of dress in New York, but, here in Boston, what would people think? The dress was daring and Sarah had a great pair of legs.

"Sarah, do you need any help putting up the pairings sheets?"

Sarah smiled warmly.

"Now, John Scranton. What would people think if you were posting pairing sheets?"

She picked up the sheets and exited the office quickly. As she left the office, she turned and flicked her hair from her face.

What a flirt, Bob thought. He turned back to Rock and Johnny.

"Get going now. We have two special guests from Wright and Ditson. They are interested in a sponsorship for the summer tour."

He leaned over and whispered to Rock, "They want Johnny and George to join the tour."

"Great idea," Rock whispered. "But let's not tell either kid until the end of the day."

At the back of the dining room, Rock paused, reflecting for a moment, and then turned toward Bob.

"We're going to make a fortune off these kids!"

Rock winked as he headed to prepare for his match.

****

George noticed a group of bookies working the crowd as he

walked across the plaza in front of the clubhouse. He approached Cyrus, who had just placed a bet with a small, wiry-haired man.

Cyrus nervously stuffed the tally sheet in his pocket.

"Hi, George."

"Lots of action today," George said.

"I heard Bob Johnson has granted 35 licenses for the match. Largest group of bookies I've seen at a tournament," Cyrus said.

George was confused.

"Bob grants a license to each bookie?"

"Yes, laddie. As the promoter, he gets a fee from every bookie."

"How does he control them?"

"That's the whole point of the license. Most of these lads are committed to responsible gambling, but there are a few bad apples. The guy I placed a bet with is first rate, but there are some lads who will try to rob you every time."

"Some players say they have been approached by bookies to throw a match. How often does that happen?

"It happens. Not often. I haven't witnessed a player take a dive in a match. But I hear stories."

"What are the odds today, Cyrus?"

"Rock and Tim are 3-2 favorites. Johnny is at 7-1, and Terry is at 9-1."

Cyrus smiled.

"I laid down a bet on your boy to win. Go make me some money."

"Good luck, Cyrus."

George headed to the bag room to clean Johnny's clubs before the match. He felt uncomfortable watching people line up to place their bets. Do these men control the outcome of each professional tournament? Has the sport become corrupted? Do players take bribes to throw matches? He couldn't imagine

Rock ever throwing a match.

As he sat cleaning a mashie, he overheard one of the bookies promise a customer that he knew who would win the tournament. The bookie turned and walked away before George could hear his answer. How did he know who would win? He didn't agree with Rock that gambling was good for the game. He'd heard too many rumors about players throwing matches, even in amateur tournaments. Gambling in golf seemed flat-out wrong. He decided to listen more closely to the banter among his fellow caddies. They'd know if the fix was in.

****

Johnny's morning match with Tim Ross was a cliffhanger. Ross took an early lead on the first hole, but Johnny countered with a great shot on the second to pull even. The lead changed hands eight times until the last hole, where they stood all square.

"What do you think? Should I use my brassie and cut the dogleg?" Johnny asked George.

"You know what Rock would say. Play it safe. But the way you've hit today, I'd say go for it. You can recover if you mis-hit it."

The wind was blowing from right to left. Johnny opened his stance and ripped into the brassie. The ball started out to the right and then began to hook around the dogleg. Johnny smiled as he finished the shot. He'd hit it perfectly. The ball landed in front of the green, less than 65 yards from the pin.

Ross decided to take the conservative route and ended 198 yards from the green. He was forced to use a long iron and his shot came up short on the oversized green, 45 feet from the pin. Johnny used a niblick and hit a low cut shot directly at the pin. The ball hit once, spun left, and stopped five feet from the cup. The crowd of spectators at the green cheered wildly.

"I'm getting goose bumps from all this applause," George confided to Johnny as they came onto the green.

Ross attempted to stymie Johnny, but he was too aggressive with the putt and the ball rolled beyond the cup.

Johnny took his time studying his putt from all angles and then carefully stroked the ball into the cup for his birdie three. Johnny took one step forward, threw his hat into the air, and twirled around on the tip of his right foot. This would became his celebratory move.

"I knew when you cut the corner that I was a goner," Ross admitted to Johnny as they stood shaking hands. "Gutsy play, young man. Can't complain about this match. One of the best I've ever played."

"Thank you, Tim. You were a tiger to the very end."

As the two golfers walked off the course, the marshal yelled into the megaphone: "Mr. Scranton wins the match one up."

****

As they came off the green, Johnny saw Bob Johnson standing with two men.

Bob patted him on the back.

"Great job, young man. Splendid win."

"How did Rock do?" George asked.

"He lost to Terry Wilder 3 and 2. Wilder made four straight birdies to close him out."

"Amazing golf," Bob said as he shook his head in disbelief.

George and Johnny stared at one another for a minute in shock. Rock was out! How could this happen?

Bob recaptured Johnny's attention.

"Johnny, I'd like you to meet two friends, George Wright and Al Spaulding." Both men were older than Bob and were richly attired. Spaulding had a Cincinnati Reds pin on his left lapel which Johnny admired.

"An honor to meet you," Johnny said. "I'd like you to meet my best friend, George Riley. Couldn't have made it this far without him."

"Yes, we've heard about George Riley. You're quite a good golfer yourself, I understand, Mr. Riley," Spaulding said.

Bob immediately intervened.

"Mr. Spaulding and Mr. Wright have been talking about sponsoring our tour this summer. They want you and George to join. We can talk later. I know you need to get ready for the finals."

"Good luck, Johnny. We're rooting for you," Wright said.

Suddenly Johnny was engulfed by reporters. He ended up fielding their questions for twenty minutes, answering everything they asked, and posing for numerous photos. George finally pulled him away to get a bite to eat before the final round.

****

The final round began at 2:30. Word spread that Johnny had reached the finals and the gallery swelled to over 2500 spectators. The round itself was anti-climactic, though. Johnny caught fire on the front side. He birdied the 4th, 5th and 7th holes and was three up at the turn. He closed Wilder out on the 15th hole by chipping in from the fringe of the green for the win. The huge gallery cheered Johnny and George as they triumphantly walked side by side down the 18th fairway. Johnny kept pumping his fist in the air all the way to the green.

****

The awards ceremony was a blur for Johnny. The post-game interviews on the other hand lasted for two hours and seemed to go on forever. What type of driver did Johnny use? How many times had he stymied a player in a tournament? One reporter even asked him what his favorite type of ice cream was.

Rock finally grabbed the boys for the drive home.

As Rock pulled the T onto the Boston-Worcester Road, Johnny said, "Rock, sorry we couldn't face each other in the final round."

"I made too many mistakes today."

A large crowd lined the road to see the champion. Rock drove slowly and stopped often so Johnny could sign autographs. Finally the crowds dispersed.

"You were great today and it's a bonus that you knocked out Wilder," Rock said with glee. "He is such a snob. During our match, he complained that my clubs looked old and worn. What business does he have to be critical of my clubs? His comments upset me and I lost focus. His strategy was to get me rattled early in the match and he succeeded. I kept thinking about his comments every time I hit a shot."

"I didn't talk to him during our match," Johnny said, as he stretched out in the front seat, the adrenalin draining from his body. He suddenly felt very tired.

As the sun set behind them, Rock pulled the T over to the shoulder of the road near the Newton town marker.

He reached into his coat pocket.

"I have your winnings, Johnny."

Rock counted out $250, then counted out more.

"And here's a special bonus for you--$500 from my share of the bets."

Johnny was stunned.

"Holy shit! Five hundred bucks! How much did you win?"

"I laid down $100 on you to win with our friend from Salem. You went off at 40-1."

"You won $4,000! The boys in Haverhill must be going nuts."

"Yes, minus the 10% commission, I received $3,600, plus my third-place finish check for $150. Not a bad three days of work."

George heard everything Rock said. This was wrong, he thought. A player betting on another player. Should he say something to Rock?

Before he had the chance to say anything, Rock turned and said, "And there's more. George, are you awake?"

"Yes. Just resting my eyes. It's been a long weekend."

"Here's a special bonus for you."

Rock leaned over and counted out an additional $500 and handed the stack of crisp new bills to George.

"You were part of this win, so you should share in the winnings."

George stared at the pile of money in his hands. It was more money than he'd ever seen at any one time in his life. Rock smiled.

George's voice quivered. "Rock, I can't accept this money."

"Do you want me to give it to the church? Take it. You earned it. I'm making a donation to your college fund. And if you join us on the tour, there will be more to come."

Johnny swung around in the seat to face George.

"Wow! We'll kick butt on the tour, partner."

George started to count the stack of bills.

"Listen, George," Rock said. "Keep the money for now. You can always give it back later." He smiled again. "Let's talk after graduation. You have plenty to do over the next few weeks. It's been a long day."

Rock engaged the clutch, released the parking brake, and eased the T out into the road, heading for Newton.

George had never seen so much money. He counted it one more time. I can't keep this. It's wrong, he thought. But my school tuition is due in a few weeks. The money would help. George decided to stuff the stack of bills into his sock. He would think about Al Spaulding's offer later. He was too tired to make a decision. He laid down in the back seat of the T and watched as the stars began to appear in the eastern sky.

****

As they approached Homer Street a huge bonfire in the middle of the block greeted them. It looked as if the whole town had come out to celebrate Johnny's victory. "I'm so proud of you," Johnny's dad said as he hugged his son.

Johnny's eyes were misty.

"Can you say a few words to the group? These folks have been waiting for over two hours. It's okay if you go to school late tomorrow."

"Okay, Dad. Love to do it," Johnny said.

George climbed out of the car and excused himself to go to the bathroom. Instead, he went directly to his room and laid the money on the bed.

Disconcerting thoughts raced through George's mind as the cheers from the crowd outside echoed through the Riley home. Did Rock throw his match? He had made ten times the money by losing that he would have made if he had won. It would probably take a regular person like George's dad five years to earn that kind of money. Was Johnny's win staged? Were Bob and Sarah involved?

Clothes still on, George lay on his bed, and drifted off into an uncomfortable sleep.

CHAPTER 12

George and Johnny became instant celebrities, and everywhere they went people asked for their autographs. George felt silly signing his name. He hadn't even played at Blue Marsh, but for some reason people asked.

Two weeks after the tournament, the boys finished their final exams. George graduated with a 94 average and finished second in the class. Johnny squeaked out a 66 average, third from the bottom of the class.

"That a boy," said George as Johnny held up his diploma after graduation. "Thought you'd never get that sheepskin, old man."

"I cruised through those finals. They couldn't keep this diploma from me. And I'm ready to be gone now that I have it. I'd join the tour tomorrow if I could. I heard you signed up for the Eastern Amateur in two weeks. What about Al Spaulding's offer to join the tour?" Johnny asked.

"I've given it a lot of thought," George said in a serious tone. "I'm not cut out for the wild life on the tour. The gambling, the drinking, the bookies, and the travel. I'm going to college and play as an amateur."

George hooked Johnny's arm, pulled him close, and quietly said, "No one can know I took money from Rock. I need it for college, but if anyone finds out, I'll be banned as an amateur for life. You haven't told anyone?"

"No way. I'd never tell. Besides, it was just a donation to your college fund. That's what I heard." Johnny winked at George.

George looked thoughtful.

"I know the pro tour will overshadow the amateur tour

someday, and I know that will be good for you, but I'm a more stay at home, keep the home fires burning type of guy."

They walked down the aisle of the auditorium in silence and then George stopped and turned to Johnny, "You need to be careful and not get sucked into any schemes by these bookies. They'll be the death of the pro tour if they don't control them. If the rumors continue about fixed golf matches, pro golf will be destroyed."

"Don't worry about me. I can handle them."

"Okay. Listen, can you caddy for me in the Eastern Amateur?" George asked.

"I can't. The team leaves for twelve weeks of tournaments and exhibition matches next week."

"Next week! I thought you were leaving in July."

"Bob's set up a match in New Haven on the new course at Yale."

"Where else do you go?"

"After New Haven, we head to Atlantic City to play the New Jersey Invitational in July. After New Jersey we go to Maryland and play an exhibition match at Columbia Country Club. Then we're off to Richmond for the Colonial and Pinehurst to play the new Donald Ross course."

"Donald Ross. That's Rock's friend, right? I hear the course is great."

"That's what I hear. Can't wait to play it. After Pinehurst, we take a train to Chicago for the Western Open. St Louis is next, and we end the tour in mid-August in Kansas City. Bob said he'd get more matches before I come back to Newport for the National in September."

"Is Sarah going ?" asked George.

"You bet. She's our traveling secretary, organizing the rooms, train schedules, luggage, and the press room at each match."

"I think she's sweet on you."

"Go on. She's five years older."

"I saw how she looked when Nancy jumped on you at the 9th hole and landed that big wet kiss. She looked annoyed."

"Get out of here. She's good looking and really smart, but she's not my type. She flicks her hair every time she talks with a guy. Drives me crazy. She's a big flirt. Might be fun one or two nights, but long term, forget it."

Nancy had returned her graduation robe and saw the boys talking in the aisle. She bounded over to them.

"What are you guys talking about?"

"We're discussing Johnny's trip, if you really need to know," George said.

"Gee, I wish I could come with you, Johnny. Three months away from each other. I don't think I can survive." Nancy pouted.

Johnny smiled.

"You'll find something – or someone to keep you company."

"Johnny, you know you're the only one for me. But I'm not going to be like George's Aunt Lucille, locked up in my room all summer."

"Now leave my Aunt Lucille out of this. Did you see her do the jig with another nun after Johnny's win? I couldn't believe it."

George rolled up his diploma and threw his sweat-soaked graduation robe onto the large pile of accumulated robes.

"Come on. Let's meet the gang at Dominic's for an ice cream sundae," said Johnny as he tossed his robe on the pile. Then he ceremoniously offered his arm to Nancy and escorted her out of the auditorium. George trailed a step behind.

"Class of 1909. I can't believe we made it," Nancy said. She turned back to say to George, "So I hear you decided on Brown."

"Yes. I signed a letter of acceptance yesterday. They offered me a small scholarship and I've saved money."

George felt a pang of guilt and he looked away from Johnny.

He knew it was wrong to take Rock's money, but he needed it. And, besides, no one would ever know.

****

There was a huge sign in Dominic's front window: "Congratulations to our own Johnny Scranton."

Dominic Ventelli had opened the first ice cream sundae parlor in the Boston area in 1901 after he had visited his aunt, who worked at Platt and Lott's Pharmacy in downtown Ithaca, New York. He spent three days with his aunt and learned how to make over twenty-six varieties of ice cream sundaes. His own ice cream parlor became an instant success. Dominic named one of his classic ice cream sundaes after Johnny–The Scranton Scramble–a combination of four different scoops of ice cream covered with blue syrup. Dominic's served the best ice cream sundaes in the Boston area.

****

A week after graduation, Rock threw a party at the club for 200 business associates. The guest list included some of the most influential business leaders in professional golf and the Boston business community: Spalding and Wright, the tour's sponsors; Harold Day, the president of First Boston Securities, Rock's financial advisors; Harry and Terry Nemcoli; Donald Ross, Rock's old friend from his English tournament days; and Charles Goodrich, Rock's ball sponsor. Belle LaCree personally supervised the preparation of the elaborate dinner, which included oysters on the half shell, roast of lamb with jubilee sauce, and a special cheesecake based on her grandmother's recipe.

"Boy there are a lot of people here," George said, as the family walked up the long driveway to the club.

"Look at the variety of cars in the parking lot," Steve said.

George recognized Belle's Pullman Model K parked near the club entrance.

"Dad, the Pullman over there was purchased by Belle LeCree last month. She paid $2,000 for it."

"Wow. That's a snazzy car. Look. There's a Cadillac Thirty, an EMF Five, and a Mora Light Four," Steve said. "I'll catch up with you. I'm going to check out a few of these cars."

"Now, Steve," Edith chastised him. "You can look at these contraptions later."

"I won't be long. You don't get too many chances to see beauties like these up close. Maggie, do you want to join me?"

He extended his hand to his daughter. Maggie skipped over to him.

"Okay, but don't be long," said Edith.

She knew that Steve wanted to buy a car, but they couldn't afford it right now.

Edith was the financial conservative in the Riley home. Steve had done well last year, made over $1,800. But $850 for a Model T or Olds Coupe was definitely out of the question.

"She spent $2,000 for her car!" Edith said as George escorted his mother into the club. "I wonder how much she spends on her clothes?"

Edith stopped in the portico and turned to George.

"Oh, my God! I'm not properly dressed for this dinner."

She dejectedly looked down at what she was wearing, a flowing brown taffeta dress which she had made herself. She had ordered the pattern from the Sears and Roebuck catalog, bought the material at Millie's Yarn and Cloth Store in Newton Center for $2.40, and sewed the dress in a day.

George tried to calm her.

"You look beautiful. Don't worry. Belle told me this was not a formal event."

"If I see one haute couture dress, I'm leaving. I can't compete with this crowd," Edith said sternly.

George leaned over and gave his mom a kiss on the cheek.

"You'll be fine. I love your broad-rim hat. It'll be the talk of the party. This isn't a stuffy crowd. No one tries to show off. It's a very down-to-earth group. You'll like them and they will fall in love with you."

George put his arm around her waist and led her into the dining room.

"I'm with the best-looking lady in the club."

Edith was amazed at what she saw in the ballroom. Men wore everything from sports knickers with wool or corduroy coats to three-piece business suits. The women wore every type of dress from long flowing mitsey skirts with blouses to evening gowns. It was an eclectic mix of dress and people.

Many of the women complimented Edith on her unique dress and asked where she had purchased it. She smiled, said thank you, and explained that she had bought the dress at a small store in Newton Center.

Belle joined Edith and guided her around the room to meet everyone.

"I love your hat," Belle said. "Can you come over next week and give me some pointers on my wardrobe?"

The wealthiest lady in Newton wanted her advice! Edith was beaming.

She heard herself say, "Belle, I just love your new car."

As they chatted, a waiter approached George and quietly asked if he could join Mr. Rockham in the Men's Grill.

George apologized to Belle and turned to his mother.

"Mom, I'll be back soon. Will you try to find Dad and Maggie?"

Edith laughed and waved George away.

"I'm sure they're fine. They're probably still goggling at the new cars outside."

****

George raced down to the Men's Grill and found Rock, Johnny, and twelve other men seated at two tables. The group included Spaulding, Wright, Greg Packard from Brookline High School, and Byron Grove from the Goodrich Company.

Rock stood holding a bottle of Remy Martin cognac in his left hand and gesturing to the assembly with his right hand. When George joined the group, Rock raised the decorative bottle above his head and announced:

"Gentlemen, this is a very special occasion. We are here tonight to honor two outstanding young players – Johnny, on his great win at the Blue Marsh, and George, as an outstanding amateur player. Greg Packard and I would like to offer a challenge to them."

Rock paused, lowered the bottle, and cradled it under this arm.

"We will store this cognac for ten years, and the player who wins the most tournaments over this period of time will be declared our champion. This very bottle will be awarded to the winner at the 10th-year reunion dinner for the Newton High School Class of 1909.

"Now, to be counted as a win, the tournament must be a regional, state, or national tournament played under USGA or

R&A rules. The tournament must be a complete tournament. No rain-shortened wins will be counted. Greg Packard has agreed to be the scorekeeper for The Challenge."

Rock looked to Packard and nodded, then continued.

"Luckily I've purchased two bottles. This bottle I'm holding is to be set aside in a cabinet in the club bar to be opened ten years from today by the winner of The Challenge. I've also got a second to be used to toast our agreement tonight. For those unaware, I have selected this cognac because of its special designation."

He raised his eyebrows dramatically and raised the bottle again.

"And I might add that, at $58 a bottle, only Belle can afford to replace it if we break it."

Rock feigned dropping the bottle and the group howled with laughter.

"So what do you think, George? Johnny?"

George looked at Johnny, who was standing at the bar.

"Okay by me," said Johnny.

"I'm going to kick his butt," George said.

The group laughed.

"If anyone is going to do some butt kicking, it will be me," Johnny responded.

Rock let out a loud deep laugh and waved the bottle in the air.

"Well, a feisty lot we have, gentlemen. Let's have a toast to our two challengers – and let the best man win."

Rock opened the second bottle and poured each man at the table a shot of cognac.

"To Johnny and George. May they take the golf world by storm and may they represent the best golf has to offer."

"Hear, hear," the group said in unison.

Each man took a sip of the finest cognac in the world. Johnny chugged his cognac in one gulp and extended his glass to Rock.

"Slow down, laddie," Rock yelled. "This is sipping cognac, not some cheap whiskey. At $58 a bottle, you don't guzzle this stuff." Rock refilled each empty glass and raised his glass in a toast. "Gentlemen, let the Challenge begin."

CHAPTER 13

George stood on the 17th teeing ground and looked at the crowd massed around the par 3 green. He was on the verge of winning his first major amateur tournament. He had Frederick Marsh from The Littleton Club dormie in the final round of the Eastern Amateur Match Play Tournament. The Eastern had become one of the premier amateur events in the country and had started with a huge field of 98 players. Now it was down to just George and Marsh.

George had opened the first day with a 74, followed by a disastrous 82 in the afternoon round. Miraculously, he qualified for the match play round when two players defaulted by signing incorrect score cards. George played well during the next three rounds, winning his matches 4-3, 3-1 and 5-4.

"Okay, George. One more hole and we have him," said Ira Runyon, his caddy, as he came onto the teeing ground.

George was ashen white and looked dazed. It was a hot, sticky day, well into the upper 80's.

"George, you look awful. Are you okay?"

"I'll be alright. I need to sit for a few minutes," George said.

Ira dunked a towel into the water bucket on the teeing ground and placed the cold towel around George's neck. "Wow!" George said. "That's cold."

He shivered and felt refreshed after a few minutes of rest.

"Okay, let's go," he said as he pulled the towel off his neck.

George selected a spade mashie to use for the 136-yard hole, which was heavily bunkered in front of the green. He hit a high, looping shot, which sailed past the front bunker, skipped twice, and stopped eighteen inches from the cup. The crowd burst into long applause, and George smiled, knowing that he had hit the best shot of the day.

Marsh looked dejected as he began his routine. As the club descended, his left arm collapsed and he almost topped the ball. The ball ended 30 yards from the front of the green. He pitched onto the green, twenty feet from the cup, but he missed his par putt. As a gesture of good sportsmanship, he conceded George's putt.

"Ira, you saved the day," George said as they walked back to the club house for the awards ceremony. "I couldn't believe how much that towel helped."

"You looked as if you were in a different world, George," Ira said. "You needed something to snap you out of it."

"You're right, Ira. I drifted into a different state of mind."

George vowed to maintain his concentration in the future. He would not let this happen again in a competition. On hot days he would take salt pills and lots of water and pace himself.

****

George was invited to meet some of the club members after the awards ceremony. Bernard Reynolds, Secretary of the Hyde Park Country Club and the First Vice President of the Massachusetts Golf Committee, greeted him at the entrance to the men's grill. Reynolds, in his early fifties, was impeccably dressed in a wool jacket and corduroy brown knickers.

"Mr. Riley. Come in. Congratulations on your fine win today. Let me get you a drink. Lemon saspirilla okay?"

"Fine," George said. "Thank you."

Reynolds escorted George to a large table where six men sat in a semi-circle. "I'd like you to meet some friends," he said.

The six men served as the Executive Board of the Massachusetts Golf Committee. The Committee had been formed in 1905 to promote amateur golf and to prohibit professionals from tournaments in Massachusetts.

An elderly gentleman rose from the end of the table and addressed the assembled members.

"Mr. Riley, I am Horatio Cliveburn from The Chase Club. We've asked to meet with you to discuss a serious matter."

A frown appeared on George's forehead as he leaned forward.

"George, if I may call you by your first name"–Cliveburn didn't wait for a reply before he continued–"We've learned that you were offered a position as a team member on the exhibition tour organized by Bob Johnson. There's a rumor that you accepted money from him to become a member of his professional exhibition tour. Is this true?"

George was stunned at the allegation. Who were these men and why were they asking him these questions? George paused, sat straight up in the chair, put his hands flat on the table, and took a deep breath.

"I declined to accept his offer. I will attend Brown University in the fall. I've decided to play in amateur tournaments only."

After a moment, Reynolds spoke.

"George, you should understand that we're deeply concerned about the growing influence of professional golf in the game. Golf is a sport for gentlemen and there is no place in this game for the professional. The honor of the game must remain secure and we mustn't allow it to become the province of these scoundrels. These hooligans must be stamped out."

"What's wrong with professional golf exactly?" George asked, curious to hear their response.

"They are not gentlemen, sir. They have no honor," Cliveburn said in a stern voice. "They don't respect the traditions of the game. There are bookies at every professional tournament, betting is rampant, and loose women follow these exhibition tours from city to city. Players are known to receive bribes to throw matches, and these promoters are scoundrels."

His face became ruby red and he pounded on the table.

George decided he needed to make a statement. He looked directly at Cliveburn and did not bat an eye.

"In response to your earlier question, I repeat, I have not received any money from Bob Johnson to join the exhibition tour."

Then he waited for the follow-up question: Had he ever accepted any money from Guy Rockham? But the question was not asked.

Instead, Reynolds stared at George with condescension.

"I should tell you that we're concerned about your relationship with Johnny Scranton," he said. "You caddied for him at the Blue Marsh tournament."

George looked defiant in his response.

"It was only one tournament," George said. "He's my best friend. He needed a caddy with playing experience. I don't plan on caddying for him again."

"Good," said Cliveburn. "Our members will be glad to hear this news. We believe you are one of the future stars in this glorious game. I'm glad to hear that you have not been tempted by these greedy professionals."

Reynolds looked around the table.

"Gentlemen, do you have any additional questions for George before we let him go?"

An older gentleman in a gray Windsor jacket raised his hand.

"George, my name is Charles Reisling Cox. I'm from the Nahant Club. Are you planning on playing collegiate golf when you enter Brown?"

"It depends on my studies. I hope to play in a few amateur tournaments in the fall and we will see about the college team next spring."

"Well, I hope you join the team. I'm a Brown man myself, class of '81. Good luck at school."

Reynolds looked ready to close the meeting. He rose from his chair and rubbed his hands together as he approached George.

"George, thank you for coming in today. We will be following your golf career closely. I for one feel relieved that you are staying in the amateur ranks. And I'm sure I speak for all of us when I say that you are an example of the true honor in our game. Keep up the good work and best of luck this fall at Brown."

George decided to be gracious. He thanked them for their time. But as he left the room, he couldn't help think what a pompous group of hypocrites they were. They praised the professionals at their clubs for their teaching skills, but treated them as hired staff. The professional game is coming, he thought, and these men are holding on to honor, status, and social class as weapons against the professionals.

George was met by his dad in the parking lot.

"What did they want, son?"

"They wanted to make sure I had not received any money from Bob Johnson to join his exhibition tour."

"Well, that's just crazy. How could they think you had accepted money? You're not a professional."

Steve looked directly at George, whose eyes darted away from his father.

"George. Did you accept any money?"

George pulled his father aside and looked around to see if anyone could hear them.

"Dad, you've got to promise me that you will tell no one what I'm about to tell you. If you do, I'll be through as an amateur and it will affect my future employment. Do you promise?"

Steve stared for a moment at his son. George had a deep frown on his face.

"Of course, son, I'll tell no one."

"Rock gave me $500 after the Blue Marsh Tournament."

His dad looked shocked.

"You got what? Where is the money?"

"I hid it in my room. Only Johnny and Rock know."

"My God. That'll pay for your entire college tuition."

"I was going to tell you before school started. Now you can use the money you saved for college to start your own business."

His father was dumb-founded.

"That was very generous of Rock. But, George, if anyone finds out, they'll strip you of this title. Is that why the committee wanted to talk to you?"

"Sort of. But, they never asked me if Rock gave me any money. They only asked if Bob Johnson had given me money to join the exhibition tour. And I said no."

Steve looked down at the trophy George carried by his side.

"So you didn't lie. You just didn't tell the whole truth."

"Yes, I guess."

Steve thought for a moment.

"This will be hard to keep from your mother," he said. "I think it's best if we don't tell her. Mum's the word for now."

Steve gently pulled George to him and gave his son a hug. It was the first time Steve had hugged George since he was a little boy.

"Oh, by the way," he said, "Congratulations on your win today." He clutched his son's trophy. "I'll be damned if the honorable gentlemen take this away."

George smiled.

"Come on, Dad. Mom's waiting on dinner for us."

****

The next day the headline in the Boston American sports section read:

> *RILEY WINS EASTERN AMATEUR*
> *YOUNGEST PLAYER EVER TO WIN EVENT*
> *SCHOOL BOY FRIEND OF JOHNNY SCRANTON*

On the following page, below the fold, the Boston American ran a smaller story:

> *BOSTON"S OWN JOHNNY SCRANTON*
> *SECOND AT PINHEURST INVITATIONAL*
> *SHOOTS RECORD SETTING 69*

Later that evening, George received a telegram from Johnny at home:

> *Congrats On Great Win, Stop*
> *Now We are even on bet, Stop*
> *Amateur or Professional you are one of best, Stop*
> *Keep Up Good Work, Stop*
> *On to Chicago for Western, Stop*
> *Wish you were on bag , Stop*
> *Johnny*

CHAPTER 14

Archibald Sargent sat in the mahogany-lined grill room at the Rockford Country Club sipping his first Dewars and water of the day. An 8:30 Sunday morning meeting of the Board of Directors for the New England Golf Commitee had never been scheduled before, and the members were irritable as they filed into the grill room. Sunday mornings in July were sacrosanct as prime time for golf, not stuffy board meetings. As Sargent tapped the side of the glass, even his index finger seemed angry.

Sargent was already a legend in New England golf history. He had won four New England Amateur tournaments in the 1890's and in 1904 had won the state amateur championships in Vermont, Rhode Island, and Connecticut. Sargent was 6'2" and lanky, with prematurely silver gray hair. Thirty-nine years old, he already looked to be an elder statesman. He was from one of the first established Massachusetts families who had settled in Manchester on the north shore in the early 1700's. As President of the New England Golf Association, he had called the emergency meeting of the Board of Governors.

"Gentlemen, we have a serious problem," Sargent said in a stern voice. "This pro game is growing like a cancer. Pros such as Willie Anderson, Alec Smith, Guy Rockham, and Johnny Scranton are constantly in the papers. They are an abomination on the good name of golf. New professional tournaments and high stake matches are popping up every day. We must do something to stop the pro game and especially this new young star, Scranton."

The twelve men seated at the table represented the major

country clubs in New England. There were representatives from Rockford, The Chase Club, Winthrop, and Hudson in Massachusetts; Newport and Portsmouth in Rhode Island; the Yale Club and the Madison Club in Connecticut; the Irvington Club in Vermont; Oyster Bay in Maine; and Dover and Essex in New Hampshire.

"I agree, Archie," said Bob Woolman from Portsmouth. "We had one of these pro tournaments near us and the promoter controlled the entire game. I heard the tournament leader tanked on the last hole of the match and collected a nice check from the promoter. It's despicable. They're ruining the good name of this sport. Scranton's a nice kid, but I'm sure he's being manipulated by these promoters."

Sargent interrupted his friend from Portsmouth.

"Rumors won't do. We need incontrovertible proof that players are cheating. So far we only have anecdotal evidence. I propose we hire private investigators to follow these pros and find hard evidence on cheating at these tournaments. We can take this information to our legislatures and get these tournaments banned."

"Are you suggesting we start lobbying for an outright ban?" Woolman asked.

"Yes. I don't see how we can stop this affliction without orchestrating bans state by state."

George Rappaport from Hudson folded his arms and frowned.

"What will this cost?"

Sargent leaned forward, his arms spread on the massive conference table.

"I propose that each club contribute $5,000, and I will personally pledge $10,000 to the campaign."

"Very generous on your part, Archie. I think I can get my

club to contribute," said Woolman.

"All in favor, say aye!"

A chorus of ayes filled the room.

Sargent leaned away from the table, settled back into his chair, and smiled. He took a slow sip from his Dewars and water.

"Thank you, gentlemen," he said. "I'll hire the private investigators tomorrow. Let's meet in two months to review our progress."

CHAPTER 15

Johnny was shaken from a sound sleep by a fire engine's bell in front of the hotel. He heard a man in the hall shout, "Get out of your rooms!" There was a putrid smell in his room.

"Get out! Evacuate the building!" the man shouted again.

Johnny stumbled to his feet and opened the door to see people running everywhere. A man stood in the hall directing traffic.

"Come, sir. The hotel is on fire. You only have a few minutes to get out."

Johnny ran back into his room and grabbed the nearest shirt. He stuffed a small bag containing his winnings from the previous night's poker game into the front of his pants.

"Where are the stairs?" he asked the man in the hall.

"Right this way."

Johnny started down the hall and walked quickly toward the small stairway the man had pointed out. As he moved down the first few steps, a blast of flames shot up toward him from the stairwell. The fire had started on the first floor, near the dining room, and spread upward. A second arch of fire burst up the stairwell. A woman below him on the stairs screamed.

"Oh, my God, I'm going to die!"

"Not today, lady," Johnny said.

He grabbed her elbow and turned her to face him.

"Come on, follow me."

They bolted back up the stairs to his room. The roof of the adjacent building was close and there was a wide ledge outside his window. Johnny threw a chair through the window, pushed the shards of broken glass away, and climbed out on the ledge.

He extended his hand to the woman still inside the room.

"Come on," he yelled.

The woman began to sob uncontrollably.

"No. I can't," she cried. "I'm scared of heights."

"You can do it. We can jump over to the next building from the ledge."

Suddenly, an intense ball of flames burst through Johnny's door. The woman froze as the fire and smoke surrounded her. Johnny climbed back into the room. As he lifted her onto his shoulders, flames swept through the room and ignited his shirt. He leaned back out the window with the woman slung over his shoulder, planted one foot on the ledge platform, and leapt as far as he could. They crashed onto the corrugated tin roof.

"Oh, my God–your arm–it's on fire!" the woman cried.

Johnny ripped off his shirt.

He turned back to the hysterical woman.

"Are you alright?" he said.

A fireman helping others who had jumped from the burning building ran over from another section of the roof.

"That was a spectacular jump, son. I didn't think you would make it."

He looked down at Johnny's right hand. It was badly burned.

"Shit, my hand." Johnny said.

"We have a doctor downstairs who can look at that. I'll take care of the young lady if you're okay to get yourself down there."

Johnny just stared at his hand for a moment.

The fireman asked again, "Are you okay?"

Johnny took a deep breath.

"I'm okay," he said. "I can get downstairs on my own. Thanks."

He staggered down the three stories to the first-floor lobby, where a local doctor was treating victims of the fire.

A small man in a white jacket approached him as he entered the lobby.

"I'm Dr. Paul Anderson. Let me take a look at your hand, young man."

Johnny curled his right fingers into the palm of his hand in order to reduce the pain that was now spreading up his arm into his shoulder. Blisters had started to form on the inside of the hand near the base of the palm. The doctor looked carefully, but didn't touch the hand.

"Are you Johnny Scranton, the golfer?" the doctor asked.

Johnny looked puzzled.

"Yes, I am. Do I know you?"

The doctor motioned for Johnny to turn his hand over so that he could see the other side.

"I saw you play Sunday at Piedmont in the finals," he mumbled. "Brilliant match. Best golf I've ever seen."

"Thanks. I got lucky on the 18th."

"Well. I'm sorry to say this burn is going to sideline you, son."

"How long, Doc?"

"It's a third-degree burn. They can take weeks to heal. You'll have pain for about ten days as the blisters heal. But it's going to be longer than that before you can play golf again."

Johnny stared at the blistered hand and sighed.

"I'm ready for a rest anyway. All these women and late night poker games have worn me out."

"A young fella like you, worn out? Come on."

Johnny looked away as the doctor put cream on the burns and wrapped his hand with a cloth bandage.

The doctor reached into his bag and pulled out a bottle. He handed it to Johnny.

"Take three spoonfuls, twice a day. It'll numb the pain."

"What is it, Doc?" Johnny asked as he read the label. "Dr. Paul's Magic Elixir. I've seen this stuff. My dad used it for a bad cold last winter."

"The narcotic in the Elixir will help. It's one of my best products."

"You're Dr. Paul?"

"Yes, sir. I've sold the Elixir for fifteen years."

Anderson chose not to add that over those fifteen years the Federal government had been trying to shut him down. He handed Johnny a card with his name, address, and phone number on it.

"That's enough Elixir for two weeks. Contact me if you need more. I can ship it to you. Keep the hand dry for at least a week. And the bandage needs to be changed every week. If you're still in town, come see me and I'll change it myself."

Johnny moved to a window and looked outside at the smoldering building across the alley.

"Thanks, Doc. Do you know what started the fire?"

"They say a person smoking near the kitchen ignited the grease pot and the fire spread quickly."

As soon as he got outside the building, Johnny took a large gulp of the Elixir. Rock spotted him standing on the curb and noticed his bandaged hand.

"Are you okay?" Rock asked. "Why is your hand bandaged?"

"Burned it trying to escape from the fire."

"Shit. How bad is it?"

"Hurts when I flex it, but the Doc says I'll be okay in a couple of weeks."

"A couple of weeks! We have a four-ball match scheduled this weekend with the Royal Club. Those Lake Shore Drive guys love to throw their money around."

"Well, I guess I'll be a spectator for awhile. Might even take the train back home for a little vacation."

Rock reached into his pants pocket.

"Are you okay for money?"

"Sent $3400 back home two days ago. They have this new service where you can wire money from one bank to another. It was easy. Anyway, I'm okay. I've got more money than I ever thought I would."

Johnny drew in a long deep breath and let it out slowly, a little shaky.

"I'd been thinking about taking time off to be ready for the National in September anyway."

"Okay," Rock said. "Don't worry. Go home and get well. We'll find someone to replace you. But first we need to find a new place to stay."

Rock saw the hotel bellman standing across the street watching the fireman rolling up their hoses. When the bellman saw Rock and Johnny, he quickly came over to them.

"Hi, Mr. Johnny, Mr. Rock. Are you alright?"

Johnny said, "We're okay."

The bellman smiled.

"That's good," he said. "The owners are moving everyone to the St. Regis. Whatever we could save are lined up around the corner. We grabbed them before the fire got too hot."

Rock nodded his approval.

"Thanks. The St. Regis, first class. I like that." He turned toward Johnny. "Thank heavens the clubs are at the golf course."

"Come on, Rock," Johnny said. "I need to change and get a drink. Maybe I can even find someone to tend to my injuries tonight."

Johnny winked.

Rock was sure Johnny would score that night. There are always those women who love an injured man, especially a young, handsome, very rich man.

CHAPTER 16

Edith began to cry as the train pulled out of South Station.
"Why are you crying, Mom?" George asked.

She hugged him and gave him a big kiss on the forehead.

"George, I'm so proud of you. My son is going to Brown University. This is the happiest day of my life."

George had visited Brown in late August and found a rooming house across from the college. The landlady, Mrs. Coppin, rented rooms for $7.50 per month. He had also found a part-time job at the Wick Center bussing tables.

George, Edith, and Steve arrived in Providence and walked up College Hill to the boarding house. Mrs. Coppin greeted them on the front porch.

"I run a tight ship with my guests," she said. "No loud parties and no women are allowed in the rooms after 11 p.m."

Steve and Edith felt comfortable leaving George in Mrs. Coppin's care.

Mrs. Coppin was an elegant woman in her early seventies with beautiful silver-gray hair. Her husband, a fisherman for 35 years, had died during the '04 nor'easter. He had been washed overboard and his body was never recovered. Edith could see the pain in Mrs. Coppin's face as she discussed the accident.

"Your parents are welcome to stay the night," Mrs. Coppin said.
She turned to Steve and Edith.

"I have an empty guest room you could use."

"Thank you for your kind offer, but we need to get home," Edith said. "Our daughter Margaret is staying with friends today and we need to pick her up."

Steve tapped his finger on Edith's shoulder to indicate it was time to leave. George walked with them to the train station.

"Study hard," Steve said. "Call if you need anything. The long distance rates have dropped, so don't hesitate to call."

Steve grabbed his son's hand with a firm grip.

"We're proud of you, son."

George smiled. It was the first time his dad had ever really praised him.

"Thanks. I'll write."

George turned and headed toward the end of the platform. He found himself whistling as he exited the station.

****

George plunged into his studies. He only played once a week at the local nine-hole course near Mrs. Coppin's house because he was overwhelmed by the amount of homework. Some nights he would stay up until 2 a.m. preparing for class the next day. He became a regular at the college library.

One day, as he was leaving the main library, he accidentally dropped his books in the doorway. As he bent over to pick them up, the door suddenly opened and knocked him down the stairs.

George looked up to see a young lady with long radiant blonde hair looking at him with stunning aquamarine eyes.

"Oh, my God," she cried. "I'm so sorry. I didn't see you. Are you okay?"

George jumped up and brushed off some dirt from his slacks.

"Yes. I'm okay," he said, feeling himself redden. "It was all my fault."

"No. It was my fault. I shouldn't have opened the door so quickly. I'm so sorry."

Their eyes met. Something about his azure blue eyes

immediately attracted her. She held out her hand.

"I'm Jennifer Smitson. What's your name?"

"George Riley."

"What form are you?"

"First form," George said.

He couldn't take his eyes off of her. She was short and slender and wore a tailored wool jacket with an ankle-length skirt.

"I'm also first form – at Pembroke."

"Nice to meet you."

George was wearing his old tweed jacket and baggy corduroy pants. I look like a bum, he thought.

"Can I make it up to you?" Jennifer said in a timid voice. "I'm off to the Cleary House. Let me buy you a cup of tea."

She surprised herself by her invitation. This was the first time she had ever invited anyone to tea, much less a young man.

"Sure," George said, feeling a little more composed. "I've got two hours before my next class. Lead the way."

As they crossed the diag in front of the library, George asked, "Where are you from?"

Jennifer moved closer to him.

"Warwick, Rhode Island. How about you?"

There was something about this guy that fascinated her.

"Newton. Just outside Boston."

"Do you live on campus or commute?" George asked. Some of the women lived in Ivory Hall. He was curious if she was one of them.

"No. I commute. My dad works downtown and he drives me in each day. I ride home with him each night."

As they walked across the quad, they talked about their families and which classes they liked and they discovered that they both loved world history.

Midday tea at Cleary House was a Brown tradition. George never seemed to have enough time to attend, but Jennifer was obviously a regular. The waiter greeted her by name and knew that she only drank Earl Gray.

Jennifer was bright and articulate, and she was conversant on a variety of topics. They talked for over an hour before George realized he had only five minutes to make his Latin class.

George screwed up his courage. He asked, "Do you enjoy football?"

Jennifer smiled the most beautiful smile George had ever seen.

"I love football."

Just ask her, George thought. This isn't hard.

"I have an extra ticket for the game Saturday against Yale. Would you join me?"

"What time's the game?"

"1:30."

"I'd love to go."

"Great!" George said, maybe a little louder than he meant to.

Jennifer smiled that beautiful smile again.

"I'll meet you before the game at The Statue, if that's okay," she said.

"Sure. Great," said George. Then he looked puzzled.

"By the way, what statue?"

"The statue of Charles Brown, silly."

"Oh, that statue," said George. He could feel himself turning red from embarrassment. "I knew that."

He couldn't stop thinking about those gorgeous eyes and that bright smile as he walked across the quad toward his Latin class. There was something special about this girl.

CHAPTER 17

The intercom rang in Archibald Sargent's private office.

"Mr. Wilson is here."

"Good. Send him in."

Pete Wilson was the lead investigator for National Investigations. He was a small, wiry man and appeared to be in his late fifties. He wore a charcoal-colored, three-piece suit and carried a black bowler hat. Sargent recognized the bowler hat from the company ad. Every investigator wore the same hat.

Wilson nodded hello.

"Mr. Sargent, good to finally meet you."

Sargent stood up from his chair and came around his desk to offer a handshake to Wilson. The detective's hand was small and clammy. He seemed nervous.

"Good to meet you, Mr. Wilson," Sargent said. "So, do you have anything for me?"

"We've assigned our best agents to your case, sir. For the past two months we've followed the three players day and night. You should have received our report on Johnny Scranton's accident in Chicago. We recently learned that he is using heavy doses of the Elixir daily. Our agent believes he's become addicted to the stuff."

"I followed Willie Anderson personally and discovered that he plays poker with known bookies in New Haven three nights a week. Our agent following Alec Smith has reported no illegal activities."

"Have you found any evidence of cheating or bribes? We need that kind of evidence."

"No, not yet. I've told my men to start talking with caddies and players though. Someone must know if they are taking bribes or cheating during a matches."

"I can't believe you haven't found anything yet. You've got to dig harder."

Wilson looked embarrassed.

"Yes, sir," he said. "We will. We'll find something."

"Just keep me informed," Sargent said crisply. Then he dismissed him with a casual wave.

Sargent turned his chair and stared out the window of his office at the fading daylight.

Damn it, he thought. We need more than that little shit Scranton hooked on Elixir to go after the tour. He took a cigar from the humidor. He paused before lighting the Cuban and pondered. He leaned over and pressed the intercom.

"Sandra. Come in with your steno pad. We need to send some telegrams."

CHAPTER 18

Johnny missed the 1909 U.S. Open due to his injured hand. In October, he accepted a teaching job as assistant pro at the Citrus Country Club on the condition that he could play in professional tournaments. The club gladly accepted Johnny's requirements in order to have this emerging star on their staff.

For three months in late 1909, Johnny worked with three doctors and two physical therapists to rehabilitate the damaged hand. The third-degree burns had created a deformity in the lower part of his palm. He was left with two thick scars and tender areas that didn't heal, and the doctors were unable to completely eliminate the persistent pain. Johnny adapted his grip by floating the right hand over the club in a modified Vardon grip and he used the Elixir to dull the pain. Each week a new shipment of Elixir arrived from Chicago. Johnny was convinced that the medicine helped, but others were increasingly concerned that he seemed to be forgetting people and places more frequently.

The next nine months were difficult. Johnny played sporadically in local tour events in Florida and a few exhibition matches with Rock in North Carolina. He adjusted his slashing-style game to accommodate the pain in his hand, but the floating grip made it difficult to control the club, and his play became erratic. One day he would have a brilliant round and the next day shoot an 80. He finished in the money in only three tournaments and lost over $10,000 in stakes matches.

Finally, he decided to take some time off and rest his hand. For two months he didn't touch a club. He would start the day with a large dose of Elixir and would throw down more and more as the day wore on. The Elixir was soon disappearing by the case rather than the bottle.

But by early September, he was back on the practice range and the hand seemed better. He no longer needed to use the floating grip and he had more consistency in his shots. He was convinced the Elixir had helped him. After winning a local pro tournament near Tampa, he decided he was ready for the big stage again. He registered for the 1910 U.S. Open.

****

The porter arrived at Johnny's compartment to take his bags to the exit.

"Broad Street Station, Philadelphia, next stop, Mr. Scranton."

"Thank you, Samuel. Do you know where I can catch a cab to the Philadelphia Cricket Club?"

"There's a cab stand outside the main entrance to the station. They have Checkers and local buggies."

Johnny handed Samuel a $20 bill.

"Thanks for all your help this trip. I'll see you in a few days on my return to Tampa."

"Thank you, Mr. Scranton. It's been a pleasure to assist you. Good luck in the Open."

Johnny caught a Checker outside the train station for the twenty-minute cab ride to the hotel. He spotted Chick Evans as he stepped out of the cab in front of the Hotel Wyanno. Johnny waved and yelled out to him.

"Chick, how the hell are you?"

Chick waved back and came over to the cab.

"Hi, Johnny. How's the hand?" Chick asked. He had been in Chicago the night of the hotel fire.

"It's been a difficult year," Johnny said. "The hand is better though. I can feel my fingers."

Chick nodded.

"That's good. I'm glad to hear it," he said.

The friends walked together toward the hotel.

"This is an incredible field," Chick said. "The 15th Open has attracted 85 players who each paid ten bucks for a chance to win the cup. I counted 65 professionals. The amateurs are being overrun."

"Yes, the Open has come a long way since1895."

The U.S. Open began as an afterthought at the Newport Country Club in 1895, tacked on to follow the prestigious National Amateur Tournament. The organizing committee arranged it as a one-day affair that would allow pros and amateurs to play together. That first year it featured all of ten professionals and one amateur. They played four 9-hole rounds in a stroke-play competition. The winner was Horace Rawlins, a professional from England, who shot 173 for 36 holes and won $150. By 1910, 267 clubs had joined the USGA, and the U.S. Open was expanded to 72 holes. The Open became the tournament for professionals because the National was still restricted to amateurs.

"Chick, nice to see you," said Johnny. "Good luck tomorrow. I've got to practice. I hear the greens are tricky."

"Good luck to you, Johnny. Hope your hand holds up."

****

Johnny was paired in the first round with Alec Smith from Scotland. Alec was a small, ruddy man with stubby legs who was a master around the greens.

"Johnny, I'm glad to play with you," Alec said with a strong Scottish brogue. "I'm nervous. This is my first tournament in this country. I arrived three days ago and only played the course yesterday."

"I hear you Scots don't need a lot of practice."

"Aye, laddie," Alec jabbed back. "We Scots come out of the womb with a spoon in our hand, ready for the 1st teeing ground."

Both men laughed.

Johnny felt a sharp pain in his upper hand as he gripped the driver on the 1st teeing ground. He started to rub his hand to try to get circulation going in his palm. The blisters had completely healed, but it still hurt when he grabbed the club, and his hand periodically was numb. As he started his warm-up swing, his grip slipped and he hit the ground in a sharp angle with the club. He felt an intense pain radiate up his forearm into his shoulder.

Johnny's caddy, Brian Jameson, a burly seventeen-year old kid from the docks of Hoboken, saw the wince on Johnny's face.

"How's the hand, Johnny?" Brian asked as they waited to tee off.

Johnny glanced at the crowd and noticed a pretty young lady. She reminded him of Nancy. His mind wandered.

Brian said, "Johnny?"

"I'll need another dose of Elixir before I tee off," Johnny said. "It'll help relax the muscle."

Brian took a bottle from the bag and Johnny took three large swigs. He could immediately feel the warmth from the Elixir begin to numb his hand and the rest of his body.

Johnny had tried something new to help him grip the club. He had taken an old leather glove and cut the top off each finger. He eased the glove over his swollen hand, and the leather acted as a cushion for the scars.

The starter approached Johnny and Brian.

"Mr. Scranton, you're up."

The starter escorted Johnny to the 1st teeing ground and announced through his megaphone: "Now teeing off, from Newton, Massachusetts, and the Citrus Country Club, the defending Teaneck Invitational Champion and winner of six professional golf championships, Johnny Scranton."

There was a boisterous and enthusiastic cheer from a large contingent of young ladies who had come specifically to watch Johnny play.

He took three slow practice swings and, after each practice swing, he adjusted the glove's strap tighter and tighter. Brian noticed that Johnny's fingers started to turn blue.

"What's that on your hand, Johnny?" a man shouted from the gallery.

"A secret weapon," Johnny responded. "Pretty soon, everyone will be wearing one of these to play golf."

Now Johnny was feeling good. He stepped up and hit a booming tee shot with his brassie, dead center in the fairway. Smith drove his ball little more than half as far and off to the right of the fairway.

"Maybe I should wear a glove if it will help me hit a shot like that," Smith said as they walked down the fairway.

"How did that feel, Johnny?" Brian asked.

"Couldn't feel a thing. I feel light-headed and can't feel my feet," Johnny said as they approached his ball.

Things went downhill from there. He missed his par on the 1st hole and sliced his tee shot on the 2nd hole into deep rough. It took two shots to get back to the fairway and he finished with a double bogey.

As he stood on the 3rd teeing ground, waiting for the group in front to hit, Johnny noticed a man in a black bowler hat standing in the crowd.

"Do you see that man over there?" he asked Brian.

"Yes. I see him."

"Do you recognize him?"

"No, Johnny."

"I've seen guys in bowlers at other tournaments. There was this guy with the same hat at the Teaneck tournament," Johnny said. "Now that I think about it, there was one at Jacksonville in July."

Johnny wondered if these men were following him. It was strange. The same bowler hat at different tournaments.

Throughout the round, Johnny found himself thinking about the men in bowlers or looking off into the crowd for the girl that looked like Nancy Marchand. Once he got confused and thought for a moment that he was playing with George. He didn't play well. He shot 83. The four swigs of the Elixir he downed during the round didn't seem to help.

As he came off 18, a young boy approached.

"Mr. Scranton, can you come with me to the grill room? Commodore Pinkert would like to have a word with you."

"Who is Commodore Pinkert?" Johnny asked, a little irrtated.

"He's the chair of the Rules Committee. He asked me to fetch you."

Johnny wanted to get into a dark room with a soft couch where he could lie down and take a nap. But this came first.

"Okay. Lead on."

Johnny followed the boy through the full length of the clubhouse and descended the back stairs into the men's grill room. The walls were covered with mahogany paneling, and large walnut tables with Hancock style chairs were scattered throughout the room. At the end of the room, there was a long mahogany bar and two ornate English oak Thurston billiard tables.

An elderly man with white mutton-chop sideburns and a handle-bar mustache met him at the door.

"Mr. Scranton, I'm Commodore Royce Pinkert from Acorn Hills Golf Club on Long Island. I'm the Chairman of the USGA Rules Committee."

Pinkert was elegantly dressed in a Brooks Brothers three-piece worsted suit and wore brown wing-tipped leather shoes with white spats. Johnny could tell the social status of a man from the type of shoes he wore. Pinkert was clearly well-to-do. Johnny figured the shoes alone must have cost him twenty-five bucks at Brooks Brothers.

Five members of the Rules Committee sat at one end of a round table. After Commodore Pinkert introduced all of the members, he asked if he could see Johnny's glove. Johnny untied the strap and peeled off the glove.

"Why are you wearing a glove?" a white-haired gentleman inquired.

"I had an injury to my hand. I don't know of any rule that prohibits the use of a glove."

"We've had a lot of interest in your glove, Mr. Scranton," the Commodore said. "We've had a formal challenge to your using it."

Pinkert didn't disclose who had filed the challenge. Peter Wilson, the agent hired by Archibald Sargent to follow Johnny, had contacted the Committee earlier and had lodged a formal complaint.

"This is an artificial help to the player," Harold Wilcox from Pine Bluff Country Club stated vehemently.

Pinkert gently raised the open palm of his left hand toward Wilcox as if to signal for him to slow down. He passed the glove among the Committee members.

"Harold, we don't have a prohibition on the use of a glove," he said. "How can we penalize Mr. Scranton if we don't have a rule against its use?"

"How long have you used a glove?" asked a rotund, bearded man seated next to Pinkert.

"This is the first tournament I've used it."

"Very interesting," Wilcox said, in a more measured tone than before. "I think we need to discuss this issue in private, don't you, Commodore?"

"Yes, I agree. Mr. Scranton, can you excuse us? If you wouldn't mind waiting outside, we'll decide this question right now. Anything you'd like to add for us to consider?"

Johnny felt light-headed but he gathered his thoughts carefully.

"I don't believe a glove assists a player," he said. "Many players will never feel comfortable wearing a glove. I'd rather not wear it myself. You don't get the same feel for the shot that you do with bare hands. I'm using it to keep my hand from swelling up due to the burn."

The bearded man stood up, came over to Johnny, and escorted him to the door.

"We'll make sure you know as soon as we decide," he said.

Once he had left the grill room, Johnny felt dizzy. His stomach was upset and his shirt was wet from sweat. He felt cold. He lay down on a bench in the locker room and tried to calm himself. He was asleep when Brian found him.

"Johnny, you look terrible. Are you going to be able to continue?" he asked as he shook him out of his morphine-induced daze.

"I'm okay," said Johnny. "Just get me the Elixir. It'll help settle my stomach."

Brian ran outside and grabbed a bottle from the bag. Johnny

took two large gulps.

Brian took the bottle back from Johnny and scanned the label.

"It says you're only supposed to take three spoonfuls a day," Brian said. "You've taken six big gulps already."

"It's okay, Brian. It's okay," Johnny kept repeating.

Brian shook his head. He wasn't sure what to do.

"Johnny, time for the second round. You don't look ready," Brian said.

Johnny jumped unsteadily up from the bench and spread his arms out in mock triumph. His eyes were red and his hair was matted and sweaty.

"Lead on. I'm ready."

Commodore Pinkert met them near the 1st teeing ground. Johnny looked a bit dazed.

"Mr. Scranton. The committee has voted. You are authorized to use the glove during this tournament. We'll discuss this issue at our Rules Committee meeting in January and make a recommendation to the USGA Executive Committee. Very interesting topic, sir. I for one do not believe it helps a player, and that's how I'll vote."

"I agree. Thank you for your deliberations," Johnny said.

"Always the diplomat," Brian whispered, as the Commodore headed back to the clubhouse.

Johnny smiled darkly.

"If they had ruled against me, I would have told that old son of a bitch what I thought about his committee and where they could all go."

Johnny spread his arms outstretched and let out a faint crowing sound. Brian wasn't sure what Johnny meant by this act, but others in the crowd seemed amused.

****

Johnny shot a 79 in the afternoon round and made the cut in the stroke-play tournament. The next day he shot an 81 and then ballooned to a 92 for a four-round total of 335. He finished 37 shots behind the winning score. His opening round partner Alec Smith shot 298 and took the first place prize of $550 home to Scotland.

Despite his poor showing, Johnny paid Brian $400 for his work. Brian was shocked when Johnny handed him the money. It would have taken him months to earn the same amount working on the docks.

"Johnny, I don't deserve this much."

"Yes you do. You helped me through a pretty tough time. I'm heading back to Tampa for the winter, but I want you ready to join me next year. Okay?"

"You bet! Whenever you're ready, I'll join you. Just call me and I'll hop a train. Deal!" Brian slapped Johnny's hand, then realized he had hit the center of his right hand. Johnny winced. Brian looked terrified.

"Sorry, Johnny," he said. "I'm so sorry."

Brian thought, don't blow this deal now.

Johnny's face was red, but he re-assured Brian.

"It's okay. It was my own fault. I need to learn to shake hands with my left hand."

He forced a smile.

"Don't worry, Brian. I'll call you early next year. We're going to make a fortune."

******

Peter Wilson followed Brian and Johnny to the train station

and posted a message to Archibald Sargent at the Western Union Telegraph office:

> *Scranton played poorly at Open. Stop*
> *Witnessed him use illegal glove. Stop*
> *Tried to get Rules Committee to disqualify him. Stop*
> *Rules Committee refused to disqualify. Stop*
> *Witnessed using Elixir during match. Stop*
> *Full Report to follow. Stop*

CHAPTER 19

Junior year at Brown proved to be the toughest for George, and his Latin final exam was especially difficult. Jennifer anxiously waited for him in the quad outside Ripley Hall. She ran up to him when she saw him approaching.

"How did the exam go?" she asked.

"I think I did well," George said. "Professor Schmidt even put a bonus question at the end."

"What was the question?" Jennifer asked as they walked toward the Van Wickle Gates.

George pointed directly ahead.

"He asked us to list the inscription from Cicero on the Van Wickle Gates."

Jennifer turned and smiled.

"You know that."

"Ah, yes. But do you know the answer, my dear?" George fired back in a taunting manner. Jennifer and George loved to play trivia games, especially about Brown-related trivia.

She made a show of looking as if she were pondering a great and important question.

"Give me a minute. I know this."

Built in 1901, the gates were a gift from the estate of Augustus Stout Van Wickle, Class of 1876, who died in a skeet-shooting accident in 1898. They stood at the south entrance to the quad.

"Haec studium adolescentium alunt, senectutem oblectant, secundas res ornant, adversis perfugium ac solacium prebent," Jennifer said.

"Very good, but you missed one word," said George as he

stroked her long, shiny blonde hair.

"No way! What word?" Jennifer asked as they walked around the outside of the gates to view the inscription. She spotted her mistake immediately.

"*Studia*! I said *studium*," she said. "I hope you didn't make that mistake!"

Jennifer gave him a playful shove, which almost knocked him over.

"But not bad for an English major," she said proudly.

Jennifer opened a copy of the Daily Herald as they walked down College Hill.

"We're in the Herald today. Do you want to see?"

"Yes."

George anxiously opened the page to the Junior Prom committee's report. He read in a loud voice the list of attendees.

"Mr. George Riley of Newton, Massachusetts, and Miss Jennifer Smitson of Warwick, Rhode Island."

George gave a wry smile.

"I was checking to make sure they listed the right girl."

Jennifer hit him gently on his shoulder.

"I have to pick up my prom dress after tea. Do you want to come along?"

"Sorry, I can't. I have my final fitting this afternoon at Cousins' Tailor Shop." This would be the first tuxedo George had ever owned, and it had to be right. He wanted the Junior Prom to be a special night.

George and Jennifer had been constant companions since the day they had first met on the steps of the main library. Jennifer invited him home for dinner two weeks later and, just as she herself would, her family fell in love with George.

During these visits, George learned a great deal about the

often shy, but articulate Jennifer Smitson. She was an only child. Her parents had lost two other children to typhus, so the Smitsons' were especially protective of their baby. Still, Jennifer was an active child. She loved to walk in the woods and collect butterflies. Her collection grew to over 200 types. George was fascinated by this collection each time he saw it. She was also an accomplished gardener. She loved to grow different varieties of hydrangea each year. There were hydrangea plants throughout the Smitson home. George began to feel right at home in the Smitson house after the first few visits.

****

George entered the small custom tailor shop near the bottom of College Hill. He was greeted by the proprietor, Phillip Cousins, an elderly man with a slight stoop. He had been making gentlemen's clothing for over thirty years.

As George slipped on the half-completed jacket, Cousins asked, "First tuxedo you have purchased?"

"Yes. How'd you know?"

"I usually receive a gentleman's measurements from his hometown tailor. In your case, I had to start from scratch."

"I don't have a tailor back home. My mother is an excellent dress maker who makes all of my clothes."

Cousins was impressed with this polite, unassuming young gentleman. He had never met a Brown student whose mother made his clothes.

"Do you have any children?" George asked.

"Yes, I have a son. He's a senior at the Portsmouth Priory."

Phillip paused as he kneeled down to take a measurement in the back of the coat. "He's been accepted to Boston University. First member of our family to attend college. Wants to study engineering and play golf."

"Ah, he's a golfer?"

"Yes. Why do you ask?"

"I play golf."

"My son thinks he's Johnny Scranton."

George tried not to smile.

"I grew up with Johnny Scranton. We've played together many times."

"My son saw Johnny play an exhibition match in New Haven last month. He's a member of the Priory's Glee Club and they were in New Haven for a concert. Sam met Johnny after the Glee Club show and watched him play the next day. He likes the slashing style that Johnny uses. I'll tell my son that you know him, if you don't mind."

Mr. Cousins stood up and stepped back from George.

"All finished. Your tuxedo will be ready tomorrow. Do you want me to deliver it to you?"

George looked a bit uncomfortable. He had still not gotten used to being treated with such deference by his elders, no matter what the situation.

"Deliver it? Oh, no. Thank you, sir, but I can pick it up. Thank you."

******

George headed back to his dorm after the fitting. During his sophomore year he had applied for a room at Hawthorne Hall and moved from Mrs. Chapman's boarding house. As he entered Hawthorne Hall, someone yelled his name.

"George Riley, phone call."

Must be Jennifer, he thought. He rushed to the phone on the wall near the main bathroom.

Brown had recently installed new phones in the dorms and had spared no expense by installing the latest technology. The University had signed a long-term agreement with American Bell to install direct dial phones. They were the first direct dial phones installed in Providence. George was still getting used to not going through an operator for all of his calls. He hesitated, then leaned into the microphone.

"Hello."

"Hello, Mr. Riley? This is Sam Cousins. My dad is making a tux for you. He said you know Johnny Scranton."

"Yes, I do."

"Can I come over and talk to you about Johnny?"

"Right now?"

"It's very important that I speak with you. I can be there in ten minutes."

"Well, I guess. Room 34 in Hawthorne."

"Right. I got it. Be right over."

George hung up the ear piece on the hook. This was strange. What could he want?

Ten minutes later, George answered a knock at his door.

A small boy with wavy blond hair and brown eyes immediately extended his hand to shake George's hand.

"Hi. I'm Sam Cousins," he said.

George shook his hand and motioned toward the bed.

"Would you like to sit down?" he asked.

Sam stepped across the room warily.

Sam looked nervous, his hands shaking as he sat on the edge of the bed.

"Since you're a friend of Johnny Scranton, I wanted to talk to you," he said.

"About what?"

"Well."

Sam hesitated. He wet his lips.

"About Johnny and the money he owes me."

George was caught off guard.

"What money? What has this got to do with me?"

George sat down at his desk and stared at Sam.

"He owes me seventy-eight bucks and I need my money. Do you know where I can find him?"

"That's a lot. Why does he owe you money?"

"I met him at an exhibition match in New Haven."

"Yes. Your dad told me."

"After the match, he invited me to a poker game at the Yale Club. Johnny was drinking a lot during the game. He kept pouring Elixir into his scotch. Anyway, the pot got really big. It was down to Johnny and me in the last hand and I pulled a full house. It beat Johnny's three of a kind."

Sam shifted on the bed. He wet his lips again.

"He didn't have any money, so he gave me a marker. He said he'd pay me after the exhibition match."

Sam was clearly frustrated. His voice got louder and cracked a bit.

"I was stupid to believe he was honorable."

George didn't like what he was hearing and he decided he didn't like Sam Cousins.

"Go on," he said. He heard the irritation in his voice as he spoke.

"The next day, I followed Johnny's match. He won a $100 Nassau five ways. After the match, I came up to Johnny near the club house and asked for my money. He said he didn't know me. Two club members grabbed me by the arms and threw me off the property. I haven't seen him since."

"I can't believe this happened," George said.

"Mr. Riley, I need to find him. He has to pay me what he owes me. I can't afford to lose this money."

George sat quietly at his desk. He didn't know what to say. He was stunned.

Sam leaned forward from his seat on the bed. He raised his eyebrows.

"You know, he's a morph head, right?"

"A what?"

"A person who gets high on morphine. We use Dr. Paul's to get high all the time at the Priory. That's what Johnny was dumping in his scotch. It's loaded with morphine."

Not Johnny, thought George. He didn't want to think Johnny was using morphine. He wanted to get this settled and get rid of this annoying twerp.

"Do you have the marker?" he asked.

"Yes."

Sam took the marker out of his wallet and gave it to George. George instantly recognized Johnny's handwriting:

> *I, Johnny Scranton, hereby agree to pay Sam Cousins the sum of $78 from my share of the winnings at the New Haven Exhibition. – JM Scranton.*

George went to his dresser and pulled out the box where he kept the "donation" from Rock. He looked back at this small intruder sitting on his bed.

"Your dad says you're going to Boston University next year to study engineering."

"Yes."

"So you don't want to be a tailor?"

"Hell, no. Always kowtowing to some rich boy."

George glared at him. Sam shook his head and held his hands up.

"Sorry, I didn't mean you. He said you were very nice. But some of these snobs really gall me. They treat him like shit. Make him come over at all hours to fix their leggings or make a new jacket on a one day notice for peanuts. I'm getting out of here."

George counted out $78 exactly.

"The Priory is a very good school," he said absent-mindedly.

"It's okay. Very strict and stodgy."

"Why not go to Boston College?"

"No more Jesuits for me. I'm up to here with Jesuits," Sam said as he gestured with his hand out flat up against his chin.

George stepped closer to Sam and showed him a wad of crisp bills

"Here's the money Johnny owes you," he said. "Can I have the marker, please?"

George sat down on the bed next to Sam.

"One condition, though," he said. "Not a word to anyone about this or what Johnny said to you. Do you promise?"

Sam looked small and a little scared.

"Yes, Mr. Riley. I promise."

George handed him the money. Sam counted each bill then hurriedly stuffed the money into his coat pocket.

"Thank you very much, sir," he said. "I need to pay off some debts of my own."

I'm not surprised, thought George. He pointed Sam toward the door, then he stopped him to ask a question.

"I'm curious. You said Johnny didn't remember you or know anything about the marker?"

"Yes. He denied everything. Acted as if we never met."

Sam stepped out of the room and into the hall.

"Bye. Thanks again."

George watched as Sam walked down toward the stairway. How many markers were out there? Had Johnny gone over the top using the Elixir? What had happened to Johnny?

CHAPTER 20

May was a hectic month for George: studying for finals, attending the Junior Prom, and playing regional golf tournaments. Still, George found time to play on the Brown golf team. The schedule included matches with each Ivy League school and three other schools – Middlebury College, the University of Rhode Island, and Providence College. George was the low medalist in two tournaments and shot a course record 74 during his match with Middlebury. The team went undefeated and George was selected to the All-American Collegiate Team.

During his junior year, George had became enamored with history and economics. He impressed his professors with his knowledge and with his keen insight into complex socio-economic issues. George's favorite teacher was Professor William MacDonald, his American History and Economics professor. Billy Mac, his students' nickname, was one of the most progressive teachers at Brown. His American History classes mixed geo-political theory and economic analysis.

MacDonald was so impressed by George that he recommended him to a friend with the First National Bank of Boston. During spring break, George was invited to meet with Vince Snediker, an Executive Vice President at the bank, who happened to be a recent convert from tennis to golf. George's golf credentials made Snediker's decision only that much easier. He offered George a summer internship at the interview and promised to give him time off to practice and play in golf tournaments. It would be the perfect summer job.

* * * * * * *

In late May, George received an invitation to play in the North-South Amateur at Pinehurst, North Carolina. Though it was during the last week of classes, George decided to play in this prestigious tournament. It was George's first trip outside of New England and he was nervous as he boarded the train in Providence. He had reserved a coach seat rather than the more expensive Pullman seat. He eased back in the slumber seat, listening intently to the rhythmic sound of the train's wheels clacking along the rail splits. He loved the smell of the steam locomotive, and he was exhilarated by the sense of controlled speed. As he daydreamed, half awake, half asleep, he felt a tap on his shoulder.

A middle aged man with a strong Southern accent was standing next to him.

"Ticket, sir?"

"Yes. I have it here," George said as he handed the ticket to the conductor.

The conductor glanced at the ticket and then held it up for George to see, as if maybe he hadn't seen what it said.

"I see you're going to Pinehurst. You'll need to change trains at Penn Station for the East Coast Limited. It leaves from Track Number 17. We'll arrive on Track Number 5 and you'll have an hour before the Limited departs."

George nodded.

"Thank you. Do you mind my asking how long you've served on this train?"

"Nine years on this run. I served four years on the New York to Atlanta run. That's why I know the schedule so good. Can I get you anything, sir?"

"No. I'm fine.

The train had reached full speed and George sat back thinking as the scenery flew by. Part of the reason he had decided to take part in the tournament was because Bob Johnson had scheduled an exhibition match in Southern Pines for Johnny's team during the same weekend as the North-South. George had written Johnny and asked to meet with him before the tournament started.

Rock wouldn't be there. He had decided it was time to stay home and devote his time exclusively to pursuing Belle. To take Rock's place, Bob had found a new player, Walter Hagen, who had joined the tour in December 1911 as the fourth man. Hagen was a year younger than George and Johnny, but he had already won three tournaments in Rochester. Word was that Hagen and Johnny were similar in their life styles – flamboyant, aggressive players who loved to party and had the girls swooning all the time.

George needed to meet this Walter Hagen. He could present a problem for Johnny.

****

In New York, the East Coast Limited was delayed for two hours due to union picketers blocking the trains. The new mechanics' union for the Southern Railway had been on strike for two weeks. There had been periodic violence between the union and the Pinkerton guards hired by the Southern Railway. The union decided to leave Penn Station when 100 Pinkerton guards arrived to quell the demonstration.

The train ride south was long and laborious. The thrill of the trip faded a bit in the nine hours it took the train to make North Carolina. George peered through the darkness and saw few lights as the Limited pulled into the Aberdeen station. He was the only person to get off the train. A brass lantern swayed in the breeze in front of the station manager's office at the end of the platform. George walked down toward the light, looked in the window of the office, and saw a rumpled figure slumped in a chair, feet up on his desk, sound asleep.

George knocked loudly on the manager's door, which was partially open.

"Excuse me, sir," he said. "Can you tell me how to get to the Carolina Hotel?"

A burly-faced man with spectacles dangling from his nose sat up in the chair and stretched.

"You just arrived on the Limited?" he asked.

"Yes. I'm inquiring about a cab to the Carolina Hotel."

The man yawned and stretched again.

"Harold was here earlier. He said he'd be back to pick you up."

"Who's Harold?"

"He's the senior porter at the Carolina Hotel. Have a seat. He'll be here shortly."

George sat in the empty station and read a brochure about the Pinehurst Resort. Founded by James W. Tufts, the former President of the American Soda Fountain Company, the resort encompassed 6000 acres. Between 1895 and 1897, Tufts had constructed four hotels and thirty other buildings around a village green designed by Frederick Law Olmstead. The most impressive of them, the Carolina Hotel, was the largest hotel south of New York City. It had 230 guest suites. Besides fine accommodations, the resort offered tennis, archery, skeet shooting, and horse racing. In 1900, Tufts hired Rock's friend Donald Ross to build the first golf course at Pinehurst, and in 1907 the second course opened. In less than ten years Pinehurst had become one of the premier golf resorts in the United States.

After a short time had passed, George heard someone

outside call, "Mr. Riley."

George walked out onto the platform. An elegant black man was walking toward the office. He had white hair, stood well over six feet tall, and wore a white linen dinner jacket.

"Mr. Riley," he said. "I'm Harold Jackman. I'm with the Carolina Hotel. Welcome to Pinehurst, sir. Let me store your bags in the back of the carriage."

Harold picked up George's bags and led him down a few steps to the road side of the platform. The shuttle service consisted of a large carriage pulled by two white stallions waiting patiently for their driver and passenger. Harold opened the door and motioned for George to climb inside.

"The ride to the hotel will only take twenty minutes," he said. "Please sit back and relax, sir. I'm sure you're tired after that long train ride."

CHAPTER 21

The dark ride through the tall pines was magical. The moonlight glistened off the tree tops and George heard a hoot owl screech as the carriage climbed a long winding hill. George laid his head back as the two stallions plodded along a well-worn path up to a crest where the Carolina Hotel came into view.

The hotel was massive, its entrance illuminated with a long row of brass torch lamps. The main part of the building was four stories tall with window after window set into white-washed clapboard siding beneath a bright red tile roof. The center of the hotel was an enormous five-story conical copper dome. As the carriage approached the entrance of the dome, a suited porter jumped from his seat on the porch and waved to Harold. When Harold had brought the carriage to a stop, the porter quickly pulled the bags from the back and disappeared with them inside the hotel.

"Thank you, Harold," George said as he discreetly handed him a dollar.

Harold looked amazed.

"Is that enough?" George inquired. "I'm sort of new to this."

Harold smiled brightly and nodded.

"Yes, Mr. Riley, it's more than enough," he said.

He folded the bill and carefully slipped it into the upper pocket of his coat, and nodded again.

"I've never received this large a tip before. You're very generous."

As he entered the foyer of the hotel, George paused to drink in the elegance of the lobby. The room was huge. Suspended from the soaring ceiling was a beautiful crystal chandelier surrounded by modern electric lights. Massive dark leather couches and matching over-sized club chairs were arranged in seating groups throughout the richly carpeted expanse. There were large potted ferns scattered throughout the room.

A large man emerged from behind a group of ferns off to George's left.

"George, you've finally arrived," the man called out in a slight German accent. "I heard you had been invited."

George brightened at once.

"Heinrich! How are you?"

Heinrich Schmidt was a handsome, statuesque man, and he sported a distinctive handle-bar mustache. His booming good nature made him an immediate friend to everyone he met. He was also the longest hitter George had ever played golf with. He had once seen him drive a ball on the 14th at Salem Country Club that cleared the double fairway bunkers, a carry of at least 260 yards. That was at the Massachusetts Amateur, the most recent of the four matches the two had played. Heinrich beat George on the last hole of their match and won the tournament the next day.

George extended his hand to greet his friend. Heinrich's hand was massive and George winced as Heinrich pressed his hand down.

"When did you get in?" George asked.

"About an hour ago," said Heinrich. "I'm beat after my train ride. I left Worcester at 6 a.m."

"I'm tired too, but I'm also famished," George said. "Will you join me for dinner?"

Heinrich shook his head no.

"Thank you, I'll pass. I need my beauty rest."

The big man delicately ran his fingers back through his hair and smiled.

"But let's meet for breakfast. I hear it's quite a spread. How about 8:30 in the dining room?"

"Sounds great," George said.

He was a little surprised at how much it mattered to him to see a friendly face. "It's great to see you, Heinrich. I look forward to catching up."

Heinrich turned and walked toward the stairs across the lobby, headed for his room.

A middle-aged man wearing a pressed white jacket with gold braids and standing behind a long polished mahogany counter at the back of the lobby had been waiting patiently while George and Heinrich were talking. When Heinrich walked away, he caught George's attention.

"Can I help you, sir?" he asked.

George strode briskly to the counter.

"Hello. I'm George Riley. I have a reservation."

The man smiled, pulled some papers out from beneath the counter, and then placed them on the glass-covered top for George to see. He laid a pen on the papers.

"Yes, Mr. Riley," he said. "We've been expecting you. You're in Room 302. Please fill out the registration form and I'll have a bellboy show you to your room."

He turned around and reached into a set of numbered cubbies behind the counter and pulled out another piece of paper, this one folded and sealed. He handed it directly to George.

"I believe I have a message for you, as well, sir," he said.

George broke the seal and unfolded the note.

Join me for a drink in the pub on the lower level. Johnny.

George was tired and hungry, but he wanted to see Johnny as soon as possible. He hadn't seen him in over eighteen months, and he had heard too much about his friend that worried him from too many people he trusted.

George folded the note and pushed it into his right pants pocket. He followed the bellboy to his room, unpacked, and changed his clothes. He put on a sport jacket and the blue open-collar shirt that Jennifer had purchased especially for the trip. The shirt represented a bold move for George, who was used to only wearing starched, high-collar shirts. He studied the new look in the mirror on the bathroom wall and ran his fingertips down the top edge of the folded collar. I don't know, he thought. He'd give the shirt a try. He ran a comb through his hair and then stepped out into the hall.

He was anxious to see his friend.

****

As he entered the pub, George was shocked by what he saw. Johnny was sitting with three other young men at a table covered with half-empty bottles and dirty glasses. He had aged dramatically. He had lost weight, at least twenty pounds. He looked haggard and his face was drawn. He was holding a full glass in his left hand and he held a cigarette in his right hand. He was leading the group in a boisterous chorus of "Alexander's Ragtime Band."

Johnny immediately saw George as he entered the pub. He looked up at George from the table through blood-shot eyes.

"George!"

He jumped up from his chair and grabbed George's arm.

"Come over and meet the gang!"

George was speechless for a moment. Despite what he had heard, he hadn't expected this awful ghost of his best friend.

"Hi ya, Johnny," he blurted out.

Johnny dragged him closer to the group.

"Hey, guys, I want you to meet my best friend, the infamous George Riley."

Johnny put his right arm around George and spread his left arm toward the men sitting at the table. The cigarette almost burned George's new shirt.

"George, this is Patrick McCarthy from Illinois, Walter Hagen from Rochester, and Sal Mangioni from Brooklyn."

Johnny suddenly swung toward the bar and yelled out for a new round of drinks.

So this is Walter Hagen, thought George, as he sat down at the large wooden table. Hagen was average height and what George judged to be about 185 pounds. He had fine features and thick, jet-black hair that he slicked back with gel. He exuded a casual confidence, and he looked smart in the finest linen jacket George had ever seen. Even in the dim light of the pub, George could see how the girls would find him attractive.

"How was your trip?" Johnny asked as he passed out the new drinks to the table.

"Fine," George said. "No major problems. I love the train. It was an adventure." He heard himself rushing. He consciously slowed his speech down. "I saw Heinrich upstairs when I arrived."

"How is old Heinie? I haven't seen him in ages. Beat the pants off me in the quarter finals of the New Hampshire Open two years ago."

"You were at a disadvantage. You played that round with only two hours of sleep," said George.

"I thought that was your recent style," Hagen chimed in with a slight laugh. "I didn't know you were a veteran insomniac."

Hagen leaned toward George.

"I have the same problem," he confided.

George turned to face Hagen more directly.

"I had heard that you joined the exhibition tour. How's it going for you?" George asked.

"The tour is going very well," Walter said as he nudged Johnny. "We've made a killing in some of the tournaments. I'm holding up Johnny's sorry ass every date."

"Oh, yeah?" said Johnny with mock disdain. "Who was it again that discovered the Cannon sisters in Birmingham?"

Hagen laughed again and raised his glass to Johnny.

"You are the master in that regard, Mr. Scranton," he said in an officious voice.

Johnny bowed his head a bit.

"Thank you," he said.

He looked over to George, raised one eyebrow comically, and smiled.

"Now you know our little secret," he said. "Hagen wins matches and I troll for the women. A great combination."

George nodded uncomfortably. He wanted to change the subject.

"Is Bob here?" he asked.

"Arrives tomorrow with Sarah," said Johnny. "They're finishing the arrangements for a match in Atlanta with members of a new club, Eastlake. There's this young player by the name of–what was his name, Walter?"

"Bobby Jones," Walter said.

"Yeah, that's his name. Bobby Jones. They want us to play a match with this fourteen-year-old kid. The club members are putting up $2,000 for a two-day match. It should be easy money. Have you heard about this prodigy?"

"No, can't say I have," George said.

"He's made a name for himself in the Atlanta area. They say he's a natural player, not like Hagen and me."

George nodded again. He remembered that Francis Ouimet was fourteen when he and Clyde Rothschild had beaten Rock and Donald Ross. That felt like a long time ago.

"So, when do you play at Southern Pines?" he asked.

"We start tomorrow," said Johnny. "You should come over and watch."

"I'll try. But I have to practice here before the North-South starts."

George noticed that Johnny was pausing before each sentence and that his speech was slurred. His lower lip quivered and he was constantly scratching the back of his neck as they talked. He used his left hand to drink and rested his right hand on the table when he wasn't taking a drag from his cigarette.

Johnny suddenly became more animated again.

"Hey," he said, "how are your folks – and especially the beautiful Miss Jennifer?"

"They're fine. They send their regards."

"He's a Yale man," Johnny said to Hagen. He stretched out the word Yale so that it sounded as if it had about four a's in it.

George was shocked and a little annoyed.

"I go to Brown, Johnny. Not Yale," he said firmly.

"Oh, yes. Brown. I always get them confused."

After some loud discussion, the group decided to move to a larger table in the corner and order dinner. George noticed that Johnny was matching Hagen drink for drink throughout the meal. By the end of dinner, each had downed five large scotches and three beers. George was content with his one drink.

After dessert, Johnny pleaded with George, "Come on, buddy. Join us for cards on the outside porch. It's a lovely night."

"No thanks," said George. "I'll see you tomorrow."

"Okay, pal," Johnny said quietly.

Then he awkwardly lurched toward George and gathered him in a long hug. When he finally let go and stepped back, his eyes were watery and he looked as if he might cry.

"It's so good to see you, George," he said.

****

As George walked down the long corridor to his room, he thought about the Johnny he had seen in the pub and the Johnny he had always known before. He would see Bob Johnson tomorrow. There was no question that they should implement the plan immediately. It was time to save his friend.

CHAPTER 22

George got up early and headed to the practice range to hit drives and try the unique Southern greens. He hit about two hundred balls, religiously following the routine he had worked out with Rock when he was in high school. Heinrich joined him on the range for the last fifteen minutes and hit a dozen or so balls. He stood chest out and with his hands on his hips as he watched the last one disappear in the distance.

"Good enough," he said. "Come on, George. I'm starved. Let's get some breakfast. It's a ritual down here."

"That's all your practice for today?" George asked as he toweled off the sweat on his forearms.

Heinrich shrugged.

"I don't want to wear myself out."

Breakfast at the Carolina was indeed elaborate. The staff wore white dinner jackets and the chefs were decked out in their master and senior chef cooking hats. Set out in a buffet, there were six different types of egg dishes, three varieties of hominy grits, huge buttery biscuits, sausage, bacon, ham, and an assortment of locally grown fruits.

"George, you must try some of these hominy grits," Heinrich said. "You'll love them."

George looked skeptical as he examined the grits lying in a sea of white cream sauce. Heinrich piled a huge serving of grits on his plate, then added three sausages and a large slice of Southern ham.

"If I eat this way every morning, I'll not be able to swing a club," George said as they moved to an empty table in the cavernous dining room.

The sunlight streamed through the beveled-glass windows recessed into the ceiling of the ornate dining room, and George admired the craftsmanship of the bamboo furniture scattered throughout the brightly colored room. Twenty-two Ionic columns were set at its edges and the floor was made of inlaid mahogany polished to a high sheen.

As they sat eating together, George was impressed not only with Heinrich's appetite but also with the single-mindedness with which he attacked his breakfast. He realized too how little he really knew about the eating machine across the table from him. They had talked about golf in the past but little else. He liked Heinrich and was curious about his background.

"Heinrich, I don't know what you do for a living," he said.

Heinrich stopped shoveling food for a moment and held his fork up in the air, as if to signal an official break in his pursuit. He took a breath.

"I'm the general manager of a printing company in Worcester. I stumbled into the trade by accident after I graduated from Holy Cross. My family had emigrated from Dresden when I was twelve. My father was a typesetter in Germany and he taught me typesetting while I was in high school. After college, I couldn't find a job during the 1904 crash, so I started at the printing company as a part-time typesetter. Seven years later, I'm the general manager. I'm lucky too: the owners love golf so they give me time off to practice and play in tournaments."

Heinrich slathered an enormous slab of butter on an especially large biscuit, then licked a little off his knife.

"How about you, George? I read that you were the medalist in the first Ivy League Tournament this season. Congratulations. When do you finish Brown?"

"I have one more year."

"Do you know where you want to work?"

"I'm not sure. I have an internship this summer with the First National Bank of Boston. "

Heinrich pursed his lips.

"I'm impressed," he said. His eyes got big. "Hey, maybe you can help me get a loan at the bank. We're trying to buy new printing equipment for our business, but the banks in Worcester are so stingy. They never give loans for new equipment."

"I can talk to someone at the bank, Heinrich, but I'll just be an intern."

Heinrich decided to drown his disappointment in a second helping of eggs Benedict, three more sausages, and another bowl of grits.

****

After breakfast, George caught a ride with one of the bag room attendants to Southern Pines, which was seven miles from the Carolina Hotel. George saw Bob Johnson standing near the 1st teeing ground, waiting for the exhibition match to begin. He got close before he called out to Bob.

"Hi, Bob."

Bob turned to look at George directly behind him.

"George, you startled me. How are you?"

Bob reached out, clasped George's right hand with both of his, and shook it heartily.

"Great," said George. "How are you?"

"I'm good," said Bob. "A little busy right at the moment."

"I need to talk with you as soon as you're free," George said anxiously.

Bob sighed and nodded to show he understood.

"I'll meet you in a few minutes over at the scoreboard," he said. "Go over and say hello to Sarah. She's by the 18th green."

George found Sarah behind the information table passing out literature.

"George!" she cried.

Sarah leapt from her chair and flashed a luminous smile.

"It's so good to see you."

She kissed him on the cheek.

George blushed.

"Hi, Sarah. How are you?"

"I'm great," she said.

She flicked her hair then affected a serious face.

"These tournaments are starting to wear on me though. I've already told Bob that this will be my last season on the tour."

"What will he do without you?"

"He might settle down and run this operation from Boston."

They moved away from the table and closer together.

"Thanks for the reports on Johnny," George said softly. "I spent last night with him and he's worse than I imagined. We need to implement the plan immediately."

Bob came over to the table just as the wind picked up and blew Sarah's hair into her face. She turned, flipped her head, and her hair settled back in place.

"George thinks we need to implement the plan," Sarah said.

Bob touched George's arm.

"You saw him? And you agree that Johnny has deteriorated?"

George was surprised that Bob felt the need to ask.

"Definitely. I almost didn't recognize him. How has he been playing?"

"Erratic. Some days he's brilliant, but some days he can barely swing the club. Last week, in Birmingham, he shot 90, 98, and

89." Bob rolled his eyes. "Thank God for Hagen. He shot 71, 72, and 70 to win the match."

George thought, why does the winning matter so much to Bob when Johnny is like this? Oh, the money. He looked out over the green expanse of the course and let out a long breath.

"Okay, I'm in. How do we start?"

Bob put his hands in his pockets.

"As soon as we finish the exhibition matches tomorrow, we'll all go to my rented house in Mid Pines. I've met a local man who has experience with drug addicts, Rev. Bill McIntyre, the pastor of the Trinity Episcopal Church in Southern Pines. He'll lead the meeting."

"What about the tour?" George asked.

"I've briefed all of the players. I told them it was your call. I have a new player ready to replace Johnny in Atlanta," Bob said.

"Where are we taking him?"

"The Linthicum Institute, about 30 miles north of here in Holly Springs. It's one of the best rehab centers in the country, and they specialize in treating morphine addiction. They'll de-toxify him – get it out of his system."

"How long will he be there?" George asked. "I read that it can take nearly a week to completely withdraw from the effects of morphine."

"That's just for the last dose. It takes a lot longer to break free of the addiction to the junk. He'll stay at Linthicum for at least three weeks before we can head north to Rhode Island. Did you firm up plans for the doctor?"

George nodded.

"I have. I've arranged for Johnny to meet Doctor Avil Hartman, a plastic surgeon at Mercy Hospital in Providence. He has extensive experience with burn victims and he thinks he can help with Johnny's hand."

Sarah had been listening carefully.

"I can't believe he can get the Elixir so easily without a prescription," Sarah said in a low voice so no one else could hear her.

"He gets it by the case from this guy in Chicago," George said.

"When are they going to ban the use of morphine and coca?" Sarah asked.

"Congress is trying to control this stuff," George said. "For God's sake, Coca Cola has started to add real coca to their soda."

"We have to help Johnny," Sarah said.

"It's going to be hard to convince Johnny that he has to go to the Institute," George said. "He won't go if anyone in the golf community knows, especially the press."

Bob interrupted him, "Sarah's been working on that."

"I've developed a cover story," she said. "Johnny has left for Boston to visit a sick relative. He may not be back for a few weeks."

George nodded.

"Sounds good. The doctor said he'll be laid up for at least two months. After the surgery, we'll move him to Harwichport for the summer so he's away from the press or anyone who might know him. If the press finds out he's in recovery, his career will be ruined."

George looked around to make sure no one was listening to them.

"Do you think he'll be okay with this?" Sarah asked.

"He'll be mad at first. He's too proud to admit he needs help," Bob said. "I'm hoping that 98 might wake him up though. I've never seen him so down after a match."

Sarah looked worried and unsure.

"Do you think this is the right time?" she asked George. "You know him better than anyone else does."

"We need to do it now," George said quietly but emphatically. "He's slipping away. If we wait, he may never recover."

Bob drew a deep breath and looked first at George and then at Sarah.

"Okay, we'll meet at my house at 7:30 tomorrow night."

"Okay," said George. "And I don't play until the next morning, so I want to come with you to Holly Springs."

"George, how are you set up now?" asked Bob. "Do you have a ride back to Pinehurst?"

"I'm staying to watch some of the matches. Don't worry. I'll find a ride."

Sarah walked silently back to the table and sat down. She looked as if all the life had been drained from her. Bob nodded to George sadly and headed off somewhere to take care of some pressing minor concern. George walked slowly toward the 1st teeing ground.

****

George followed Johnny for fifteen holes. It was the worst golf he had ever seen Johnny play. On the 5th hole, Johnny sculled a spade mashie and the ball careened deep into the woods. He had a triple bogey on the 11th after hitting two consecutive shots into the water. Twice George saw him sneak swigs of the Elixir. George decided he'd seen enough. If it hadn't been obvious in the pub the previous evening, it certainly was now. Johnny was a mess and there was no doubt in George's mind that the plan had to go forward.

As he walked back to the clubhouse, he met Walter Hagen. Hagen looked tired.

"I hear Johnny is having a terrible day. I thought I'd give him some moral support," Walter said.

"It was horrible to watch," George said.

Hagen looked serious and concerned.

"What you plan to do for Johnny is wonderful," he said. "He really needs help. I know I have a drinking problem. I'm trying to deal with it. But, Johnny. He's in total denial. He believes that the stuff really helps him."

He sounded sincere, but George was confused.

"Thank you, Walter," he said. "But I don't get it. You say you think he needs help, but last night you were matching drinks with him."

Hagen looked away for a moment. He looked uncomfortable.

"I was worried about Johnny last night too. I have a secret to tell you. The bartender waters down my drinks. I tried to get Johnny to do the same thing, but he refuses. He even asks for doubles."

Hagen looked a little sheepish.

"Let me know if I can help."

He looked away again, the confident glow from the previous evening now entirely gone.

"Good luck in your match tomorrow," Walter said. "I'm off to pick up the pieces."

George patted him gently on the shoulder.

"I'll keep you informed. Thanks for your candor, Walter."

Hagen headed over the hill toward the 16th.

This was not the Walter Hagen George had expected. Whatever his own problems, this Walter Hagen cared about Johnny. George smiled as he walked down the 18th fairway. Maybe they would pull this off and help their friend recover.

CHAPTER 23

The moon was rising behind the Carolina Hotel as Sarah picked up George in a new Olds Touring Car. The car was white with a red leather interior. A large replacement tire was mounted on the running board next to the parking brake.

"Wow, snazzy car, Sarah," George said as he got into the passenger's seat.

"These folks go first class. This is the club manager's car. He let me borrow it for a few days."

Sarah giggled as if she were a school girl on her first date.

George loved her giggle. It sounded honest and joyous. And it wasn't only the giggle. It was the whole package. George had been smitten with Sarah since the first day they had met in Natick.

After a few minutes drive, Sarah got to the point.

"George, you're Johnny's best friend. You need to be strong tonight."

"What do you mean by strong?"

"Strong, as in tough. You need to tell him that he's let you and his family down. His drug addiction is destroying his health. Tell him he looks like shit. He'll listen to you. He won't listen to me."

George closed his eyes. He wasn't looking forward to the next few hours.

The drive to Mid Pines took twenty minutes. As they turned into the driveway of the rented house, Sarah asked, "Do you think we are doing the right thing? I mean pulling him out in the middle of the tour. We could wait until the fall when things have settled down."

"No, this is the right time," George said flatly. "We can't wait. He needs help now."

Sarah didn't have time to respond before Bob and Johnny pulled up behind them.

"Boy, am I hungry," Johnny said as he got out of Bob's Model T. When he saw the Reverend's car parked close to the house, he asked, "Who else is joining us tonight?"

"A friend," Bob said.

They greeted one another and then entered the cottage-style house directly into the living room. George saw that six chairs had been set up there in a circle.

Johnny laughed.

"What! Bob, are we having a revival meeting?" he asked.

George moved close to Johnny and guided him toward one of the chairs.

"Not exactly," George said. "Come on, Johnny, sit over here."

A gaunt man dressed in a gray suit with a white collar came into the living room from the kitchen. Bob walked over to shake his hand and thank him for coming. Then he turned to Johnny.

"Johnny, this is Reverend Bill McIntyre from Trinity Episcopal Church in Southern Pines," Bob said. "I invited him to join us tonight."

Johnny nodded hello to McIntyre.

"Nice to meet you," he said, a little suspicion in his voice. He began to scratch the back of his neck, then he turned back to Bob. "Do you have anything to drink?"

Before Bob could say anything, McIntyre interrupted.

"Johnny, Bob and your other friends here have invited me tonight to help you deal with your addiction to drugs and alcohol." He spoke softly with a pronounced Southern accent.

Johnny turned to George and Sarah and let out a muffled laugh.

"Okay, folks. Is this a joke?"

"No, Johnny," George said. "We're very concerned about your health and your well-being. We want to help you get better."

Johnny started to rise from his chair.

"Shit. I don't need help," he said angrily.

George moved behind Johnny and grabbed his shoulders to force him back down into the chair.

Johnny looked startled.

George spoke in as calm a voice as he could muster.

"Johnny, please listen to these folks. They care for you. You need to sit."

Johnny was shocked that George had grabbed him. He had never seen his friend so determined. He felt cold.

McIntyre pulled his chair close to and directly in front of Johnny. He spoke firmly but his voice was soothing.

"Johnny, your constant use of the Elixir has created a morphine dependency."

Reverend McIntyre paused to allow his words to sink in.

"The morphine has taken a toll on your mind and your body. You're addicted. You're anxious all the time. You constantly scratch the back of your neck. You experience severe insomnia."

He paused again.

"Stop me if I'm wrong," he said.

Johnny didn't say a word. He sat bent over in his chair, staring down at the floor, his elbows on his knees and his hands tightly clasped together.

McIntyre started again.

"You regularly vomit. You have a difficult time remembering things, places, people."

He stared at Johnny and waited. After a few moments, he said, "You need to get this under control, or else."

Johnny looked up and his eyes were beet red.

"Hell, I have it under control," he said, his voice shaking slightly. "I only use the Elixir when I play."

McIntyre moved his chair back from Johnny a bit, then he looked around at the others and nodded.

"Johnny, that's not true," Sarah said. "You take it four to five times a day. I've seen you chug it down after dinner."

Johnny's right hand began to shake uncontrollably as he sat slumped in the chair. Sarah looked panicky.

"We love you, Johnny, and want you to get better," she said quickly.

Johnny started to rock from side to side.

"I really hate this. I hate what's happened to me," he mumbled.

He began to sob uncontrollably.

George moved around from behind Johnny's chair and crouched down in front of him. He pulled Johnny forward and hugged him. Johnny buried his face in George's shoulder. Tears came to George's eyes as he held his friend.

"Okay. It's okay," George said softly. "We're here for you."

"You're a shit for doing this to me," Johnny said as he continued to sob.

"Yeah, I'm a shit and you're a bastard. Now let's move on."

McIntyre leaned forward again.

"Johnny, deep down inside you want to get better," he said. "We're here to help, but you need to make the commitment to get better."

Johnny pulled back from George and looked up, bewildered.

"But how? I've tried to quit. The pain in my hand keeps coming back and I can't play golf. I need to play golf."

Suddenly, his face brightened.

"Okay. You're right. I'll stop using the Elixir."

Bob stepped closer to Johnny and cleared his throat before he spoke.

"We've heard that line before, Johnny," he said. "You need professional help. And you need to take some time off to get better."

Johnny nodded and tried to sound unconcerned, but his voice was cracking.

"Okay, Bob. You're right. Whatever you say. Right after we play in Atlanta."

Bob spoke quickly, almost cutting Johnny off.

"You've already been replaced on the team, Johnny. Byron McGee has agreed to stand in for you," he said.

Johnny's eyes flashed with anger. He pulled himself entirely free of George.

"What! Does Hagen know about this?"

Bob tried to stay calm, as McIntyre had told him to do.

"Hagen knows. I've already briefed the team," Bob said matter-of-factly. "They're the only people outside of this room who know our plans."

Johnny was fidgeting, his eyes darting around the room. He looked ready to leap up from his chair.

"Your plans!" he yelled. "What the hell does that mean?"

Sarah slowly moved from her chair and leaned closer to Johnny. He was now tightly surrounded by his friends.

"We've set up an appointment for you at the Linthicum Institute," Sarah said. "It's one of the best drug rehabilitation centers in the country."

Johnny's anger seemed to drain and he looked puzzled.

"A rehabilitation center? What do they do?"

Sarah looked directly into his eyes.

"Johnny, you are an addict. And you can't get better alone. These folks at Linthicum will help you get better."

Johnny's lower lip quivered. His eyes welled up again and he dropped his face into his hands.

"I admit it," he mumbled. "I never thought of myself as an addict until a few months ago."

He took a deep breath, sniffled loudly, and rubbed his eyes.

"I can't stop taking the Elixir. I can't sleep. I'm always tired. My mouth is dry. My right hand shakes all the time."

George exchanged glances with Bob. He could see a tear rolling down Sarah's cheek.

McIntyre spoke after a short silence.

"It's not going to be easy, Johnny. You'll experience intense pain during the withdrawal period. The professionals at the Institute will help with natural sedatives. After you stay for a few weeks at the Institute, George will take you up to Providence for an appointment he's arranged with a plastic surgeon there."

George leaned down to make eye contact with Johnny.

"I've found this great doctor who thinks he can help. He thinks the skin below your scar is dead and is pressing on the nerve. He knows how to help with that."

George paused to give Johnny time to comprehend what he had said.

"We've rented a place on Cape Cod for after the surgery. The surgeon says the recovery will last two months."

Johnny suddenly sat straight up in his chair. He looked panicky.

"Two months! I can't afford to be away from the game for two months! What about my job in Tampa?"

Bob moved over to crouch directly in front of him.

"You're in no shape to play on the tour. But the team has agreed to divide the winnings in Atlanta five ways–less my commission, of course. This was Hagen's idea and everyone agreed. And I've talked with the club president at Citrus and he's agreed to let your assistant run the pro shop until you return. I told him you needed to take care of a family matter in Boston for a few months. He told me in confidence that some members had requested that you be fired. If you don't get better, you'll be out anyway."

"Johnny, if you continue to use the Elixir, there will be a tragic end," said George. "I need you to be alive if you're going . . . ," George paused for a second ". . . to be my best man."

Johnny's eyes lit up.

"Best man? This is great news. When's the ceremony?"

"I haven't asked her yet, but if Jennifer says yes, we'll get married next year."

Johnny looked thoughtful.

"Johnny Scranton, sober at a wedding. That'll be a first."

Johnny hung his head down between his knees.

"I'm not sure I'm strong enough to go through with this."

Sarah gently lifted his face up with her soft hands.

"We'll be with you every step of the way," she said.

She stood up and moved behind him to massage the back of his neck. Johnny closed his eyes.

"Okay, let me sleep on it," he said as he leaned his head back against Sarah's lap.

"Oh, no," said George. "We leave tonight for the institute. We leave now."

Johnny straightened up in his chair, startled by George's statement.

"Tonight? I'm exhausted!"

Reverend McIntyre immediately sensed that there was an opening. He moved forward quickly.

"You need to tell us that you want to get better," he said. "You need to show us."

"I do. I really do!" Johnny exclaimed.

"Then you need to make a commitment tonight, or the program won't work."

Now Johnny began to cry in earnest.

"Yes. Yes, I want to get better. I'll try." Tears rolled down his cheeks.

But McIntyre pressed even further. He jumped to his feet and his voice boomed as if he were delivering the Sunday sermon.

"This is not good enough, Johnny Scranton!" he roared. "You must resolve tonight that you will beat this addiction with all your might."

Johnny was transfixed.

"Yes. I will do what needs to be done to get better."

McIntyre grabbed his shoulders and shook him.

"You can! You can!" he shouted in Johnny's face.

Johnny slumped into the chair and all he could do was nod.

McIntyre stepped away from Johnny and turned to Bob.

"Now, Bob," he said simply.

Bob's eyes were wide and his mouth hung open.

"Now, Bob," said McIntyre a second time.

This time Bob turned to Sarah.

"Get the car," he said.

They quickly gathered their coats and piled into the cars for the short trip to Linthicum.

Johnny, George, and Sarah piled into the Olds and Bob followed in the Model T.

Johnny settled into the deep back seat of the Olds and closed his eyes. He looked exhausted. George noticed that a certain calm had settled over his face. His lower lip was not quivering.

"I don't know what I'd do without you guys," Johnny said softly.

"Guys, is it?" Sarah said, as she negotiated the narrow roads. "I'm a lady, and don't you forget it."

George looked over at her. She was radiant. Someday she would find Mr. Right and he would be a very lucky man. The thought lingered for him as they headed north to Holly Springs: if he had not met Jennifer.

Chapter 24

There was a discreet sign for the Linthicum Institute at the entrance to the grounds. Sarah guided the Olds up a long, winding driveway to a large plantation-style home set on a hill dotted with tall elm trees and surrounded by gently rolling fields of clipped green grass. Lanterns hung along the porch that stretched across the front of the house. An elderly gentleman with long white hair met them as they approached the front door.

"Good evening, y'all," he said.

He had a thick Southern accent that was difficult for George to understand.

"Welcome to the Linthicum Institute."

He directed them into the hallway of the house. "Let's shut that door, please, so we don't let the night air in the house."

"Night air?" George whispered to Sarah.

The man leaned forward and extended his hand.

"My name is Dr. Charles Pritchard. I'm the director of the Institute. Reverend McIntyre called to let me know that you were on your way."

He turned to Johnny.

"I assume you're Mr. Scranton?"

Johnny approached cautiously, but said nothing. Pritchard reached out with his right hand to offer a handshake while placing his left hand softly on Johnny's shoulder.

"Nice to meet you, Mr. Scranton," he said. "We have your room ready on the first floor."

A slim, short-haired woman wearing a blue nursing blouse and long, tailored pants appeared from the rear of the house.

Johnny had never seen a woman in pants. She looked sexy.

"Come with me, Mr. Scranton," she said. "I'll get you settled."

As soon as they left, George asked about the nurse wearing pants.

"We don't lock the rooms so patients can feel comfortable during their stay. The nurses wear pants to free them to interact more closely with the patients and be able to catch up with our runners."

"Runners!" Sarah said.

Pritchard pointed to the field outside a nearby window.

"As drug addicts withdraw, they can lose all sense of reality and begin to hallucinate about being free. Some have described the feeling as floating in a sea of clouds. It is at this point some patients take off and want to run into the imagined clouds. I've had patients get as far as the outer drive of the property before we catch them."

"Don't you restrain patients?" Sarah asked.

Pritchard shook his head.

"No. Restraints are not part of our therapy. Patients are free to roam around the house unattended. They just can't leave the grounds. We have over 200 acres, so they have a long way to go before they get off our property. We try to instill in each patient a sense of responsibility so he'll take charge of his life."

Bob joined them from parking his car just as Pritchard was escorting George and Sarah out onto the front porch.

"It's good for you to leave now so that we can get Mr. Scranton settled," the doctor said. "The longer you're here, the more likely he is to want to leave with you. It's wise to remove that possibility as quickly as possible."

"Can we at least say goodbye to Johnny?" asked Sarah. She was wringing her hands and sounded as if she might start to cry.

"That's not a good idea," said Pritchard softly but firmly.

"You can see him for a little while tomorrow."

George stepped closer to Sarah and gently put his arm around her. She leaned into him and pressed her face into the crook of his shoulder. She didn't make a sound, but he could feel her crying.

"What happens to Johnny tonight?" George asked.

Pritchard patiently laid out the details in a measured, sure tone that suggested he had answered this question many times before.

"Tonight we'll take some information from him and he'll be observed by our staff. Then we'll start detoxification therapy early tomorrow morning," he said.

He led them down the porch steps toward the cars then stopped to speak again.

"Tomorrow will be a tough day for him. For morphine addicts it usually takes three to four days of intense detoxification to clean out their system. He'll start with a good breakfast, he'll sauna three times during the morning, and he'll receive massage therapy in the afternoon. And every patient receives a heavy dose of vitamins, especially vitamin C, which will help to flush the morphine out of his system."

He paused again and seemed to be looking past Bob as if he were wondering about the cars that were parked in front of the house. There was a long silence. Just as George was ready to thank him and say goodbye, Pritchard twitched, sighed loudly, and started talking again.

"The worst part will be during the second day, when his cravings kick in and he begins to withdraw from the drugs. On the fifth day, we'll start our counseling services. Altogether, he'll stay with us for three weeks working with our counselors, exercising, and learning how to live with his addiction."

He fell silent again. Sarah lifted her head from under George's shoulder.

"Isn't there anything we can do for him tonight?" she asked.
Pritchard shook his head and spoke very sweetly to her.

"No, really, dear. Nothing tonight. But if you can come back mid-day tomorrow, I think that will be when Johnny will need your help. He's going to experience some tough withdrawal over the next few days. A friendly face always helps with that."

Sarah rubbed her eyes and sniffled. She nodded.

"Okay, Doc," Bob said. "One of us will be back tomorrow."

****

"George, why didn't you join us on the tour?" asked Sarah, as she parked the Olds near the entrance to the Carolina. She had pulled up just short of the soft light provided by the few late-night torches still burning across the front of the hotel.

"It would have been great if you had been with us," she said.

She shifted the car into neutral, then reached out and engaged the parking brake. She turned toward George and then moved across the front seat to be closer to him. George turned to his left to face her and leaned back against the flat of the passenger's door. He gave a shrug.

"I'm content playing as an amateur," he said. "I'm not cut out to live the life of a traveling pro."

Sarah looked down at the seat and ran the slender fingers of her right hand across its smooth leather. She raised her eyes to him without lifting her head.

"Well, what about me?" she asked. "Are you cut out for me? I've always thought that you might " –she seemed to be searching for the right words–"like me."

Before George could answer, she slid closer and moved her right hand around to the back of his neck. She began to rub gently. Her hand felt soft and smooth as it caressed him. He loved it when she played with his hair above the collar.

"Now, Sarah, we mustn't, " George said a bit embarrassed.

But his voice was failing and he could feel his face reddening. He glanced down at her silk blouse. He could see the outline of her breasts clearly through the silk.

She edged closer and suddenly she leaned across the small space left between them and kissed him gently on the lips, just for a short moment.

Then she tilted her head back so that she could look into his eyes. She ran her hand languidly from his neck around to his face so that it rested tenderly on his cheek.

George felt a rush as he held this beautiful woman in his arms.

"Is there any chance we could be together, George?" she asked, her voice low.

George's heart was racing and his palms were sweating. He tried to respond to her question, but no words came out. This seemed wrong, but the urge to kiss her welled up inside him.

He heard himself whisper.

"Oh, Sarah," almost inaudibly.

Then he pulled her against him and they kissed a long, slow kiss. Her lips were moist and warm and seemed to melt into his. She shifted in the seat until she was nearly on top of him and pushed herself against him. He could feel her breasts pressing into his chest and the heat of her leg against his thigh. He moved his right hand to her breast and gently ran his fingers along its supple curve. The breast was small but firm. She whimpered and pressed even closer. Then she leaned back to look into his eyes again. She was breathing heavily.

He reached down and slowly unbuttoned the top button on her blouse.

She sweetly smiled and they slowly kissed again.

George gently pushed her back and unbuttoned the second button. Sarah looked directly into his eyes.

"I want to be with you," she murmured. "Let's go back to your room."

George ran one hand up to the small of her back and Sarah responded by wrapping her arms tightly around his neck and their lips came together again. George felt himself drowning in her heat.

Suddenly he pulled back. Pangs of guilt overwhelmed him.

"No. I can't do this," he said breathlessly. He grabbed her shoulders and gently pushed her away.

"I can't be with you."

He laid his back hard against the car door and looked away from her.

"You are the most desirable woman I've ever met," he said quietly.

He shook his head slowly.

"But I'm committed to Jennifer. I plan to marry her. I can't betray that trust."

Sarah took a deep breath. A drop of sweat rolled down her cheek. She ran her right hand down along George's left arm and looked down at the seat. After a moment, she looked back up at him, her lower lip quivering. Her eyes were watery.

"I didn't hear you say you loved her," she said in a sultry voice.

George looked at her in surprise.

"Of course I love her," he said.

Why didn't I think to say that? he thought.

Sarah nodded, then bowed her head and slowly, carefully adjusted the buttons on her blouse.

George watched her for a long moment without speaking. She was beautiful.

Finally he said, "I've got to go." When Sarah didn't respond, he added awkwardly, "Thanks for the ride."

He opened the door and quickly climbed out of the car. He leaned through the window to look at Sarah and say good night again. He kissed her on her forehead.

She stared at him for a moment, then smiled weakly. She reached up and this time kissed him on the forehead, then again on the check.

"You're a temptress, Miss Knowles."

The urge to pull her out of the car was intense. But he resisted.

"Good night, George," she said reluctantly.

George smiled. Her blonde hair sparkled in the torch light.

"Go, before I change my mind," George said.

She sighed, then she shifted the car into gear and drove off.

A myriad of disturbing thoughts and feelings raced through George's mind as he walked up the steps to the Carolina Hotel.

What would it be like to be with Sarah? Had he made a mistake in pulling back?

No, he had done the right thing. He loved Jennifer and he was committed to her. That was never going to change. In the clearer light of morning, he would have regretted betraying her.

But then he found himself thinking, don't let Sarah go. It's only for tonight. Jennifer would never need to know.

The confusion lingered as he turned and watched the taillights of the Olds grow smaller in the distance.

CHAPTER 25

The alarm clock startled George as he lingered, half asleep, half awake. He glanced at the clock. It was 9:30. He had less than 90 minutes to get ready, warm up, and be on the 1st tee. He jumped into the shower, dressed quickly, and rushed down to breakfast before the match.

On the patio outside the dining room of the hotel, the committee had set up a buffet for the players. George hurried through the line, filling his plate with eggs, sausage, and bacon. He was famished.

"Quite a solid breakfast, Mr. Riley."

Heinrich's voice resonated from behind the breakfast bar.

"I think you'll need your best game today. I see you play with Chick Evans and Arthur Pamponon at 11."

Heinrich took three pieces of bacon and wrapped them around a sausage. He joined George at a table near the back of the room. His plate was piled high with breakfast treats.

"You look tired, George," he said, not looking up from the table. His eyes were focused on the feast in front of him. "I hear Johnny is in town. Did you see him last night?"

"Yes. We had dinner. He's doing fine. Sends his regards."

Heirich looked surprised as he glanced up for a second.

"That's not what I hear."

"What do you mean?"

Heinrich chose his words carefully. He had a deep frown on his forehead. It made him look as if he were in pain.

"There are lots of rumors. Many believe Johnny is washed up due to the drugs and booze. Some members at Worcester don't even want him playing at the club. I think he needs some help if he's going to continue to play golf for a living."

George thought for a minute as to whether he should tell Heinrich about Johnny's rehab, but he decided not to mention it.

"He was fine last night."

Heinrich looked relieved. His face broke into a broad smile.

"That's good to hear. Statements from you about his condition will be a comfort to many people."

"That's nice of you to say," George said.

Heinrich poured ketchup on a large mound of eggs Benedict.

"Have you tried putting on the sand greens?" he asked. "They just rolled the practice green and it's lightning fast."

Heinrich quickly polished off the eggs Benedict.

"I practiced on them yesterday," George said. "They're certainly different from our greens. It's strange to play on a green without any grass, isn't it?"

Heinrich nodded as he devoured his second German sausage of the morning.

"And I still can't get used to the rectangular shape of the greens," Heinrich said.

"They use a roller each day to press the sand down, so the greens are true, but they don't hold the ball. You need to bounce the ball in front of the green and let it roll up onto it."

Heinrich began his assault on a large pile of buttermilk biscuits.

"How do they keep the sand so firm?" asked George.

"They add an oil mixture to the greens before they roll them in the morning. After each group plays a hole, a caddy drags a piece of carpet across the green to keep the green smooth for the next group. They keep the carpet tucked in boxes next to the greens."

"Are all the greens flat?" George asked.

"All the greens are flat as a pancake, both the old course and the new course."

Heinrich waved his forefinger as a warning.

"But some of the greens have built-up areas in the middle. If you go off the back of the green, the ball will roll into the rough, or worse, the pine straw. I found it very difficult to hit a shot out of that stuff."

George looked at his watch. He needed to warm up and hit a few balls before his match. He quickly finished his breakfast and stood to say goodbye to Heinrich.

"Don't go and try to shoot the medal round today," Heinrich said. "Drink lots of water and don't overeat. It gets unbelievably hot here in the afternoon."

Heinrich headed back to the buffet for another round of eggs Benedict as George left for the practice tee.

****

A handsome young black man with short cropped hair was standing next to George's bag at the end of the practice tee.

"Hi, Mr. Riley. My name is Willie Smith. I'll be caddying for you today."

George held out his hand to shake Willie's hand.

"Hi, Willie," said George "Glad to meet you. How long have you caddied at Pinehurst?"

"This is my third season, Mr. Riley. I'm the best greens reader out here."

George nodded.

"Good. I'll need help with these sand greens. They're far different from the greens I play on up North."

"Yes, sir. You can't be too aggressive on your approach shot. These greens are fast. They'll eat you alive if you fly the ball directly at the pin. So hit short and let the ball drift into the pin. They added oil to the mixture last year and the new gas-powered rollers really pack the sand."

"Let's see if I can execute with your help."

George found an open tee area and stretched for five minutes. Once he was warmed up, he started his practice session with his niblick and worked his way up to his brassie. After hitting his warmup shots, he decided to keep the shafts whippy instead of adding shellac because the air was so heavy due to the high humidity.

He heard the starter call his name.

"Damn," he muttered. "I didn't leave enough time to get in some practice putts."

He cursed under his breath.

As they walked toward the teeing ground, George hoped Willie was as good a reader as he said. I'm going to need lots of help, he thought.

Chick Evans was standing to the right of the starter when George walked onto the 1st teeing ground. George had seen Evans play in 1910 in a semifinal with Bill Frownes at The Country Club. He had completely collapsed during the last three holes of his match. He was two up with three to play when his putter gave out. Frownes played brilliant golf the last three holes to beat Evans on the final hole.

Evans was short and slender with muscular forearms. He was now one of the hottest amateur players on the circuit, having recently won four tournaments, including the French Amateur and the Chicago Amateur. He was also the defending North-South champion.

George walked up to Evans and held out his hand.

"Hi, Chick. I'm George Riley."

Chick smiled and shook George's hand.

"Hi, George. Nice to finally meet you. I've heard a lot about you from Francis, Johnny, and Heinrich."

"This is the first time I've played in the South," George said. "It's going to be a challenge."

Evans nodded.

"Don't worry. These folks run a great tournament."

He turned and laughed. "And they are so hospitable to us Yankees."

They waited patiently to tee off as the group in front was slow getting off.

"I saw you play in 1910 at The Country Club," said George. "I was with Francis Ouimet."

"Yes. Not one of my best days," Evans admitted. "I let that match with Bill Frownes slip away. Let's hope today is better than that day at Brookline."

Arthur Pamponon joined them in the teeing ground. Pamponon towered over George and surely weighed over 300 pounds. When Pamponon shook George's hand, he felt as if the giant would break it off.

Evans whispered to George, "He doesn't talk much, but he can hit the ball a mile."

The starter appeared with three straws in his hand. The player who selected the longest straw teed off first. The player with the second longest teed off next and the third player teed off last. This process of selecting honors was a unique tradition at Pinehurst. George pulled the shortest straw and Evans pulled the longest.

The sun had started to emerge from behind the heavy clouds that had covered the course during the early morning. The heat and humidity were already stifling. It was 90 degrees and Willie said it was only going to get hotter.

George jumped out quickly with three pars and did a good job of adapting his putting style to the the unique greens. Willie was a big help, directing him where to hit each approach shot. Evans and George each shot even par 36 on the front side. Pamponon took the turn with a 39. He had gotten into trouble on the seventh hole when he hit a tree trying to cut the dogleg.

By the 9th hole, George's shirt was soaked with sweat, and he felt faint as the group headed to the 10th teeing ground. His legs started to shake and he started to have chills.

"You okay, Mr. Riley?" asked Willie.

"I'm a little dizzy," said George.

Willie laid the bag on the grass and guided George to the shade of a nearby tree. He helped him down into a crouch then handed him a bottle of water.

"Drink this," he said.

The caddy pulled two salt pills from his jacket and held them out to George.

George stared down at the pills in his hand.

"Where did these come from?" he asked.

"From me," said Willie. "I always carry salt pills. You're not used to this heat, sir. You need to take more water and keep your salt levels up. Let me get you a wet towel."

Willie walked over to a bucket at the far edge of the teeing ground.

Evans and Pomponon and their caddies had moved into the shade near George.

"Boy, is it hot," Evans said as he stretched, holding his brassie over his head with a hand on each end and twisting his torso back and forth to keep loose. "I can't get used to this heat."

"Doesn't bother me," Pamponon said flatly.

The big man looked with concern at George.

"Son, you don't look very good," he said. "Need anything?"

"No, thanks, Arthur," said George. "Willie's gone to get a cold towel. I just drank some water and took two salt pills. I just need to sit here for a few minutes."

Willie returned and laid a cool, wet towel on George's neck. He thanked Willie, then he stood up and drew a deep breath. He was already feeling better. He was determined to play through the intense heat.

A thermometer next to the yardage sign registered 102.

****

The 10th hole was a 402-yard par 4 with long fairway bunkers. George played a slashing shot with his brassie. The ball faded left as it left the club face and caught the edge of the outer fairway bunker. The ball lodged firmly under the front lip of the bunker.

George couldn't get home with his second shot so he decided to blast the ball out into the fairway with his niblick. He successfully exited the trap but it left him with a blind, uphill shot to a small green protected by large trees on the right side. He checked the top of the trees on the far side of the green. They were moving left to right. He grabbed a pinch of grass and threw it into the air. There was little wind where the ball sat, but he would need to compensate for the wind near the green. He turned to Willie.

"How far would you say we are?"

Willie stood with one hand on his hip while he balanced the bag with his other hand. He squinted.

"About 170 to the hole, Mr. Riley. The pin is cut in the middle of the green, so you'll have lots of room in back. You should fly it to the front edge of the green and let it feed into the cup."

George was in between clubs – should he use a full mid mashie or a spoon? He decided to hit a cut shot with his spoon. He played the ball forward on his left foot in order to keep the ball low, and he hit down on the ball so he would get top spin as the ball landed. The ball leapt from the spoon and stayed about 15 feet off the ground – then bounced in front of the green and curved left to the pin. As the ball hit the flat sand green, it skipped twice and checked up. Neither George nor Willie could see where the ball had landed because they were downhill, well below the front edge of the green.

Willie smiled.

"You hit a great shot, Mr. Riley. It's in the hole."

"How would you know that?" George asked in amazement.

"I have a sense about such things."

When they got to the hole, George checked the cup. Sure enough, his Haskell Comet 3 was in the bottom of the cup.

"I can't believe that shot, George," Evans said. He shook his head in disbelief. "Great shot."

George plucked the ball from the cup with two fingers and kissed it.

George turned to his caddy and grinned.

"Keep putting those cold towels on my neck."

"Yes, sir. Keep hitting shots like that," Willie said. He winked at George.

George and Evans played the next eight holes one over while Pamponon got into trouble again and finished with a 43. Evans shot 74. George shot 73, for the low gross score in the qualifier. Pamponon finished with a disappointing 82.

Sarah walked out to meet George on the 18th green as he finished. She flashed George her perfect smile and comfortably looped her arm around his. He chose to read that as an indication that all was well between them. Her blonde hair fluttered in the light afternoon breeze

"Not bad for a walk in the hot sun," she said.

"Yes. I got lucky today."

They walked toward the scorer's tent arm in arm.

"How's our patient?" George said, once they were clear of the others.

"He's in the withdrawal phase," Sarah said. "He asks for you constantly."

"Okay. I'll sign my card and meet you in the parking lot in 10 minutes."

As they came out of the scorer's tent, three men in rumpled, sweat-soaked suits waved and then rushed toward George.

"I'm Carl Rowe from the New York Times, Mr. Riley," said one of them. "Any comment about your round?"

George wanted to get this over with.

"The course was in excellent condition," he said, "but it sure was hot out there. I'm from Boston and it never gets this hot."

Rowe's followup question caught George unprepared.

"You're friends with Johnny Scranton, aren't you? There are rumors that he disappeared last night. He didn't show for his round at Southern Pines today. Do you know where he is?"

George paused before he answered. This was what they knew would be coming. He tried to sound casual.

"I saw Johnny early this morning. He left for Boston due to a family emergency. I know for a fact that he talked with Bob Johnson before he left. Have you talked with Mr. Johnson?"

Rowe looked skeptical.

"That's the official story, Mr. Riley. I thought you might have a more personal insight, if you know what I mean."

Sarah suddenly stepped forcefully between the reporters and

George, but she spoke sweetly.

"Thank you, gentlemen. I think you've got the story. And Mr. Riley needs to get out of this heat."

****

When George left the Carolina Hotel after the match, Chick Evans was relaxing on the front porch.

"Coming to the dinner tonight, George?"

"I need to see a friend, but I hope to be back in time. Save me a seat, will you?"

"You're the medalist, George," Evans said with a broad, friendly smile. "You can sit wherever you want."

George loped down to the Olds and climbed inside. Sarah gunned the engine as they sped off down the driveway.

Strange, thought Evans. He shoots a great round and then rockets off without telling anyone where he's going. He had heard the rumor that Johnny Scranton had disappeared, but his version didn't include a trip home to Boston.

CHAPTER 26

During the second full day at the Institute, Johnny started to hallucinate from the withdrawal. At the same time, he had so much morphine left in his system that his stomach muscles began to contract when he was deprived of his usual dose. He went into convulsions and began to throw up everything he ate. The convulsions lasted an hour or more at a time, and they were the most intense pain he had ever endured. The doctors at the Institute administered a natural herb supplement which slowly helped to settle his stomach, but his stomach muscles felt for days afterwards as if they had been pounded mercilessly with a baseball bat. Getting better was no fun.

******

At Pinehurst, George won two matches on the second day of the tournament to advance to the semifinals on the third day. He lost that match though, 2-1, to Ben Mathews from Mobile, Alabama.

The match was close. George was two up through the 13th hole when Mathews rallied with three straight birdies. George's mind started to wander and he made a number of mental errors. Mathews closed him out on the 17th with a magnificent putt to save par.

Willie and George walked quietly toward the clubhouse after the match.

"Mr. Riley, you seemed to lose your focus," said Willie. "Thinking about Mr. Scranton?"

George stopped in the middle of the fairway.

"What did you say, Willie?"

Willie tilted his head and pursed his lips. His tone was apologetic.

"I thought you might be upset about your friend, sir," he said. "I know that he's in the hospital up in Holly Springs. You've been visiting him every night."

"How did you find out?" George asked, shocked that Willie knew about Johnny.

"I have a friend who works as a gardener in Holly Springs. He told me."

"Who else knows?" George said, more sharply than he meant to.

Willie shook his head and held up his free hand.

"No one else, Mr. Riley. Your secret is safe with me."

He looked very upset.

George started to walk down the fairway again.

"Willie," he said more calmly, "It's important to keep this a secret. He's going to get better and some day he'll play again. I don't want his reputation ruined."

"Don't worry, Mr. Riley," Willie said quickly. "We have a sacred code down here. We don't tell stories about our players. We make our living carrying a bag. Those caddies who violate this rule don't last very long at Pinehurst. Your secret is safe with me."

Willie crossed his heart and held up his hand. After a few moments of silence, he spoke again.

"You're a good man, Mr. Riley – and a good golfer, too," he said. "I'm amazed that you could play so well with all you've been doing for your friend."

****

Johnny was sitting in an old cane rocking chair on the front porch when George arrived at the Institute.

"So, how did it go?" Johnny asked in a hushed tone.

"Lost to Ben Mathews from Alabama 2-1. I made too many mistakes."

The color had returned to Johnny's face. He looked tired but he seemed relaxed.

"You're looking better," said George.

"Am I? I can't remember much about the last few days," Johnny confided.

George smiled.

"I heard a lot of foul language. What a mouth."

Johnny sighed and looked away toward the lawn beyond the porch.

"How did you get me to do this?" he asked. "I can't remember that part very well either."

George sat down into a chair next to Johnny's.

"I laid down a challenge to you," he said. "Like when we were kids playing a match next to the cemetery."

Johnny seemed confused.

"Like the challenge we played finding gutties as kids?"

"No," said George, turning toward Johnny and resting his forearm on the arm of the rocking chair. "You really don't remember, do you?"

George turned back around into his chair and looked straight ahead.

"I challenged you to be the best man at my wedding. But there was one condition. You had to be sober and drug free."

Johnny folded his arms and shivered. George couldn't tell if the shiver was real or a dramatic touch. Then Johnny let out a low laugh.

"A sober Johnny Scranton at your wedding," he said. "Impossible!"

Johnny threw up his hands in despair. George turned to face him again.

"Johnny," he said, "this is serious. You're going to lose your job at Tampa if you don't change. Some clubs are already planning to ban you from tournaments. And that's just golf. The doctor here said you could have a heart attack from an overdose. The morphine could literally kill you."

Johnny sighed again. Drug free and sober. The past four days had been the worst days of his life. This was going to be even harder than he had thought.

****

George attended the champions dinner and received the qualifying medalist award. The dinner was well attended and George asked Sarah to join him at his table. She wore a sexy blue chiffon dress that came to mid calf. She was the most beautiful woman in the room, and a local photographer took their photo.

"Maybe we'll be in the society section of the Globe," Sarah whispered as they waited for the photographer to complete his picture.

George looked concerned.

"Let's hope we aren't in the Providence Express," he said softly. "What will Jennifer think?"

Sarah looked up at him with a faint smile.

"Don't worry, George," she said, a hint of irritation in her voice. "I'll explain to her that you're the only guy who ever rejected my advances."

George politely danced with Sarah whenever she asked him. And she pressed herself close against George whenever the chance arose. If only . . . , George thought.

CHAPTER 27

George returned to Providence on the overnight train and his first order of business was to meet with Doctor Avil Hartman. A graduate of Harvard College and Harvard Medical School, Hartman had served his plastic surgery residency at the Massachusetts General Hospital in Boston. In 1903, he moved down to Providence to become the Chief of Plastic Surgery at Mercy Hospital. He established a clinic there that specialized in reconstructive surgery for burn victims.

Hartman was fascinated with Johnny's case. At their first meeting in his office, he had laid out clearly for George what needed to be done. He laid an anatomical illustration of the hand on his desk and pointed out relevant details of it as he spoke.

"This is not an easy operation," he said. "I need to remove the dead tissue and make sure I don't cut or nick these nerves in the palm of his hand. He needs them to be able to feel the club."

Hartman certainly seemed to know what he was talking about, and he had an air of confidence that was reassuring. George came away convinced he had found the right man to treat Johnny.

George finished his last exam, arranged for Johnny's arrival, then headed to Boston to begin his summer internship.

****

It was Vincent Snediker, the Senior Vice President, who officiously greeted George on his first day of work at the First National Bank of Boston. Snediker explained to him that summer interns rotated every three weeks to a new department in order to learn the various aspects of bank operations. Snediker himself had developed the summer rotation system as an opportunity for senior management to evaluate the interns and decide if they wanted to offer an intern a future position with the bank. Snediker was sure that George would do well in the program.

"You seem like a bright young man," he said and then he dashed off to another meeting.

George's first rotation was in the index vault, a cavernous room in the basement of the bank where over 50,000 bonds were stored. The supervisor of the vault was Robert Watson, a graduate in finance from Wesleyan, who recently had been promoted to division chief. He was a large man with a pot belly. His nickname among the clerks was "Rolly."

George's first assignment was to compile the weekly registration sheets for the bond traders. He pulled bonds which were about to mature and recorded the bonds' registration numbers on a call sheet. The call sheets were then sent to a bond broker on the first floor, who would contact the clients and see if they wanted the bonds cashed or renewed. George found himself surprisingly fascinated by the complexity of the process: bond maturity dates, yield ratios, rollover rates, and attachments.

"So who do you know around here to land this plum assignment?" Watson asked George as they reviewed a series of older bonds from the 1880's. "When I came to the bank with a completed degree, it took almost eight months before I was assigned here. Worked in the options index room."

He made his face long and rolled his eyes and stretched out the word: "Boring."

George had already decided he was going to be up front with anyone who asked how he got the job.

"I was recommended by my history professor at Brown. He

knew someone in management."

Watson nodded to show he expected as much.

"Mr. Snediker told me I'm to give you time off this summer to play golf. So you must be the sports star this season," he said.

"What do you mean?" George asked.

"Each summer Snediker hires an intern who also happens to be an excellent athlete. Last summer he hired a badminton champion. The guy won three national titles before he was eighteen and was the defending Ivy League Champion from Yale. Our public relations department loved this guy."

"Did the bank offer him a job after the summer program?"

"No," said Watson, but he ended up being offered a pretty nice job in a bank in New York City."

George found the story of the badminton player disquieting. Was he hired only because of his skills as a golfer? He didn't like to think that. He would prove to Vince Snediker and the bank managers that he was a valuable employee for the bank and a team player. He would show himself eager to learn as much as he could about the bank during the next nine weeks.

CHAPTER 28

Johnny's operation took three painstaking hours, a test in his weakened condition. He had been anesthetized, and as the ether wore off, he launched into a long series of convulsions and dry heaves.

"Shit," he said, as Sarah dabbed a cold towel on his forehead, "You didn't tell me I was going to be in worse shape than I was during withdrawal."

"Try to rest," Sarah said. "The doctor says this will pass. He said we can take you to Harwichport tomorrow."

Sarah looked tired. She had shadows under her eyes and she was pale. The past three weeks of taking care of Johnny had been very trying for both Sarah and Bob Johnson.

"You look as if you haven't had much sleep," Johnny said. "This is no way to find Mr. Right."

"Maybe I want some time off to be with a friend."

Sarah raised his unbandaged hand and slowly ran her fingers up and down the length of his arm. Johnny smiled

"Johnny, I'm so proud of you. The past three weeks you've been courageous. This is the Johnny I knew and fell in love with."

"Fell in love?"

Johnny looked surprised.

"Are you getting sweet on me?" he asked with a sly grin.

"I've always been sweet on you," she said, smiling back at him warmly. She lowered her eyes as if embarrassed.

"Remember the time that guy in Birmingham had his hands all over me at the bar? I was shaking like a leaf. You stayed with me and held me until I calmed down."

"Yeah, I remember that," Johnny said. "I always sort of thought you'd slug me if I put the moves on you, though."

Sarah laughed and gently placed his arm back on the bed.

"I think you were probably right."

Her face became more serious.

"I don't really think we would have done well as lovers, do you? You're better as the brother I never had. You can think of me as your sister."

Johnny offered an exaggerated frown.

"Yeah. The gorgeous sister I'll always protect."

His voice got quiet.

"Thank you for all you've done."

Sarah noticed a small tear form in Johnny's right eye. She leaned over and softly kissed him on his forehead.

"I do love you."

****

Donald Smitson couldn't find any information at the library about road conditions on Cape Cod. He did find a guide to roads in Southern New England. It said that the road to Fall River was paved but the road from Fall River to the Cape Cod Canal was still packed dirt.

He had recently purchased his first car, a Model T, and he treated it as if it were their second child. Jennifer had spent two weeks lobbying her dad for permission to use the T to take Johnny to Harwichport. Donald reluctantly agreed with two conditions: that Jennifer would not go alone and that she would call him as soon as she arrived in Harwichport.

The driving fell to Jennifer since George couldn't take time off from the bank so early in his internship.

Jennifer loaded her bags in the storage compartment of the

T while Bob Johnson paced around the car. Jennifer noticed her father's worried look.

"Daddy, don't worry," she said. "I'll be back on Friday. And Bob and Sarah will help drive."

"Now you need to be careful near Fall River," her father said firmly. He held up his book to show her. "The guide says that the wooden bridge sometimes floods. We had a lot of rain last night. It might be under water. Don't cross unless you have enough clearance under the wheels."

"Yes, Daddy. I'll be careful."

Bob thought it was a good time to change the subject.

"I love the Brewster Green color of your car, Don," he said. "I haven't seen a Model T this color before."

"The salesman told me it was the first one he sold this year," Don said. "It was $690 to start, then I ordered the special snap-in canvas windows for the back seat. That was extra. How do you like the brass grill? Cost an additional $25."

"I'm amazed how much the price of the T has dropped," Bob said. "When Guy Rockham bought his car in 1908, it cost $850. And they're nicer now, too."

He moved to view the front of the car. The car had brass headlights and two brass carriage lamps.

"I think the brass grill looks very smart," Bob said, admiring the detail work on the grill. "Ford has made lots of improvements to the car since it was first released in 1909. I like the brass rearview mirror on the driver's side. Is that an extra this year?"

"No," Don said. "The mirror comes standard with the car. Can you believe it? And this year they introduced the new vanadian steel frame. It's the same steel being used in the Rio Grand Touring car, and that costs $1800."

Jennifer put her duster coat on and slid into the driver's seat from the passenger side of the vehicle.

"Daddy, we need to go," she said. "We need to swing by the hospital and get Johnny and Sarah."

She adjusted the clutch and hollered "ready" as Bob cranked the engine. The four cylinder turned over and purred like a kitten.

"Much quieter than the earlier model T's," Bob said.

Don gave his daughter a big kiss.

"Drive carefully now, sweetheart," he said. "I love you."

Jennifer smiled a little-girl smile and whispered, "I love you too, Daddy."

Then she released the brake and headed toward downtown Providence to pick up Johnny and Sarah.

Don looked worried.

CHAPTER 29

The trip to Cape Cod took longer than Jennifer had expected. The Falmouth Road was partially washed out and it took over an hour to travel the sixteen miles to Falmouth Center. They arrived at sunset and Bob pulled the T into an Esso station on the eastern edge of town. An old man in greasy overalls appeared from behind the station to help with the fuel pump.

"How far to Harwichport?" Bob asked him.

"About 30 miles east."

The sun was going down fast.

"How's the road?"

"Part of the road is paved," said the old man, "but most of it's unpaved. Difficult to travel at night."

"Are there any lights on the road?" Sarah asked.

"Let's see."

The old man rubbed his chin.

"The only lights are in Hyannis Center. Harwich has no lights on their roads. Falmouth only has lanterns a half mile east of town."

Bob turned to Jennifer.

"We should stop for the night."

Jennifer nodded her agreement. Bob turned back to the old man.

"Can you recommend a place to stay?"

"Mrs. Parker's house on the village green. She takes in boarders. Makes a mean pot roast, too," the old man said in a drawn out New England accent.

"How far is Mrs. Parker's house?"

The man pointed down the road.

"Turn left onto Main Street and proceed into town," he said. "Mrs. Parker's house is the third house on the left. I'll call and tell her you're coming."

"Thank you, sir," said Bob.

The man finished pumping the gas.

Jennifer asked, "How much do we owe you?"

"Let me see. She took a total of 15 gallons. So that'll be $2.40. I'll call Agnes."

Bob counted out the money and handed it to the old man.

"Thank you again, sir. Can you crank her over, please?"

The old man moved to the front of the car and pulled the crank handle out. He turned the engine over and Bob released the brake and eased the T out onto Main Street.

******

The Parker house was a large, yellow clapboard Victorian with a wraparound porch. There was a widow's watch near the peak of the roof. A distinguished gray-haired woman greeted them at the door.

"Well, you must be the folks with the gorgeous Model T. Earl called and told me you were coming." She moved back from the door. "Please, come in. I'm Agnes Parker. Welcome to my home."

Jennifer stepped in first.

"Thank you," she said.

She peered into the parlor. The room was elegantly furnished with oriental rugs, Chippendale furniture, and a baby grand piano. It smelled fresh and clean.

"I have two rooms available," Mrs. Parker said. "Earl said you're traveling to Harwichport."

Jennifer nodded.

"Yes. It's too late to travel," she said. "So we decided to stop for the night."

Bob and Sarah came through the door supporting Johnny on their shoulders.

Mrs. Parker looked concerned.

"Is he alright? What happened to him?"

"He had an operation," Bob said. "He'll be okay."

Mrs. Parker looked out through the door to see if any more people were in the group. She saw the green car sitting out front. She shook her head and frowned.

"I don't know how you young people dare drive those contraptions," she said. "My Charles hated them. They seem to be everywhere these days. I don't like the sound or smell, and they spook my horses."

"We'll try to be quiet when we leave tomorrow," Bob said.

Mrs. Parker shook her head again, but this time she laughed, an almost girlish giggle.

"Listen to me going on," she said. "Come, I'll show you the rooms."

Mrs. Parker shook her head one more time, as if to clear out the cobwebs. Jennifer touched her lightly on the arm.

"Can I use your phone, please?" she said. "I need to call my dad. I'll reverse the charges."

Mrs. Parker smiled and pointed to a doorway at the back of the parlor.

"The phone is in the kitchen, dear."

Sarah and Bob helped Johnny up the stairs.

"Guys in the first room. Gals in the next room," said Sarah.

"Always the organizer," Bob kidded her.

CHAPTER 30

Jennifer woke to the sound of a rooster crowing behind the Parker house. She decided to get up early and take a walk around town. She was met by Mrs. Parker as she descended the stairs.

"I make the best Danish in town. How about a bite, dear?"

Jennifer decided she could delay her walk.

"I'd love some, thank you."

Mrs. Parker sat at the kitchen table drinking tea while Jennifer ate her Danish. Mrs. Parker almost immediately expressed her interest in Johnny.

"Your friend is in pretty bad shape, my dear. He should rest today," she said emphatically.

"Thank you," said Jennifer, "but we really need to get him to Harwichport. We have a nurse there who'll take care of him."

Mrs. Parker was looking down at her tea as she slowly stirred it with a small spoon.

"Do you mind my inquiring about what happened to him?" she asked.

"He had an adverse reaction to the ether they used during his hand operation."

Mrs. Parker looked up from her tea.

"He looks familiar," she said. She paused and put her finger up to her mouth. "I think I've seen him before."

Jennifer shook her head no.

"Probably not," she said. "He's not from around here."

Mrs. Parker poured Jennifer another cup of tea.

"Where are you from?"

"Warwick, Rhode Island."

The old lady smiled dreamily.

"Oh, I do love Providence," she said. "My late husband and I used to stay there on our way to Newport for tournaments."

"Tournaments?" Jennifer asked.

"Yes. My husband was an avid amateur golfer. He played in all of the national tournaments."

Jennifer stared directly ahead.

"Golf tournaments?"

"Yes. Charles Rogers Parker. You may have heard of him. He won a number of tournaments before he died last year."

"He died," said Jennifer, her voice trailing off. "I'm so sorry. How did he die?"

Mrs. Parker put her spoon down onto the teacup's saucer and stared at the table.

"He was at a tournament in Haley, Massachusetts. A man shot him during a poker game."

She let out a long sigh.

"My Charles loved to play his poker," she said quietly.

She became more animated.

"The man claimed it was self defense," she said more loudly. "It was a ridiculous claim! My Charles didn't even own a gun."

"That's horrible," said Jennifer. "I'm so sorry for your loss."

Mrs. Parker became more agitated.

"No one was charged in his murder. He was murdered, I say."

She tried to gather herself. She pushed down on the front of her starched blouse as if she were rubbing out wrinkles.

"I'm going to make sure that every man involved goes to jail," she said adamantly.

"Did the authorities investigate?"

"Yes. They questioned three men, a Harry Roundcroft, a Walter Hagen, and a Johnny Scranton. I'll never forget the names."

Jennifer held back a gasp. She looked away so as not to give away her shock.

Mrs. Parker was talking more softly again.

"My Charles was a good man. I do miss him."

So much for my walk, thought Jennifer. She needed to get back upstairs immediately and tell Bob and Sarah this lady's story. They needed to get out of the house quickly.

She stood up from the table and stretched her arms.

"Well, thank you for the Danish. It was delicious," she said. "But I think it's time I wake my friends and we be on our way."

Mrs. Parker looked upset.

"No. No," she said. "I've made breakfast. You can't leave before you've eaten breakfast."

"We'll have to grab a bite to eat on the road," Jennifer said nervously, as she backed out of the kitchen. "It's a long drive."

She climbed the stairs and pounded on Bob's door. He answered in his night gown.

"What's the matter?" he asked.

"We have to leave now," Jennifer whispered. "Mrs. Parker's husband was shot dead by a man playing cards. Guess who was at the card table."

She quickly told Bob the story.

He looked dumbfounded.

"None of them ever told me anything about this," he said. "You're right. We need to leave. Get Sarah up. I'll have Johnny ready in five minutes."

Jennifer pulled a scarf over Johnny's head before they came down the stairs. Mrs. Parker stood at the front door. Her arms were folded and she was tapping her foot.

"You sure I can't make you breakfast?" she said.

Bob reached into his wallet and paid for the rooms.

"No thank you, Mrs. Parker. You've been very kind, but we really need to go."

Mrs. Parker followed them onto the porch. She looked suspiciously at them.

"Where are you staying in Harwichport?" she asked. "I know it pretty well. I have relatives in town there."

"Near the beach," said Bob as they shuffled Johnny out to the car. "I'm not sure of the address."

He quickly jumped into the front seat of the car. Jennifer and Johnny climbed into the back seat and Sarah hand-cranked the engine. The T started immediately. The sound of the engine startled Mrs. Parker.

"Thank you again," Bob said. He shifted the car into gear and gunned the engine. The T lurched forward, and they rolled down the street away from Mrs. Parker.

Once they were well out of sight of the house, Bob pulled over to the side of the road. A buggy passed as he swung around to face Johnny.

"Okay, Johnny," he said sharply, "what happened with Charles Parker?"

Johnny looked angry.

"How did you find out?" he snapped. "Did Hagen tell you?"

"We stayed with his widow last night," Jennifer said. "She told me the story."

Johnny turned pale.

"Did she recognize me?"

"No, but she's determined to see you, Hagen, and Roundcroft in jail," Bob said. "So what happened?"

Johnny shrugged his shoulders.

"Hagen and I met a couple of guys at a bar and we started to play poker. After about two hours, this guy Roundcroft accuses

Parker of cheating. I remember I lost two hundred bucks."

"$200!" Jennifer said.

"So Parker pulls out a gun, a small gun." Johnny held his hands a few inches apart to show how small the gun was. "They start yelling at each other. Parker raises this little gun and points it directly at Roundcroft. He says he's going to blow his head off."

Johnny was holding his left hand up, finger pointed, like it was a gun.

"Roundcroft suddenly pulls a gun from his boot and fires at Parker. Hagen and I dove for cover. So now Parker fires a shot and hits Roundcroft in the arm. We heard another shot and then Parker crumpled over the table."

Johnny spoke more softly.

"There was blood everywhere. The manager of the club applied towels to Parker's stomach to stop the bleeding, but by the time a doctor got there, he was dead."

Everyone in the car was quiet, transfixed by Johnny's story. Bob broke the silence after a few moments.

"What happened to you and Walter?" he asked.

Johnny waved his good hand to show his open palm.

"The town constable took us down to the station and questioned us. He had us write down what we saw. The next morning the State police showed up and said we could go, so we left for New Jersey and the next match."

Johnny took a breath, then shook his head and shrugged.

"They've never even asked us to come back and testify," he said. "That lady's wrong about our being involved. We just happened to be there when it happened."

He looked as if he had been struck with a sudden insight.

"Boy, if she knew who I was she might have made a scene. Good work getting me out of there."

Bob stared at Johnny for a long moment, disgusted at what he had heard. He turned back to the steering wheel and let out a long sigh, then he engaged the clutch and eased back onto the road.

"Let's get out of here," he muttered.

****

After driving for two hours on deeply rutted roads through Hyannis, Yarmouth, and Dennis, they crossed over the Herring River Bridge and soon entered Harwichport. The Pilgrim Congregational Church, its tall white steeple gleaming in the sun, was the most prominent building in the center of the village. The Church and its vestry had been built in 1855. Its steeple was visible to fishermen ten miles out into Nantucket Sound.

The house George had rented was located a block beyond the church at 18 Sea Street. It was a small Victorian built on the bluff 200 yards from Nantucket Sound. A graceful woman walked down from the porch as they pulled up to the house.

"Hi, I'm Marjorie Walker," she called. "I'm the nurse George Riley hired to take care of your friend."

Jennifer slipped out of the car and shook her duster.

"Hello," she said. "I'm Jennifer Smitson. This is Bob Johnson. Sarah Knowles and Johnny Scranton are in the back seat."

Marjorie looked into the back of the car and waved. Then she looked back to Jennifer.

"George called last night. He hadn't heard from you. He was concerned."

Jennifer pursed her lips and let out a breath.

"Oh, God, I forgot to call him. We stayed in Falmouth last night. Do you have a phone out here?"

Marjorie smiled wryly.

"Yes, dear," she said. "We have electricity, too." She sounded sarcastic.

"I'm sorry," said Jennifer. "I've never been here. I didn't know."

Marjorie smiled more sweetly.

"That's okay, dear. Everyone thinks we're so isolated that we don't have any modern conveniences. We like to keep this place a secret."

Johnny looked groggy and unsteady as he tried to climb out of the car.

Marjorie immediately moved over to him, took his arm, and guided him to his feet.

"Johnny, I'm Marjorie. Let's go into the house and take a look at the wound. I need to change your bandages. Dr. Hartman called and we discussed your recovery plan."

She turned back toward Jennifer.

"Dear, the phone is in the parlor," she said. "I left George's work number next to the phone."

Jennifer stepped out onto the wraparound porch after she had called George and looked out toward the ocean. It was the most beautiful stretch of coastline she had ever seen. A vast expanse of sand dunes lay below the house. The afternoon sun was shimmering off the surface of the water and she could hear the waves crashing on the beach beyond the dunes. To her right, there was a large bluff. A Queen-Anne-style house was under construction on its edge. To her left, the beach extended in a broad crescent to a harbor and breakwater. This was the perfect spot for Johnny's recovery. It was a place where no one would recognize him, it was secluded, and it was quiet. The loudest sounds were those of the waves that rhythmically crashed on the shore.

****

Pete Wilson parked in the church parking lot and watched as Jennifer helped Johnny from the car. He had been following Johnny for three weeks and he was tired. The early morning departure from Falmouth had caught him by surprise. Why did they leave so early? he wondered. He had been sleeping in his car across from Agnes Parker's house when he was startled by the sound of the T as Bob Johnson gunned the engine during their getaway. It looked as if Johnny was going to stay at the house on Sea Street and this was his chance to head home for a short break. He found a telegraph office in Dennis, down Cape from Harwichport, and sent Archibald Sargent an update.

Scranton moved to Cape Cod. Stop
Recent operation in Providence on hand. Stop
No tournament play while recovery. Stop
Ready to start rumor program. Stop
Full report to follow. Stop

CHAPTER 31

August 3, 1912 • Newton, Massachusetts

"Number please?"

George immediately recognized the voice of the telephone operator as he placed his call to Rock.

"Hi, Beth. Can you please connect Newton 413. How are you today?"

The August heat was stifling in the house. He anxiously tapped his foot as he waited for the call to be connected.

"I'm fine, George."

George had never met Beth in person, but he felt as if he knew American Bell Operator 14. He had learned over the years that she was a single mother with two children: a boy, Joshua, fourteen, and a girl, Irene, sixteen. Beth lived in Waltham with her mother and had joined American Bell eight years earlier. She worked evenings so she could be with her kids when they got home from school each day. Her mother took care of the children when she went to work. She had just recently been promoted to chief night operator for central Newton and Brookline.

"Sorry for the delay, George," Beth said. "The lines are wet after the big storm yesterday. It's been taking a few extra minutes for the connections to go through." She was quiet for a moment. "Now I have a light. I'll connect you." George heard the familiar ring, then Beth said, "Rock, I have George on the line." Pause again. "Go ahead, George."

"Hi, Rock. What are you doing this weekend?"

"Nothing special. You want to hit the course?"

"Well, actually, I was thinking that it's been six weeks since we got Johnny settled in Harwichport. I thought we might drive down this weekend and surprise him."

"Sounds great," said Rock. "I can drive. I'll pick you up at 7:30 a.m. Saturday."

"Okay. See you then."

****

The Massachusetts Road Commission had recently paved the Boston-Plymouth Road. Rock floored the gas pedal and the T accelerated to 44 miles per hour, the fastest Rock had ever driven. George was exhilarated by the speed.

"The new T's will go over 60 mph," Rock yelled as they raced past a billboard for Plymouth Rock. "I may buy one. Do you think I should get another Ford?"

"I like the new Buick Roadster," George said.

"It's a nice car, but it's $600 more than a T," said Rock. He laughed. "You're quick to spend my money, George. That's a serious piece of change, even for me."

As they approached Sagamore, they saw in the distance an enormous power shovel lifting loads of dirt and dropping them into an adjacent railroad car. Rock pointed to the dusty construction surrounding them. It seemed to spread in all directions.

"This is where they're digging the Cape Cod Canal," Rock said. "When it's finished, it's supposed to cut shipping time between Boston and New York by three hours."

As they drew closer, he pointed more directly at the huge machine looming in front of them.

"That's the same type of shovel they're using to dig the Panama Canal," he said.

George always found himself amused by the odd variety of things that Rock knew.

"How the hell do you know about this canal?" he asked.

"I'm giving lessons to a guy who works for the engineering firm that designed it. He wants me to invest in the project. Says we'll make a killing."

Now Rock's interest made more sense to George: there was money in it.

"Are you going to invest?" he asked.

Rock shook his head.

"No way," he said. "I'm just stringing the guy along. He's a terrible golfer. I figure as long as he thinks I'm interested, I can get at least 20 more lessons out of him before he decides to quit."

George couldn't help laughing.

"And he's got the money," Rock said. "The project is way over budget."

The road narrowed and a flag man directed them to the side.

"How long will we be delayed?" a frustrated Rock asked.

The man answered in a heavy Portuguese accent.

"We're going to let a few cars cross over the unfinished section of the canal. Tomorrow, they cut the last section of the isthmus and the only way across will be over the new bridge at Bourne. Please follow the man in the buggy. He'll lead you through the uncut section of the canal."

Rock engaged the T, and two cars followed them onto a narrow section of the uncut isthmus. They could see three more of the massive power shovels operating in the bottom of the dug-out area for the canal itself. The last open section was only 200 yards wide, and they passed within 50 feet of one of the gigantic machines.

"These shovels are made in Ohio, the largest steam shovels in the world," Rock said as he steered directly behind the man in the buggy. "They've had a lot of problems with the shovels because of all the rock in this area of the Cape."

The trip across the isthmus took 30 minutes. They had to stop several times when the small-gauge railroad servicing the big power shovels blocked them.

"Augustus Belmont–he's this rich industrialist from New York who is building the canal," Rock said. "He's supposedly spending $5,000 a day on the construction. I heard that he's close to filing bankruptcy. The Federal government may bail him out."

"$5,000 a day!" George said. "They'll need lots of ship tolls to cover that cost. Taxpayers shouldn't bail this guy out."

Rock nodded his agreement.

The conversation struck him as a good lead-in to something else he had been thinking about. He had been helping Belle with some of her investments. She'd been unhappy with the cousin she was using as a financial advisor, and it occurred to Rock that George might be helpful to them in his new situation at the First National Bank. Conversely, Belle knew a few people at the Bank, and Rock thought that maybe she could make a few calls to cement George's position there. Good for everybody.

"What types of investments have you heard about at the bank?" he asked.

George thought for a moment.

"There are two new investments I thought sounded sort of interesting," he said. "The first is a bridge over the Mystic River and the second involves a new steamship line to Europe."

Rock smiled.

"Tell me more about the steamship line."

******

They cleared the construction site and drove along the Brewster road on the north shore of the Cape. At Brewster, Rock turned south until they entered Harwich Center. Rock spotted a bar and pulled into the parking lot.

"Where are you going?" George asked.

"To take a leak, then to get a shot of whiskey to cut the dust."

"Rock. I thought we agreed that we weren't going to drink around Johnny."

"We did, and we won't," said Rock. "But we haven't seen him yet." He slid across the seat and pushed on George to get out. "Come on. The first drink is on me."

George held up his index finger to stress only one.

"Okay, one drink," he said reluctantly.

Rock climbed down from the car and patted his duster. A dirty cloud formed behind him as they walked toward the bar entrance.

"Damn," he said. "I wish Ford made an enclosed car so we could get rid of these damn dusters. Every time I drive anywhere I end up covered with dirt."

"I heard they're going to offer a fully enclosed model next year," George said.

Rock sneezed twice as they entered the bar.

Al's was a fisherman's hangout, a large dark room with a fish grill behind the bar and a large pot of clam chowder simmering on a table just inside the door. The daily specials were listed on a chalkboard near the entrance and featured an all-you-can-eat fish fry and clam chowder.

George and Rock worked their way through the boisterous crowd to get close to where an attractive woman in her mid-twenties was tending bar. She had long chestnut-brown hair and wore one of the new lace blouses, cut low to show the top of her breasts.

"A shot of whiskey, darling, and a draft for my friend," Rock yelled over the din. The bartender deftly filled the order while

Rock's gaze surveyed her every move. "What's your name, sweetheart?" he asked.

"Mary." She had big brown eyes that contrasted with the reddish tint in her hair.

"What's yours?"

"I'm Rock and this is George."

Mary smiled and nodded hello.

"You're new in town. How long are you staying?"

"Until Monday," said George.

Rock scanned the packed room.

"Why are there so many people in here on a beautiful Saturday afternoon?" he asked.

Mary had started to dry a glass with a clean white linen towel. She looked surprised at the question.

"Tonight is the start of the annual eel tournament. I thought that's why you boys are here. All the boats have come in early to get ready for the tournament."

Rock laughed loudly.

"Eel tournament! What's that?" he asked.

Mary looked at Rock as if he must be kidding.

"It's a tournament where you catch eels," she said slowly, as if she were talking to a child or perhaps someone who didn't understand English so well.

"You get four hours to catch as many eels as you can. Whoever catches the most – by weight, not by number – gets the first prize of $200 and a trophy."

George and Rock looked unconvinced.

"Eels?" said Rock. "Really?"

Mary made herself look insulted.

"It's a big deal down here," she said. She straightened up and put on a proud smile. "My uncle won last year."

"But eels?" said George. He made a disgusted face. "They sound horrible."

Mary pointed the glass she was drying at George. She gave him an exaggerated look of disapproval, then put the glass down on the bar in front of him.

"I'll bet you've never had one properly cut and cooked. You'd love it," she said.

"The town throws a big party tonight in front of the fish market pier at the end of Bank Street," she said. She raised her eyebrows and her eyes lit up. "You guys should come. Starts at 9:30. There's a big bonfire. Lots of fun."

Before either of them had a chance to respond, Mary turned and nodded to a scruffy little man a few seats away who had been calling her by name. She walked over to him, poured him a beer, said something to him, and then quickly returned to the men. She leaned over in front of Rock, set her elbows on the counter, and rested her chin on her folded hands. Rock noticed a bead of sweat trickle into the dark crease between her breasts.

"So if you're not here for the eel tournament," she asked, "why are you in town?"

"We're visiting a sick friend."

Mary nodded knowingly.

"The guy on Sea Street. We call him the recluse. He doesn't leave the house."

"How do you know?"

"Everybody knows everybody and everything in this town," she said, again a trifle slowly to make her point. "Maybe you guys can coax him out for the party."

"How do we get to Sea Street?"

"When you leave our parking lot turn right on Bank Street. Drive one mile to Main Street. Turn right again. At the Pilgrim

Congregational Church – you can't miss it – turn left. The house is halfway down the hill on the right across from Marjorie's Queen Anne." She slowed down. "Marjorie is who's caring for him. She won't tell us a thing about him." She made a mock-serious face and wagged a finger in the air. "Very secretive."

The boys finished their drinks and Rock left $2 on the bar.

"Maybe we'll see you tonight," he said.

Mary flashed him a big smile.

"Starts at 9:30," she said. "Thanks for the tip, boys."

As Rock and George approached the car, Rock looked back at the bar entrance.

"Now that is one pretty woman," he said. "Did you see those breasts? I'd like to get some of that tonight."

George laughed and punched Rock in the arm.

"What would Belle think?"

"I'm not a saint, son," he said. "I can look, can't I? Besides, Belle and I have an understanding. She can see other men and I can see other women. Don't you have the same arrangement with Jennifer?"

George shook his head emphatically.

"No way. I'm a one-woman man," he said as he walked over to crank the engine. The engine suddenly backfired and startled a horse that a man was riding down Bank Street. The horse started to neigh loudly and turn in tight circles.

"Sorry. It needs a tuneup," Rock yelled to him as the man dismounted and tried to calm his frightened horse.

Rock was sure that there would soon be a ban on riding horses on the main roads.

CHAPTER 32

Agnes Parker was looking through newspaper articles six weeks after Johnny, Sarah, Jennifer, and Bob had stayed at her house. She spotted the picture of Johnny accompanying a story titled *Johnny Scranton and Guy Rockham Low Gross Best Ball Team*.

"That's him," Agnes cried out. She collapsed to her knees and crumpled the paper in frustration. The murderer had been in her house! She needed to do something. He needed to be put in jail.

She tried to calm herself so that she could remember. Why were they on the Cape? Where were they going? It was Earl that had called about them. He would know. She stormed to the kitchen, ready to phone Earl, when she remembered: Harwichport! There was a nurse there he had to see.

She rooted through her cabinet for the phone book, then placed the call to her cousin Brian in Harwich. He was the assistant constable for Barnstable County. He would find this monster and bring him to justice.

****

Johnny heard the faint rumble of a car coming down Sea Street and immediately recognized it as Rock's old T. He jumped up from his rocker on the second-floor porch and leaned precariously over the railing.

"George!" Johnny yelled. "What the hell are you doing here?"

George waved hello.

"Hi, hot shot," Rock called as he got out of the T. "Get down here and welcome your guests properly."

"Rock! You son of a bitch. I'll be right down."

Johnny disappeared through a large window. George exited the car and stood back, arms on his hips to examine the house. It was exactly as Jennifer had described, a small Victorian with blue shutters and yellow-painted window frames. The clapboards were light gray and the front of the house faced Nantucket Sound. A large porch wrapped around two sides of the house, and there was a widow's watch on the roof. George could see a pier at the end of the road where a group of men were loading barrels onto a small boat.

Johnny immediately bolted out of the house and down the steps of the porch.

"My God. It's great to see you," he said. "I've been going stir crazy out here. I thought you'd never come. Why didn't you call?"

"We decided to surprise you," said George.

Johnny crashed into George and hugged him, shaking him violently. He stepped back and caught his breath, then turned to Rock and poked him hard in the shoulder. He stood there grinning broadly at his friends.

Finally he said, "The old T is looking mighty fine, Rock."

"Yes, sir. Belle hates riding around in anything but first class."

"How's the second richest woman in Newton?"

"Well enough that she's now the richest woman in Newton," Rock said with a quick laugh. "She's made a fortune in rocks."

"Rocks!" Johnny laughed. "That seems about right!"

"She invested in her nephew's business in western Massachusetts. He bought a granite quarry then negotiated a sweet contract with builders in New York and Chicago to supply the granite for their skyscraper facades and interior floors. The orders have been pouring in and Belle's reaped a bundle in dividends."

"Well, good for her," Johnny said. He waved his hand in

the direction of the house. "Come on, guys. Come in and have a drink."

George was shocked.

"A drink!"

"Don't worry. Only lemonade or sarsparilla in this house. The warden, Marjorie, makes sure there's no alcohol."

George could see the six weeks here had been good for Johnny. He looked rested and the color in his face had returned. It looked like he had gained back most of the weight he had lost while he was hooked on the elixir.

"How do you feel?" George asked.

"I feel stronger every day," Johnny said. He smiled and held up his right hand. "I don't have any pain in my hand and there's no pain when I grip."

He grabbed a walking stick near the door and squeezed it to show his friends.

"Do you have any urges to drink or use the elixir?" Rock asked.

Johnny laughed softly and smiled again, this time more ruefully.

"Sure I do. Every day," he said. "But I've used the techniques they taught me at the institute to overcome the urges. And Marjorie has been a big help. She's the first person who's really listened to me."

Johnny headed toward the kitchen to get his guests' drinks. He suddenly stopped and turned, realizing what he had just said.

"Except you guys. You're my best friends in the world. Thanks for coming down."

He stood staring at them for another moment then grinned and disappeared into the kitchen. He returned a few minutes later with a pitcher of lemonade and some glasses.

"Can't get dehydrated," he said. "Any golf news?"

"Hagen and the team did well in their last four exhibition matches," Rock said.

Johnny nodded as he poured the lemonade and handed out full glasses.

"I figured they must be doing well. I've been out of action for nine weeks and the money just keeps rolling in. I don't know how to thank you guys."

Rock shrugged.

"You can always donate the money to my academy if you don't want it."

Johnny laughed.

"No way."

Rock took a sip of the lemonade. It was the best lemonade he had ever had.

"You know," he said, "Hagen has decided to leave our team and play on the new Mid-American golf tour starting in February."

"Is that tour really going to happen?" asked Johnny.

Rock nodded yes emphatically.

"Oh, it's going to happen," he said. "They already have twelve tournaments scheduled for next year."

Johnny looked excited by the news.

"I want a piece of that action," he said. "I need to get back in shape. Do either of you know a place I can practice down here?"

"The Port Club has a nine-hole course," said Rock. "I'm sure we can use their practice range. I know the pro there."

"But we hear you never go out," George said. "The town folks consider you a mystery."

"How do you know that?" Johnny asked.

"We stopped at a local place on the way into town to ask for directions," George said. He didn't want to admit that they had stopped at a bar. "We told the waitress we were looking for a sick friend. She called you the recluse."

"The recluse!" Johnny said, clearly annoyed by the moniker. He had started to enjoy the peace and solitude of the beach. He didn't want it compromised by the gossipy interest of some dried-up old ladies.

"Forget that," George said. "Let's get up early tomorrow and go for a short workout over at the club. Dr. Hartman said to tell you to start using the hand so atrophy doesn't set in. I brought your clubs."

"Deal," Johnny said.

George wandered closer to an open bay window to taste the cool breeze blowing in from the ocean. From his new spot he could see the sea grasses spread in front of the cottage and the golden strands of light bouncing off the thin wispy clouds on the western horizon to his right.

"Johnny, this view is spectacular."

"Yeah. I love to sit on the second-floor porch and watch the passing of the day. It's very peaceful."

The three friends paused to survey the beauty of the view.

Finally Johnny said, "We need to get ready for dinner."

"Dinner? When's dinner?" Rock asked.

"Marjorie serves dinner at 6 on the dot every night."

"Well, we have a surprise for you," Rock said. "We've been invited to a beach party in front of the fish pier at the end of Bank Street. The bartender invited us."

"What bartender?" asked Johnny.

Rock laughed and pushed at George a little.

"George's 'waitress.' The one he told you about when we stopped for directions."

Rock looked excited as he told Johnny the more detailed

story of meeting Mary at Al's. "And she's the bartender there," he said. "She's a knock-out."

"Oh, boy. Somebody's going to get laid tonight," Johnny said as he clapped his hands.

George smiled.

"She certainly took a shine to Rock," he said.

Rock shrugged.

"She was only being friendly. Truth is, she's a little skinny, not my type."

"I don't care what type she is," Johnny said. "I've been a monk for the past six weeks. All I need tonight is a warm body."

****

"Hi, Agnes," Eloise asked in a perky voice. "How are you tonight?"

"Hi, Eloise," said Agnes. "Can you place a call to Harwich 38, for me please?"

"That's your cousin Brian's number."

Eloise had an impressive memory. Everyone in town knew not to talk about private issues over the phone.

"Okay, dear. The call is going through," Eloise reported.

A young voice answered the phone. It was Ben, Brian's youngest son.

"Sorry, Agnes, Dad's not home."

"Ben, you be sure to tell him to call me. It's very important."

****

George heard footsteps on the front porch and then a knock at the door. From where he was standing near the window, he could see the silhouette of a slim woman with perfect posture through the screen. Johnny moved quickly to greet her.

"Come in, Marjorie," he said. "Meet my friends from Boston. This is George Riley and the mug over there is Guy Rockham."

Johnny smiled and lightly placed his hand on Marjorie's back to guide her toward them.

"This is my guardian angel, Marjorie," he said warmly.

Marjorie appeared to George to be about 50, about the age of his mother. But she was beautiful and elegant in a far different way than any son could comfortably regard his mother. She had long gray hair, still thick and lustrous, and stunning eyes so light blue that they were almost clear. She wore a brown hoop skirt and a stylish white blouse tucked in neatly at her small waist. The years had aged her gracefully, though she walked with a slight limp. She must have been the town's greatest beauty when she was younger, George thought.

"Nice to finally meet you, George," she said, extending her hand to him. "I feel as if I know you. Johnny has mentioned you often."

She turned back to Johnny. She couldn't resist kidding him. She nodded slightly toward Rock and said, "Johnny, the mug doesn't look like a scoundrel."

Rock laughed.

"I'm sure he's had nothing good to say about me," he chuckled.

Marjorie shook Rock's hand then turned back to Johnny.

"I can only stay for a few minutes. I came to tell you I need to go out tonight. One of my girls has just gone into labor and I need to see her."

Johnny turned to George and Rock.

"Marjorie is a midwife," he said proudly. "Her training as a nurse has helped save many babies."

Johnny turned to face Marjorie.

"That's okay, Marjorie. We can manage for ourselves tonight.

We'll walk into town and have dinner at that café you mentioned."

"Rebecca's. Best scrod on the Cape," Marjorie said.

"That sounds good to me," said George. "So, how is our patient doing?"

Marjorie smiled. Her smile was warm and deep, as beautiful as she was.

"You can see for yourself," she said. "Nine weeks sober this Sunday. He's gained back some weight and he's getting his strength back. A little longer and he'll be ready to take on the world."

"We thought we'd take him over to the golf course tomorrow to hit a few balls," said Rock. "If that's okay with you, of course."

George was surprised to hear the deference in Rock's voice. Even the great scoundrel was awestruck by this woman.

Marjorie smiled again. A man would do pretty much anything to deserve that smile, thought George.

"I think that's a great idea," she said. "He needs to get out. He's turned into a recluse."

Johnny winced.

"Yeah. I heard that's what the locals call me."

"We heard it from the bartender at Al's when we stopped to ask for directions," Rock said.

"That would be Mary Hampton," said Marjorie.

"Seems friendly," George added.

"Yes," said Marjorie, a bit sternly. "Maybe too friendly, especially with the boys, and especially in a small town. Since her steady beau left her two years ago, rumor has it that she's chased every free man in town."

"A real hellion, I guess," said George. He winked discreetly at Johnny.

"Well, anyway," said Johnny, "the guys invited me to a beach party tonight at the end of Bank Street. How far is the beach?

Should we drive?"

"Beach party?" Marjorie looked puzzled, then she brightened. "Oh, yes. I almost forgot. Tonight is the eel tournament. You won't need to drive. Just head down the path to the beach, turn left, and walk up to Bank Street."

Marjorie adjusted her voice to a softer, more serious tone.

"Now, Johnny, I want to warn you that people will be drinking at this party. You'll need to be strong. Bring a bottle of lemonade and remember our talks about self-discipline."

She turned to look more directly at George and Rock. George found himself staring at her again. She had small wrinkles around her eyes and at the edges of her mouth, but her skin still looked soft and supple.

"You can help him, I think he's ready."

Just for that moment she struck George as the beautiful older schoolmarm every boy loves. Then she quickly gave a wave and turned toward the door.

"Okay, guys. I'll be back tomorrow."

"Bye," Johnny said. He watched Marjorie walk down the steps of the porch to the street before he turned back to his friends.

"Isn't she great?" he said.

Yes, she is, thought George.

"Come on," said Johnny. "Let's change and go to dinner. This heat really makes me hungry."

CHAPTER 33

Brian Donahue rushed home to get ready for the tournament, determined to win the $200 first prize. His nemesis, Bill Varney, a classmate from the class of '97 at Harwich High, had won the tournament three years in a row. But Brian had a secret weapon this year. He had hired two high school kids and they had been charting the eel runs in the Oyster River for the previous month. Winning the money would be great, but beating Bill–now that was another matter.

His son Ben caught him just as he was ready to go upstairs to change.

"Dad, Cousin Agnes called and wants you to call her right away," he said.

Brian thought, No, not today, Agnes, not today.

"What did she want?" he asked.

"She said it was very important. It has something to do with the death of Cousin Charles."

Since Charles' death, Agnes had become increasingly irrational. She complained constantly of suspicious sounds in her yard at night, and she had periods when she imagined that people were following her. Recently she had demanded that Brian come to Falmouth and arrest a man who was sitting in the park across from her house. The man turned out to be with the town's parks maintenance department.

Brian sighed and picked up the phone.

"Hi, Rita. Can you connect me to Falmouth 47, please?"

"Lovely night for the tournament, Brian," Rita said. "Might take a moment. The lines going west have been slow today."

Brian heard a distant and tinny ring. He heard Rita say, "This is Harwich operator 4. I have your cousin Brian on the line, Mrs. Parker." A pause. "Go ahead. I'll connect you."

"Brian," Agnes shouted. "Are you there?"

"I can hear you, Agnes."

"I still can't get used to these long-distance calls," Agnes said, only a little less loudly. "Brian, I've found one of the conspirators in Charles' murder. He's in Harwichport."

Brian sighed again.

"Agnes," he said slowly, "Charles wasn't murdered. He was shot in a card game. Remember, I checked with the state police. They said it was a case of self-defense."

Now Agnes screamed into the phone.

"It was murder, I tell you! And one of the murderers is right there with you! You must put this man in jail!"

She sounded hysterical.

"Now, Agnes, calm down. Tell me about this man."

Brian could hear Agnes take and release a long breath, but her voice was still shaking when she continued.

"His name is Johnny Scranton and he stayed in my home six weeks ago. His lady friend said they were headed to Harwichport."

"Six weeks ago?" Brian said. "Why didn't you call me sooner?"

"I just realized who he was."

Brian saw his way out of this most recent crisis with Agnes.

"He's almost surely moved on by now," he said. "What does he look like?"

Agnes provided a detailed description of Johnny and then added, "He was sick and his hand was bandaged."

Brian groaned. The recluse with the bandaged hand.

"Okay, Agnes. I'll check into it. I'll call you when I have more information."

Brian's wife approached him as he hung up the phone.

"What was that all about?" she asked.

He shook his head.

"Agnes is having a difficult time. We need to get her help. I'll tell you about it on the way to the tournament."

Brian hurried upstairs to the bedroom. He carefully removed his firearm and placed it in the lockbox on the dresser. He dutifully hung his uniform on its wooden hanger and smoothed what wrinkles he could from it so that it would be ready in the morning. Then he climbed into his most worn, most comfortable shirt and trousers.

When he got back downstairs, Ben was waiting anxiously by the back door. Together they gathered the eel buckets, the wading boots, the tar-covered torches, and the long rake with the catch on the end to trap the eels. He was ready to show the town–and Bill Varney–who the best eeler in Harwich really was.

****

"There's an empty booth in the rear," George said as they entered Rebecca's.

The restaurant had been an institution in Harwichport for over 40 years and it looked it. Faded paintings of old ships adorned the walls, and a large brass chandelier that had seen better days hung from the ceiling in the middle of the single dining room. The café had long wooden tables in the middle of the room and smaller wooden booths along the walls. Leaning on a weathered bar at the far end of the room were four fishermen wearing slickers and waders and drinking beers. Rebecca's was known on the Cape not for its decor but for its two specialties: baked scrod and eel strips baked in olive oil.

"If you want a thick steak, this apparently is not the place,"

Rock complained as he looked at the menu. "Let's see what beers they carry."

George kicked Rock under the table. Johnny noticed George's clumsy attempt to control their friend.

"It's okay, George," he said. "I'm a sarsparilla guy now. Both Marjorie and the doctor told me that I need to go out with folks who drink. I need to be able to control my urges on my own."

Rock threw his hand in the air in triumph.

"There you go!" he proclaimed. "The bar is now open."

He motioned to a harried but pretty young woman at the front of the room.

"Waitress!"

She walked over and stood by their booth. She was cute, short and curvy. She had luxurious, shiny, raven-black hair tied in a long single pony tail which extended down to her waist, and velvety-black eyes.

"What can I get you guys?" she asked.

Rock had called her over, but George noticed that she glanced at Johnny and smiled.

"We want your best beer on tap, darling," Rock said.

"Narragansett or Carling?"

"Two Narragansetts" – Rock gestured toward Johnny–"and a sarsparilla for our handsome friend."

"Raspberry or cranberry?"

"Oh, cranberry, of course," Rock said, before Johnny had a chance to choose for himself. Rock smiled at the waitress. "We're on the Cape, aren't we? Home of the best cranberries in the country."

The waitress smiled back.

"I like you, big boy," she said flatly. "What's your name?"

"Guy Rockham. Maybe you've heard of me?"

She giggled and shook her head.

"No. Are you famous?"

"I'm a professional golfer."

The waitress nodded and made a disparaging face.

"Oh, golf? I don't know anything about golf. It seems sort of silly to me, chasing after a little white ball. I'd rather spend my time catching rays at the beach."

"Darling," Rock said. "You have so much to learn about the game. Lucky for you that I'm available to give private lessons."

The waitress gave a laugh.

"Yeah, I'm sure you are, Romeo," she said. "Two beers and one cranberry sarsparilla coming up."

Rock watched her as she headed to the bar.

"Not bad. A little buxom maybe."

"Yeah, as if that will ever happen," Johnny said, mocking Rock.

Rock pursed his lips and leaned toward Johnny.

"Bet I can get her to join us at the beach tonight," he said.

"Bet you can't," said Johnny.

"Ten bucks says she'll show up at the beach."

"Okay, you're on."

They slapped hands and shook on the bet.

"You guys," George said. "Always have to make a bet."

"You in?" Rock asked.

"No way. I don't want to lose ten bucks. I'm a poor student. I can't afford these big bets."

The waitress came back with their drinks.

"Have you decided what you'd like?"

Rock smiled and gazed directly into her eyes.

"I'd like to know your name," he said.

The waitress flipped her hair over her right shoulder. These guys seemed silly, but harmless.

"My name is Isabella."

"How do you do, Isabella," Rock said formally. "This is Johnny Scranton, and the young one over there is George Riley." With a quick glance, Rock saw that she was not wearing a wedding ring.

Isabella smiled and nodded at Johnny and George.

"Nice to meet you," she said. "Now, what do you want to eat?"

As they finished the order, Rock said, "I hear there's a big beach party tonight. Would you like to join us?"

Isabella frowned and stepped back melodramatically.

"We just met. How do I know you aren't some crazed killer, or worse, a gigolo?"

They all laughed. Rock made a menacing face.

"Well, we just got out of jail and we're looking for our next victim," he said. Then he put on a pleading face. "We're really just three guys who need a date."

Isabella leaned back onto her left foot and tapped her pencil on the order pad she was holding. She looked as if she were judging their worth.

Suddenly, she said, "Okay, sounds like fun. I'll meet you around 9:30 in front of the bonfire."

"Deal," said Rock. "I'll bring some drinks."

"Great. I like scotch."

She turned and headed for the kitchen.

Rock reached out and gave her a light tap on the butt.

"My type of woman," he said, loud enough for her to hear.

Isabella looked back and smiled.

"Okay, pal, pay up," Rock said, as soon as she had entered the kitchen. He extended his hand, palm up, on the table.

"You haven't won yet," said Johnny.

Rock grinned broadly.

"She'll be there. You'll see."

****

After dinner, they wandered down to Main Street. A fair-sized crowd had assembled near a bandstand located in the neatly kept park across from the Pilgrim Congregational Church. Rock spotted Mary from Al's Bar and pointed her out to Johnny and George. She was standing alone near the stage, a canvas bag at her feet. She was up on her toes, searching the crowd with her eyes, apparently looking for someone.

This is a bartender? thought Johnny. I've been going to the wrong bars. She was about 5'5" with a slender, athletic build. She was wearing a lightweight blue cloth dress that buttoned in front. Her chestnut brown hair set off golden brown eyes and was pulled back tight and tied with a blue ribbon.

They walked over to her. "Remember us?" said Rock.

"Hi," she said sweetly. "You were in the bar earlier. Did you find your friend?"

Rock nodded.

"We did indeed," he said. "Mary, this is Johnny Scranton, and you've already met George Riley."

George nodded to Mary. Johnny held out his hand and Mary took it gently in both of hers. As she held his hand, she looked down to see if he had a scar. Rock nudged George and pulled him over to a nearby display table.

"So you're the recluse," Mary said. "Lots of folks have been talking about you."

She patted his hand and spoke in a lowered voice.

"Some say you're a bank robber. Others say you're hiding from a jealous lover."

Johnny gazed at her silky hair. She smelled fresh, like flowers, like no bartender he had ever met. She was still casually running her fingers along his hand, glancing down at it occasionally.

"That feels nice, but why are you so interested in my hand?" he asked.

She looked a little embarrassed and let out a low laugh.

"I'm sorry," she said. She let go of Johnny's hand and put her hands down at her sides as if she were smoothing her dress. Now he wished he hadn't said anything. "My cousin Brian asked me about you," she said. She wrinkled her nose. "I'm his secret detective."

"Why is your cousin looking for me?"

"He's on the county police force. He said he needs to talk to you."

Johnny nodded.

"Mrs. Parker," he said.

Mary was clearly surprised.

"You know my cousin Agnes?"

"Your cousin? What's the deal?" asked Johnny. "Is everyone on the Cape related?"

Mary laughed again.

"Just about. Some go back 100 years," she said.

"Well, you can tell Brian I'm the guy and I'd be happy to talk with him."

Rock and George rejoined them. Rock was holding a flier on the tournament.

"So what's going on here?" asked Rock.

Mary used the same tone of voice that, once again, suggested Rock's inability to understand simple things.

"Well, this would be the start of the eel fishing tournament you didn't believe existed," she said.

A man standing on the stage interrupted before Rock could defend himself.

"Ladies and gentlemen," he called out. "Welcome to our 10th annual eel fishing derby!"

The crowd applauded and cheered. Mary leaned over to Johnny.

"That's Paul Rousch, the town's first selectman. A real ass."

Johnny smiled. He liked Mary's earthiness. This girl's a keeper, he thought. Rousch continued.

"We have 38 contestants tonight. The tournament will take place between Oyster Creek and Saquatucket Creek. Only eels caught in these areas will be eligible for the grand prize. Contestants are restricted to ten-pound lines with no more than four snelled hooks per line. No contestant can have more than five active lines. Total poundage caught between 9:30 and 1:30 will determine the winner. Each contestant can have one runner to bring the eels to the weigh stations, which are located up on Main Street and in the back lot at Saquatucket Creek. Only eels presented at the weigh station before 1:30 will be counted."

Rousch stopped speaking and ran his eyes across his audience. He found a wide burly man to the left of center and stared at him.

"Last year Charlie Garlie tried to slip an eel in after the 1:30 close," Rousch said. "This year, we've tried to account for Charlie by having an area roped off around each weigh station. The eel must be in the rope enclosure before 1:30 to be included."

The crowd laughed and hooted. Brian Donahue raised a hand.

"Can we use multiple racks to secure an eel?" he shouted.

"Yes. Any way you can grab the rascal. I see Ralph Doughty has brought his flat-head hammer. Are you prepared to smash them over the head, Ralph?"

The crowd burst into laughter again.

"Nope," said Ralph, waving the hammer. "This here is to keep poachers away from my spot."

As Paul read the roll of contestants, Johnny moved closer to Mary. She was lightly swaying back and forth and her hair glistened from the torch lights surrounding the stage. He heard himself sigh as he drew in her flowery aroma again. He looked around, a little embarrassed, to see if anyone had noticed. He straightened up and cleared his head.

"Why does this start so late?" he asked her. "Fishing at night!"

"Eels are nocturnal feeders who live in the salt grass," said Mary. "It's almost impossible to see an eel during daylight." Her eyes got wide. "And tonight is a perfect night for eel fishing. There's a low tide and the fishermen can wade into the marsh to drag their lines along the bottom of the creeks."

"Eels are slimy, right?" George said.

"They have a slimy coat to protect them from disease and predators. They can easily slip out of your hands," Mary said.

"How do you know so much about eels?" asked Johnny. "You don't go eel fishing, do you?"

"Sure I do. All the time. I've been eel fishing with my dad since I was little."

Johnny was fascinated with this girl. He liked her wry smile and the little dimples that became pronounced when she spoke. And she seemed to be an encyclopedia on eel fishing – always a benefit in a woman.

"How do the eelers see in the marsh? It's pitch dark out there."

"There's a partial moon tonight and they carry torches. Usually, they pick a spot and try to catch as many eels as possible in that one spot."

"How big do the eels get?" George asked.

"A mature eel is usually six to eight pounds. The record caught in Harwich is nine pounds." Mary was reeling off facts now as if she were reading from a textbook. "Eels can live in a marsh for up to ten years before they reach maturity. Then they leave the freshwater marshes and go out to sea to spawn. After they spawn, they die. They're called a catadromous fish."

"They die after spawning?" Johnny asked, intrigued by Mary's command of the knowledge more than the information itself.

"Yes. Scientists aren't even sure where they spawn."

"How do you know so much about eels?" George asked.

Mary threw her shoulders back and raised her head high for effect.

"I'm the fish warden," she said with obvious pride. "I went to school in Brockton and I enforce the fishing laws throughout the lower Cape."

Johnny looked surprised – but pleased. He nodded his approval.

"So you're a cop after all," he said. "Just as I thought."

Mary smiled.

"Sort of," she said. She hooked his arm. "But don't worry. I don't carry a gun."

"A cop. Who would have guessed!" Rock said.

Rousch finished the roll and held up his hand.

"Everyone, ready. Get set." He waited dramatically. "Go!"

The result was total bedlam. Men carrying a variety of tools, buckets, and torches ran in both directions down Main Street. One group rushed toward Oyster Creek and the other the opposite way toward Saquatucket, each man bound and determined to catch the most eels.

The band launched into a rousing rendition of "There'll Be A Hot Time in the Old Town Tonight," and headed down Main Street.

CHAPTER 34

"Where are we headed?" Ben asked as he followed his dad quickly down Main Street. Ben was eleven, blessed with bright red hair and a face full of freckles, and this was his first eel tournament. His older brother had tired of the job, but Ben was thrilled to help.

"I had Jake and Roger chart the eels for the past two weeks," Brian said. "They discovered that there's lots of them just north of the Oyster Creek Bridge. It'll be our spot. Come on, it's only a half mile."

There was a dim glow of light in the western sky as Ben and Brian reached the bridge. Brian lit one of the torches and handed it to Ben.

"Follow the trail to the creek. I set two red flags on stakes in the marsh where I want us to start."

Ben looked scared.

"Dad, it's pretty spooky out here."

"Don't worry," said his dad with a soft laugh. "We'll be okay. Ghosts don't go fishing."

Ben put his arm around his son and squeezed lightly to comfort him.

"Come on, let's catch us some eels.

****

Mary and the boys walked down Main Street, turned right on Bank Street, and continued until they reached a huge bonfire near the entrance to the Bank Street Pier.

"This year's pile of driftwood and lumber is the biggest I've ever seen," she said. "It must be over 30 feet high."

"How long does it take to build something like that?" Rock asked.

"This one took three days. The Boy Scouts scour the town for driftwood, fallen trees, and any odd leftover lumber."

Mary looked at the raging pile to make her official-sounding assessment.

"This one looks like it'll burn until midday tomorrow."

A makeshift dance floor and a stage had been built near the bonfire, and a series of tables were lined up next to the stage. George noticed a group of elderly women selling cider and local crafts and a variety of cranberry dishes – cakes, cookies, breads, and pies.

"The seven congregations in town join to sponsor the food," said Mary, pointing to the tables. "The funds raised tonight go to support our youth programs."

George looked out at the old pier at the end of the street.

"The pier looks run down," he said. "What happened to it?"

The pier extended over 100 feet into the water. It seemed barely to support the five dilapidated buildings attached to it. Thirty years before, Harwich had been home to a prosperous fishing industry. Back then, there had been six fishing piers and over 80 fishing vessels and 300 men fished the near shore off the port. Bank Street Pier was the most prosperous of the six. In the good days forty men worked full time on the pier off-loading the catch and processing salted fish. Now the near-shore fisheries were depleted and the larger boats from New Bedford and Gloucester had taken over the off-shore fishing grounds.

"This pier hasn't been used much since I was little," said Mary. "All the serious fishing now is done by bigger boats in the deeper waters offshore. We don't have the deep-water ports on the

Cape to accommodate them, so we only get a few shallow-bottom schooners off-loading quahogs and clams at Bank Street Pier."

She looked at Johnny.

"The pier near Sea Street, where you are staying, was destroyed in the '09 nor'easter."

A girlish voice called Rock's name. They saw Isabella strolling briskly down the hill, her black hair flowing freely under a broad rimmed hat. She was wearing a dress that buttoned in the front, similar to Mary's but bright yellow. Rock trotted over to greet her.

"Hi. I was beginning to think you weren't coming."

"Sorry I'm late. I had to close the restaurant."

"Hi, Isabella," Mary said. She spread her arms out to display her dress. "I see you copied me again."

They both giggled. Mary grabbed Johnny's hand as the band began an Irish jig. "Want to dance, recluse?"

"Sure."

"Good idea," said Isabella. She grabbed Rock's hand and led him on to the dance floor with a hearty "Come on, Romeo!"

****

"Where are the adult drinks sold?" Rock asked, sweating from three rounds of dances.

"No alcohol is sold during the tournament," Mary lamented. "However . . . ."

She reached down into her bag and took out a flask. She rooted around the bag a bit more and produced several small glasses.

"Courtesy of Al's," she said happily.

Johnny held his hand up. "None for me, thanks."

Mary looked surprised.

"What! A teetotaler?" she asked.

"He's a sarsparilla man," said Isabella.

"It's sort of the reason I'm here in Harwichport," said Johnny. "I don't handle liquor very well, so I'm not drinking anymore."

Mary looked embarrassed, as if she had been caught doing something she shouldn't have been doing.

"Oh, no," said Johnny as soon as he saw her response, "that doesn't mean you shouldn't drink. It was nice of you to bring it." He looked around at the silent group. "Rock wants some–don't you, Rock?"

Rock nodded.

Johnny repeated himself, this time with more emphasis, *"Don't you, Rock?"*

This time Rock picked up Johnny's cue more ably.

"Of course I do!" He was nearly yelling. "Let me have glass of that fine restorative you've been so kind to offer us, Miss Mary!"

Mary laughed. Beautiful, thought Johnny.

"You make me almost afraid to give you any," she said to Rock. She held up the flask. "Anybody else?"

They downed their drinks and then chose treats from the food table. They sat on the ground near the stage for a while, talking and taking in the music. Just as the evening was turning dark, Isabella abruptly stood up and brushed off her dress.

"Come on, guys," she said. "Let's walk along the beach."

Johnny noticed Isabella wink at Mary.

"It certainly is a lovely night for a walk," Mary said.

The half moon cast enough light so they could see their way as they headed east along the beach. A bright row of stars spread out behind the moon where the night sky grew darker. Mary leaned into Johnny as they shuffled leisurely through the sand. Before too long the two of them were alone, well behind the others. Mary was holding Johnny's hand and was lightly stroking it with her fingers as she had done earlier. She was looking out at the water as they walked.

"How did you injure your hand?" she asked.

Johnny found himself hesitating at first, not sure which parts he wanted to share with Mary, but her tender prodding soon drew out the story in detail – the fire, the Elixir, the intervention and rehab, his recovery. As he told about the addiction, it sounded bad to him, worse than he had ever really thought of it being, even after all the counseling and the kindness his friends had shown him. He felt ashamed, but, for some reason, he didn't want to lie to her.

When he was finished telling the story, they walked slowly without talking for a few minutes. He waited for her to be shocked, to move away.

Instead, she moved closer. She leaned farther into him and, they walked along, quiet for a few more minutes, then she said, "I feel awful offering you alcohol after what you've been through." Her voice caught. "I'm so sorry."

She used her free hand to rub her right eye.

"It's okay," he said softly.

When she looked up at him, her eyes were a little red.

"We should catch up," she said.

After they had rejoined the others, George pointed to the bluff above them. There were lights moving all along it.

"What's that up there?" he asked.

"That's Davis Lane," said Isabella, who now had her arm tightly wrapped around Rock's. The top of her head barely reached his shoulder. "There's a path along the bluff and the lights are the torches carried by the runners for the contestants."

"Let's sit for a while," Mary said.

They could hear distant music from the bandstand. It was soft and echoing as if it were drifting down from the clouds. They lounged silently in the sand and enjoyed the faint music mix with the sound of the waves making shore. George looked up at the moon through the slight sea mist and tasted the sweet salt air on his lips, and he thought of Jennifer. He sighed.

Isabella looked over at him.

"It's hot tonight, isn't it?" she said.

"One of the hottest days this summer," Mary said. "It got to 101 today."

Mary looked over to Isabella as if she were suddenly inspired.

"Hey, I've got an idea. Let's swim out to Shallows Island."

"What?" Rock said. He looked a little unnerved. "I don't have a bathing suit."

Mary laughed.

"You don't need one, silly."

Now her eyes were brilliant with fun. She smiled at Johnny and then turned to Isabella. "You game?"

Isabella flashed a coy smile. "Sure," she said. "Come on, Rock."

The girls jumped up, ran closer to the water, and started to unbutton their dresses as if this were their normal routine. The boys sat dumb-founded as they watched Mary and Isabella peel off their clothes. Johnny could see the moonlit outline of Mary's lithe body as she slipped out of her undergarments. Isabella seemed to be dancing and joyously throwing off apparel in all directions at the same time.

George leaned over and laid his face in his hands so he couldn't see. How did this get so out of hand so quickly? What would Jennifer think? He also didn't want to admit that he didn't know how to swim.

Mary and Isabella moved swiftly from the pile of discarded clothes into the ocean.

"Come on, guys," Mary yelled from the shallow water. "It's

low tide. It's a short swim across the channel to the island." She added a taunting tone to her voice. "You're not chicken are you?"

In the soft moonlight, Johnny could see the undulating waves washing over the smooth curve of her breasts.

"This sounds like a challenge," he said. He cracked a broad smile. "A really good one."

Rock jumped up.

"I'm game," he said. "George, are you coming?"

George shook his head. The best he could come up with was the old standby: "No way. Sharks are out there. I'm not going to be dinner tonight."

"Don't be silly, George," cried Mary as she splashed water at Isabella. "We'll be okay."

"No, you guys go," said George. "Have a good time. I'll meet you back at the bonfire."

"Your loss, old man," Johnny shouted as he ran toward the water and Mary.

George stood on the beach and watched as they swam naked toward Shallow Island.

Chapter 35

The sky was crystal clear as Brian reset the hooks after their fifth drag along the creek bottom. His informants had been right. He and Ben had already caught over 30 eels only two hours into the tournament. They worked smoothly as a team. Ben grabbed each eel with the special claw hoe and then Brian would hit the eel over the head with a hammer. Once the eel was knocked out, Ben would transfer it to one of the large buckets.

"Time to take another bucket to the weigh station," Brian said. "I'll set out a new group of lines while you're gone."

Ben beamed with purpose and pride. He was thrilled to be working with his dad in something so important.

"Okay, Dad. I'll check on the leaders while I'm down there." He ran over and grabbed the bucket. It was heavy. "We must have another forty pounds here."

"Take one of the torches," said Brian. "I don't want you falling off the edge of the road."

****

"Okay, guys. The island is less than a quarter mile across the channel," Mary said as she treaded water.

"A quarter mile," Johnny said, floating on his back. "That sounds pretty far."

Mary smiled and extended her hand to him.

"You'll be okay. Stay close to me," she said. She pulled on his hand to draw herself up to him. Under the water, her smooth leg floated up against his. "Come on, tiger. Now's the test."

Rock was still only half in the water. Isabella waded up to

him and whispered in his ear.

"Let's swim to the northern part of the island, big boy," she said. "I have a treat for you when we get there. Just follow me."

Rock gazed into her big black eyes and grinned.

"I'll follow you anywhere, darling," he said.

Isabella started swimming toward the northern end of the island with Rock in tow. Mary led Johnny to a spot closer toward the middle shore of the island. Before long, Isabella and Rock were out of sight.

The 15-minute swim was more tiring than Johnny had expected it to be, and Mary had to help him out of the water and up the island's small incline onto the shore. He collapsed onto his back on the wet sand, panting for air.

"Breathe slowly," Mary said as she lay down on her side next to him.

"That was a lot of work," Johnny gasped, his voice shaking. "I didn't realize how out of shape I am."

Mary combed his hair back with her fingers.

"Operations can take a lot out of you. I had an appendectomy and it took months for me to recover."

She took his hand and traced it along her bare stomach.

"See," she said, "you can feel the scar."

Her stomach was covered with sand, but through it Johnny could feel the softness of her skin. The scar was raised and it extended unevenly for about six inches.

"Mary, they really cut you," he said.

Mary sat up, and as she bent gracefully to wring the seawater from her hair, the shadowy play between the dark night and the light of the half moon cast her body in ethereal relief for Johnny. He marveled at how perfectly at ease she seemed naked on the beach with him – and how content he would be for this moment to last forever.

She shook her hair free and turned back to him.

"I love it out here," she said. "I feel as if I'm the only one in the world. Free and without any bonds." She lay down flat on her back on the sand. "Lie back." She pointed to the sky with excitement in her voice. "Look, there's a shooting star!"

Johnny folded his arms behind his head and looked up. Even with the brightness of the moon, he had never seen so many stars.

Mary started to draw on an imaginary board in the sky with her index finger.

"There's the Big Dipper, and there's Cassiopeia, just above its handle,"she said.

He didn't see it. "Where?"

She took his hand again and used it to point so he could follow.

"Go along the handle of the dipper until you find Cassiopeia. There. Orion's Belt is here."

"How do you know so much about the stars?" Johnny asked.

"My dad was a fisherman before he bought the bar. He would take me night fishing as a little girl. He'd point out all the constellations."

"Did you sit on the deck of his boat naked and look for shooting stars?"

Mary rolled over and gave him a gentle punch on his shoulder.

"With my dad?" she said, laughing. "No way."

After she had delineated all the constellations she could find, it occurred to Johnny to ask about something that had caught his attention earlier.

"So, back at the bandstand, what was that little wink Isabella gave you, some type of code?"

Mary shook her head to show it wasn't important.

"Oh, just a little game we play," she said.

"What type of game?"

Mary paused, then laughed.

"To see who can get a guy to swim to the island first."

Johnny was startled.

"You've done this before!"

Mary relished Johnny's surprise.

"Oh, we've tried," she said. "But no one has actually come out here before. You fellas are the first."

"No one would come?" said Johnny. "With a beautiful woman like you?" His disbelief sounded genuine to Mary. "You've got to be kidding."

Mary shrugged. But she looked pleased at his compliment.

"I suspect they were afraid we would try to corral them into marriage."

"So the Harwich boys aren't so smart, are they?" Johnny said with a smile. "I'd think that would be an incentive for them."

Mary felt her face flush red and couldn't restrain another smile. This guy made her feel special.

Johnny paused and watched a shooting star cross in front of them.

"How old are you?" he asked her.

"Twenty-three. Spinster age."

"You look younger."

"So, how old are you, stud?"

"Just turned twenty-two."

Mary propped herself up on one elbow and gave a little laugh. It sounded so unaffected to Johnny. Why couldn't more girls be this sweet?

"How do you like being with an old maid?" she asked.

"Most beautiful old maid I've ever seen," he said softly.

He gently pulled her down and gave her a light kiss. When

he drew back, she moved closer and pressed her moist lips hard against his. This time they kissed long and hard and Mary eased herself down onto him, her breasts close against his chest. Mary broke off as Johnny started to run his hand along the lower curve of her back.

"I don't want you to think that I'm a tramp, Johnny."

"I don't think that," he said. "I could never think that."

There was something about this guy. Mary felt at ease with him. Maybe this was Mr. Right, she thought.

"I'm not very experienced, Johnny," she said quietly. "You'll be only the second guy I've ever been with."

Johnny feigned surprise.

"What? Where is the rascal that stole your virginity?"

Mary looked away from his face and down at his shoulder. She lightly ran her fingers along its muscular edge.

"I was just 18," she said. "It was just once. We'd been dating for six months. We went to his house and his parents weren't home. One thing led to another and—well, you get the idea."

Mary lifted herself farther from Johnny's chest and he could see the moonlit outline of her face and shoulders above him. He took his hand and started slowly making circles around the outside of one breast.

"I'll be gentle," he whispered.

They embraced in a long, sensual kiss, and nothing else seemed to matter.

****

After three hours, Brian and Ben had caught over 50 eels and were frantically trying to catch more before the 1:30 deadline. Brian could see Ben running toward him. He was out of breath from sprinting back from his latest trip down to the weigh station.

"Who's leading?" Brian asked anxiously.

"I couldn't see," said Ben, leaning over to gulp in air. "They took the sheets down until they've announced the winner." He straightened up and took one more big breath. "Why do they cover up the standings in the last hour, Dad?"

"So they can keep the excitement building until the final moment," Brian said. Why do they do that? he asked himself. "Tradition, I guess."

Brian checked the bait bucket.

"I'm getting low here," he said to Ben. "Can you cut some into smaller pieces? They're feeding so fast we don't need the bigger chunks."

******

Johnny and Mary swam back to shore and found Isabella's and Rock's clothes already gone.

She leaned over him as he sat to put on his shoes and kissed him on the forehead.

"That was wonderful."

Johnny pulled her down toward him and they kissed again, long and slowly and deeply. Mary sank into his arms and lingered, savoring the closeness.

Once they were dressed, Mary pulled out the pocket watch her father had given her.

"It's close to 1:30. The winners will be announced soon."

They walked up the beach toward the bonfire hand in hand, not rushing, not even talking much.

"How much longer are you staying in Harwichport?" she finally asked as they neared the bandstand.

"About a week, I think," said Johnny. "It depends on what my doctor says." He squeezed her hand a little. "Can I see you again?"

"Of course you can," she said, smiling, her face lit with delight. "But watch out, Johnny Scranton. You might fall in love with me."

You might be right, thought Johnny. This girl had struck a chord in him like no other woman he had ever met. He was used to being in control, to being the one all the girls wanted; but this small-town, Cape-Cod, fish warden-bartender-tomboy had him weak at the knees.

When they reached Bank Street, they found George, Rock, and Isabella near the pie stand. George was eating a huge slice of cranberry pie.

"Hi, guys. How's the pie?" Mary asked.

"Great. You should have some."

"I think I will," said Mary. She looked up at Johnny. "I could eat a horse."

"Pie for everyone!" Johnny said.

Isabella leaned in and hooked Mary's arm.

"We thought you might miss the announcement," Isabella said. Her eyes were dancing with questions.

"We stayed longer on the island than I planned," Mary said giddily.

Isabella used her free arm to pull Rock toward her. She nuzzled her face playfully into his chest. Rock looked like a happy man.

Paul Rousch was up on the stage again, raising his hands and trying to quiet the crowd.

"Ladies and gentlemen," he cried out. "We have the results from tonight's tournament."

The crowd moved closer to the makeshift stage. Johnny could see a sizable group of dirty, tired-looking men huddled near the bonfire.

"The runner-up in the junior division, with 146 pounds,

Harry Crawford!"

There was polite applause. A straw-haired boy about 15 years old waved from the edge of the crowd.

"The winner of this year's junior division, with 186 pounds –Kyle Ramire!"

More polite applause was punctuated by a shriek from a woman in the back of the crowd. A stocky boy with olive skin and dark, curly hair loped up to the table in front of the stage and was handed a small trophy by a smartly dressed older man.

"My cousin," Mary whispered to Johnny.

"Not another one."

He laughed as she hugged him.

"Now, our runner-up in the adult division, with 345 pounds –Jim Calhoun."

More polite applause, but Mary cheered louder than before and Isabella bounced up and down and hooted and whistled. A man sitting near the top of the hill jumped to his feet and ran down to the front of the stage. Rousch leaned down from the stage and quietly said something to him and the man nodded and walked back to where he had been sitting. "There's no trophy for second place?" said Isabella. "That doesn't seem right." She and Mary cheered all the more loudly.

"A cousin of yours?" Johnny asked Mary.

"No," said Mary. "He's one of Isabella's cousins." She slapped Isabella on the back.

"Now, our 1912 Harwich Eel Tournament winner with a new derby record catch of 393 pounds – Brian Donahue!"

Mary jumped up and whistled loudly through her fingers. Then she ran up and kissed Brian on the cheek as he came to the table to collect the trophy and the $200 check. She ran back and hooked her arm around Johnny's arm again.

"Your cousin?" he said.

"My favorite cousin," she said happily.

"Okay, folks," Rousch announced loudly. "The hard cider bar is now open."

Johnny looked puzzled.

"I thought you said they didn't sell alcohol at the party."

"Not during the tournament," Mary said, enunciating the difference carefully. "It's another story after the tournament."

"They make this special hard cider," Isabella chimed in. "Now's the only time of the year it can be sold. One hour"–she whipped her hand horizontally in front of her chest to punctuate her words–"and then they cut off the tap."

Johnny nodded.

"So that's really why all these people are out here this late."

Isabella grabbed Rock and started to dance around him as if he were a maypole.

"The town shuts down until noon tomorrow," she said in a sing-song voice.

"Because everyone needs time to recover," said a man standing near them.

Mary smiled. She grabbed Johnny's hand and pulled him onto the dance floor as the band struck up a Scottish jig.

"Come on, lover-boy. The night is young."

CHAPTER 36

The cool morning breeze woke George as he lay on the front porch couch. A morning dove cooed outside and George realized he had slept only three hours. Still, he was wide awake, so he decided to watch the sunrise from the beach. In the dim morning light he found a narrow path that led through the uneven dunes in front of the house. As he followed the path down to the water, the wind whistled through the dune grass and marsh plovers darted in and out, searching for insects. The first rays of the sun streaked into the morning sky as he sat on the hard-packed sand above the high-tide line.

Slowly, the bright outer edges of the rising sun appeared on the horizon in various shades of gold and red and an occasional streak of silver. Then, all of a sudden, as if by magic, the low-lying clouds disappeared and the top third of the sun popped above the water and into the sky. It seemed as if someone had pulled the leading edge of the sun into the sky with wires.

"God, this is beautiful," George said out loud.

"Yes it is," a voice responded behind him.

He turned, surprised that anyone else was on the beach at this hour. He saw Marjorie walking toward him trailed by a broad-shouldered pointer with a mix of black and tan markings on his face and hind quarters. She was dressed in a simple cream-colored hemp dress tied at the waist with a plaid scarf. Her hair was pulled back in a bow and she looked younger than when George had first met her, but just as elegant.

"Good morning, Marjorie," he said. "What are you doing here?"

"I take my morning walk with Samuel."

She pointed to her dog.

"I saw you leave the house while I was making breakfast and decided to join you."

George held out his hand.

"Hi ya, boy."

Samuel came over to sniff George's out-stretched hand.

"He's very friendly," said Marjorie.

"I love dogs," said George.

He scratched behind Samuel's right ear.

"What type of pointer is Samuel? I don't recognize the breed."

"He's a short-haired marsh pointer. They're native to the Cape. They've been bred here for the past 200 years. They're great dogs."

Marjorie sat down next to George. Samuel immediately stretched across her legs.

"Every time I see the sun rise," she said, "I'm reminded that there must be a God who created this wonder. It couldn't be by accident."

Samuel rolled over and she scratched his belly.

"It's wonderful and spectacular all at the same time," George said as he watched the sun begin to climb.

The sun had risen halfway out of the water and bright streaks of red and yellow darted farther into the morning sky.

"So how's Johnny been doing – honestly?" asked George.

"He's really doing well," said Marjorie. George could hear her affection for Johnny in the pleasure with which she said it. "He's ready to start using his hand more. He should be ready to head home by the end of the week."

George was surprised. "Head home?"

"Yes. He told me he wants to stay with his dad and work out at Rock's club."

"I thought he would go back to Tampa," said George.

"He said there are too many temptations in Tampa. He's not sure how he would handle them."

George paused to watch the rays of the rising sun dance on the waves.

"He did great last night. He stayed with sarsparilla at the dance. He turned down everything else."

George remembered the speciality of the after-party.

"Oh, that God-awful hard cider. I don't know how people drink that stuff. It's pure white lightning."

"That's great news about Johnny," Marjorie said. She smiled a little. "And I agree about the cider. It's awful, but it's been a town tradition for as long as anyone can remember."

She looked more closely at George, as if she might be considering a deep question. Instead, she simply asked, "How about you, George? Did you have a good time?"

"I had a great time," George said. "I ate some of the best pie I've ever had."

"Let me guess. Mary Jane's pie."

"How'd you know?"

"Best pie maker in town. She's my cousin."

George nodded knowingly.

"Mary told us how everyone seems to be related."

Marjorie threw a ball for Samuel to chase. He bolted down the beach.

"It's both a blessing and a curse," she said. "Everyone knows everything about you, which isn't always the best thing." She waited a moment. "But when times are hard, they're here to help." She paused again. "These folks really helped me when my husband died. I don't think I could have made it without them."

George was drawing a figure in the sand with his finger and

stopped. He turned to Marjorie.

"I'm sorry to hear of his death," he said. "How did he die?"

Marjorie readjusted the bow securing her hair.

"He died trying to secure our boat during the'09 nor'easter."

She pointed to the remnants of a pier in front of them.

"He was swept out to sea by a wave that capsized three boats tied to what used to be that pier. I was standing on the hill with Samuel when it happened."

She pointed to a spot behind them.

"One minute he was there. The next he was gone. Four other men from Harwich died that day too."

George looked down at the sand where he had been drawing.

"That's horrible," he said.

Marjorie folded her arms and sighed.

"They searched for three days, but they never found his body. I prayed he didn't suffer. "

Tears filled her eyes.

"Here I go telling a stranger my sad story."

George put his arm around Marjorie's shoulder to comfort her. She leaned closer and wiped away the tears. They watched silently as the sun lifted completely out of the water and ascended into the morning sky.

Marjorie wiped her eyes again. She stood up and brushed the sand from her dress.

"Come on. I'll cook some eggs."

****

"I forgot to tell you about the exhibition golf match today at The Port Club," Marjorie said as they walked back toward the house. "Two of our local players are playing against two professionals. It's billed as a stakes match. What does that mean?"

George nodded to show that he knew.

"Each side puts up a certain amount of money and the winners are awarded the entire pot. Do you remember who's playing?"

"I don't recall their names. I have the paper at home. I'll get it and bring it over to the house. I do know that the match begins at 1 p.m."

Marjorie and Samuel split off toward her house to get the newspaper and George walked up the long path to Johnny's house. When he got there, he found Rock slumped in an easy chair in the front room, a damp towel laid across his forehead.

"I have the worst headache," he said as he lay his head back and tried to adjust to the least painful position.

"You drank too much of that hard cider," George said, so casually that it sounded unsympathetic to Rock. "Is Johnny up? There's a stakes match today at the Harwichport Club. Let's go and watch."

Rock let out a long, disparaging sigh.

"Who's crazy enough to play a stakes match on the Cape? These bumpkins don't have money."

Rock finished his insult just as Marjorie walked into the room. When he saw her, he groaned.

"Morning, Rock," she said brightly. "The bumpkins are playing two fellas by the name of Carl Strayman and Isaac Walker."

She handed the paper with the article on the stakes match to George.

"I'll make us some breakfast," she said as she walked into the kitchen.

"I know them," Rock said. "Strayman is a clubmaker near Brattleboro and Walker comes from Rhode Island. I saw Strayman play last year at the Narragansett Club. He finished in the top ten.

I've never seen Walker play."

Rock adjusted the towel on his head for fuller coverage.

"Boy, I'd like to get into this action," he said. "I wonder which bookie set this up." He ran some names through his mind. It even hurts to think, he thought. "Maybe Chuck Wheeler from Norton. He tried to get me to play in a series of stakes matches last year. He told me I could make $3,000 in four weeks. I'd just made twice that playing with Johnny and Walter. Nice guy, but small potatoes."

Johnny appeared in the parlor entrance.

"What's this talk about a stakes match?"

"Carl Strayman and Isaac Walker are playing a stakes match against a couple of locals today," said George. "Let's go. It might be fun to watch."

"Okay. I'll hit a few balls while you guys watch the match," Johnny said. He sat down on the arm of Rock's chair. "I didn't get to talk with you after the swim. How'd it go with Isabella?"

George stepped closer to hear Rock's response.

"We thought we were so smart. Turns out she and Mary had a bet on who would get a guy to the island first."

Johnny nodded.

"I guess she won. You were way ahead of us," Johnny said.

"Not exactly," Rock confessed.

"What do you mean?"

"We never got to the island." Rock shifted in the chair and shrugged almost imperceptibly. "I've never exactly learned how to swim," he muttered. "I never go in the deep end."

"You're kidding," George said, relieved that there was someone else who had never learned to swim. "So what happened?"

"It's a little embarrassing," Rock said.

"Well, if you can't tell us . . . " Johnny started to say before

Rock broke back in.

"I didn't say I wouldn't tell you."

Rock waved his hand in front of his face and adjusted himself in the chair again. His eyes were closed. Johnny looked over at George and raised his eyebrows and smiled without Rock seeing.

"I thought that maybe I could sort of float out to the island, but when we got to the deep water and I couldn't feel bottom, suddenly I started to panic. Isabella came back and tried to help, but I was kicking and trying to keep my head above water. I felt like I was going to drown. She grabbed me and kept my head up and pulled me back to shore." He paused for a moment and then spoke quietly. "It took a half hour before I calmed down. We got dressed and went back to the bonfire. I was really cold. Can you believe, as hot as it was last night–and I was cold? We stayed near the bonfire until you got back."

Johnny grinned. The image of little Isabella saving Rock and dragging him to shore offered so many possibilities for ribbing Rock. George understood the look in Johnny's eye and shook his head no. Johnny decided to be kind.

"So, I guess Mary won the bet," he said simply.

George pulled a straight-backed chair up, spun it around with the back facing Johnny, and sat down straddling it.

"What happened to you, hotshot?" he asked.

"I had a great time. We lay on the beach and Mary pointed out stars and constellations to me."

"You laid on the sand, naked as a jaybird, and watched the stars?" asked Rock incredulously. "Come on, out with it, boy. What else happened?"

"It would be a violation of the gentleman's code of honor to tell you," Johnny said.

His voice sounded as if he were joking, but George could tell he was serious.

How strange, he thought. Johnny usually loved to talk about his conquests in almost embarrassing detail. Was this a different Johnny? Had the intervention, the operation, the time alone out here changed him this much?

"Come on, Johnny," said Rock.

"Leave him alone," said George. "If he doesn't want to tell, he doesn't have to."

Johnny shrugged his shoulders.

"She's a special girl. I've never met anyone like her."

He smiled sheepishly and turned away from George and Rock to go into the kitchen and check on breakfast.

CHAPTER 37

The Port Golf Club was designed and built in 1898 by Aldie Strom, a local golf architect. The club opened as a nine-hole course, initially just for summer residents, but within five years it had become one of the premier courses on the Cape. The clubhouse was small but functional and Strom had built a separate practice area.

In 1908, the club recruited Harry Long as its summer resident pro. Long had competed with Rock on the English and European golf circuit for five years before he injured his left foot and was forced to retire from competitive golf. He turned out to be a master instructor and, despite his injures, he developed a prosperous teaching practice that catered to the rich families that summered in Harwichport.

After a long breakfast, the boys grabbed Johnny's bag from the car and walked up the hill into the village. The golf club was a five-minute walk from the Congregational Church. It lay in a secluded grove of poplar and oak trees. Rock commented to Johnny as they walked up the worn path to the clubhouse that the residents of the village seemed to be walking slowly, undoubtedly recovering from the aftermath of the earlier cider celebration.

"Do you know where I can find Harry Long?" Rock asked a young man sitting on the clubhouse porch.

The young man pointed to the far side of the clubhouse.

"He's down at the maintenance shed working on the tractor before the stakes match begins."

"Thanks."

Rock motioned to Johnny and George to follow him quietly.

Once they were near the shed, they saw a small, wiry man with long white hair seated on a bucket while he adjusted the rear linkage of a red tractor. Rock found a small pail by the shed, filled it with water from the nearby pond, and stealthily approached the man from behind. Rock doused him with the bucket of water and stepped back to laugh as the man erupted in anger.

"What the hell! I'll kill the son of a bitch who did this!"

He shook his head to clear the water and turned to see Rock. Rock pointed at him and laughed even louder.

"That's for the time at Royal St. Lotham when you doused me just before I teed off," Rock yelled.

Harry looked shocked. He was breathing heavily and shaking off water like a dog. "Rock, you son of a bitch!"

Then his tone completely changed.

"How the hell are you?"

They began to laugh together. They stepped forward and hugged. Harry was small enough that Rock lifted him completely off the ground. When he set him back down, he turned him toward Johnny and George.

"Harry, I want you to meet my friends, Johnny Scranton and George Riley."

Harry ran his hand through his hair to get rid of some more water and nodded hello.

"My honor, gentlemen. I'm proud to have players of your caliber visit our humble little course."

George detected a slight Scottish accent in Harry's voice.

"Harry, can we use your practice range?" asked Rock.

"Sure," said Harry. "I'm sorry I can't join you though. The stakes match begins in less than an hour and I still need to mow one section on the 9th."

"I thought they only used horse-pulled tractors on the

Cape," George said.

"You're right. All the courses on the Cape use horses, except for us. One of my members donated this tractor to the club. When it works, it gives a much smoother cut, and it takes half the time."

"This is quite a long way from your playing days in Europe," Rock said.

"That's certainly true, laddie," said Harry, smiling wistfully. "But I really love teaching and I've settled into the rhythm of the town. I finally got married, you know. We have a four-month old baby boy."

Rock looked surprised.

"That's fantastic, Harry. Can you join us for dinner so we can catch up?"

"Where are you staying?"

"18 Sea Street."

Harry nodded.

"Across from Marjorie. That's where the recluse is staying."

Johnny winced. Harry paused to wipe off his hands with a rag from his back pocket.

"I'm the recluse," Johnny said. "Tell us about the stakes match."

"Chuck Wheeler. You remember him, Rock?" Rock started to say something, but stopped as Harry continued. "He's organized the event. They're playing for $2,000 a man."

Johnny's jaw dropped.

"$2,000 a man! That's more than Hagen and I ever play for. How did the locals come up with that kind of money?"

"It's not Harwichport money. It's Hyannis money. I found two members to sponsor our lads. I get ten percent. Wheeler gets ten percent for organizing the match, and he keeps the marker bets. The sponsors get a fifteen percent premium, and our local lads can make over $500 per man if they win."

"Sweet deal all around," Johnny said. "I need to get Hagen up here."

Rock and George smiled as Harry finished fixing the rear linkage of the tractor.

"Do you expect a crowd in this heat?" Rock asked.

"Golf has taken off on the Cape, Rock. I wouldn't be surprised if we get upwards of 400 people today." Harry cleaned the grease off his hands again. "I've already sold over 200 raffle tickets," he said proudly.

"Raffle tickets?" said George. "What are the raffle tickets for?"

"A new set of Wright and Ditson woods."

Harry picked up the empty water bucket and tossed it into the back of the tractor.

"Sorry, lads, but I've got to get to work. See you tonight for dinner."

Harry climbed up on the tractor and pointed to Rock.

"Can you crank her for me?" he said.

Rock walked to the front of the tractor and gave the handle a sharp turn. The sound of the unmuffled engine was deafening.

"And don't worry about shagging balls today," yelled Harry as he shifted into gear. "I have a kid who collects range balls for me. Terrible golfer, but a very hard worker."

******

Johnny headed to the practice tee and Rock and George walked over to the course to watch the match. A surprisingly large crowd surrounded the 1st teeing ground and extended along the first fairway. The two local players, Ralph Williams and Buddy Carlson, looked nervous as they stood on the teeing ground waiting for their opponents to arrive.

Ralph recognized George standing near the clubhouse entrance.

"George," he called. He walked over and extended his hand.

"We played against one another years ago in Braintree."

"I remember. How you been?" George asked.

"Great," said Ralph. "I'm a bit nervous today. I've never played in a professional match. I decided to turn pro this month after I lost my job as a teller at the Nauset Five and Dime Bank. There was a run last year and they laid off most of the staff."

George shook his head. "I'm sorry to hear that. Maybe you can win today and take some of the sting out."

Strayman and Walker arrived ten minutes late and started to take practice swings.

"You better go, Ralph," said George. "Good luck."

"Strayman and Walker are pulling a Hagen on these guys," Rock said to George. "He always arrives late for a match so he can mess with an opponent."

Carl Strayman was a lanky man who used an extra-long driver. Strayman didn't waste any time. He hit a rocket straight down the middle of the fairway. George estimated that his ball traveled at least 240 yards. His partner, Isaac Walker, was shorter, but with broad shoulders and huge biceps. His drive also landed in the middle of the fairway, about 30 yards behind his partner's ball.

Ralph began to shake as he addressed the ball. He backed off and took three deep breaths to try to regain his composure. He played the ball off his left toe. As the driver descended, the shaft turned in his hand and the ball shot out to the right, just 60 yards from the tee. Ralph looked embarrassed and dropped his head as he placed his driver back in his bag.

His partner, Buddy Carlson, was no more than 5' 3" and looked as if he were only 14 or 15 years old. He hooked his drive into the parallel fairway and ended in a deep bunker.

As they walked down the fairway with the players, Rock counted 23 clubs in Carl Strayman's bag. What does he do with all of those clubs? Rock wondered. Rock heard that Roger White, the 1912 Western Open champion, carried 31 clubs. Rock carried 18 clubs in his bag. There was some talk at the USGA about restricting the number of clubs to 14. Rock was definitely opposed to this rule change. The more clubs the better.

******

Johnny spent an hour on the practice tee before he decided to rest for the day. He was amazed at how exhausted even this short workout left him. He sat in the clubhouse for a while and then found a small tree and sat down in the cool of its shade. George sauntered up to him about twenty minutes later.

"How was the match?" Johnny asked.

"Strayman and Walker closed them out on the 17th."

"Where's Rock?"

"He started to talk with a young lady on the 6th hole. He'll join us soon. How was your practice?"

"My hand feels great, but I'm exhausted. This may take longer than I thought to get back in shape."

A police car pulled into the clubhouse parking lot. Officer Brian Donahue, the new eel champion of Harwich, climbed out and ambled over to Johnny and George. His uniform was crisp but he looked like he had had a long night. He tipped his hat to Johnny.

"Mr. Scranton, my name is Brian Donahue."

Johnny stood up and offered his hand. Brian shook it.

"Marjorie told me you had come to hit a few balls," Brian said, as he watched the crowd file out after the stakes match. "Never could understand this game. No offense, but it's always seemed silly to me, chasing a little white ball out in the sun."

"None taken," said Johnny.

Brian took off his hat and wiped the sweat from his brow with the sleeve of his forearm. "Can we talk?"

"I'll find Rock," George said.

By the time George had returned with Rock, Johnny had finished with Brian and was anxious to get home.

Rock put his arm around his sweaty friend.

"Johnny, I've got an idea," he said. "I'm amazed at how many people came out to see the match today. Harry says they got over 400 spectators–and no one knows these guys. What if we organize a stakes match with four players people know, players they want to see? We could make a fortune."

"How would we raise the money?" Johnny asked.

"We'll get sponsors and the players will need to post"–Rock thought a minute–"at least $2500 each as their share."

"Who do you think might play?" Johnny asked.

"This is a natural for you and Walter. I think Alec Smith would be perfect, and I'll have to think about the fourth man. Think about the publicity we would get, the greatest stakes match in history."

Johnny wasn't sure he could raise that type of money, and just an hour's practice had made clear that he had a long way to go before he would be ready to play competitive golf again. But a stakes match like that would be a great goal.

"Come on, Rock" he said. "We can talk all about it after we have a swim."

On their walk back to Sea Street, George was curious about

Johnny's talk with Brian.

"So how did the meeting with the sheriff go?" he asked Johnny.

"There's no problem there. He just wanted to assure me that the case was closed." He added as an afterthought, "Brian's a cousin of Mary's."

"So, what about crazy Agnes?" Rock asked.

"He told me not to worry. He'd take care of Agnes."

CHAPTER 38

For the next five days, Johnny and Mary were constant companions. They sailed to Chatham Lighthouse, took a trip to Dennis, and fished on the Herring River. It was a glorious week. On Friday, Mary borrowed her dad's car to drive Johnny to Hyannis to catch the train to Boston. She arrived at the beach house three hours before the train departed. As Johnny put the last bags into the back of the car, he pulled her toward him.

"This has been the best week of my life."

Mary leaned forward and kissed him.

"I'll stay in Boston until early October," he said. "I'll try to get back here to see you, and you can visit me any time you want."

He brushed a stray hair from her face with his hand. "But then I have to go back to Tampa for the season."

Mary felt herself go cold. She knew he was going back to Florida. They had talked about it before, but she hated to hear it.

"Tampa," she said, her voice sounding weaker than she wanted it to. "That's so far away."

Johnny lightly stroked her chestnut brown hair.

"I need to get back to work and make money so I can pay for your train ticket to visit me down there."

She looked up and smiled. This was new. She had never visited anyone off-Cape, let alone Florida.

She threw her arms up around his neck.

"Visit? When? How long?"

"Whenever you can come," said Johnny.

Mary felt like she might start crying. Over this simple thing. She gathered herself and started to plan instead.

"I'll talk with my dad to see when he won't need me," she said. She took a breath and sorted it out. "February will be the best time to leave the bar. Business is slow and it's so cold." She looked up at Johnny, her eyes big. "And it'll be a great time to escape to the sunny South."

Just then, Marjorie came out on the porch carrying a broom. She was cleaning the house for the next tenant.

"I want to say goodbye," Johnny said. "I'll be right back."

Marjorie saw him coming up the steps and put down the broom. She waited patiently for him to come over to her.

"Thank you for all you've done for me," he said. He let out a loud breath. "I think I'm ready to take on all the temptations out there."

"I think you are too," said Marjorie. She smiled at him, her eyes watering. "Trust yourself, Johnny. Remember that you're the best judge of what's right or wrong. Don't let people tell you differently."

Johnny leaned closer and hugged her gently.

"I won't," he said softly.

Then he pulled an envelope out from his jacket.

"I almost forgot," he said. "This is for you."

Marjorie put her hands up, palms toward him.

"No," she said. "George paid me before he left on Monday."

"This is something special for you," he said. "I bought it at Monahan's Jewelers."

He folded her hand around the envelope.

"The jeweler told me you're second cousins."

"Bless you, Johnny." Marjorie smiled again. This time a tear trickled down from the outer edge of her eye. She sighed. "Now be off with you or you'll miss your train."

Inside the envelope, she found $200 and a silver medallion

depicting St. Jude, the patron saint of lost causes. The inscription on the back of the medal said *To Marjorie, My Friend and Healer, Johnny.*

She pressed it close to her heart.

****

For the next two months Johnny worked out feverishly at the Commonwealth Club. Once he was back in a good routine, the old form returned quickly. In October he returned to his old job in Tampa and began teaching. He thought about Mary often and called her three times a week. The time flew by until early January when Mary confirmed her February visit.

Johnny anxiously waited on the railroad platform for the West Coast Limited from St. Augustine. The train was running fifteen minutes late due to heavy thunderstorms that had ripped through the area the previous night and flooded low sections of the tracks. As he paced the platform, Johnny's mouth was dry and he had butterflies in his stomach.

The Limited came in fast, slammed on its steam brakes, and stopped on the outer edge of the platform. A porter stepped down from the middle car and placed a wooden step near the train door. Mary was the first person off the train, bounding down the steps, all smiles and energy. She was wearing a sleeveless lavender summer dress and had her hair cut shorter in the latest bob-weave style.

God, she looks gorgeous, Johnny thought, as she ran to him and leapt into his waiting arms. They hugged and kissed, and kissed again.

"Oh, darling, I missed you," she said.

Mary pressed her body firmly against his and they kissed again. Mary suddenly pulled back and exclaimed, "A palm tree!

The first palm tree I've ever seen."

Off to her left a slender king palm swayed in the gentle afternoon breeze.

"Everything is so green."

Johnny cupped her face gently in his hands to look at her more closely.

"God, how I've missed you," he said. He put his arm around her and led her away from the platform.

"We had three weeks of rain. I hope the weather gets better for your vacation."

Mary laughed.

"It's got to be better than Harwich. We had ten inches of snow three days ago." She was talking fast now, excited, emphasizing the near disaster. "I was afraid I wouldn't be able to get off the Cape." She slowed back down. "Brian drove me to Hyannis to catch the train. He said to say hello."

A station porter brought Mary's six bags to them and Johnny directed him to his car. He and Mary hooked arms and walked down the ramp to the parking lot.

Johnny pointed to a royal-blue Buick Touring Sedan with white-rimmed wheels.

"So what do you think of my new car?"

"Snazzy," she said, her eyes widening for effect. "I love it. When did you get it?"

"Last week. George knows all about this stuff and he convinced me to buy the Buick instead of a Ford. This came with an automatic starter and a canvas roof."

"Neat. And I love the color."

Mary jumped into the passenger seat and Johnny dropped her bags into the back seat one by one. "Did you pack for the season?"

Mary laughed.

"I have some good news," Johnny said.

"Tell me."

"Rock has organized a stakes match in early June at the Rockland Club near Newport. Hagen and I will play Alec Smith and Fred McLeod."

"Johnny, that's fabulous," Mary said. "I can come see you." She narrowed her brown eyes. "Who are Smith and McLeod?"

"Two of the best professional golfers in the United States. Smith won the U.S. Open in '06 and '10. McLeod won in '08. It'll be the richest stakes match in the history of golf, $10,000 per man. With outside bets and pushes, I figure the winning team can pocket over $30,000."

Mary was shocked.

"$10,000 a man! You don't have to post the entry fee, do you?" she asked in a disapproving voice.

"No. No," said Johnny. "Rock has raised $15,000 from outside investors. Hagen and I only need to post $2,500 each."

Mary looked concerned. "Only $2,500! That's still a lot of money to risk."

"I have four months to make my share. I'll be okay."

"How does Rock make money on this?"

Johnny laughed.

"You never need to worry about Rock," he said. "He gets ten percent of the purse, the proceeds from the Calcutta on Friday night, registration fees from the bookies, and the proceeds from the gate. It's a sweet deal."

Johnny pulled out of the parking lot and Mary leaned over and rested her head on his shoulder. She ran her hand along his jacket.

"I like the jacket you're wearing. It's smart. What's the fabric?"

"They call it poplin. I knew you'd like it."

Johnny turned off the main road and entered the circular driveway in front of a Spanish colonial-revival house with an off-white stucco facade and red tile roof.

"Here we are."

Mary was stunned.

"This is your house?" she said.

The house was a single-story cottage built on a bluff overlooking Tampa Bay. A massive mahogany and stucco portico extended from the front door. The entrance had red crustacean tiles, and the front lawn was dense with a variety of flowering plants.

"Johnny, this is gorgeous. I can't believe this is your place."

"What do you mean?"

She chuckled.

"I envisioned a bachelor's pad."

"Come on. I'll show you everything," he said. He leaned closer to her as she climbed out of the car. "Especially the bedroom."

"You devil, Mr. Scranton."

Mary laughed as Johnny picked her up and carried her into the house.

****

George sat in his dorm room after supper studying for a philosophy exam. The temperature had dropped to 16 degrees and a heavy snowstorm was forecast for the next day.

A loud voice echoed through the halls of the dorm: "Special delivery for George Riley."

George rushed down the hall to retrieve the envelope.

"Can you sign here, please?"

He checked the return address. It was from the First National Bank of Boston. He turned the letter over in his hands for a few moments, staring at it, as if he were divining its contents by handling it. Then he nervously opened the envelope. He unfolded the paper inside and read it.

Dear Mr. Riley:

We are pleased to offer you a full time position with the First National Bank of Boston. You will be assigned to our commercial loan division as a Junior Associate. Your annual salary will be $2,800 per year. We will endeavor to accommodate your amateur golf schedule and give you time off to participate in national and local golf tournaments.

Please contact Harvey Rothman within two weeks to indicate if these terms are acceptable. Mr. Rothman will discuss a start date and our benefits package with you.

I look forward to welcoming you as a full-time member of the First National Bank of Boston family.

Sincerely,
Edward Hogan, President

George collapsed in a small chair in the hall. He couldn't believe he had gotten the job. He ran to his room, grabbed his coat, and sprinted the four blocks to Jennifer's house at 120 Brown Street.

The Delta Gamma house was a large yellow colonial with three prominent dormers on the second floor. The house had been donated to the sorority in 1909 by Helen Risling Cooper to provide suitable off-campus housing for Pembroke women. Jennifer had moved from the family home her junior year and liked the security and companionship of the sorority.

As he rang the doorbell, George realized it was past the weeknight curfew for visitors. The sorority mother answered the door. Mrs. McAndrews was an imposing, formal woman of indeterminate age. She was stern-looking, but she had a soft spot for George.

"Good evening, Mr. Riley," she said.

"I'd like to see Ms. Smitson, please, ma'am."

"It's beyond visiting hours, dear."

"This is extremely urgent. May I see her just for a moment just this once?"

She didn't like to make exceptions, but this had to be important if George were so concerned.

"Alright. I'll call her. Please wait in the parlor, Mr. Riley."

The rules for male visitors to the house were strict and numerous. First of all, no men were allowed beyond the parlor of the Delta Gamma house, not even the girls' fathers. Men who were admitted to the parlor had to be wearing a sports coat or a suit. And no loud talking or signs of public affection – including holding hands – were allowed. Even when no visitors were present, the women were not allowed to wear dresses shorter than ankle length in the house, and open-collared blouses were prohibited. Even on weekends, sorority members had to be back in the house before 11 p.m. unless they had a note from their parents. George found the place and its myriad of restrictions stifling, but Jennifer loved the house.

Jennifer walked into the parlor and looked concerned.

"Hi," she said. "What's wrong? Why are you here so late?"

It still felt odd to George that he couldn't so much as give her a light kiss hello here.

"I have great news," he said quickly. He smiled and held up the letter. "I've been offered a Junior Associate position with First National."

Jennifer grabbed the letter from him. Her eyes raced through it then she threw her arms around his neck and hugged him.

"What are you doing?" George said. "The matron!"

Jennifer let go of him and broke into a huge smile.

"Forget Mrs. McAndrews," she said with a laugh. "This is wonderful news. Now we can make plans."

"Are you sure you don't mind leaving Providence and your family?"

"George, we've talked about this," she said firmly. "My place is with you." Her voice softened. "I love you, George. I don't care where we live."

Jennifer brightened and suddenly hugged him again.

"Let's go for a walk and talk about where we want to live."

"What about Mrs. McAndrews? And don't you need to study?"

Jennifer made a face to show that none of that mattered.

"She'll let me out for a short walk. And my Latin can wait." She rolled her eyes. "Herodotus and Ovid."

George looked surprised.

"My high school Latin teacher wouldn't let us read Ovid. He said he was too racy."

Jennifer winked as she left to retrieve her coat.

"He's quite graphic," she said, with a coy smile. "We should read him together."

CHAPTER 39

The 1913 professional golf tour opened in late February with the Southern Invitational at the Breakers Club in Palm Beach, Florida. The Breakers Club had opened in 1905. The course was short – only 6140 yards – but it was difficult when the wind blew on shore. Wind gusts buffeted Palm Beach all four days of the tournament. Johnny used a combination of low pitch-and-run shots and precise putting to shoot an opening round 71. He played steady golf the next three days and won the tournament by three shots.

As he raised the winner's trophy, his first win since 1910, he thought of Mary and of all his friends who had supported him throughout his recovery. He had been sober now for nine months. Brad Caswell, a local playing pal of Johnny's and the defending tournament champion, spoke at the awards ceremony.

"A different Johnny Scranton came to play this week," he said, obviously happy for his friend. "He's fit and controlled, and he plays with a fire in his belly." He raised his glass to toast Johnny's triumph. "Look out, world. Johnny Scranton is back."

Over the next six weeks, Johnny played in four professional tournaments. He won at Pensacola and Sarasota and finished second at Naples and third at Vero Beach. In six weeks, he won more than $4,000 in prize money and $3,000 as his share of the Calcuttas. He was getting in shape, on the course and in the bank, for Rock's big stakes match.

******

George was doing his best to get Mary and Jennifer out the door of the Delta Gamma house. "Come on, ladies. We need to leave now or we'll be late for the train," he said.

As they passed the Van Wickle Gates, Mary grabbed his arm to get his attention.

"I read in the paper that the stakes match will be a four-ball tournament. What does that mean, George?" she asked.

"Johnny and Walter play as a team and Smith and McLeod play as a team."

Mary seemed confused.

"Is this where they hit each other's shots?"

"No," said George. "That's an alternate shot match."

He was walking so fast that the girls were almost trotting to keep up.

"In four-ball, each player plays his own ball, but only the best score per hole for each team counts. The team with the lowest score for that hole wins the hole. The team that wins the most holes during the two days wins the match."

Now Jennifer was confused. She had hold of George's hand but was trailing him by a few feet, so she spoke more loudly than normal to make sure he heard.

"So it doesn't matter if your team has the low overall score, just how many individual holes you've won?"

"Exactly right," George said, looking straight ahead as if he were an arrow headed for the train station. "Each hole becomes its own single point. It can really change your strategy."

"When will Smith and McLeod get here?" Jennifer asked.

"They arrive tonight," George said. "There's a practice round tomorrow."

Mary suddenly swung herself around so she could face George and Jennifer as she talked with them. She was skipping backwards to stay ahead of them. How does she do that? thought George.

"I'm so excited," she said, clapping her hands. "I haven't seen Johnny since February. He calls me twice a week and we talk forever." She looked concerned for a moment. "I worry about his long-distance phone bills."

Jennifer let out a little laugh.

"I think he can afford a few long-distance phone calls."

They arrived at the station about two minutes ahead of the New Haven Limited. Before the train had come to a complete stop, Johnny jumped off it and ran to meet Mary. They collided in mid-platform and embraced for what seemed like an eternity to George.

Jennifer leaned over to him, her eyes smiling. "I like her very much," she said. "They're made for each other, don't you think?"

George nodded and put his arm around her.

When Johnny and Mary finally stepped away from each other, George and Jennifer joined them. After hellos and hugs, Johnny asked, "Do you know if Hagen's arrived?"

"I saw him yesterday," George said. "He was wandering through Brown's village shops and I ran into him by accident. Two gorgeous women were with him. He said they were his nieces."

"Good old Walter. He has 'nieces' in every town."

"I need to meet this Walter Hagen," Mary said in a stern voice, hooking Johnny's arm with hers and pushing into him. "He might be a bad influence on you."

"Walter's okay. Most of his antics are for the press." He made a funny choking sound and bulged his eyes out. "Now where can we get a sarsparilla? I'm thirsty."

****

The New England Golf Committee was assembled in the great oak room at the Newland Country Club for an emergency meeting. Archibald Sargent was angry and he wanted to let the assembled committee members know it. He sat fuming at the head of the long dark table.

"How could you let this happen? A major stakes match right here in Rhode Island? This is unacceptable, gentlemen."

He pounded his fist on the table and blew some air out of his nose like a human locomotive.

"Shit."

He leaned back and pulled down on the lapels of his vest to calm himself.

"Avery, why in the world did you let Rockland get away with hosting this damn stakes match? I thought we agreed that all member clubs would be prohibited from staging pro events."

Avery Harmistand from Newland was the president of the Rhode Island Golf Committee. He was universally liked because he did his best never to offend anyone. He was seated at the other end of the table from Sargent but it was apparent that he was uncomfortable with Sargent's anger.

"We tried to get the governor to support a ban on stakes matches, Archie," he protested. "But he's a fan of Johnny Scranton and refused to help." He let out a loud sigh. "Our bill never even got out of the Senate committee."

"You don't need a damn bill," said Sargent sharply. "Just clamp down on the clubs."

Harmistand shook his head and held up his open hands to show he was helpless.

"We adopted the ban on pro tournaments in January. But Rockland stands to make so much money from this one event that they voted to resign from the association." He looked truly sad. "That club had been a member since '02."

"How much are these sleazy thugs paying Rockland?" Joel Baumgardener asked.

"$4,000 and a percentage of the gate receipts."

Baumgardener looked impressed.

"Shit. That is a lot of money for two days of golf," he said.

Sargent glared at him then raised himself up out of his seat to address the members of the committee.

"Gentlemen," he said, his voice low and measured, "We've spent four years and almost $50,000 on our efforts to stamp out this plague on golf." He pulled in a deep breath and let it out as he spoke. "We've failed to get one single state in New England to ban golf for money." He paused. "We've failed to find cheaters." He paused again. "We've failed to get Johnny Scranton banned from tournaments."

The way he dropped back down in his chair clearly exhibited his disgust.

"Not one of these approaches has done us any good." He clenched his fists on the table. "Now one of our own member clubs has defied our rules."

Baumgardener tensed up waiting for the explosion.

But Sargent didn't explode. He was staring down in front of him at an imaginary spot on the table.

"We need a new strategy," he said simply.

Ted Martin from the Surry Club raised his hand.

"I think it's time we suspend our surveillance of Scranton and the other pros. The private investigators are costing a fortune and we're not getting any useful information."

"I agree, Ted," Sargent said quietly. "All in favor of ceasing surveillance?" Sargent pronounced the verdict as unanimous without looking up to check hands. When he did look up, his eyes narrowed and his voice hardened. He had been thinking of a new strategy for weeks. Now was the time to present it to the committee.

"I propose that we direct our local committees to adopt a new policy. Any club member who associates in any way with a professional promoter or any golf business will be banned from playing in any tournaments sanctioned by us – or the USGA."

He leaned over the table and stared directly at Avery Harmistand.

"We need to find a few prominent amateurs who associate with these thugs and make a very public example of them."

A chorus of like voices rose from all the men at the table: "Hear, hear."

Sargent smiled for the first time.

"Now, let's make a list of gentlemen to consider banning."

CHAPTER 40

Rock and Johnny stood in the shade of an umbrella and looked out from a distance at the 1st teeing ground of the Rockland Club of Newport. People milled up and down the edges of the fairway.

"I can't believe how many people have come out to see the match," Johnny said.

"We've sold over 8,000 tickets already," said Rock. He raised his eyebrows and smiled. "And 25 bookies have paid license fees."

Johnny could feel the brisk wind on his face and through his hair. Not good, he thought.

"How much did you collect at the Calcutta party last night?" Rock smiled again.

"$14,000. It was a wild night."

He laughed and slapped Johnny on the back.

"We're going to make a fortune, my friend," he said. "But you need to get ready. We begin in less than an hour."

"I'll be ready."

They turned to walk back to the clubhouse.

"I hope the wind dies down," Johnny said. "It must be gusting over 20 miles an hour. Those last five holes will be a bear. "

Rock nodded.

"You'll need to hit low runners today," he said. He stopped and pointed a finger at Johnny. "It's going to be on you, boy. Smith and McLeod are masters in the wind, and this weather doesn't favor Hagen's high ball game."

******

Rock was right. Smith and McLeod broke out to an early lead, shooting birdies on the first three holes, largely because they were better at accounting for the wind. But Johnny and Walter countered with an impressive string of four birdies and an eagle on the back nine, and at the end of the first day, after 18 of the 36 holes, Scranton and Hagen were one up.

The next day, the wind was worse. There were periods of strong gusts, then the wind would die down for brief periods. It seemed to be blowing in different directions. Smith and McLeod came out confident and they made up their deficit immediately, taking the first hole, and the match was back to level.

For the rest of the day, some 10,000 spectators witnessed some of the best shot-making they were ever likely to see. Despite the swirling wind, McLeod aced the 4th hole on a spectacular 85-yard pitch-and-run to the cup. Hagen holed out on the 8th from 160-yards for an eagle. On the par-5, 502-yard 11th hole, Johnny missed a double-eagle by inches when his second shot grazed the cup and rolled to the back of the green. By the time they reached the 36th hole of the match, Smith and McLeod were one. They needed only to tie the hole to win the richest stakes match in history.

The 18th hole was a 394-yard par 4 with a narrow entrance between three large open traps. The pin was tucked in the back right corner of a two-tiered green. Smith and McLeod hit dead straight tee shots and landed in the middle of the fairway. Johnny's drive landed on the right edge of the fairway. Hagen pulled his tee shot left and ended in a deep pot-hole bunker. He blasted out of the trap, then hit his third shot thin. His ball hit the face of the wind and dropped precipitously, 20 yards short of the green. When McLeod and Smith both hit their second shots on, McLeod beyond the pin and Smith beneath it, Hagen was effectively out of the hole.

Johnny knew, as he examined his second shot, that he had to make a perfect shot in order to send the match into extra holes. He stood staring at the distant flag whipping around in the swirling wind as it came off Narragansett Bay.

"What do you think?" he asked his caddy.

"You saw how Mr. Hagen's shot was knocked down by the wind. The wind is still heavy into you," he said. "I'd hit one more club to make sure you get back to the pin."

He pointed toward the upper tier of the green.

"If you don't land on that second tier, you won't have a chance for the birdie."

Johnny stood for a long time trying to determine where exactly to place the shot.

"Give me a mashie iron," he said finally.

He decided to play a low cut-shot so the ball would bite quickly. He shifted his weight forward and shortened his back swing. As the ball left the club face, Johnny knew that he had hit it perfectly. The ball stayed under the roiling wind, hit the right edge of the green, skipped once, and landed seven feet above the cup.

The crowds surged toward the 18th green as Hagen joined him near the narrow entrance to the green.

"Sorry, partner. I caught it thin. It's up to you now."

"That's okay," said Johnny. "I have a shot at the bird."

By the time Johnny and Walter got to the green, Smith and McLeod were already assessing their putts and talking strategy. McLeod left Smith crouched by his ball and walked over to them with an admiring smile on his face.

"Nice shot, mate," he said to Johnny as he circled behind the hole in order to determine the exact break at the cup. "You didn't let us off easy."

Smith had a 25-foot straight uphill putt from the lower tier for his birdie. McLeod's second shot had landed twenty feet above the hole, beyond and to the right of Johnny's ball.

"I had the same putt yesterday," Smith said as he conferred with his partner. "It's risky to go for it. There's a tricky break near the cup, and the ball's down the slope if you overshoot. You could end up down by me."

They walked to the front of the pin to look at the angle left for McLeod by Johnny's position near the cup. Smith crouched down again and used his putter to point from the pin to McLeod's ball, then swept his club back along an imagined line to a spot between Johnny's ball and the cup.

Johnny and Walter watched from a polite distance but they knew immediately what the plan would be, even before Smith suggested it.

Smith stood upright, worked his jaw around, then looked at McLeod and said, "I think you should go for the stymie. Johnny's been too hot with his putter to give him a chance at a clear seven-footer."

McLeod nodded.

"I think you're right," he said. "I'll shoot short of the cup and try to block him. If it rolls a little too far and goes in, all the better."

McLeod was an acknowledged master of the stymie. He had stymied Harry Vardon on the last hole of the 1908 Open and had won the Burkdale Invitational in 1910 with an 18th-hole stymie of Jerry Travers. But this shot was more difficult than the others: he needed to place the ball nearly perfectly on the top edge of a small incline. He walked over once more to make sure he knew the spot where the treacherous slope began. Then, with surprising speed and confidence, he set himself, squared his bullnose putter, and gently stroked the ball.

As if by magic, the ball stopped on the edge of the slope, one foot from the cup and directly in the path of Johnny's ball. Johnny was stymied.

McLeod had placed his ball so close to the cup that Johnny didn't have the room to curve his own ball around the stymie and reach the cup without it rolling away down the incline. His only option was to try to lift the ball over McLeod's and catch the edge of the cup straight on. He motioned to his caddy to bring him the special Wright and Ditson beveled putter that he had used at Blue Marsh four years earlier.

He felt the weight of the club in two practice strokes, then he stepped up to the ball, leaned back on the putter with most of his weight on his right side, and gently lifted his ball directly over McLeod's. The ball looked headed for the center of the cup but a sudden gust of wind swept across the green and the ball veered left and landed two inches off the far rim. It caught the green for a second then rolled down the incline.

Johnny leaned over to watch his ball come to a stop, then he stood for a moment with his hands on his knees. Hagen came over and consoled his friend.

"We can't control the wind, Johnny" he said with a shrug of this shoulders.

Then they walked over to McLeod and Smith, and Johnny offered a handshake to the man who had stymied him.

"I concede your putt, Fred," he said, pushing forth a smile. "Congratulations. Great match and great stymie."

McLeod was characteristically gracious. "We all know that the wind won this for us, Johnny. Great match."

****

The next day The Providence Express had a banner head-line proclaiming the match to be *"One of the Greatest Displays of Golf Ever Seen."*

"Scranton and Hagen Defeated by the Best Players in the World," the Boston Examiner headline read.

The Boston American announced, *"Johnny Scranton misses by inches a putt on the 36th hole which would have sent the match into extra holes."*

The New York Voice, in bold lettering, referred to the match as, *"The finest hour for professional golf in America."*

"A new day is dawning for American golf," The London Herald reported.

And the New York Daily proclaimed, *"We can play with the best from England."*

Johnny and Walter shared $12,000 from the Calcutta, and Rock magnanimously added another $4,000 per team from his bookie fees.

"My God, Johnny!" Mary screamed when he opened his leather bag and shook out more than $8,000 in cash on the bed in their hotel room. She was covering her mouth with her hands and jumping up and down. "I've never seen so much money. You're rich! You're rich!"

"No, I'm not," said Johnny.

Mary stopped jumping. She looked confused.

"What do you mean?" she said. "Look at all this money."

"I'm not rich," he said.

He paused.

"We're rich."

Mary's hands were still clasped together in front of her mouth. She looked as if she might be praying. She slowly repeated what Johnny had said.

"We're rich. What do you mean?"

"I mean,"–Johnny stepped nearer to her and knelt down on one knee–"I mean . . . will you marry me?"

Mary pulled down on her lower lip with the fingertips of her clasped hands so that her open mouth formed a perfect O. She looked dazed for a moment, then her O turned to a brilliant smile and she threw her arms around Johnny's neck and pressed her face into his chest.

"Yes, yes, yes, my love," she cried. "I've been waiting for you to say those words since our first night on the beach in Harwichport."

She leaned her head back and looked up into his eyes.

"I fell in love with you that first night."

Johnny gazed into her sparkling eyes.

"I now realize that I also fell in love with you that night. It's taken me this long to get up the nerve to ask you."

A small tear appeared in the right corner of his eye. Mary gently brushed it away and their kiss was sweet and tender. Johnny brushed the money off the bed and lifted her into his arms. They missed their dinner date with George and Jennifer.

* * * * * *

The phone rang in George's hotel room, waking him from a sound sleep.

"George, I need you and Jennifer to meet me at the courthouse in downtown Providence at 2."

"What's up?" a groggy George asked. He looked at his pocket watch. It was 6:45 in the morning.

"I'll tell you at the courthouse," said Johnny.

George could hear Mary's voice in the background.

"Oh, yeah, I almost forgot," said Johnny. "Be sure to wear

something nice. See ya."

Jennifer figured it out before they ever entered the grand foyer of the courthouse. Walter Hagen was talking with Johnny and Mary near the clerk's office. All three were dressed to the nines and Mary was holding a small bouquet.

"Johnny, I can't believe you two are doing this right now," Jennifer said. "What about your dad? What about Mary's dad?"

Mary smiled. She was swaying back and forth in excitement, slowly spinning the bouquet around in her hands.

"They're okay with it. Johnny called my dad this morning and asked for my hand over the phone," she said. "We're heading back to Harwichport this weekend and we'll renew our vows this summer with the whole family. That'll be the big wedding, but this is the one that counts."

"My God," said Jennifer, her face lighting up with happiness. "You're really going to do it. Can I see the ring?"

They had purchased the ring at Sheridan Jewelers near the railroad station. Mr. Sheridan worked miracles to get the ring ready by 2. Mary had selected a polished gold setting with a large diamond in the middle and two smaller diamonds on each side. Jennifer had never seen anything like it. It was the most expensive ring Mr. Sheridan had sold in two years.

"Come on, gang," Walter said. "I have to catch a train back to New York. Let's get these folks hitched."

Mary took charge.

"Jennifer, will you be my maid of honor? And, George, of course, you'll be Johnny's best man."

"Of course," said Jennifer, obviously thrilled.

She curtsied.

"It will be my pleasure, ma'am." She was almost giggling with excitement.

Johnny pulled George away from the group for a moment while they waited for the clerk to process their marriage certificate. Once apart, he looked upset. He spoke quietly to his oldest and closest friend.

"I'm sorry, George," he said. "Mary sort of jumped the gun there. She's pretty excited. But I wanted to ask you myself."

George smiled. This mattered to him.

"Thanks, Johnny," he said. "But I didn't think any different. We're best friends and we always will be."

George gave him a hug. "She's a great girl. Congratulations."

The ceremony lasted ten minutes. The Chief Magistrate of the Court cancelled his lunch plans and presided at the wedding. It was not everyday that the Magistrate's Office had such storied personalities visit his court. Walter had leaked the story to a friend at the Providence Express, and a photographer was stationed at the clerk's office. The Magistrate asked the photographer to take a few photos during the wedding which he planned to use in his next election brochures. The next day the paper ran a front-page story about the stakes match and the surprise wedding.

"Do you think they'll cover our wedding in the same way?" George asked as he read the article.

"I hope not," Jennifer said with a slight smile. "Elegant but quiet for us, darling."

CHAPTER 41

George was anxious as he waited to meet Charles Pierce, Senior Vice President of the First National Bank of Boston. Pierce was the youngest account executive appointed to a Senior Vice President level in the bank's history. He directed the Special Projects Division, which was currently focused on two investment portfolios: golf course construction and corporate business parks.

The waiting room outside Pierce's sixth-floor office was lined with photographs of the bank's executive staff. On his first day on the job George had seen the photo gallery and vowed to have his picture on the wall within five years. As he sat waiting to meet Pierce, he reflected on the previous hectic three weeks – his graduation from Brown, Jennifer's graduation from Pembroke, and their wedding just one week later. They were married in a quiet ceremony at the Pawtucket Yacht Club and a sober Johnny Scranton served as George's best man.

"I want to get Riley immediately involved in the Special Projects Division," Pierce said, as he talked with Horace Sullivan, the head of the commercial loan department, before they met with George. "I want him to go through the commercial loan training program on an accelerated basis. With all of his golf contacts, this kid can be a gold mine for the bank." He spoke to Sullivan as if he were sharing privileged information with him. "You know, Belle LaCree just moved her portfolio to the bank and she made it clear that she wants Riley managing some of her investments."

"We made a commitment that he would get time off to

practice and play in tournaments," Sullivan said, looking straight at Pierce to see his reaction, hoping that this had been the right thing to do.

"Good. That's part of the plan. He'll make contacts and create business for the bank that we'd never have access to without him."

Pierce tapped on a folder on his desk.

"Golf experts estimate that over a thousand new golf courses will be built in the United States in the next ten years. There's going to be more than two million new golfers. The popularity of the sport is exploding, and I want us to be positioned to provide construction and operating loans for these clubs."

Pierce picked up his intercom.

"Edith, can you send in Mr. Riley, please?"

Pierce and Sullivan stood to greet their new protégé as he was shown into the mahogany-paneled office. Pierce thrust out his hand to shake George's hand.

"George, welcome to the Bank of Boston," he said.

"Thank you, Mr. Pierce," George said. "I'm happy to be working here."

"Good," said Pierce. He picked up the folder from his desk. "We have lots of things planned for you to do. First, let's talk about your golf assignments."

******

George reveled in his new duties at the bank. Each week he was involved in a new project and even enjoyed the numerous corporate golf events he was assigned to in order to pitch new products offered by the commercial loan department. Some days he would arrive home at 10 p.m. and be out the door the next day for an 8 a.m. meeting. He made sure he balanced his work duties with his family responsibilities – each week he was home at least two evenings for dinner, and Saturday and Sunday were reserved exclusively for the family.

Denise Brower, George's secretary, became the vital link in keeping him organized and on schedule. She had been chosen to work with the new young star of the bank upon his arrival in the commercial loan department. She was in her mid-forties, diminutive, had long, silky red hair down to her shoulders, and spoke with a slight Southern accent. She had been with the bank for 22 years and had most recently been senior secretary in the commercial loan audit division. The "girls" in the typing pool were jealous when she was chosen to be George's new secretary.

"George, Mr. Pierce's secretary called. He wants you to join him in ten minutes in his office."

"Okay," said George, looking up from the stack of papers on his desk. "I just need to finish this work-up on the Saugus commercial loan."

Denise stepped farther into the room. She was an impeccable dresser. She wore a white silk blouse with a high starched collar, a blue wool jacket and matching mitsey skirt.

"I just read the article in the Boston Traveler about the South Shore Amateur yesterday. Did you really shoot a 71, one under par, George?"–she pronounced his name "Geoge," as if the "r" was silent. "That's fantastic."

"I got lucky. I kept the ball in play and didn't get in trouble."

Denise was thrilled to be assigned to George. He was modest and sweet and polite, like her own son would be if she had one, she thought. And he was good-looking and a hard worker to boot. You could do a lot worse in the bank than to have George as your boss.

George finished the paperwork and then rode the elevator to the sixth floor. "They're waiting for you. Go right in," said Edith.

When George entered the office Pierce was half sitting and half leaning on the front of his desk. He seemed to be staring off into space. Bill Rice from public relations was seated in the corner reviewing a press release.

"Hi, George," said Pierce, snapping back to the moment. "Come in and sit down."

He looked toward Rice.

"You're up, Bill."

Rice was an affable, comfortably handsome man and the hands-down best dresser at First National. George enjoyed thinking of him as the Walter Hagen of the bank.

Rice stood up and moved to a chair that was located closer to George and Pierce.

"I guess you're wondering why we asked you up here," he said. "I understand that you've registered to play in the U.S. Open next week at The Country Club."

George nodded.

"Yes. I sent in my application last week. They say it's going to be the largest field in the history of the tournament."

"That works for us," said Rice. "We plan to invite our best commercial customers to a meet-and-greet dinner at the Ritz on Wednesday night before the tournament begins."

"The qualifier is Tuesday and Wednesday," George explained. "The field is so large that they've decided to divide the qualifier into two days, two rounds on Tuesday and another two rounds on Wednesday."

Pierce passed a paper to George.

"This is a list of the players we'd like to invite. What do you think?"

The list included some of the best players in the world: Harry Vardon, Ted Ray, Alec Smith, Robert McDonald, Jack Hobens,

George Sargent, Jim Barnes.

One name was notably absent.

"I don't see Walter Hagen's name on the list," said George.

Pierce and Rice exchanged glances.

"I hear he's a bit wild," said a skeptical Rice. "Do you think it's a good idea to invite him?"

George found it amusing that the Walter Hagen of the bank mistrusted the Walter Hagen of golf. He shook his head and then smiled.

"Walter's fun," he said. "You don't need to worry about him. He'll be the hit of the party." He looked over the list again. "You should also invite Heinrich Schmidt from Worcester too. He's a new client."

"Okay, George. They're both on the list," said Pierce.

"And you can take Johnny Scranton off," said George. "He's not playing in the Open this year. He's injured."

George didn't mention that Johnny had fallen off a ladder and had broken his arm while hanging a picture for Mary. Being a husband was taking a toll on the new Johnny Scranton.

Pierce leaned back in his chair and lit a pipe.

"I hear Vardon and Ray are the men to beat."

George nodded.

"The USGA specifically rescheduled the tournament from June until September so they could play," he said. "They've played six exhibition matches at The Country Club since they arrived last week and haven't lost yet. Vardon shot a 71 in his match with Nipper Campbell and Louis Teller."

"Who else do you like?" asked Rice.

"You never know who'll get hot," said George. "But Campbell, Teller, Barnes, MacDonald Smith, Jerry Travers, George Sargent – they all have a chance."

"You beat Sargent at Myopia last month in the Hunt Club Invitational, didn't you?" said Rice.

Good memory, thought George. He nodded in response.

"I did. I got a lucky break when his birdie putt on 18 lipped the cup. I went on to win the extra hole."

George had, in fact, played well all summer. In four amateur tournaments, he had won two and finished in the top ten in the other two.

"Of course, there'll be the local favorite," George added. "Alex Campbell, the head pro at The Country Club. He knows the course backwards and forwards."

"What about your friend Francis Ouimet?" Rice asked.

"He's a solid player and a great guy," said George. "I hope he does well, but it's unlikely that Francis will win this tournament. This is his first time playing on a stage as big as the Open."

"This is a great opportunity for you," Pierce said. He smiled broadly as he guided George toward the door. He patted him on the back as he added with some emphasis, "and for the bank."

He walked with George all the way to the elevator, something he had never done before.

"I'm counting on you to get these players to join us Wednesday night, George. It will impress our clients to no end."

As he rode down the elevator back to his own office, George felt confident that he could get the players on the list to show up for the meet-and-greet. What he wondered about was how he would measure up against the best golfers in the world.

CHAPTER 42

Because of the large number of entrants for the 1913 U.S. Open, the players trying to qualify were divided: 84 players were scheduled to play their two qualifying rounds on Tuesday, and 84 players were scheduled for Wednesday's qualifying rounds. George was scheduled to play on Tuesday. As he entered the clubhouse, he suddenly felt a wave of nausea wash over him. He had never had this reaction to pressure before. Why now? he thought.

As he sat in the locker room changing into his golfing clothes and trying to settle his stomach, he spotted Francis Ouimet.

"Francis, how are you?" he asked in a muted tone.

Francis peeked over the locker-bay railing.

"Hey, George. Nice to see you." Francis sounded genuinely pleased. "How've you been?"

"Very well, thank you. They keep me busy at the bank."

"How's Jennifer?" Francis asked. "I'm sorry that I couldn't make it down to Pawtucket for the wedding. I've been working at Wright and Ditson. They're so good about giving me time off for tournaments that I feel like I should be working almost all the other days."

George smiled. His stomach grumbled.

"I know what you mean. It's the same with me," he said. "I saw where you won the Massachusetts Amateur, and you had a great showing in the National Amateur at Garden City."

Francis nodded.

"I've been fortunate to play well this summer–except for the last two days."

"What do you mean?"

"I played two practice rounds at Wellesley and shot 88 both days. Can you believe it?"

"You're kidding. You set the course record there, 66, right?"

"Doesn't matter now," said Francis. "I just hope I got all the bad golf I had in me out of my system." He laughed softly, then he remembered something. "Hey, I thought Johnny would be here today. I didn't see his name on the board."

"He broke his arm doing chores around the house. He's laid up for a few weeks."

Francis laughed again. Then he looked a little embarrassed.

"I'm sorry," he said. "I don't mean to laugh. I wish he could play. But Johnny Scranton married! What'll they think of next?"

George couldn't help but laugh too. It was funny when you thought about it. Francis bent over to tie his shoe.

"I saw Walter Hagen's name on the list of qualifiers."

"Yes, he'll be here. I haven't seen him yet, though," said George.

"Will you introduce me? I've never met him."

"Sure. But, don't worry: when Walter arrives you'll know him. He makes a huge splash." George reached over for his bag and his stomach made a gurgling sound. "Come on," he said. "Let's hit some balls. We need to steady our nerves."

He put his arm on Francis' shoulder and guided him out of the locker bay.

******

On the practice tee, Francis spied a dapper young man dressed in a white silk shirt, a plaid bow tie, white flannel pants with the cuffs turned up, and white buckskin shoes with thick red rubber soles. He was driving ball after ball long, high, and

HONOUR

311

straight. This must be Walter Hagen, he thought.

"Walter!" George cried out. "It's great to see you again."

Hagen immediately walked over to them, a wide grin spread across his face.

"Hi, George. Last time I saw you, you were dodging the bouquet at Johnny's wedding," he said, his voice close to breaking with laughter.

George smiled but didn't laugh. He gestured toward Francis.

"Walter, I want to introduce you to my good friend and neighbor, Francis Ouimet. Johnny and I have played with Francis since high school."

Hagen flashed his winning grin again.

"Francis, I'm glad to finally meet you," he said warmly.

Francis was impressed by the strength of his handshake.

"And me, you," said Francis. "Somehow we keep missing each other. I've followed you, though. That was a great match you and Johnny played against Smith and McLeod in Newport. I wish I could have been there."

"I'm still upset over that loss," Walter said, looking pained. "Truth is I didn't help Johnny much down the stretch. I went cold at the end." He shook his head. "I thought his putt on 18 was going in."

Just then Walter was distracted by a young lady in the gallery who had been waving to him and calling his name. She wore a lace dress with cutoff sleeves that flattered her well-tanned arms. Hagen pointed to her.

"As you can see, one of my nieces needs my attention before I tee off," he said. He smiled again. "Nice to meet you, Francis."

He winked at George and then trotted off toward the gallery.

****

George opened with a solid 77, but during the afternoon round his confidence faded. He struggled to hit his drives straight and he lost consistency with his mid-irons. He could feel himself lose focus, and no matter what he tried he couldn't get back on track. He shot nine over par on the last five holes alone and closed out with a disappointing 89 for a two-round total of 166.

Heinrich Schmidt was standing near the scorer's tent as George walked out after signing his card. George gave him a meek wave.

"Heinrich, hello. How'd you do today?"

"Hi, George." Heinrich shrugged and shook his head. "I didn't play well. Shot 80 this afternoon on top of an 81 this morning. How about you?"

Just the question seemed to depress George. He put his hands in his pockets and looked disgusted.

"I shot a 166. I don't know what happened. I couldn't make a shot on the last five holes. I've never played this badly before when it mattered."

Heinrich nodded to show his empathy.

"I know the feeling. Same thing happened to me in the Western Massachusetts Amateur. I was playing well and suddenly I started hitting erratic shots. The more I concentrated, the worse it got. It's never happened again, thank goodness." He slapped his massive mitt of a hand on George's back. "So let that go. It's done. Let's just hope we make the cut and play better on Thursday."

George nodded yes weakly. Heinrich pulled a small pad of paper from his coat pocket.

"George," he said, "can I ask you a few questions about your round? I'm a special correspondent for the Boston Traveler during the tournament. They want me to write about the local guys."

Heinrich a correspondent? That's interesting, thought George.

"Sure," he said. Then a question occurred to him. "Do you happen to know how Francis did today?"

"Ouimet?" Heinrich flipped through his pad. "74 and 78 for a 152. Finished just behind Harry Vardon at 151."

"That's great!" George exclaimed. That Francis had done so well made George feel a bit better. At least someone from the neighborhood had a good day.

Heinrich had produced a pencil and was licking its point. It looked tiny in his hand.

"Now. Tell me about your round, please."

****

Tuesday's cut line was set at 166, so George and Heinrich were among the players selected from the Tuesday qualifiers. By Wednesday night, the full field of 66 players was complete.

George rushed home from work on Wednesday evening, changed into fresh clothes, and headed to the bank's party at the Ritz. News had spread quickly about First National Bank's George making the cut, and he became the cause celebre at the party. Senior staff from the bank patted him on the back and offered congratulations. He was embarrassed by all the attention, so he was glad when Walter arrived accompanied by two young ladies who were in the touring company of the Broadway hit "Angel."

Hagen immediately replaced George as the center of attention. He was wearing a white tux with tails and the women wore long flowing gowns as if they were outfitted for an evening whirl at the swankiest New York hot spots. He exuberantly regaled the enraptured guests with stories of his exploits and conquests on and off the course. In all, seven of the nine players George personally invited attended the party, including Harry Vardon, who made a brief appearance before he retired for the evening.

Pierce was beaming, delighted at the success of his plan and of his protégé.

"How did you get all of these guys to come?" he asked George.

"I promised them good food and expensive drinks, and I made sure to remind them in person earlier today," George said. He smiled. "And I gave their caddies a copy of the invitation with ten bucks slipped inside. The caddies are really the key."

Pierce was smiling as his car came around to pick him up after the party. He envisioned a sparkling future for his young associate – and George's success would reflect well on his mentor.

CHAPTER 43

The 19th U.S. Open was scheduled with the first two rounds to be played on Thursday, September 18, and–with the field reduced by cuts–the final two rounds to be played Friday, September 19. Play began promptly Thursday with Charles Murray and Wilfred Reid teeing off at 8 a.m. George was paired with William McDougal, and they followed the Murray/Reid twosome. Heinrich was in the twosome directly behind George, and the two friends chatted as they waited to tee off.

George saw Francis walking briskly towards them.

"I came to wish you both good luck today," he said in a slow, deliberate tone. "I'm sorry that I couldn't join you last night at the Ritz, George."

"You missed a grand party, Ouimet," Heinrich declared, much more loudly than Francis was speaking.

"When do you tee off, Francis?" George asked.

"I'm with Karl Keffer at 10:30. You guys can set the pace."

"It's more the fox being chased by the hounds," Heinrich lamented. "And there are lots of talented hounds out here." He counted on his fingers. "Ted Ray was medalist in the qualifier at 148. Wilfred Reid and Robert McDonald both shot 72's in one of their rounds yesterday. Harry Vardon shot 75 and 76. And John McDermott, he's won the title the last two years. All tough acts to follow."

"Don't forget Francis," George interrupted.

He shoved Heinrich's shoulder.

"He shot 74 and 78. He was in the top ten qualifiers."

"So now I guess I've become one of your hounds, Heinrich!"

Francis laughed as he headed off to the practice tee.

****

Neither George nor Heinrich played well during the first two rounds on Thursday and were far below the Friday cut-line of 49 players. George was more consistent than during the qualifier, but not to any great benefit: he shot twin 82's, and his 164 total missed the mid-tournament cut by a stroke. Heinrich faired far worse, shooting 81-96-177, with a mortifying 11 on the 16th hole in his afternoon round. In fact it was a difficult day for most of the 66 men who had qualified. Two-thirds of the players failed to break 80 in either round, and only nine players were within five strokes of the daunting 147 put up by co-leaders Harry Vardon and Wilfred Reid. The leading amateur was Brookline's own Francis Ouimet, who shot a respectable 77-74-151. Half way through the tournament, he was in seventh place, tied with Walter Hagen, four strokes off the lead.

******

On Friday, the trolley from Newton to Brookline was packed with spectators headed to the Open. A cold front had swept through overnight and heavy rain had fallen, turning the grounds into a sea of mud. The Boston Examiner proclaimed in its front page headline, *Advantage English Players At Brookline*, and touted Vardon and Ray as the odds-on favorites to win the tournament. As he walked up to the grounds of the Club, George noticed Lucas Griffin, the bookie from Salem, taking bets outside the front gate. He had not seen Lucas in four years, since the tournament at Blue Marsh.

George stepped up behind him and tapped on his shoulder. "This is God awful weather to be selling bets, Lucas."

Lucas smiled as soon as he saw who it was.

"George! How are you? I haven't seen you in a long time."

Lucas was nervously looking around to see if anyone was near. He had been roused by agents for the club earlier and had become more careful about his business transactions. George could see that he was uneasy.

"I've noticed they have extra guards for this Open," he said.

"Believe me, I've noticed too," Lucas said with disgust. "Look at this crowd. I could be making a fortune if I was inside."

The frustration was clear in his voice.

"There must be 10,000 fans here and it's only 8 a.m."

George felt bad for Lucas but he had come to favor a total ban on bookmaking at tournaments. Once it was allowed at all, there seemed to be no good way to control it, and the game was awash in tainted gambling and unscrupulous pool selling. In England there had recently been a series of scandals in which bookmakers were accused of giving players bribes to throw matches. George wanted nothing to do with this type of competition. There was no point in sharing his opinion with Lucas at the moment, though. Better to make small talk, he thought.

"I heard they're cracking down on gambling at tournaments," George said.

Lucas misunderstood.

"Don't worry about it, George," he said quickly, his eyes darting around. "I can take your bet."

He produced his book and read off his odds.

"I got Vardon and Ray at 1-3, not much to earn there. Reid's 1-2. Everybody else can make you some cash, though. Barnes is 3-1, Ross 4-1, Teller 5-1."

He looked up at George's face expectantly. "Who do you like?"

George's curiosity was pricked.

"How about Francis Ouimet? What are his odds?"

Lucas nodded.

"That's right, you boys are friends," he said. "I have Frances at 9-1. It's a good payoff, George" – he made a sad face – "but to tell you the truth, I think this weather kills his chances."

"Francis might surprise a few people," George said. He held his hand up and waved it slightly. "But no bets for me, Lucas."

Lucas nodded again.

"You're not really a betting man, are you, George?"

George shook his head no and turned to leave. He turned back around and said, "Don't get caught by the Pinkertons. I hear they're brutal."

He was against gambling, but he didn't dislike Lucas.

****

During Friday's morning round, only seventeen of the remaining 49 players in the field broke 80. George followed Vardon for the first nine holes, then switched over to follow Hagen. Both played well in horrible conditions–Vardon shot a 78 and Hagen a 76. The surprise of the third round, though, was Francis, who slogged through the heavy morning rain to shoot an impressive 74 to catch Vardon and Ray. After 54 holes the three shared the lead at 225.

The crowds swelled as word spread that a local boy from Brookline had surged to the top of the leader board.

Ray and Vardon went off early in the fourth and final round that afternoon, and they posted identical scores of 79 for four round totals of 304. Hagen began the fourth round in spectacular fashion, scoring the only eagle of the tournament on the 4th hole. He hit his drive down the middle of the 300-yard hole and then hit a mashie directly into the middle of the green.

The ball hit dead stick and dropped into the hole for an eagle 2. He birdied the next three holes and as he took the turn, he too had pulled even with Vardon and Ray.

George rushed over to watch Walter as he walked down the par-5, 10th to his second shot of the hole. Hagen chose his brassie from his bag, having decided to go for the green despite the fact that it was partially obscured by the fog that had set in with the rain and cold. As his club descended, Walter slipped on the wet turf and the ball scooted wildly about 60 yards down the fairway. Walter threw up his hands in disgust.

"Shit! I can't stop slipping in these shoes," he cried, loud enough for the fans lining the fairway to hear.

His outburst drew George's attention to his red rubber-soled shoes. He was wearing snazzy two-tones that looked as if they had been chosen to match his sweater. Walter's love of fashion was coming back to haunt him on the soggy back nine.

George was standing to the front of the crowd, and directly behind him.

"Walter!" he called out. "Do you want me to run back and get you a different pair of shoes?"

Walter looked around, confused for a moment, and then he saw George.

"No thanks, George," he shouted back, shaking his head and waving him off. "I'll be okay."

Hagen headed to his third shot, still shaking his head and now saying something to himself. When he got to the ball and saw his lie, he stared at the flag for a moment then suddenly kicked the turf hard with his right foot. At that point he was so frustrated that he topped the third shot and went on to double bogey the hole. He finished the hole three shots off the pace of Vardon and Ray, who had already finished as the leaders in the clubhouse.

Meanwhile George crossed over to follow Francis. He had heard that he had played a tough front nine and also had lost ground to the leaders. George caught up with him as he lined up a niblick for his second shot on the 330-yard 13th hole. He mis-hit the shot and the ball landed 30 feet short of the hole in the tall rough to the right of the fairway.

"I hit that one fat," George heard him say to himself.

George knew exactly what Francis was feeling. Hitting a niblick off the heel of the club face was probably one of the worst feelings in golf.

Francis spent a considerable amount of time examining his next shot. He walked up to the flag and bent down to gauge the break. He played with the clubs in his bag for a minute or two before he finally selected a mid iron. Smart, thought George: take it easy, give yourself time to calm down. Finally, a fully composed Francis walked up to his shot, cooly cupped the head of his club in, and chipped the ball with a short snap of his wrist. To the excited cheers of the spectators, the ball hit the stick and dropped into the cup.

A smiling Francis saw George on the walkway to the 14th tee ground and waved.

"Maybe I can get a string going," he said as he walked by him.

A string was what he needed, Francis was still two strokes behind Vardon and Ray. He needed two birdies and no bogies over the last five holes to pull even. It wasn't a day that was giving up pars, much less birdies, very easily.

By the 17th, Francis had pulled even. He shot par on the 18th to end tied with Vardon and Ray after the full 72 holes. The three would play an eighteen-hole playoff the next day.

George found Francis in a throng of ecstatic well-wishers in the locker room. He was rain-soaked and looked tired, but

George had never seen him look happier. Francis pushed himself away from the crowd and came over to George.

"Francis, I'm so proud of you. The kid from the neighborhood came to play."

"Thank you, George," said Francis. He let out a long breath. "It's a long way from our days at Blue Hills."

The next day, once again in pouring rain and on a soft, muddy course, George witnessed what he would always regard as a miracle. Ted Ray shot a respectable 78. Harry Vardon shot a solid 77. And Francis Ouimet, the 20-year-old amateur who lived across the street, playing against two of the most famous and accomplished golfers in the world, shot an astonishing 72 to win the 1913 U.S. Open. At the conclusion of the round Francis was lifted by the crowd and carried off the green to thunderous applause. Golf in America would be changed forever. Francis Ouimet, the humble, quiet kid who could be any boy in any neighborhood, became the national symbol of that change. His win was great for golf–and especially amateur golf.

CHAPTER 44

June 17, 1915 • Citrus Country Club • Tampa, Florida

Harold Crosby noticed a lone figure standing on the practice tee as he closed the door to the maintenance shed. As head groundskeeper at the Citrus Country Club, Harold was always the first to arrive and the last to leave. The season was winding down now and few members stayed late in the heat and humidity. The club was to close June 25 and Harold was looking forward to his two months off to travel and relax with his family before they reopened in early September.

The light was fading and the radiance from the new moon cast a glow over the course. Harold hopped into his car and drove to the practice tee to check on this mysterious person. Who in his right mind would be out hitting balls at twilight? Harold wondered. As he approached the practice area, he could see a haggard-looking Johnny Scranton hunched over two half-empty buckets of balls.

Harold parked the T at an angle so the lights wouldn't shine in Johnny's eyes.

"Johnny," he shouted, "How long have you been out here?"

Johnny turned toward the car lights.

"Hi, Harold. It's going to be a beautiful night. I'm almost finished."

Harold got out of the car, sensing there was something wrong with his friend. Harold had been one of Johnny's strongest supporters when he had been having his problems. He had lobbied the club president to keep Johnny as head pro during his rehabilitation period, and he had taken it upon himself to help him stay on track once he'd returned to the club in 1912.

For two good years, Johnny seemed healthy and happy whenever Harold saw him. But what he had seen in these last six months concerned him. Johnny had become increasingly moody and withdrawn and looked tired all the time. Harold hadn't seen him using the Elixir or drinking, but he'd had some problems himself, and he knew the signs of a relapse. He walked over to the practice tee and sat on a nearby bench. He spread his arms out across the top of the bench's back and settled in.

"How you doing, my friend?" he said. "I only ask 'cause you look like shit."

Harold didn't see the point of pulling punches with people. It made more sense to him to say what he thought.

Johnny smiled.

"I've developed this loop at the top of my swing. I've tried every trick I know, but I can't get rid of it. It's driving me crazy."

Johnny had gone on a tear during 1913 and 1914. He had played in over twenty tournaments and stakes matches, won seven, finished in the top ten in twelve of the tournaments, and won over $138,000 in two years. By January, 1915, however, Johnny's right hand had started to shake and he was having difficulty sleeping. Mary made an appointment with a neurological specialist in Tampa. After extensive tests showed no new damage, the best the doctor could suggest was for Johnny to take time off to rest himself and his hand.

Johnny thought differently. He'd always solved his golf problems with more practice, and he insisted to Mary that this was just a golf problem. He tried to satisfy her protests by withdrawing from a tournament in Fort Meyers at the end of January. But then he shifted back into high gear: he played in nine of the remaining winter tournaments dotting the South from February through May. He failed even to make the cut in six. And as he pressed on, his swing developed this strange loop because he needed to compensate for the shaking in his hand. So Johnny had heard it before when Harold offered his opinion.

"You need to take some real time off, buddy," Harold said. "Why don't you go to the Cape for the summer until we start up again in September? Don't play, just rest. It would do you good."

Johnny gave Harold's suggestion an unenthusiastic shrug.

"I don't know, Harold. Maybe I'll take off August, but I have this tournament in Jacksonville next week, and then I join George up in Worcester for the Cary Invitational the following week."

Harold indicated his disagreement by waving his right hand without moving his arm from the back of the bench.

"Screw Jacksonville," he said. "And you know George will understand if you drop out."

Johnny became more adamant. "I can't. I've made commitments and I need to honor them."

He tapped his driver on the ground at his side. He started to talk fast, as if more to himself than Harold. "I just need to be more consistent. I've shortened my back swing to keep the club head steady at the top. I'm beginning to get rid of this damn loop. I've talked with Rock and it's like he's always said—work through it and the loop will disappear."

"Yeah." Harold drew the word out and made a quiet smacking sound at the end of it. "I'm not talking about your swing, Johnny." He spoke slowly—almost harshly, to Johnny's mind. "Maybe your body's telling you to slow down because you're tired."

Johnny looked dazed. He stood without answering for a long moment, out of rhythm with the conversation. Then he said, "Okay. I hear you. I hear you." Almost as an afterthought he added, "Mary's found this natural herb that helps people sleep. I'm going to start using it before Jacksonville. We'll see how it works."

Harold looked unconvinced, but he saw no reason to push any harder. Johnny was going to do what Johnny was going to do. He stood up from the bench and stretched his neck and shoulders.

"Well, if you insist on working in the dark, like some kind of damn raccoon," he said, "the least I can do is give you some light."

He climbed into the T and drove the car all the way up on to the practice teeing area behind Johnny so he would have enough light to see what he was hitting. For the next hour, Harold slept in the car while Johnny worked on his swing.

****

Mary accompanied Johnny to the Jacksonville tournament the following week, and as soon as the last round was complete, they left the club to catch the overnight train to Boston. The train was late arriving at South Street Station, and Johnny's dad had waited on the platform for over two hours. There was a chill in the late June night air as the remnants of a cold and rainy spring lingered into early summer. The big New Haven Railroad locomotive screeched to a halt, and the first off the slumber car were Mary and Johnny.

Mary walked quickly up to Charles and gave him a big kiss on the cheek.

"Hi, Dad."

Johnny gave him a hug but said nothing. Charles stepped back from his son to look more closely at him. Johnny looked drawn and gaunt.

"How was your trip, son?" he asked. "You look tired."

Mary could hear the concern in Charles' voice. She took his arm so he would turn toward her.

"We were delayed in New York because of the railway strike," she said.

Charles frowned. He was convinced that unions were a bad idea in general. If you made your own money, you had a right to spend it the way you wanted to. He shook his head.

"These unions are always flexing their muscles."

He caught himself. He didn't want to start arguing with them right away. "How long can you stay?"

Johnny sounded tired when he responded.

"George and I play in the Cary National Pro-Am in Worcester next week. Then I catch the tour at its next stop in Canton, Ohio, the first week in July."

"I wish you could stay longer. You could rest up. I know you've had a tough run."

Johnny didn't say anything. Mary waited for him then looped her arm in his.

"It's been a difficult year so far," she said, nodding. She offered her proudest smile. "But we have good news. Johnny won the tournament yesterday in Jacksonville."

Charles perked up at the announcement.

"Great!" he said. "Tell me all about it on the way home."

Johnny moved slowly as they put the bags in the car. Charles noticed that his son was pale and that his hand would occasionally shake. He silently prayed that this wasn't because of drinking or, God forbid, drugs again.

****

The phone at the Scranton home rang early. Johnny and Mary were sound asleep when his dad knocked on the door.

"Johnny. Bob Johnson is on the phone."

"What the hell does he want this early?"

Johnny stumbled to the first floor phone.

"Bob. Is everything okay?"

"Hi, Johnny," said the familiar but scratchy and distant-sounding voice on the phone. "I got a call from Buddy Rollins, the Rules Chair at Jacksonville. He said he's been trying to find you."

Johnny yawned away from the phone.

"We left for Boston right after the tournament ended. I didn't attend the awards dinner. I just grabbed the check and we darted for the train."

"He said they'd gotten a complaint from one of the players that you'd used an illegal ball during the final round. They tried to contact you but you were already gone, so they talked with your caddy. He told them that you used the Victor 31 just for that round. They disqualified you and awarded the championship to Jimmy Smitten."

"What! They disqualified me over a golf ball?"

Johnny laughed, part in disbelief and part in anger.

"I switched to the Victor when the wind started to blow. It's heavier than the Flyer I usually use. But there's no restrictions on the weight of the ball."

"I know. But Rollins told me their committee adopted their own rule on weight, apart from the U.S.G.A. This ball supposedly violated their rule."

"What? When? No one told me about any new rule. And nobody from the committee was checking clubs or balls anyway."

Johnny could hear himself shouting. He tried to calm down.

"The wind started to blow and I needed a ball that could cut through it. I've used the Victor in other tournaments and there's never been a problem."

"Well, I think it's bullshit," Bob said. "We'll fight it. I just thought you should know about it as soon as possible." He said something quietly to someone on his end of the line. "Listen, Johnny, I've got to go now. I'll talk to you later."

"Thanks for calling, Bob."

Mary was starting to make a pot of coffee when she heard Johnny slam the phone down on the desk. She went into the parlor to find out what was going on.

"Shit. They stripped me of the title. Damn."

Johnny repeated for her what Bob had told him about the committee's decision. His anger rose again as he told her the story. But finally he seemed to run out of energy to be angry.

"I worked hard to win that tournament," he said, sinking into the desk chair and looking down at the floor. "This is a screw job. And they better not come after me for the prize money. That $900 is mine."

Mary stood at the back of the chair and wrapped her arms around him. Her hands gently traced circles around his chest as she tried to reassure him. She then raised her hands and slowly massaged the back of his neck. The tension in his neck began to ebb.

"We'll fight this," she said as she leaned over and kissed him on the top of his head.

Johnny was exhausted.

"I'm going back to bed."

"Don't worry," she said, her eyes filling with tears as she watched her dejected husband head back up the stairs to their bedroom.

She had been concerned for months about Johnny's depression. It didn't seem to be getting better and this wouldn't help. She made a decision. After the Cary, she would press him to stay with her on the Cape for a longer rest and to meet with a psychiatrist in Providence. She was determined to prevent him from slipping back to the old Johnny.

CHAPTER 45

"George, what time are you and Johnny leaving for Worcester?" Jennifer asked as she potted a new group of gardenias in the sun room.

"Johnny and Brian are coming over at 8:30."

George was standing in the hallway near the entrance to the sunroom. He was holding a small metal file. He had been checking his clubs for nicks or scratches, carefully inspecting them one by one, a ritual he performed before each match. If he found a nick or gouge on the face of a club, he would use the file to smooth out the imperfection.

"I didn't know Brian was out."

Brian Jameson had just been released from prison in New Jersey after serving four years for assault with a deadly weapon. He had gotten into a brawl in a barroom and clubbed a man with a broken chair leg. It was his bad luck that the man turned out to be the son of the local district attorney. He was paroled in large part based on letters from George, who vouched for him, and from Johnny, Walter, and Brad Rothchild, who promised that they would employ him as a caddy.

"He got out Saturday," George said. "It'll be good to see him. He got railroaded down in Paramus for that fight. He didn't start it and the guy he hit came at him with a knife."

"I've always liked Brian," Jennifer said. "I hope he's not bitter. Jail can change a person."

"So now you're a sociologist!"

"You know what I mean. Go. You'll be late. Good luck today." She kissed him on the forehead.

"Just a peck? We're getting to be an old stuffy couple," George said.

"I didn't want to get you started," she said with a coy smile.

"I'll show you, Mrs. Riley."

George pushed her against the wall and gave her a long, passionate kiss.

"Mr. Riley!" Jennifer exclaimed, out of breath. "You need to go. You'll be late."

Jennifer knew that her face must be flushed. She could feel the heat. And her knees felt a little shaky. George still had a way of surprising her when she least expected it.

George grabbed his bag and loaded his clubs and shoes into the back of their new Studebaker touring car. He had purchased it in March after he had received his first bonus check from the bank. The car had black leather upholstery, a stained-wood dashboard and large bulbous tires. Johnny and Brian walked up the driveway just as George walked around to the front of the car.

"Great car, George," Brian said as he ran his hand along the headlights.

"Hi, guys. How we doing this morning?" George asked. "Good to see you, Brian."

He put out his hand to shake Brian's.

Nice to see you, George," Brian said. "Thanks for your letter to the parole board. Both your letter and Johnny's offer helped. I'm indebted to both of you."

Johnny didn't say anything. He looked tired.

"I didn't think you got a fair shake at the trial," George said. "You were only defending yourself."

Brian nodded. He stood smaller than George remembered him, more drawn into himself.

"Right or wrong," he said, "I learned a lot about humility in the last four years."

George patted Brian lightly on the back and could feel him flinch from the contact.

After an awkward moment of silence, George said, "We need to get going."

George got into the driver's seat and turned over the engine. Brian climbed into the back seat and Johnny got into the front passenger seat. George engaged the clutch and glanced at Johnny.

"Okay, partner, ready to take on the best teams in the country?"

"I guess. Let's get going," a sullen Johnny Scranton answered.

George adjusted the side mirror and slowly released the hand clutch as he carefully

backed the car out of the driveway. Johnny curled up in the front seat and closed his eyes, then he abruptly straightened up in his seat.

"What's that sweet smell, George?" he asked.

"It's from the new leather seats. The salesman said it would disappear in a few weeks. My first new car. Doesn't it smell grand!"

George double-clutched and the Studebacker climbed a small hill as they entered the Worcester Road. As they approached the Devonshire Hill, George gunned the engine. The 30-horsepower, four-cylinder motor had enough power to climb the hill at over 40 miles per hour. When they reached Blue Marsh, Johnny was amazed at the new houses that lined the front of the property.

"My god, what have they done to the place?"

"The members had to sell the front parcel in '14 to keep the club operating through the recession."

"I hope they haven't ruined the course."

Johnny slumped down in the seat and closed his eyes again. Twenty minutes later, as they approached Framingham Center, Johnny suddenly sat up and blurted out, "They think I cheated in Jacksonville, George."

George pulled the Studebaker over to the side of the road. He turned to face Johnny, his own face animated by his disbelief.

"What are you talking about?"

"They think I cheated."

Johnny told George the entire story.

"By now, everybody on the tour knows I was disqualified," he said. "It's so embarrassing. They'll think I cheated."

"Nobody's going to think that, Johnny," George said firmly, doing his best to console him. "The way Jacksonville went about it, it could have happened to anybody. And besides, it was a stupid rule, and everybody will see that."

George's outrage and certainty buoyed Johnny, made him feel stronger, but it was his own anger that fed a determination he hadn't felt in months.

"I'll show them, George," he said. "We're going to kick butt today."

"Okay," said George. "Let's show them how two Newton boys can play this game."

As he kicked the car into gear and swung out onto the road, George noticed Johnny's neck had turned bright red and he was scratching his forehead as if it itched.

******

The Cary International at Worcester Country Club had become the premier pro-am tournament in the country. Players from around the world were invited each year to play in the best-ball competition, each team consisting of a prominent amateur and a ranked professional. Worcester had not only broken with the New England Golf Committee on their policy to exclude professionals in tournaments; they had, in the eyes of the Committee, perpetrated the most unpardonable of sins by arranging a tournament in which by its very design pros played alongside amateurs. That the Club restricted betting to a quiniela game after each round and conducted it under precise supervision in the club's massive ballroom might have seemed to many a step in the right direction as far as gambling was concerned - but to Archibald Sargent's group, it was little more than insult to injury.

George and Johnny arrived at the club with plenty of time to warm up and hit a few practice balls. Cyrus Clyde met them as they entered the men's locker room.

"Well, good morning, lads," he bellowed.

"Cyrus!"

Johnny was pleased to see his old friend. Cyrus wasted no time on small talk.

"Heard you had a problem in Jacksonville, laddie."

"I'm innocent, Cyrus," Johnny said. "You know me. I always play by the rules. Those bastards took the title away and never gave me a chance to defend myself."

Cyrus swung his arm around Johnny and squeezed his shoulder.

"You don't have to defend yourself to me, lad," he said, shaking his head. "I know you and I know a pile of shit when I smell it. As far as I'm concerned, it's Jacksonville's got the explaining to do."

George could see Johnny's eyes tear up and a smile come to his face for the first time that day. Cyrus shook Johnny with the arm he had wrapped around him and then gestured toward George.

"I see you have your steady mate with you," he said. "Hi ya, George. Good to see you too." He threw his hand out to shake George's.

"Hi, Cyrus," George said.

George could see that Cyrus had aged even since he had seen him the previous summer at the Massachusetts Open in Athol. Cyrus' hair, always pale, had gone completely white, and he walked with a guarded gait.

"How've you been, Cyrus?" George asked.

Cyrus bobbed his head back and forth, side to side. "Not great, laddie. I have gout. They want to take my right foot, but I say no."

"I'm sorry to hear that," said Johnny. "Isn't there something else they can do for it?" It was the first time since his return from Tampa that George had seen him take a real interest in anyone else.

"I see this specialist at Mass General, so we'll see," said Cyrus. His face tightened up and he let out an audible breath. "It's crap to get old." Then he looked embarrassed and abruptly picked up a pack of papers clipped to a board.

"Did you bring a caddy?" he asked.

Johnny nodded.

"Brian Jameson is with us. He'll carry for both of us."

"I thought he was still in jail," said Cyrus. "I'm glad to hear he's out." He looked down at his papers. "Are you sure you won't want to use one of our lads? Shame. I have a great group of caddies, and they know the course."

"Thanks, Cyrus, but we're okay," George said. "What's the field look like?"

It's cracker jack," Cyrus said. "Some of the top amateurs in the country are here; Chick Evans, Russell Wolcott, Barry Jones, James Corcoran. And some of the leading pros, Travers, Rivers, Johnson, Billy Maybrier."

Cyrus made a notation on his list. George assumed it was

the meticulous log of caddies that Cyrus prepared for each tournament.

"I'll leave you lads to get ready. Good luck."

Cyrus hobbled off to check on his boys.

****

A 36-hole medal-qualifying round was scheduled for the first day of the tournament. Johnny and George shot 65-66-131 and easily qualified for the 16-team match-play round to follow, which consisted of single-elimination matches over the next two days.

On the first day, they won both matches 3 and 2, as Johnny dropped key putt after key putt. On the second day, George and Johnny played Chick Evans and Walter Seizmore in the semi-finals in the morning round. Evans and Seizmore took an early lead, winning three of the first seven holes, but slowly Johnny and George came back. On the 12th, George hit a perfect second shot with a mashie to within two feet of the cup to win the hole with a birdie and pull even in the match; and on the 13th, Johnny contributed his own birdie by chipping in with his niblick, and they had the lead. They closed out Evans and Seizmore by going two holes up on the 17th when George made two brilliant shots to birdie again.

"Well, partner, we made it into the finals," George said as they approached the locker room to rest before their championship match. "Do you have any more golf in you?"

Johnny slapped him on the rear and laughed, the first time he had laughed in weeks. "You know I do, partner," he said confidently. "They're going to know not to let two Newton boys on the same team after today."

George had missed this camaraderie. It felt good to see Johnny looking and acting more like the Johnny he had always known.

"We take the shots," George said, laughing loudly. "We make the shots."

Johnny pumped his hand into the air.

"Whatever it takes to win!"

Johnny winked at George.

****

The final match began at 2, Johnny and George playing the team of Jack Sullivan and Charles Hollis. Sullivan had been the 1914 Atlantic City Open champion and had won three pro tournaments in the previous five months. He was 5'10", a lanky, fit man universally respected for his geniality as well as his shot-making. Hollis was the defending Pennsylvania Amateur Champion. He was from Pittsburgh, a tall man with a pug face and muscular build, and every time he swung a club, his biceps rippled under his tight-fitting shirt. The four men gathered near the first teeing ground about ten minutes before the match was to begin.

"George, nice to see you again," Hollis said, as they shook hands. "I haven't seen you since Pinehurst in April." He looked toward Johnny. "And I suppose this is the famous Johnny Scranton I've heard so much about, or should I say, the infamous Johnny Scranton I've heard so much about." He stressed the word *infamous* and grinned as he said it.

Johnny had been wiping off the head of his driver. He looked up. He had never met Hollis before, but he could judge pretty quickly that there wasn't much chance of their becoming friends. He moved close to Hollis and glared at him.

"What's that a reference to?" he said, his voice quiet but cold..

Hollis shrugged as if his comment were no big deal. "I heard you had a problem in Jacksonville."

The back of Johnny's neck was getting red, and he moved closer still to Hollis, but before he had a chance to respond any further, George had stepped between the two and Sullivan had grabbed his partner's arm and was pulling him away.

"Let's just play golf," George whispered to Johnny. Then he turned to Sullivan and gave him an uncomfortable smile.

"Jack, it's an honor to meet you," he said. "I'm George Riley, and I believe you know Johnny."

Sullivan stepped away from Hollis and walked quickly over to Johnny. He grabbed Johnny's right hand and shook it heartily while clasping his right shoulder with his left hand.

"Hi ya, Johnny," he said with obvious warmth. "How you been?"

Johnny re-composed himself and concentrated on Sullivan.

"I see you're back and snatching a few tournament wins," he said. He took a breath. "How's the family?"

"I've got three kids now," said Sullivan. "How's your lovely wife Mary? Connie had a grand time with her in Chicago. I think they compared notes for three days."

Hollis was standing about ten feet away, rocking back and forth. He hadn't realized that Scranton and Sullie knew each other quite so well and now he was feeling awkward about having taunted Johnny. He was trying to decide whether it was better to look bored or disgusted. Apologizing would never occur to him.

"Mary liked Connie very much," Johnny said. "We should all get together soon." Johnny leaned toward his friend and whispered, "I don't like your partner, Jack. Starts insulting me right off the bat."

Sullivan didn't seem surprised.

"Was that about Jacksonville? I told him you were set up

down there. It's an outrage what they did. A lot of the players never got word about their special rule. You weren't the only one, you know ñ they disqualified five other guys without a hearing."

Johnny hadn't heard that part before. Somehow it made him feel better.

"We need to fight this," Sullivan added. "Might have happened to any us."

"Thanks, Jack. I appreciate the comments." Johnny paused, then said loud enough for Hollis to hear, "I still don't like your partner."

Sullivan laughed.

"He can be a hothead, but wait til you see him play. Good luck, my friend."

****

As they approached the 1st teeing ground, Johnny whispered into George's ear. "Whatever it takes, I want to win today," he said, his voice almost menacing. George could see that Johnny's neck was still bright red.

"Calm down," George told him. "You want to be upset with this guy or do you want to play good golf? You're reacting exactly the way he wants you to."

Johnny nodded. He motioned to Brian to bring him a cold, wet towel, and then walked off by himself for a few moments and took long, slow breaths, just like they'd shown him during rehab. All the same, it wasn't until the 3rd hole that he really had himself back under control.

In the meantime, it was up to George to keep them in the match. By winning the difficult 4th by shooting par, George erased the one-hole advantage Sullivan and Hollis had built while Johnny was still gathering himself over the first three holes.

From that point on, the match became a see-saw: first Johnny and George would go one up, then Sullivan and Hollis would win two straight to go one up, then Johnny and George would come back and win a hole or two. By 17, the match was level.

The 17th hole at Worcester was a brutal 378-yard par-four with a sharp dogleg to the left nicknamed "Mound a plenty" because of the over-sized, grass-covered mounds dotting the fairway. The entire length of the right side of the bumpy fairway, a considerable stretch of rough, and even the elevated green were all rimmed by a long stand of dense trees. Johnny teed off first and pulled his drive down the left side into the dogleg. George hit a poor drive, slicing the ball right and into the deep woods. Assuming the ball was lost, he had started to play a provisional second stroke from the tee when Brian, out as a fore-caddy, waved a towel to signal that he had found George's first ball deep in the woods. That saved George a stroke but it didn't leave him in any great position for his second shot. Sullivan and Hollis played safe drives down the right side of the fairway and were left with straight shots onto the elevated green.

George's second shot was blocked by the trees, so he was forced to punch out into the middle of the fairway. To make matters worse, he hit his third shot into a pot-hole bunker to the right of the green. With both Sullivan and Hollis sitting so well, he knew he was almost certainly out of the hole.

Johnny had already trekked the 50 yards up the fairway to examine the dogleg, so George walked with Brian to check on Johnny's ball. It was buried deep in a divot a good two inches below the level of the fairway around it. He decided to join Johnny.

Johnny was trying to gauge the direction of the shifting wind. "Sorry, partner," George said. "I came up on that shot. You're our only hope."

Johnny didn't looked fazed.

"Don't worry about it," he said. "Do you think I can make the turn, or should I pitch to the right front of the green?"

"You have a difficult lie back there," George said. "I think you should run it up to the right of the green and hope for a good pitch. You'll never get it to turn fast enough coming off your lie to make the green."

They stared at the raised green. It had a steep slope on its right side that ended in the trees.

"Better to go for the chip shot than risk putting it in the woods."

"I don't know," said Johnny. He was feeling good. "I think I can make this shot. The wind's shifted behind us."

George watched him walk briskly over to check his ball. He exchanged a few words with Brian then confidently pulled a spade mashie from his bag. As George came back over the hill, he was amazed at how quickly Johnny got set and addressed the ball. From where he was, he could see that the ball was no longer in the divot. It was sitting on the fairway about six inches from where he had last seen it. He was about to say something, but Johnny dragged the club back slowly and turned the face of the club inward. As he hit the shot, his whipping action produced a lateral spin to the ball and it jumped off the club face. The ball started out to the right then suddenly hooked left around the dogleg. It landed on the green, bounced once, and stopped three feet from the pin.

George rushed to join Johnny in the fairway.

"Johnny," he said in a voice lowered almost to a whisper, "that was a great shot, but what about the lie?"

Johnny looked surprised. "What about it?" he said. "It was a perfect lie for that type of shot, a little up hill."

"But it was sitting in a divot."

Johnny shook his head. He looked awat from George.

"No. It was sitting up."

George was stunned at Johnny's response. He stopped to catch his breath and contemplate his next move. He caught up with Brian and found his own ball buried deep in the bunker.

"Looks as if you need to smash this one out," Brian said.

George knew that didn't matter much at this stage. He asked Brian outright, "Did Johnny move his ball out of the divot?"

Brian paused for a second, looked confused, and then looked directly at George.

"Johnny wouldn't do that," he said. "Why would you say that? He hit a fantastic shot. It hooked perfectly."

Now George was angry. He pointed his finger at the ground as he spoke.

"That ball was in a divot. How the hell did he pull that shot off out of a deep divot?"

Brian looked lost. He didn't want to be in the middle between George and Johnny. He was shaking his head back and forth slowly.

"It wasn't in a divot, George. The divot was six inches away from the ball."

George shook his head.

"I know what I saw, Brian."

Brian moved over to the bag away from George.

"I don't know what to think," George said, more to himself than to the caddy.

He leaned over and tried to calm down. After a few minutes, he blasted out of the bunker and two-putted for a bogey 5. Hollis finished with a par and Sullivan missed his birdie putt by inches.

George rushed over to Johnny and pulled him to the back of the green, away from any spectators.

"You have to call a penalty on yourself, Johnny."

"What are you talking about?"

"Johnny, I know what I saw. That ball was in a divot."

Johnny sighed. "George, whatever you think you saw, that ball was lying on the grass when I hit it," he said in a quiet but commanding voice. He moved over to line up his putt.

"George, will you help me?"

George stared at Johnny and then stepped away.

"No. This is all yours."

Johnny was stunned. They had always helped each other line up putts as partners. This was too much. What was going on?

"Okay. To hell with you," he said loudly enough that everyone around the green could hear.

George stormed off toward the 18th teeing ground without waiting to see him putt. He wasn't sure what to do. He was convinced that Johnny had moved the ball. He had never witnessed such a flagrant violation of the rules, but only Johnny could call this penalty. George was not going to condone his actions by helping him win the hole.

He heard a loud roar behind him as Johnny dropped the ball into the back of the cup for his birdie to win the hole and take the lead for them.

* * * * * *

The 18th hole was a slight dogleg left, a 340-yard par 4. Four large oaks protected the left side of the fairway and blocked shots directly from the that side into the two-tiered green. George decided that the only honorable thing to do was to lose the hole and hope Johnny played poorly enough to send the match into extra holes. This would right the terrible wrong that Johnny had just perpetrated.

Johnny had been teeing off before George, but as he came up to the teeing ground, George grabbed his driver and placed his ball on a sand tee. Johnny hooked him by his shoulder.

"Why change the order now?" he asked. "We're on a roll."

George glared at him. "No. I want to hit first."

Sullivan and Hollis glanced at each other. Hollis didn't bother to restrain a smug grin.

George knew how to rattle Johnny. He had seen him often enough follow a poor shot with another poor shot when pressed. So George took two quick practice swings, then he deliberately let loose at the top of his back swing, and the ball sliced into the deep rough along the right side of the fairway. There would be no way to get out to the green on his next shot. George hoped that Johnny would do something similar.

To help add to the pressure, he said, "Don't follow me. We need a good lie."

Johnny took his time setting up to hit his drive, but his shot sailed directly toward the same deep rough as George's had, as if it were drawn there on the same string. But when it landed, they heard a loud "crack" and the ball ricocheted back to the middle of the fairway.

"Boy, did you hear that?" Johnny said, open-mouthed. "It must have hit a rock or something."

George couldn't believe it. He could see the ball from the teeing ground, sitting on the middle of the fairway on a downslope, no more than 110-yards from the green. How did that happen? But maybe Johnny would still make a mistake.

George slowly walked up the fairway toward the rough. He decided that he and Johnny would have it out later. This was a honorable game. Somewhere along the way, Johnny had forgotten this basic tenet. Maybe Jacksonville had changed him. Was this Johnny's revenge for being disqualified?

Johnny hit a perfect second shot that landed ten feet from the cup. All they needed on this hole was a tie, so the match was all but over. George hit his second shot wide of the green. Sullivan and Hollis both hit safely, but they landed 25 and 30 feet from the hole. Only a miracle could send this match into extras.

After Sullivan and Hollis both missed their long putts, George conceded Sullivan's remaining putt for a par. Johnny played safe and lagged his putt to within six inches of the cup. After Sullivan and Hollis conceded Johnny's remaining putt for par, the hole was tied and the match was over.

George had a sick feeling in the bottom of his stomach as they walked up the path to the clubhouse. He roughly pulled Johnny into a small office as soon as they entered the locker room.

Johnny's eyes flashed with anger.

"What the hell is wrong with you?"

"You stole that match today," George said. He was infuriated.

"Shit. I'm your best friend and you don't believe me."

George's face was beet red and his hands were shaking. He tried to keep his voice from cracking as he spoke.

"I saw what I saw. The ball on the 17th was in a divot and then suddenly you make this miraculous shot."

George threw his hands into the air.

"No one could make that shot. It was impossible."

Now Johnny's face was getting red.

"You're accusing me of cheating?"

"That's right. You stole the hole and you stole the tournament."

Johnny swept his fist across the nearest table and knocked off the table lamp.

"Screw you," he shouted. "I've never cheated in my life. I can't believe this."

Johnny turned from George in frustration and then suddenly spun back around to confront him. His eyes were filled with tears.

"This coming from someone whose always cheated to get ahead."

"What the hell are you talking about?" George said.

"You know what I'm talking about," Johnny yelled. "You took Rock's money and violated the amateur rules. You lied to the committee at South Shore. Why, you even lied about how you got the job at the bank!"

"The bank? What did this have to do with the bank? thought George. This was out of hand, but he couldn't stop himself.

"That's bullshit!" George stepped in close to Johnny, almost chest against chest. He poked him with his finger. "I didn't lie and I got that job after hard work. To hell with you!"

Johnny pushed him off in disgust.

"You're such a hypocrite," he sneered.

George pushed back with both hands but held off the round-house punch he wanted to throw.

"We're through. Don't ever call me again."

He turned and burst out through the door, almost knocking over two locker-room attendants who were eavesdropping outside.

Johnny collapsed into a worn leather chair in the corner of the office. He felt betrayed. How did this happen? He couldn't believe that his best friend didn't believe him. He replayed the hole in his mind. Did he accidently move the ball? he wondered. He decided he should check with Brian.

He realized too that he had said things in his anger that he already was sorry for. But he would talk to George after he calmed down. He would apologize. They would work it out.

******

George couldn't sleep after the argument. He kept waking up, replaying the afternoon match in his mind. Around 4 a.m. he awoke in a cold sweat. He went down to the parlor and flicked on the overhead light and paused to stare at the new Tiffany incandescent lamp that hung from the ceiling. He stood there in the doorway, turning the light on and off, again and again, and pondering what to do. He didn't see any way around it: Johnny had dishonored the game, and until he confessed to his transgression, George wouldn't have anything to do with his now former best friend.

At 6 a.m. Jennifer heard a banging downstairs and was surprised to find George in the kitchen cooking eggs. He looked awful, tired and pale.

"What on earth are you doing up so early?" she asked.

"I've made up my mind," he said as he stared down at the eggs he was flipping in the hot skillet.

Jennifer sighed. She had heard the story four times the previous evening.

"He's made a mockery of the game! We're through."

She walked over to him, stood behind him at the stove, and started to rub his back. She spoke softly, sadly to him.

"I thought we agreed last night that you'd meet with Johnny and try to resolve this."

"No. I've made up my mind. I'll have nothing to do with him until he confesses."

"But, George," Jennifer said, leaning her cheek against his back, "he's your best friend. Even if he did cheat, you can't abandon him, not now. You don't want him to go back to his old self." She waited for George to say something, but he didn't. Finally she tried a different tack. "Mary and I talked last night after you went to bed. She feels awful about what happened. And Johnny told her he didn't cheat. I don't think he would lie to her."

"He's a cheater," George said firmly, as if he were incapable of hearing what his wife was saying. "And I won't associate with cheaters."

Jennifer had never seen George so angry. She decided it was best just to give him more time. And more sleep.

****

Mary called Jennifer the next day.

"What are we going to do?" she asked.

"They're like two little boys who had a fight in the sandbox," Jennifer said. "I've never seen George this mad. Maybe Rock can get them to talk."

"That's a good idea," said Mary. "I'll call Rock."

CHAPTER 46

By the summer of 1915 it had become increasingly clear to Archibald Sargent that he was losing ground in his attempts to ban professionals from golf tournaments. Upon reflection, he realized that he had made the mistake of not being true to himself, of attacking the problem too subtly, so he decided to return to the two simple business principles that had made him a rich and powerful man to begin with: he would ruthlessly expand the scope of his plan and doggedly double his effort. Now he would urge member clubs to include in their definition of a golf professional anyone who in any way derived income related to golf: architects, manufacturers, salesmen, promoters. He would travel extensively and personally preach the gospel of amateurism. By January, 1916, he had arranged to have himself appointed chair of the National Golf Committee on Amateur Status, a new group supported by 234 clubs that had agreed to adopt a code of conduct that would more rigorously define amateur standing. By the following September, Sargent's hand-drafted code had been adopted by the Committee's Executive Board, and the new rules effectively applied to all sanctioned tournaments, both national and local.

"This new code of conduct will purge from our ranks the growing menace of professionalism which has crept into golf," Sargent boldly stated at the news conference to announce the new code. "Each player who wishes to be sanctioned as an amateur will be required to sign a pledge which promises to abide by the new rules. Those who refuse to sign the pledge will be barred from the amateur game."

Sargent bristled at a reporter's suggestion that this was a witch hunt. "We mean to leave no room for the thugs and rascals who seek to squeeze profit from our game," he said. "Golf is a gentlemen's sport and those who degrade it will not be welcome."

He was furious as he was driven away from the press conference.

"Get me the name of that reporter who called the code a witch hunt," he barked at his administrative assistant, Sandra Nace. "I'm going to write a letter to his editor."

Sandra was a petite woman in her early thirties who had worked with Sargent for five years. She had flowing black hair that framed an open, friendly face accentuated by a perky smile. She was a precise counterpoint to the austere and imperious Sargent.

"This is a marvelous accomplishment, Archibald," she said sweetly as she noted his request in her stenopad. She sat with him in the back seat of the Rolls Silver Ghost limousine, smiling, legs crossed, her lavender slip slightly exposed. "After all the time you've spent trying to discredit the professionals, you finally have the full weight of the National Committee behind you."

"Thank you, Sandra," he said, affecting as much gratitude as he allowed himself. "I couldn't have accomplished this without your help."

Sargent smiled and stroked her hair gently. He glanced down at her ankle and noticed her lacy slip.

"You're wearing the silk slip I bought you."

He was looking forward to later in the day when he would see the full slip up close.

Their relationship had begun five years before. They were cautious and very discreet. Sargent happily paid for her small but elegant apartment in the Back Bay so that they could ensure privacy, and they scheduled carefully so that their afternoon trysts always ended at 4:30 sharp, allowing Sargent to be home for dinner with his wife and children. Sandra was satisfied in what she regarded as her temporary role as his mistress because she was sure that before long she would replace the current Mrs. Archibald Sargent. It was only a matter of time and she was willing to wait in the comfort of the Back Bay.

"Now the hard work begins," Sargent muttered.

Sandra leaned over and rubbed the back of his neck. "You mean the Ouimet issue?"

Francis represented a particular problem for Sargent and his Committee on Amateur Status. He had become something of an American hero since his unlikely U.S. Open championship three years before. He was by far the most recognizable face in amateur golf, and Sargent appreciated that his unaffected sense of gentlemanly courtesy and honor reflected well on the game. But the new code of conduct specifically barred golf equipment manufacturers and salesmen from the game, and Francis owned a sporting goods business and, worse, was not shy about publicly promoting it. If he refused to leave the concern behind, the Committee would look impotent if it didn't debar him.

"Yes," said Sargent. "He and the other Woodland members clearly violate the new rules." Sargent paused as he gazed out the window. "Damn. Why does it have to be Ouimet? He's so popular."

Sandra offered her suggestion couched in the least directive terms, as she had learned was best with Archibald. "Would it be a good idea to meet with him before you make a final decision on his status?"

"Yes. You're right," said Sargent. "I was thinking that myself."

He gazed into her dark brown eyes. He knew that today's assignation would be rousing. Sandra loved to reward him with special favors when he made her feel helpful.

"Call him and set up a time to meet next week. Maybe I can convince him to find some other business."

****

It was a crisp fall day as Francis walked the four blocks from his office to meet Sargent for a drink at the Parker House Hotel. He had never met Sargent, but he knew of his relentless campaign to ban professionals. He couldn't help but wonder why Sargent would want to meet with him.

Sargent was waiting for him in the lobby. The Parker House, opened fifty years before by Harvey Parker, was the most elegant hotel in the city. Sargent had chosen it for the meeting because he felt at home there and he expected Francis to be impressed by it. He snuffed out a cigar when he saw him come through the door. He walked over and reached out to shake hands. Sargent had a firm grip and his handshake lasted longer than most, and he expected that to impress Ouimet as well.

"Thank you for meeting with me, Francis," he said. Then he smiled what he regarded as his most winning smile. "I hope you don't mind me calling you Francis. I feel as if I know you."

"Not at all, Mr. Sargent," said Francis.

"I would guess that you haven't been here before," Sargent said, trying unsuccessfully to hide his condescension as he guided Francis towards the Colonial Bar adjacent to the lobby.

"Yes, actually, I have," said Francis. "I was here last year for a party thrown by Walter Hagen on behalf of the Boys and Girls Club of Boston."

"Oh, yes. I remember that party," said Sargent. He resisted an outright scowl. "Three people were arrested and Hagen was asked to leave the hotel."

"I guess I left before the fireworks began," said Francis, a slight smile coming to his face. "I do remember that Walter donated $5,000 to the Boys and Girls Club for their youth golf program. I was delighted to accept the check on behalf of the Club."

Sargent looked flustered. This wasn't going as he had intended. He needed to start over. He chose an empty table in the corner away from the rest of the patrons. A young waitress approached and took their drink orders, and he got down to business as soon as she walked off.

"Francis, I've asked to meet with you to discuss a serious issue," he said. "As you know, the National Committee has adopted a new code of conduct for all of its members. The new code bars anyone from being a member who is directly involved in a golf-related business."

"I haven't read it, but I've heard about it."

Francis glanced at the couple seated near them in the corner of the bar to see if they were in range of their conversation. He had heard too many stories about Sargent's ugly involvement in trying to discredit Johnny Scranton to trust him.

"The Committee requested that I meet with you. They asked if you would consider closing your sporting goods business."

Francis was stunned. This was what the meeting was about?

"They want me to close my business? You can't be serious."

He shifted in his chair and stared at Sargent, assessing this self-important autocrat. He chose his words very carefully and spoke slowly.

"I haven't taken any money to play golf, and my business interests are entirely separate from my golf interests. I've been very careful not to mix any business with golf activities."

Sargent nodded.

"I agree, Francis. No one's suggesting that you've profited from your golf notoriety."

He leaned in on his elbows and spread his hands open to show he meant no ill will.

"Grantland Rice calls you the pinnacle of American golf virtue."

There. That should help, he thought.

"But the Committee is concerned about any golfer having any business dealings that relate to the game."

"Pardon my French," said Francis, his voice growing loud and defiant, "but that's bullshit."

This wasn't the young, malleable Francis Ouimet that Sargent had expected. He looked around and held up his hand.

"Please, Francis, what will people think?" he asked.

Francis paused to compose himself.

"I'm sorry. You're right," he said. He spoke more quietly but very firmly. "I'm not sure how it works for you, Mr. Sargent, but that store is my livelihood. It's what allows me to play amateur golf rather than turning professional."

Francis paused again. He shook his head.

"No. I won't give up the business."

"Francis, if that's the case, I don't know if I can keep the committee from voting to debar you."

Sargent tried his best to provide an expression of helplessness that suggested the decision was out of his hands.

"I'm just hoping to find an accommodation that's not embarrassing to you or the committee."

"Damn right it will be embarrassing."

Frances paused a third time to regain his composure. He smiled but he was glaring at Sargent.

"You can tell them I respectfully decline their suggestion."

Sargent leaned back in his chair and nodded. He had given him a chance. He had done what he knew he should do, what the committee would expect him to do. If this was not the preferable outcome, there was an upside: by debarring Ouimet, he would send a clear and decisive message that the Committee was in charge and that the rules applied to all, no matter how popular. They would be criticized, but in the long run, this would be good for American golf.

Sargent changed the topic abruptly to allow Ouimet the chance to tell him about the upcoming Boston junior golf awards, a function of some committee the young man chaired. After a few minutes of half-listening, Sargent looked at his watch.

"I need to run," he said with a manufactured sigh. "I'll let the Committee know your decision. I wish it were different. I don't know how they'll vote."

Sargent stood to leave but decided to throw one last barb before he left. As he counted out and dropped a few bills on the table, he said, "By the way, the Committee is also investigating your Woodland teammates J. H. Sullivan, Jr. and Paul Tewksbury."

Francis's mouth went slack in disbelief. Now he stood, leaning on his hands across the table toward Sargent.

"I can't believe that. Paul's just a salesman at Wright and Ditson. J. H. is an architect. Neither of them has ever profited by playing in a tournament."

Francis could feel his anger rising at the injustice.

"These are honorable men who love golf."

Sargent nodded smugly.

"I'll convey your thoughts to the committee. You'll hear shortly about their decision." He offered his hand to shake. Francis shook it politely as a matter of course, hardly thinking, feeling numb.

"Well, I'm off, Francis," said Sargent, nearly jovial. "It was good to finally meet you."

Francis sat down, dumbfounded, as Sargent strolled out of

the bar. The "honorable gentlemen" of the game he loved were clearly planning to debar him. He'd have to think about what his next steps should be. Francis smiled sardonically. Maybe, he thought, I should just turn pro. That would show them. He decided it was time for a good stiff drink. What would people think? What was he going to tell his father? How would it affect his business? He sat in the bar for a long time while pondering his future.

****

"Denise, can you please place a call to Francis Ouimet at his sporting goods store?" George asked.

Denise had the number handy. She knew that Francis and George were friends, but Ouimet also was a client. When Francis had left his old employer, Wright and Ditson, and partnered with his father to open a sporting goods store on Landsdown Street in Boston, George had arranged for their first loan. The business prospered by selling a wide variety of sports equipment, but it specialized in supplying golf clubs to pro shops, and Francis had contracted with several ball manufacturers to be their exclusive wholesaler in the Boston area.

As he sat in his office re-reading the report from the National Committee and waiting for Denise to put the call through, George tried to calm himself. He rarely lost his temper, but this was outrageous. Francis had barely had a chance to say hello before George started yelling into the phone.

"Have you seen the final report from the National Committee regarding your amateur status?"

"Yes, George. I got a copy yesterday."

"You're banned from playing any national sanctioned tournaments, Francis."

"I know."

There was a long pause. George was so angry that he couldn't find words. How could Francis be so unruffled?

"I got a call last night from Harold Rivers," said Francis. "He officially informed me that my amateur status has been revoked by the USGA based on the National Committee's recommendation. I'm not sure yet what I can do."

"We need to fight Sargent's rules," George said, bringing his voice back to normal volume. "They're using you to make a point. It's just wrong."

"I'll fight them. But I've got other options, too," Francis said. "I may end up playing in the Western Golf Association. Bill Strenchum called me this morning and invited me to play in their amateur championship."

The Western Golf Association, based in Illinois, had split from the New York City based USGA in 1910, and a contentious rift had developed between them. Playing in their tournament would not help Francis's position with the USGA, but it would allow him to play.

"That's a good idea," said George. "These guys need to wake up. There's going to be a huge public outcry if they keep you from playing in the East."

"George, there's another possibility." Francis waited before he said it. "I'm thinking of turning pro."

George's silence made it seem as if the line had gone dead.

"George, are you there?"

Francis could hear George draw in a long breath.

"I'm here, Francis," he said. "Did I hear that right? You might turn pro?"

"I've got to consider it, George. I can't give up the business, and I still want to play competitive golf."

George wasn't sure what to say. But this sounded like the wrong course to him. Francis loved the amateur game, and the game needed him.

"Francis. You don't need to decide right now. You don't really want that life, do you?"

"The way they've handled it, it's not exactly a question of what I want, is it, George?" Francis said. "I may be forced into the pro game, unless things change."

George understood that what Francis was saying made sense. He just didn't want it to be so. How could a committee of old men keep the most famous amateur in the game from playing? Didn't they understand the good will the game would lose if they forced Francis Ouimet to turn pro? What were they thinking?

"I'm going to the board meeting next month to file a formal protest," George said. Francis could hear the pleading in his voice. "Please don't do anything that can't be undone. First, let's see if we can get this ruling reversed."

"Don't worry, George. I'm not rushing into anything," Francis said softly.

George let out a breath. "I'm sorry, Francis, but I've got to go. I've got a client waiting for me. I'll talk to you soon."

"Bye, George. Thanks for the call – and for your support."

George hung up the phone and slumped back in his chair. His next call would be to Heinrich. Together they would get this insulting decision overturned.

******

Bernard Deacon, a columnist with Golf Times, joined the campaign to reinstate Francis and wrote often about the travesty of barring him from tournaments and demanding that the decision be reversed. In one column he described the USGA's decision as akin to Brutus stabbing Caesar in the public forum. Francis remained above the fray, a gentleman throughout the campaign. He made no statements to the press and refused to publicly criticize the committee.

Francis accepted Bill Strenchum's invitation to play in the 1917 Western Amateur in late October. He played brilliant golf, a win over Ken Edwards on the last hole of the match. Heinrich Schmidt, the defending champion, presented the winning trophy to Francis and once again urged the USGA to reinstate the greatest player in the game to his rightful status. Francis stood mute at the presentation. Always the gentleman, he believed in quiet diplomacy.

The campaign by George, Henrich, and others lasted two years before the Francis Ouimet was finally re-instated as an amateur. No one from the USGA ever publicly apologized to Francis or his family.

CHAPTER 47

When the personal strife between George and Johnny began in the summer of 1915, most of the world had already been embroiled for nearly a year in what would become the most extensive conflict in the history of man. More than 60 million combatants from more than one hundred countries were already fighting in the Great War before the United States entered the war in April, 1917. Five million Americans were mobilized in less than a year in the greatest effort the country had ever seen, and every man and woman in the United States was somehow affected. Two weeks after Congress declared war, Walter Hagen placed a call to Johnny in Tampa Bay.

"Johnny, can you hear me?" Walter asked, yelling into the phone from his home in Rochester, New York.

"Yes, Walter," said Johnny. "I can hear you loud and clear. You don't need to shout."

"Have you thought about what your plans will be now that we're at war?"

"I was thinking about enlisting, of course," said Johnny. "I heard that Congress is already working on a plan that would re-institute conscription anyway. What are you going to do?"

"That's what I called about," said Walter, the excitement in his voice palpable even over the phone connection. "I got a call from Frank Ryan with the PGA in New York. He's been asked by Secretary of the Treasury McAdoo to organize a series of exhibition matches to sell bonds they're going to issue to help pay for the war. McAdoo thinks we could raise enough money that we'd be more valuable at home playing golf than going overseas with the troops." Walter saved his capper for last. "And they want us to play as partners, just like the old days, if that's okay with you."

Johnny thought it through quickly. This would be a quite different way of doing his part in the war than he had imagined, but it did make sense. And Mary would certainly be relieved that he wouldn't be in danger in Europe, so far away and so out of touch. He also had to admit to himself that traveling and playing golf with Walter would be hugely preferable to anything the army could offer: time spent with Hagen inevitably turned out to be entertaining, to say the least.

"What's the plan?" he asked.

"The PGA and USGA have already canceled this year's tournaments," Walter said. "Our first match would be in Atlanta in three weeks. Do you think you could make it?"

"Sign me up," said Johnny, feeling his own excitement taking hold. "You can cable me with the details."

"Great!" said Walter.

"And, Walter," said Johnny slowly, enunciating carefully, "not entirely like the old days, if you know what I mean."

Walter laughed. "Don't worry about that, pal," he said. "We've both got promises to keep."

"See you in Atlanta, Walter."

"I'm looking forward to it."

Mary came into the room as Johnny finished the phone call. Her hair was loose and she was wearing a blue sun dress that always reminded Johnny of that first night on the beach in Harwichport. He smiled at her and hung the phone up slowly.

"Who was that?" she asked.

"Walter. The government wants us to play golf to help sell war bonds. I'd be away from home but not overseas."

Mary's face brightened as the good news sunk in, and she walked quickly over to him and buried her face in his chest. "That's wonderful," she said, her voice breaking slightly.

Johnny slipped his arm around her, his hand at her trim waist. "Come on. Let's go for a dip before dinner. I'll fill you in at the beach."

****

Both the amateur and the professional golf communities turned out to support the massive drive to sell Liberty Bonds. In Boston, George teamed up with Francis to coordinate weekly fund raisers throughout New England. Francis worked three days a week selling sporting goods and traveled the other four days a week selling war bonds. The bank allowed George the time off he needed – and used the resulting good will to promote their own mortgage program for new homes as "a patriotic alternative to renting." Their own exhibition matches extended through the summer and into the fall and carried over through the spring and summer of 1918. By the end of the war in November of that year, George and Francis had played in over 30 exhibition matches and had sold nearly $200,000 in bonds. The team of Hagen and Scranton, touring the country almost non-stop, played in 56 matches and raised over $300,000 to benefit the war effort.

****

The months following the argument between George and Johnny had turned into years and they had only grown farther and farther apart. Jennifer could see that George missed the fellowship and counsel of his best friend, but as the months passed, he became more and more resolute that Johnny had cheated and was undeserving of his friendship. His disappointment with

Johnny and his anger at him was so constant and obvious that friends were apprehensive about even bringing up his name in George's presence. Johnny had climbed out of his depression fueled by a recuperative summer at the beach and by Mary's unrelenting devotion to him, but she could still feel his enduring unhappiness at being deprived of his closest friend. When he was asked about the feud, Johnny would simply say, "Ask George. He knows what's wrong."

George mulishly insisted on following through on Jennifer's plans to build a house in Harwichport, on Pilgrim Road, one block from Bank Street Beach. There on the Cape, Mary and Jennifer steadfastly maintained their connection with each other, but even that was made difficult because George and Johnny went out of their ways to avoid each other. Now families, each with two small children, they lived barely a quarter of a mile apart during the summer, yet the two former best friends refused to acknowledge each other.

Jennifer and Mary would meet for lunch with the babies or go to the farmers' market, but George and Johnny each worked hard to avoid the other. If George saw Johnny walk down Main Street, he would slip into a storefront or an alley until Johnny had passed. Johnny made sure he didn't patronize the same restaurants as George, and it became his habit to send a family member into a store before he entered in case there was any possibility of a George sighting. Before they were fully able to talk, each man's children had learned not to mention Uncle Johnny or Uncle George in their father's presence.

It was not until 1919, on a cold February day, months after the end of the war, and nearly four years after their falling out, that a crack appeared in the wall between them. Late in the day, a letter was delivered to the Riley home in a tattered envelope addressed in typeset to *George Riley, Newton Highlands, Massachusetts, U.S.A.*

The return address at the top left corner of the envelope read simply WAR DEPARTMENT. At the top right corner, there was a three-cent stamp. Below the stamp, at a skewed angle and surrounded by a blocked outline, was imprinted OFFICIAL BUSINESS. On the other side of the envelope someone had scrawled "Verdun, France" in black ink.

George called Jennifer into the living room before he gently opened the envelope. They stood together silently in front of the couch. What could this be? George wondered. There were two pieces of paper inside the envelope, the first a hand-written letter on American Expeditionary Forces stationery. It read:

George and Johnny,

I need to make a confession. I'm lying here in a hospital in France. I'm pretty shot up and I'm afraid I'm going to die. Sister Rose Marie is helping me. I don't want to die with this on my conscience.

I'm the one who moved Johnny's ball at the Cary National. It was in a divot, like you said, George. I kicked it out when no one was looking. Johnny didn't know.

I don't have a good excuse. I stood to make $400 from bets and I needed the money. And I thought Johnny needed a win. And there was no way anybody was going to make that shot from the divot.

Once I did it, I was afraid to admit it. I thought I'd never caddy again and that things would be worse for Johnny. So I lied to you, George. I didn't know you'd be so angry with each other.

I'm so sorry (the words were crossed out and replaced with a new sentence) *I am sincerely sorry for lying to you both and for violating your trust. I have asked God for forgiveness and am trying to make it right. Please don't let my mistake ruin your friendship.*

Your friend,
Brian Jameson

George dropped the letter on the coffee table and collapsed on the couch behind him. He folded his hands over his head and bent forward to rest his face on his knees. Jennifer picked up the letter and urgently scanned it. Then she carefully sat down beside George and laid her arm gently across his back.

"George," she said softly, "you've got to call Johnny and tell him about this."

George felt as if he were barely capable of breathing, much less responding to his wife. All these years. He'd been so wrong. He'd been so foolish. He'd been so unfair.

"I can't believe it," he said faintly.

"There's a note," Jennifer said, as she took a smaller piece of folded paper from the envelope. It was from Sister Rose Marie.

21 Decembre, 1918
Romaqne-Gesnes, France

Brian died three days ago. He was wounded on November 9, 1918, during the Battle of the Muse. He's buried in the American Cemetery outside of town. He was very brave. He eliminated a German machine gun position which saved many American lives. After we wrote this letter, he seemed at peace. He's with God now.

George got up from the couch and slowly walked upstairs. Jennifer didn't know what to say.

******

For hours George sat unmoving in the gray overstuffed chair that filled the corner of their bedroom and tried to decide what to do. He replayed in his thoughts the horrible accusation that he had cast at Johnny with such unbending certainty, how his anger had blinded him to what he should have known—what he should have trusted–about his friend. What failing was it that had allowed him to so thoroughly discount all the years he had experienced Johnny's essential honesty? As George sat somberly in the darkening room, he felt drained and lost, as if the life map he had laid out for himself with such determination and certitude had crumbled before his eyes.

Three times he raised himself up out of the chair to go downstairs to place a call to Johnny in Tampa, and three times he hung up the phone before letting the call go through. Finally, after a long sleepless night, he decided that if he were to repair their friendship, if he were to redeem himself in any meaningful way, he would need to do it face to face. He packed a small bag, slipped the letters into the breast pocket of his coat, made a quick call to Denise at the bank to cancel his appointments for the next few days, and then boarded the afternoon train to Florida. Jennifer saw him off at the station.

She look at him and smiled as he boarded the train, and in an instant he was reassured.

"This is the right thing to do."

George leaned over from the pullman's first step and kissed her. They held the kiss for a few extra seconds.

"I'll call you when I get to Tampa. Love you."

As the locomotive slowly made its way south, George looked out at the passing scenery and remembered that first train ride south to Pinehurst in the spring of 1912. It had been seven years since the intervention. George had seen Johnny ravaged and weak then, shaking, owned by his addiction–a curse cast unfairly upon him for risking his life to save someone he didn't even know. He had seen him climb out of that addiction, and since then he had seen him again and again struggle with the pain his hand still caused him.

He had seen how often and tenaciously Johnny had worked to remake himself to keep doing what he loved, to keep swinging a golf club. He had seen him withdrawn and depressed, grasping to conquer the ignoble demons that infested his life. But amid all those years and all those trials, George realized, he could not think of any instance in which there had been even a remote indication that Johnny had cheated at golf, not even of a moment that suggested he had sacrificed his honor in any way. And yet he had been willing to condemn Johnny so curtly, so completely. Why?

The train ride seemed to be never ending. He tried to sleep, but he kept mulling over and over how he would approach Johnny and what exactly he would say. But now he began to think about what he had been not thinking about, what he realized he had been avoiding thinking about. His own life, which he had formed so carefully to plan, with the right school, the right wife, and the right career, was rooted inexorably in a few crucial moments of which he could not be proud. All his successes, all that he had gained and could set forth as proof of his goodness, in that moment seemed to him to be every bit as dependent on his failings as they had been on his hard work and virtue.

Somehow Johnny had looked past all that: he knew George had cut a corner when he took Rock's money and he knew the advantages George had gained by withholding the truth from the committee at Brockton. Yet he had never brought either matter up to George, apparently never judged him the way George had been so quick to judge Johnny. And now he came to the humbling realization that it wasn't just that he was wrong about Johnny's cheating: even if Johnny had cheated, to hold him so starkly accountable for a failing confined to a game of golf seemed now to George unimaginably cruel and uncharitable.

****

George arrived in Tampa early the second morning of his trip, tired and sore. When he looked at himself in the mirror of the men's room at the Tampa train station, he saw a drained, washed-out visage that reminded him as much of Johnny at the intervention as of himself. He scrubbed his face, wet his hair and pushed it into place, and shaved, then changed into a fresh shirt and smoothed his rumpled coat as best he could. He stepped out from the station into the cool, sunny winter morning of Tampa and hailed a cab. It was early so he decided to call Jennifer after his meeting with Johnny.

He had never been so far south, and just like Mary before him, the palm trees and rampant untended verdure were a delight to him, however muted his enjoyment was by the circumstances. He had the cab driver drop him at the front of the property, and once he was walking up the drive to the house, surrounded by the lush gardens and drinking in the fresh Gulf air, he felt his mood lifting as an almost physical sensation, just being there finally and being ready to set things right as well as he could. He stepped up to the door, put his bag down next to him on the porch floor, pulled the letter out from his coat pocket, and knocked loudly.

Mary answered the door in her night gown. Her surprise made her look for a moment as if she had no idea who he was, then alarm washed suddenly over her face.

"George," she said, "you look terrible. What's wrong?"

She stepped out to him and placed her right hand on his left arm and gently pulled him into the front hall of the house.

"Are Jennifer and the kids alright?"

George nodded and meant to say something to reassure her, but no words would come out. He handed her the letter and cleared his throat. When he spoke, his voice sounded weaker to him than he had meant it to be.

"Hi," he said. "Sorry to disturb you so early, but you and Johnny need to read this."

Mary held the envelope in her hand and stared at it as if it were some delicate but dangerous new creature in her life. When she raised her eyes back up to look at George, she looked wary and confused.

"Johnny's out for his morning walk," she said slowly, quietly. "He'll be back in a few minutes."

She guided George deeper into the house.

"Come in, George. I'll make some coffee."

Mary led George to the kitchen, a large sunny room that had windows open to a stone patio and a stretch of flat green lawn that dissolved into brilliant sky. Even without seeing the water, George could tell from the sweet smell of the breeze and from the unbroken blue in the distance that the house sat on a bluff overlooking the bay. They sat at the kitchen table and Mary read the letter and then the note. When she was done reading them, she folded the letter back up along its creases and ran her fingers along its length. George sat with his hands locked together and resting in front of him on the table and waited for her to say something. When she looked back up at him, her eyes were filled with tears.

"My god."

She reached across the table to George and tenderly laid her hands on top of his.

"Let me talk to him before you do," she said. "I'll walk out and meet him."

Without saying anything more, Mary got up from the table and disappeared into another part of the house. A few moments later, George heard her go out the front door.

Riding all those hours on the train George had constructed and re-constructed exactly what he planned to say when he came face to face with Johnny. Now, there in Johnny's home and with the moment at hand, everything he had projected seemed suddenly, woefully inadequate to him. How was he to blot out the terrible mess he had made, the awful slur he had cast on his best friend? How was he to restore nearly four years of their friendship drowned in bad feelings and anger? As he paced around the kitchen, he was at last struck with the discomforting conclusion that there was no way he could undo his betrayal and no avenue to make it right. Brian's sin could never mitigate his own. He stood staring out the window of the kitchen toward where the sea must have been and decided that he would apologize without excuse – and he would hope for the generosity of spirit that he had denied Johnny, and that Johnny had always shown him.

A lengthy fifteen or twenty minutes after Mary had left, George heard them come into the house. When they came into the kitchen, George could see streaks from where tears had streamed down Mary's face. Johnny was walking behind her, his eyes down, and he was holding Brian's letter. Mary stood quietly by the table for a moment, then George became aware that she was gone, so soundlessly removed as if she had not been there at all.

Johnny stared at George without saying anything, not even hello. It occurred to George that he had not been this physically close to Johnny since the round at Worcester, how healthy he looked, how different from how he himself must look to Johnny right at this moment. It's Pinehurst in reverse, he thought. He gathered up his voice and stepped closer to him. George held up his right hand, palm open, meaning to show that he was about to explain, but it struck him immediately that this might seem as if he were offering to shake hands. That seemed wrong, presumptuous, so he dropped his hand back to his side. He sighed and then began his apology.

"Brian moved your ball," he said. "But the way I acted, the things I said."

George looked for some reaction in Johnny's face, but he couldn't gauge what he was thinking. Johnny was just staring at him dispassionately. In his discomfort, George looked down at the floor.

"I shouldn't have doubted you. I should have believed you."

He could hear his voice cracking.

"And even if I couldn't, I should have been a better friend."

He had to catch his breath and clear his throat before he continued.

"I'm so sorry. I hope you'll forgive me."

Johnny was quiet for a long time, a stretch that George knew felt even longer to him than it was. At last Johnny drew in a long breath and cleared his throat. George looked up at him. Johnny rubbed his forehead and then pushed his hand back through his hair. He spoke very slowly.

"You were a son of a bitch at Linthicum," he said, meaning to sound firm but with his voice catching. "And you were a son of a bitch at Worcester."

Johnny's eyes moved around the room as if he didn't want to look at George, as if he were searching for something else to focus on. Then he shook his head and stepped closer to George and fixed a steady gaze on him.

"And you're still a son of a bitch."

He stared at him for a few moments, the sadness in his face so unmistakable that George thought he was about to cry. Then he put his hands on George's shoulders and drew him into a hug, close and strong.

"But, you're my best son of a bitch and I've missed you," he said, almost inaudibly.

As if they had emanated from someone else, George could hear his own sigh of relief and he could feel the tears on his cheeks.

After a moment, Johnny gently pulled away from George to look him in the face and asked, "Are you crying?"

There were tear stains on his face as well.

"Of course not," said George, wiping his face with his hand.

"Good," said Johnny. "Neither am I."

Then they sat with Mary in the kitchen and had a late breakfast. They traded stories about their kids and about golf, and they laughed together for the first time in nearly four years. It was as if the previous four years had miraculously washed away.

Suddenly George realized that he hadn't called Jennifer.

"Can I make a call to Jennifer?"

Johnny turned to Mary who was clearing the table of the dishes. "He comes all this way to apologize, mother, and now he wants me to pay for a long-distance call," Johnny said in a stern voice. Then his tone suddenly changed. "Of course. It's in the hall. Request the East Coast Relay Operator. They're faster this time of day."

Mary directed George to the hall.

"Let me talk to her after you've finished," Mary said. "It's so good to have you here, George. I hope you can stay a few days."

George smiled as Mary kissed him on the forehead. She had a sparkle in her eyes which he had never noticed.

"Let's see what the boss says."

George winked as he picked up the receiver and dialed the operator.

CHAPTER 48

Greg Packard checked and re-checked the meticulous log he had kept on every tournament Johnny and George had played in the previous ten years. He and his wife Doris had religiously filled scrapbooks with newspaper articles he had found about their matches – a total of eighteen scrapbooks crammed with news accounts, commentaries, and line scores that had taken over their own corner in his home study. Some would say the Packards were obsessed with the Challenge. Some days they would spend hours maintaining the records they kept. But still, as the tenth anniversary approached, Greg was worried that he had made a mistake in his calculations. His wife Doris came into the room and saw he was upset.

"What's wrong, dear?" she asked in her unwaveringly calm manner. She had a soothing voice that always helped Greg collect himself during his most stressful moments.

"For ten years I've been keeping a running score of their tournament victories and I was sure they were tied," he said. "But now when I count their wins, Johnny's ahead, 42 to 41."

"I'm happy to help you go back and check each tournament and see how you marked it," Doris said sweetly. She listed the possibilities out loud. "Maybe you counted a tournament win where you shouldn't have counted it, or didn't count one where you should have, or maybe Johnny really just did win."

She loved solving this sort of puzzle. She was the volunteer bookkeeper for their Lutheran church and her fellow parishioners called her "the bulldog" because she stayed at the books so assiduously until they balanced perfectly. It would never have occurred to anyone to question her figures because they knew that if there were a discrepancy, she would spend hours going back over the records to find the mistake.

They spent the next two hours poring over the articles they had collected and comparing them to the charts and notes that Greg had made before he found the error.

"Here it is!" he cried. He held up an article from Scrapbook 12 with a triumphant smile. "Johnny played in 247 tournaments that met the Challenge rules. George played in 166. As of April, I had Johnny with 42 wins and George with 41. But I had listed the 1910 Missouri Invitational as a win for Johnny when it wasn't a completed tournament. The rule is that a tournament had to be completed to be counted in the Challenge."

He shuffled through some more papers and pulled out another article.

"The first report that I got on that tournament was from the Kansas City Herald" – he quickly scanned the lengthy account in his hand – "which just reports that Johnny won the tournament."

He held up the first article he had found. "Now I see a separate article from the Herald that I don't remember. It says that the last day of the tournament was cancelled and that the leader after the third day – Johnny – was awarded the winner's prize. So Johnny's win can't be counted under Rock's rules."

Doris leaned over and pointed out her initials on the margin of the scrapbook.

"Yes, dear," she said. "I remember. You were sick that week and I helped organize the mail for you. I don't think I showed it to you. I'm so sorry."

Greg threw his hands in the air, cocked his head to the side, and shrugged to show that her oversight didn't matter.

"So it's a tie," he said with satisfaction. Then he suddenly grasped the picture beyond the triumph of his bookkeeping and his face fell. He turned to Doris, now clearly distraught, and blurted out, "There are no tournaments scheduled for either of them before the reunion on June 12. After 10 years we have a tie. A tie proves nothing." He started to pace around the room. "No one's going to be satisfied with a tie. The grand presentation will be ruined. What are we going to do?"

Doris immediately swung into calming mode.

"It will be alright. Maybe they could have a playoff," Doris said with a twinkle in her eye.

The next day Greg called Rock, Johnny, and George to let them know the disappointing news. Their individual reactions startled him.

"A tie, you say?" said Rock. "That's great!"

"A tie?" said Johnny. "Wouldn't you know?"

"A tie? After ten years we end up in a tie?" George said. Then he erupted into laughter.

Greg decided to call Bob Johnson and suggest a playoff. There was no better golf organizer on the planet. He'd solve the problem.

****

The phone ringing in the Riley home on an early Sunday morning was unusual. George grabbed the candlestick phone next to his bed and pulled the receiver taut to his ear.

"Hello?" he said. He could heard a clacking on the line, but no voice.

"Hello? Anyone there?"

"Mr. George Riley, please."

"Yes, hello. This is George Riley." George was only half awake and there was a strange echo on the phone line.

"This is the Boston Telephone Exchange toll operator 31

on a relay call from the American Telephone Association inter-regional exchange. I have a call for you from Tampa, Florida. I have a Mr. Johnny Scranton on the line for you. Can you take the call, sir?"

"Yes, operator. I can take the call now."

"Go ahead, Mr. Scranton. I'll clock in the toll line starting now."

It had taken Johnny over forty minutes to relay the call through five different operators on the East Coast. His usually reliable East Coast Relay was not answering, so he was forced to switch to the ATA Association exchange.

"George, can you hear me?"

"Yes. What's wrong, Johnny? For God's sake, it's Sunday morning!"

Johnny laughed.

"Nothing's wrong. I've just had a long talk with Bob Johnson and he has a marvelous idea. I officially challenge you to a game to decide who wins the Remy Martin cognac. We'll play what he calls a charity match the weekend of the reunion. He's checked with Rock and we can get the club for the match."

"A what? It sounded to me like you said a charity match. What is that?"

"It's like when we raised money for war bonds," said Johnny, "but for this we'll raise money for some local group of our choice. I think we ought to give the proceeds to the Boston Boys and Girls Club Scholarship Fund. Stroke-play match, 18 holes, winner is the Challenge champion."

"I like the idea," said George. "I officially accept your challenge, Mr. Scranton. It'll be like old times." Then he laughed. "You better get ready, my friend. I'm going to whip your ass."

"So he starts off talking like that," said Johnny. "I like it.

Bob's going to organize and thinks he can get lots of press. He'll send you the details next week. Get to work, old man. You'll need it. See you in June."

"Bye, Johnny," said George. "See you in June."

The line abruptly went dead. George rehung the earpiece and placed the phone on the night stand. Jennifer rolled over, curious about the call.

"Johnny challenged me to a match. Wants to play the weekend of the reunion in a charity match."

"What's a charity match?" Jennifer asked in the midst of a yawn. She could hear that the children were awake.

"Some new tournament Bob Johnson has concocted," said George as his wife got up and slipped on her robe. As she walked past him he grabbed her by her arm and pulled her back into bed.

"The little monsters will be okay. Let's spend the day right here."

"Shame on you, George Riley," she said with artificial shock in her voice. "It's the Sabbath! You need to get ready for church."

She smiled and kissed him on the forehead.

"Get dressed. Breakfast will be ready when you come down."

George gazed at her long radiant hair bouncing from side to side as she headed out the bedroom door. He reached over for the phone and dialed Greg's number. So far, the new direct dialing system was only available in Newton, but it was going to be expanded to the entire Boston area by the end of the year. It was difficult getting used to dialing a three-digit number rather than having the operator connect the call, thought George, but such was the cost of progress. It only took a few seconds before he heard Greg's phone ring.

"Hello?"

"Greg. This is George. Sorry to call so early. I thought you should hear what Bob and Johnny have concocted for the Challenge."

Greg didn't let on that he already knew.

CHAPTER 49

Nancy Johnson – the one time Nancy Marchand – sat next to her husband counting the gate receipts for the Challenge Match.

"Bob, this was a brilliant idea," she said.

Bob offered her a sly smile. "Who'd guess that I would be involved in a charity event?" he said.

Nancy gently hit him on the right arm. "You know you love this. What can feel better than helping out the Boys and Girls Club?" Then she smiled. "And think of the publicity for organizing an event like this. I'll bet we get five new contracts for matches after today."

Bob had always been a hard worker, tireless in promoting his tournaments, but he appreciated that Nancy saw different angles that didn't always occur to him. They made a great team.

By 8:30 over 1,000 spectators had flooded the Commonwealth Club and accumulated donations to the event had reached $30,000. Bob had worked the phones for weeks and the money had rolled in from companies and individuals throughout the Boston area. The Boston American described the match as one for the ages:

George Riley and Johnny Scranton, boyhood friends and world-class golfers born and bred on the same street in Newton, will face off today at the Commonwealth Club in a medal tournament to benefit the Boys and Girls Club of Boston. This is a once-in-a-lifetime opportunity to see one of the best amateur players in the world go head-to-head against one of the best professional players in the world.

Johnny and George were escorted to the first tee by Francis

Ouimet, the Honorary Marshall, for the opening ceremonies. Governor Calvin Coolidge presented Johnny and George with a state proclamation honoring the two men for their outstanding service to the Commonwealth and the nation.

"Governor, will you start the match by flipping a coin?" Francis asked, sensing that George and Johnny were anxious to get started. As the Governor flipped the coin in the air, George called "heads." The coin landed heads and George smiled as he prepared to hit.

"The honor won't last long," Johnny said as the crowd roared with laughter.

"We'll see," George fired back.

George selected his Wright and Ditson driver and hit a slight fade down the middle of the fairway. Johnny used his whippy Robush driver recently shellacked for the match. He hit a booming shot which carried more than 30 yards past George's ball and landed in front of the fairway pond.

"Always a great feeling to get that first drive off. Rock would be proud of us," Johnny said as they walked down the first fairway.

Johnny started off par, birdie, birdie, par, and George matched him with two birdies and two pars. The 5th hole was a long uphill par 4 with large double mounds separately protecting the left and right sides of the landing area. The two-tiered green sloped from back to front, and the pin was set six feet from the back of the second tier.

Johnny hit a tremendous drive down the middle of the fairway, spaced perfectly between the twin mounds. George pulled his drive and landed on the downslope in the middle left of the twin mounds. The wind swirled at the top of the hill and it was difficult for the players to judge the speed of the wind from below. Johnny hit a soft spade mashie and the ball hit the down slope of the first tier and spun back, ending at the bottom of the green, far short of the cup.

After watching Johnny's shot, George decided to be more aggressive and selected a mashie. He played the ball forward in his stance, crooked the blade inward, and cut straight down on the ball. The ball stayed low off the twin mounds and ran up the hill onto the second tier of the green within six feet of the cup.

Johnny had left himself a 35-foot, uphill putt with a nasty break on the second tier. He boldly stroked the putt, but he underestimated the speed of the green and the ball landed five feet beyond the hole. He decided to finish and firmly stroked the ball directly into the back of the cup.

George faced a short putt, but it was deceptively difficult because of the way the green broke sharply at the top of the ridge near the cup. George examined the putt from every angle, then carefully guided the ball to what seemed like the right spot beyond the cup. The crowd erupted as the ball looped around the hole and fell in to the cup for his birdie.

"Nice putt," Johnny said as they walked to the 6th teeing ground. Johnny noticed how shiny the Wilson forged putter looked. "New putter?"

"I bought it three years ago, but I've only used it twice."

"What happened to Matilda?" asked Johnny. Matilda was the nickname of a long-nose putter George had used for years. For the previous two years, he had experimented with a variety of new putters, but none had the feel of Matilda, though this new Wilson was close.

"She was stolen from my bag at a tournament in Middleton, Rhode Island, two years ago. I left the bag outside the pro shop and apparently someone lifted it. Never found who took it."

"Sorry about that, George," said Johnny. "I know how much

you liked that putter."

* * * * * *

The boys took the turn with Johnny one up and nine holes to play. Johnny picked up another stroke on the 14th, and with only four holes to go and sitting two strokes behind, George knew his chances to pull even were dwindling. It was time to force Johnny's hand.

At the 15th, a 505-yard par 5 and one of the most difficult holes on the course, George decided to gamble off the tee. He knew Johnny's long game could get him home in two if he had a good drive, but he hoped he could pressure him into a mistake. The hole had a 50-yard flat landing area in the fairway and beyond the landing area there was a steep hill down to a lower-level fairway that had a stream cutting across it at an angle about forty yards in front of the green. George figured that if he could place his ball on the left side of the landing area, he had a chance to catch the downslope back to center, and the ball would careen down from the upper level to the bottom of the hill. It was a risky shot since the far edge of the left side dropped off sharply into a ravine. If the ball hooked too far left, it would be gone and he would have to take a penalty; but if he could catch the downslope just right and roll down to the lower level, he could get on in two.

Johnny came up off his drive and his ball landed 25 yards short of the hill.

This is my chance, thought George. He took a deep breath, then hit a slow draw which landed in the middle of the fairway. The ball bounced left, followed the contour of the hill, and missed by inches the steep grade into the raven below. The ball bounded down the hill and landed in the middle of the lower level, about 160 yards from the green.

"Great shot, Mr. Riley," George's caddy said. He patted him on his back as they walked down the fairway.

Johnny looked frustrated as he viewed his shot from the top of the hill. He was still over 235 yards short of the stream. He decided quite understandably that he wasn't getting home in two and chose to lay up and hope for a mistake from George.

George selected a mashie for his second stroke and he hit a beautifully lofted shot which carried the stream and landed in the middle of the green, twenty feet from the hole. Johnny tried to spin his third shot in close to the pin, but the ball hit a small mound and spun off far to the back of the green. He two-putted, settled for his par, and watched as George rammed in his 20-foot putt for an eagle that pulled him even in the match.

The 16th and 17th were difficult holes for both men. Each struggled to save par. George hit a tree on 16 but made a miraculous shot under an overhanging branch to match Johnny's par. On 17, Johnny pushed his drive right and landed in an area covered with rocks. He decided to take a drop. He then hit a shot to within four inches of the hole to match George's par.

The 18th hole measured 398 yards. A large oak tree protected the left side of the fairway and blocked a direct shot to the hole. George hit a solid drive down the right side of the fairway. Johnny took a few deep breaths before his practice swing, then he focused on putting all of his effort into this one last drive. He hit what seemed to be a perfect drive down the middle of the fairway, but suddenly the ball hooked left and landed on the far left side of the fairway.

When he got to his ball, he saw that it had landed in a deep divot.

"What do you think?" asked his caddy. "Just punch it out and play it safe?"

Just then George approached and saw the ball in the divot.

Loud enough for George to hear and with dramatically precise enunciation, Johnny announced, "You know my philosophy, my friend. Always go for it!"

He made a show of grabbing a mashie iron and curved the blade inward. Then he got serious. He knew his only hope to get home was to hit a sweeping shot and hook the ball around the oak. This was a shot Johnny had hit hundreds of times over the years, but it was certainly not a sure thing. He needed to keep his weight forward and allow the club to sweep through the ball and create spin for the hook. He stepped up to the ball, let out his breath as he swung, and caught the bottom third of the ball exactly as he wanted to. The ball leapt from the divot, curved majestically around the oak, and landed ten feet below the pin. Spectators who witnessed the shot described it later as the purest shot they had ever seen.

George shook his head in disbelief.

"See," Johnny said, with a grin on his face. "I could have made that shot at Worcester if it had been in a divot!"

George didn't know what to say. He walked to his drive, still shaking his head, as the tumultuous applause drowned out any possible retort.

George studied his shot for a few minutes. He had a difficult angle to get close to the hole. The cup was located in a trough between two mounds but there was a flat area above and to the left of Johnny's ball. If he could spin the ball onto that flat area, he'd have an opportunity to set up a blocking shot. He decided this was his best chance to stay even and his only chance to win the hole – and the match.

He selected a spade mashie, his favorite club. He hit a low draw with plenty of spin on the ball. The ball landed in front of one of the hills, skipped twice, and stopped on the flat area just above Johnny's ball. George whistled as he walked to the green. I've got him right where I want him, he thought.

The crowd was four deep surrounding the 18th green. Francis Ouimet examined the two putts.

"You're away, Mr. Riley," he said. He smiled as he walked to the back of the green.

Once he had examined the putt from as many angles as he could find, George decided that indeed his best play would be to try to stymie Johnny. He was sure Johnny would make the 10-foot putt for a birdie if he didn't, and he himself had a difficult putt which turned sharply over the mound above the cup. The only hope was to place the stymie and hope Johnny missed his next shot. George pressed down hard on the forged putter to try and place the ball precisely one foot in front of Johnny's ball. The press gave the ball a slight backspin so that it careened down the slope and suddenly stopped directly in front of Johnny's ball. George broke into a wide grin.

"I believe I have you stymied, Mr. Scranton," he said playfully. The people in the crowd laughed as they applauded.

"So you have, my friend," said Johnny, bowing slightly toward George.

Johnny walked over to his bag and lifted out his lofted putter. He tried to remember how long it had been since he had made this type of a shot. He hadn't lifted a putt over a stymie in a match for at least five years, but maybe he could pull it off. It was a delicate shot: too hard and the ball would overshoot the cup, too soft and the ball would die before reaching the hole. He played with the weight of the putter, then briskly approached the shot, dragged the head back, and cut down on the putt.

The ball leapt from the beveled club over George's ball, hit the green halfway to the hole, caught the side of the mound and rolled into the right side of the cup for a birdie. George smiled broadly as Johnny came over for a congratulatory hug.

"I never thought you could make that shot," George whispered in his ear.

"I didn't think I could make it, either," Johnny admitted.

Francis was the first to congratulate them for a match that would be remembered by everyone who saw it.

"It beats the drama at Brookline by a mile," he stated later at the awards presentation.

Greg Packard awarded the bottle of Remy Martin cognac to Johnny and the crowd lingered to savor the beauty of the course in the afterglow of a great match. George and Johnny retreated to the grill room and George grabbed two shot glasses from behind the bar.

"We deserve a taste of this stuff," he said. "What do you think?"

Johnny smiled but shook his head no.

"I can't break my promise to Mary," he said. "I've been sober for over seven years, George. I'm working on a good streak here."

Then he turned to the bartender and asked for a sarsparilla.

"I wonder how much a ten-year-old bottle of Remy is worth these days?" George asked. "Let's hope it hasn't gone bad."

George carefully opened the bottle, filled his shot glass, and raised his glass towards Johnny.

"To the honor of golf and to the honor of our friendship. May they continue for many, many years."

"Hear, hear!" said Johnny.

The cognac tasted warm and leathery with a strong floral aftertaste.

"Not bad after ten years," George said. "But not especially better than sarsparilla, I guess."

They sat next to each other at the bar, toasted their friendship, and then talking quietly about the day's game. After a short while, George said, "I have an idea, my friend. I challenge you to a re-match next year."

Johnny smiled the warm, generous smile that was loved by everyone that knew him. He held his sarsparilla high in the air.

"You're on, my friend. Now let's get to the reunion. It's been quite a day."

Epilogue

Johnny could hear the sound of the waves crashing on the rock buttress below as he drove into the driveway of the house on Ayer Road. He parked the car and sat there for a few moments, windows open, drinking in the soothing, sweet breeze, his eyes closed, his head leaning back on the top edge of the seat. He thought of Mary, how she had loved this house. They had built it in 1915 – so long ago, he thought, 57 years. Could it really have been that long?

Married two years and before the children were born, they built four bedrooms and big porches, knowing they wanted lots of kids. Mary had toured with Johnny when they were first married, but she never really liked the travel–he knew that, though she never said it–and once the kids came along, she was thrilled to spend summer after summer back on the Cape. And for all those wonderful years, the house had been the center of a joyful world for them. Mary would happily bring the kids back to her home-town after school let out and Johnny would join them when he wasn't playing in a tournament, harder for him each time to leave once he was there. Each Christmas, the entire family would gather in the Ayer Road home for a two-week holiday.

Johnny thought of the children. They had done so well for themselves, in good marriages, with fine children of their own. Kevin and Roger, the older boys, both engineers: Kevin built bridges and Roger built roads. Johnny liked to kid that no highway in the country could be built without his sons. Brian and Irene ran his business. They were really better at it than he had ever been. June, their middle child, had been taken from them so young, just four years old, in the typhoid fever epidemic of 1928. That was not easy. But life had been so good to them in so many other ways.

Johnny exited the car and decided to watch the sun set in the western sky. He sat on the patio near the bluff wall in the backyard and watched the sun slowly descend behind a bank of low lying clouds over Nantucket Sound. It was the first anniversary of Mary's death and tomorrow there would be a memorial service in her honor. She had loved this spot and he could feel her around him as he sat on the simple teak bench that she had placed there just weeks before she died. He missed her warm smile, the flowery fragrance of her hair, and her gentle touch. He missed the way she would, after all those years, still run her fingers softly along his hand, as she did that first night they met.

He sat immersed in his memories, half awake, when he was startled by a sound behind him. He turned and saw George standing behind him quietly watching the last light of the sun spread across the horizon.

"Sorry," he said. "I didn't mean to wake you."

Johnny sat up straight and shook off his drowsiness.

"That's alright," he said. "I was only half asleep. I was think-ing of Mary, how she loved this spot."

George nodded. He picked up a chair and pulled it over to join Johnny on the patio.

"Jennifer's favorite place to watch the sunset was our porch," he said. "The way the sun's rays spread out at this time of day always remind me of her long golden hair." He vividly remembered the day she had died in September, 1967–two days after they lost their boyhood friend Francis Quimet.

They sat together without speaking for a short while. Then

Johnny said, "I got a call from a reporter. He's doing a story on the Challenge. Wanted to know the results of the '59 match. I told him I couldn't remember."

George laughed.

"You always forget the ones you lost," he said. "I think you've selectively blocked out that putt on 18. You missed the twelve-footer to win and I closed you out on the third extra hole."

"Ah, yes. Now I remember," said Johnny, his eyes brightening. "But what about the '69 match? Who dropped the thirty-footer for the win? I haven't forgotten that putt."

"I must admit, that putt was spectacular," George said, smiling broadly. "I never thought you could make it. The break on that putt was enormous. And that was the year you missed shooting your age by one shot."

Johnny sat leaning on the front of the bench now, excited by the good memories.

"Say, after the memorial service let's go play nine holes at the Port," he said. "I want to try the new Persimmon driver I purchased yesterday in Hyannis."

"What happened to your old Wilson Staff?"

"I saw the Persimmon at Clyde's Golf Shop and fell in love with the feel. He's giving me a free demo for five days, so I've got to get out on the course."

"Okay. You're on. What shall we play for?" George asked.

"The love of the game."

They both laughed at that.

"Bullshit," said George. "How about twenty-five bucks? I'm feeling lucky today."

Johnny rose gingerly from his chair. He was still feeling the back sprain he'd gained lifting his grandson.

"Come prepared, Mr. Riley," he said with a wink. "I plan on kicking your butt."

"That'll be the day," said George.

LIST OF MAJOR REAL-LIFE CHARACTERS

Charles E. "Chick" Evans Jr. *(July 18, 1890 - November 6, 1979):* Amateur golfer from Chicago, Illinois. Won the U.S. Open in 1916, the U.S. Amateur in 1916 and 1920, and seven Western Amateur titles. Established the Evans Scholarship program in 1929. Played in fifty U.S. Amateur tournaments through 1967.

Walter Charles Hagen *(December 21, 1892 - October 5, 1969):* Professional golfer born in Rochester, New York. Between 1914 and 1932, he won the U.S. Open twice, the Open (now commonly called The British Open) four times, the PGA Championship five times, and the Western Open five times. Won a total of 45 PGA tournaments during his career.

Francis DeSales Ouimet *(May 8, 1893 - September 2, 1967):* Amateur golfer born in Brookline, Massachusetts. Winner of the U.S. Open in 1913, the U.S. Amateur in 1914 and 1931, and seven Massachusetts State Amateurs. Played on the first eight Walker Cup teams and was the first American elected a Captain of the Royal and Ancient Golf Club of St. Andrews.

Edward R. G. "Ted" Ray *(March 28, 1877 - August 26, 1943):* Professional player born on the Isle of Jersey in England. Winner of the 1912 Open (now commonly called The British Open) and the 1920 U.S. Open.

Donald J. Ross *(November 23, 1872 - April 26, 1948):* Professional golfer and golf course designer born in Dornoch, Scotland. Won the North-South Open three times and the Massachusetts Open twice. Designed over 600 golf courses during his career.

Heinrich Schmidt *(dates uncertain):* Amateur golfer born in Worcester, Massachusetts. Won the 1912 Massachusetts Amateur at the age of 22 by defeating Francis Ouimet 2 up.

Albert Goodwill Spalding *(September 2, 1850 - September 9, 1915):* Professional baseball player, one of the founders of the National League, and sporting goods businessman born in Byron, Illinois. Played for the Boston Red Stockings and the Chicago White Stockings. Elected to the Baseball Hall of fame in 1939. By 1905, Spalding owned eighteen stores selling golf equipment, official major-league baseball equipment, and other sporting goods. His company manufactured wooden-shaft clubs for 35 years.

Harry Vardon *(May 9, 1870 - March 20, 1937):* Professional golfer born on the Isle of Jersey in England. Winner of the Open (now commonly called The British Open) six times, and the U.S. Open in 1900. Won a total of 62 tournaments in Europe and the United States. The Vardon Grip is still the most widely used grip in golf.

George Wright *(January 28, 1847 - August 21, 1937):* Professional baseball player and sporting goods businessman born in Yonkers, New York. Played shortstop for Cincinnati Red Stockings and Boston Red Stockings. Elected to Baseball Hall of Fame in 1937. Founder of Wright and Ditson Sporting Goods in 1880.

AUTHOR'S NOTES AND CREDITS

Chapter 2

Golf Balls: There were no rules regarding the size and weight of golf balls until 1921 when the USGA set the weight at no greater than 1.62 ounces and the size not less than 1.62 inches in diameter. *www.ruleshistory.com.*

Rules of Golf: The first written rules of golf, compiled in 1744 in Edinburgh, Scotland, were as follows:

Articles & Laws in Playing Golf

1. You must Tee your Ball within a Club's Length of the Hole.

2. Your Tee must be upon the Ground.

3. You are not to change the Ball which you strike off the Tee.

4. You are not to remove Stones, Bones or any Break Club, for the sake of playing your Ball, Except upon the fair Green & that only within a Club's length of your Ball.

5. If your Ball comes among watter, or any wattery filth, You are at liberty to take out your Ball & bringing it behind the hazard and Teeing it, you may play it with any Club and allow your Adversary a Stroke for so getting out your Ball.

6. If your Balls be found any where touching one another, You are to Lift the first Ball, till you play the last.

7. At Holling, you are to play your Ball honestly for the Hole, and not to Play upon your Adversary's Ball, not lying in your way to the Hole.

8. If you should lose your Ball, by it's being taken up, or any other way, u are to go back to the Spot, where you struck last, & drop another Ball, And allow your adversary a Stroke for the misfortune.

9. No man at Holling his Ball, is to be allowed, to mark his way to the Hole with his anything else.

10. If a Ball be stopp'd by any Person, Horse, Dog or anything else, the Ball So stop'd just must be play'd where it lyes.

11. If you draw your Club in Order to Strike, & proceed so far in the Stroke as to be bringing down your Club; If then, your Club *shall* break, in any way, it is to be Accounted a Stroke.

12. He whose Ball lyes farthest from the Hole is obliged to play first.

13. Neither Trench, Ditch, or Dyke, made for the preservation of the Links, nor The Scholar's Holes, or Soldier's Lines, Shall be accounted a Hazard; But the Ball is to be taken out, Teed, and play'd with any Iron Club.

www.ruleshistory.com

The Boston Americans: Boston was awarded a baseball franchise in the American League in 1901 and the team, the Americans, played at the Huntington Avenue Grounds from 1901 until 1911. On December 18, 1907, the team changed its name to the Red Sox. The team opened its new facility, Fenway Park, on April 10, 1912, and the Huntington Avenue Grounds were demolished the same year.

Wright and Ditson: The business was founded by George Wright and Henry Ditson in 1871 as a sporting goods company. In 1891, Al Spalding purchased the company, but his company continued to market products under the Wright and Ditson name until the early 1930's.

Chapter 5

The City of Newton: Background material on the history of Newton was obtained from the archives of the Newton Historical Society, the Newton History Museum at the Jackson Homestead, and *http://www.ci.newton.ma.us/Jackson. www.ci.newton.ma.us/Jackson.*

Chapters 16 and following

Brown University: Background material for the sections on Brown University was found in the *Encyclopedia Brunoniana* by Martha Mitchell (1993) and at *www.brown.edu.* The period from 1891 until 1919 was a period of considerable change for the University. The Women's College became a department in the University in 1891, and it became common to refer to women at the University as "Pembrokers" after the name of the building in which most classes for women were conducted. In 1928, the Women's College was officially renamed Pembroke College.

Chapters 20 and following

Pinehurst Country Club: Background material on Pinehurst and the Pinehurst Resort was gathered from *Pinehurst: Golf, History, and the Good Life* by Audrey Moriarty (2005) and at *www.pinehurst.com.*

Chapters 30 and following

Harwich, Massachusetts: Background information on the early 20th century history of Harwichport was gathered from visits to the Harwich Historical Society and the Brooks Academy Museum, a review of the Brooks Free Library collection on Harwich history, and a review of the Harwich Town Reports, 1900-1919, as well as from *www.harwichhistoricalsociety.org.*

Chapters 41 and following

The 1913 U.S. Open at The Country Club, Brookline, Massachusetts: Numerous sources were consulted, including *The Greatest Game Ever Played* by Mark Frost (2002); *Francis Ouimet and the 1913 United States Open* by Richard O'Connor (1999); *A Game Of Golf* by Francis Ouimet (1921); *Golf, A Turn of the Century Treasury* by Mel Shapiro (1986); and *www.golfclubatlas.com.*

In Ouimet's book, he relates on page 45 the story of his practice round at Wellesley Country Club two days before the Open: "The Sunday before the open tournament, I played at the Wellesley Country Club with friends. I bring this up merely to show you that one's form in golf is a mercurial affair. I made two scores of 88 on a short and rather easy nine-hole course, the 88's being just twenty-two strokes higher than a record score I had established on one of my earlier rounds over the layout."

ACKNOWLEDGMENTS

A hearty thank you to the following people for their help and suggestions in producing this book:

Stephen Quinn for his editorial prowess;

Jim Morris for his outstanding cover
design and book layout;

Mary Nace, Marshall Strauss, Robert Koenig,
Sherelyn Ernst, Elaine Strauss, David B. Stinson,
Laurie O'Connor, Shannon Fairbanks,
Sally O'Connor, and Andrew Goldman
for their excellent advice and critique;

April and Patrick O'Connor for their endless
support with graphics and web design.

Made in the USA
Middletown, DE
19 August 2018